Sweets from Morocco

Published by Honno
'Ailsa Craig', Heol y Cawl, Dinas Powys
South Glamorgan, Wales, CF6 4AH

1 2 3 4 5 6 7 8 9 10

The author would like to stress that this is a work of fiction and no
resemblance to any actual individual or institution is intended or
implied.

ISBN 978 1 906784 00 3

Published with the financial assistance of the
Welsh Books Council

Cover image: © Getty Images
Cover design: G Preston

Printed in Wales by Gomer

Sweets from Morocco

by

Jo Verity

HONNO MODERN FICTION

Acknowledgements

My thanks go to all those who encouraged, advised, supported and listened:
Caroline Oakley, Helena Earnshaw, Janet Thomas and everyone at Honno; Leona Usher, Matt Powell, Stephen May, Andrew Cowan, Suzannah Dunn, Louise Wener, Louise Walsh and Catherine Merriman; the members of Cardiff Writers' Circle; and, of course, Jim Griffiths.

For Nick Evans

Chapter 1

THE RECTANGULAR GARDEN WAS DIVIDED, half-and-half, into lawn and vegetable patch and in the far corner, between the row of runner beans and the tall privet hedge, two children sat on their heels. The girl's dark-brown hair hung forward in heavy plaits, framing her solemn face, and she was frowning as, with a short length of bamboo cane, she agitated murky liquid in the jam jar which stood between them on the red soil. The boy looked on, glancing between the jar and the girl's face, seeming to seek assurance that events were on course. His hair was brown, too, but less vibrantly so, his skin, paler, his movements more hesitant, as if he were her sun-bleached replica.

She stood up, holding the jar aloft and inspecting its swirling contents, then, with her free hand, flicked the plaits back over her shoulders. 'I'll go first.'

The boy scrambled to his feet and, now that they were both standing, it was possible to see that he was a shade taller than his sister. 'Must we?'

She dismissed his question by raising the rim of the jar to her lips, pausing long enough to ensure his face contorted with revulsion before taking a hearty gulp. She swallowed and, mouth fixed in a triumphant smile, offered the concoction to him. 'Now you.'

The boy shoved both fists into the pockets of his khaki shorts and turned his head to one side, avoiding her glare.

'Lewis. Drink it.'

'But…'

'Drink it. Or I'll never speak to you again.' She thrust the jar close to his mouth.

He stood his ground but dipped his head, closing his eyes and screwing up his face as if he had already downed a dose of the disgusting brew.

'You promised, Lewis. Come on. It's only gravy browning and water.'

'And vinegar. And bi carb.'

She tried another tack. 'We could do blood-mingling instead, if you like,' but he didn't respond and she stamped her foot. 'Don't be such a ninny.'

A reedy voice put an end to the stalemate. 'Tessa? Lewis? Come and wash your hands before dinner.'

Lewis edged to the end of the bean row. 'Coming, Gran,' he shouted in the direction of the voice, disclosing their hiding place and gaining a let-up from his sister's demands.

'You know what breaking your promise means, don't you? You'll be cursed forever.' Tessa caught the back of her brother's tee shirt. As he twisted, trying to break from her grasp, she doused his feet with the contents of the jar. Some of the liquid splashed on to the ground, escaping in dusty rivulets across the compacted soil, but there was still plenty to saturate his new sandals – the second pair he'd had that summer as his feet had grown a size-and-a-half since Whitsun. He let out a squeak, like brake blocks binding on the rim of a bicycle wheel, flexing his feet, listening to the kissy slurp of liquid surging up through the patterns punched in the leather.

Tessa dropped the jar and hugged him. 'Don't cry, Lew. Please don't cry. Here, take them off.' She knelt and, whilst Lewis placed a hand on her shoulder to steady himself, she pulled the sandals off, not bothering to undo the buckles, still stiff with newness.

'It'll leave a mark. What'll I tell Mum?' he fretted.

'Mum's not here, stupid.'

'Dad then.'

She slapped one shoe against the other then placed them on the ground. Reaching beneath her gingham skirt, she dragged her knickers down to her knees then slipped them off. She scrubbed away with this improvised duster, removing as much liquid as she could before placing the sandals on the path, in full sun but out of sight of the house. 'There. They'll be dry by the time we've had dinner. Gran won't notice you've got bare feet.' She wriggled back into her knickers.

'Lew-iiis. Tess-aaa.' The calling voice rose on the second syllable of the names. 'I won't tell you again.'

'C'mon, slow coach.' Tessa grabbed her brother's hand and they ran across the lawn to the back door.

Their grandmother was in the kitchen, stationed at the gas cooker, prodding the contents of two simmering pans with a vegetable knife. She nodded towards the sink. 'Wash your hands here, where I can keep an eye on you. I don't want you disappearing again.'

Tessa ran cold water into the chipped enamel bowl and they dunked their grubby hands, drying them on the towel which hung from the handle of the larder door. Then the children took their places, side by side, at the table whilst their grandmother strained the vegetables through a colander, held at arms length to keep the rising steam away from her spectacles. For the past three weeks, the sun had blazed out of a near-cloudless sky and, as the heat built, there was talk of record-breaking temperatures. Despite this, Gran wore a cardigan over a summer dress, the whole lot swaddled in a washed out pinafore. Her hair was an improbable shade of orange, perfectly straight to within an inch or two of the cut ends where it erupted in a crinkly border. Tessa and Lewis often discussed their grandmother's hair, never daring to ask how she achieved this effect but, given its likeness to knitting wool which had been unravelled from an unwanted garment, they guessed it had been reached in a similar way.

'What's for pudding, Gran?' Tessa asked before she'd taken more than a couple of mouthfuls of food.

'Pudding? There'll be no pudding until I've seen two clean dinner plates.'

'Only two?' Tessa asked. 'What about yours?'

The woman shook her head. 'You're too sharp, young lady. You'll cut yourself one of these days.' After a short silence she continued, 'I don't know why they give you these long school holidays. And I certainly don't know what's got into you two.' Lots of their grandmother's sentences began 'I don't know why…' or 'I don't know what…' as if life were a series of conundrums to which she would never find a satisfactory answer.

Tessa knew the answers to both. Miss Drake had explained to the class that the long summer holidays had come about hundreds of years ago, to enable children to help their families at harvest time. The school that she and Lewis attended was in a suburb, where the largest garden was, at most, twice the size of theirs, making nonsense of this explanation. But, like admitting that she no longer believed in Father Christmas, it would be crazy to point it out and risk the holiday being shortened. And as for what had 'got into' her, Gran must be stupid if she couldn't work *that* one out. The birth of her new brother was what had 'got into' her.

Lewis hooked his heels over the strut of the chair and spread his toes as wide as they would go. Simply having nothing on his feet made him feel heroic. His mother told him off if he went about barefoot, warning that he would stand on a piece of glass or get splinters from the woodblock floor or catch those awful things from the swimming baths – verrucas, that was it. He'd get verrucas and the doctor would have to dig them out. This didn't make sense, though, because how could anyone go swimming *unless* their feet were bare?

He dissected the luncheon meat on his plate, enjoying the ease with which the blunt-ended knife cut through the soft pinkness of each slice. Two, four, eight. Two, four, eight. Sixteen neat rectangles.

'Don't play with your food, Lewis, there's a good boy.'

How was he supposed to cut it up? Diagonal cuts generated a series of frivolous triangles and if he rolled a slice up and jammed it in, she would surely shout at him for overfilling his mouth. There *were* grownups – Uncle Frank, for example – whom Lewis knew would be happy to discuss this dilemma, but not Gran. So in order to secure the bowls of strawberry jelly and evaporated milk that he'd spotted on the slab in the larder, he let it go unchallenged.

'Gran?' Tessa stirred the contents of her bowl, reducing it to an orangey-pink liquid, marbled with bright red. 'When's Mum coming home?'

Doris Lloyd's face took on the soppy expression of someone seeing an orphaned puppy. 'Are you missing her? Not long now. But she needs to get her strength back. She'll have her hands full with you two *and* your new baby brother.'

Tessa continued stirring, clattering her spoon in the glass bowl whilst Lewis looked on uneasily. 'We don't want a brother. Or a sister. We never asked her to get one, did we, Lewis?' She nudged him.

He shrugged.

'Don't be ridiculous, Tessa,' their grandmother said. 'It'll be wonderful, having a baby in the house again.'

'Why? Babies don't do anything. They just cry and wet themselves.'

Doris Lloyd stood up and gathered the empty bowls. 'That's enough of that. Off outside, you two. I've got things to do.'

The children returned to the garden. Lewis's sandals had dried but, when he put them on, they felt stiff and rubbed his heels and the tops of his bare toes. To make matters worse, Tessa's vigorous buffing had removed the polish and, as he had feared, a white tide mark wavered across the insteps. 'Mum'll be mad.'

Tessa shook her head. 'No, she won't. She won't even notice. The baby'll take up all her time and she won't bother with us any more. Or love us.'

Lewis tugged at his ears, a sure sign that he was anxious. 'What about Dad? He'll still love us. Won't he?'

Tessa had two fathers. One told them adventure stories about a sister and brother, played never-ending games of I-Spy, made bows and arrows from hazel twigs, and showed them how to fold a sheet of paper into a boat that really floated. The other banished their friends from the house, retreated behind the newspaper and refused to listen, flew off the handle at nothing at all and slapped the backs of their legs. Lewis said that their father would still love them but she wasn't convinced.

His sudden tempers scared her. Once, smarting from what she considered to be an unjust outburst, Tessa had run crying to her mother. 'It's hard to explain,' her mother had said, 'but Dad gets fed up sometimes. His leg gives him pain. It stops him sleeping and he gets … crabby.' She'd heard the story many times. When he was fourteen, Dick Swinburne had been playing cricket in the street and had skied the ball on to the roof where it had lodged in the guttering. He'd volunteered to get it back but the ladder he was using slipped and he fell, injuring his hip and breaking his leg. As a result of the accident, he wore a built-up shoe and walked with a jerky limp. Tessa barely noticed it but her friends stared and whispered when they came to the house. Her father's leg might be the cause of his bad moods but there was no call to take it out on her and Lewis. They hadn't even been born when the ladder slipped.

Heat smothered the garden and drove the children back into the house. They took out a jigsaw and began sorting the pieces, but jigsaws were for rainy days and they gave up, creeping upstairs to read comics from the box that they kept beneath Tessa's bed, poring over the beloved characters who were more part of their lives than the next door neighbours.

'It's not fair,' Tessa grumbled, flopping back on her bed. 'Everyone's away.'

The Swinburne family usually spent two weeks every summer in a caravan in Devon or Dorset. When school broke up, the children waited for their mother to begin filling two battered suitcases with shorts and sunhats, bathing costumes and pakamacs. They'd been saving sixpences in a draw string purse – a Christmas present to Tessa from Diane, her current best friend – to buy a model sailing boat and they planned to change the surplus into pennies for the slot machines on the pier. The previous year, Lewis had perfected his technique for launching one game's tarnished ball bearings and he managed to get them to clunk into the metal cups every time. This success returned his stake money and earned him another try. By the end of the holiday, he had amassed a profit of one shilling and tuppence, which he spent on ice creams for the family.

This year the suitcases had remained in the attic and, when Tessa pestered, her mother had given an inadequate but ominous explanation. 'The baby's due very soon and I have to be near the hospital. Perhaps we'll go next year.'

Tessa and Lewis's knowledge of human reproduction was based on the opaque statement 'babies grow inside their mother's tummy' and, over the past months, their mother's stomach *had* swollen alarmingly. Voluminous dresses replaced gaily patterned skirts and pretty blouses, giving free rein to macabre imaginings. What was going on beneath those swathes of gathered fabric?

She'd also taken to patting the swelling each time she said the word 'baby' which Tessa took to be a kind of ritual, like saluting a solitary magpie or crossing fingers when telling a fib. But once the baby had been born, the urge to know the ins-and-outs of the birth had diminished. 'Probably something to do with her belly button,' Tessa ventured but couldn't square her theory with the inconvenient fact that men possessed these intriguing features, too. In his turn, Lewis wasn't keen to dwell on any of it, afraid that it might be distressing like the animal carcasses he tried to avoid seeing when they passed the butchers' stalls in the Central Market.

They messed about for the rest of the afternoon, unsuccessfully pestering their grandmother for biscuits and pop, finally returning to the far end of the garden to hunt for caterpillars on the leaves of the wilting sprout plants.

Dick Swinburne – only his schoolteachers had ever called him Richard – finished work at the General Post Office at five-thirty but for the past week he'd gone straight to the hospital, not getting home until well after Tessa and Lewis had finished tea. Once he'd given his mother-in-law the latest news, she was released from duty and went to catch the bus back to her terraced house on the other side of town.

'Have you two behaved yourselves for Gran?'

'Did she say anything?' Tessa asked.

Ignoring her question he turned to Lewis. '*Have* you?' he repeated.

'Yes, Dad,' Lewis answered, thankful that his stained sandals were hidden in the shadows under his bed.

'Good, because I've got some news.' He settled in his shabby leather chair, patting the wide arms where the children perched when there were stories to be told or news to share. 'Jump up.'

Tessa could tell from his tone that he was in a good mood as she and her brother took their places, draping their skinny arms around the back of the chair behind his head. 'What?'

'Can't you guess? I'll give you a clue.' He shut his eyes and leaned his head back and she marvelled at the tufts of gingery hair which burst from his nose and ears and the darker bristles, erupting from his chin. 'Let's see. Something rather special is happening tomorrow.'

'We're going on holiday?' Lewis suggested.

Tessa, understanding immediately what her father was hinting at, was delighted with her brother's innocent remark and prolonged the episode. 'You're taking us to the circus?'

'Come on. Think hard.'

His good humour was dissolving so Tessa gave the answer he was looking for. 'Mum's coming home?'

'Well done, Tess. Mum and *Gordon* are coming home.'

'Who's Gordon?' demanded Lewis. The only Gordon he'd ever heard of was a blue train in the books he borrowed from the library.

'Gordon is your new brother. We've named him Gordon John after your granddad who died in France. I think you're going to like him.'

The children hadn't been allowed to visit their mother. Lewis could only assume that this was because the place was in some way terrifying. If he went by his grandmother's description – 'He's a bonny little chap. He's got your dad's nose.' – all he could picture was a kind of blancmange with tufty nostrils.

Worse than that, he and Tessa had not been consulted about the name. Choosing a good name for the succession of pets that had swum, slithered and hopped in and out of their lives, had always been a serious process, not least because of the wheedling involved to get their parents to agree to the budgie, goldfish, white mice or whatever in the first place. Current pets were Pip, a spiteful ginger cat who lacerated anyone foolish enough to get within arm's length and Speedy the tortoise, who did nothing much. The family had, for three weeks or so, owned a bright-eyed Cairn terrier called Pete who had made a permanent getaway by slipping his lead when supposedly moored to the lamp post outside the library. Lewis thought that 'Pete' would make a jaunty name for a new brother. Easy to spell, too. His father's disclosure that the baby's name had already been decided was further confirmation that family rules were being re-written as Tessa had warned.

'So, it's an early night for you two. In the morning you can help me get the place ship shape and set up the cot in our bedroom. The little chap'll be sleeping in with us for a while.'

Lewis was optimistic, at least for the first five minutes. Their mother looked pretty much as she had before she'd swollen up and, as soon as she came in, she pulled him and Tessa down to sit either side of her on the sofa, hugging them and laughing. 'I'm sure you've both grown an inch while I've been away.'

He longed to tell her how much he'd missed her and that Gran's mashed potato wasn't quite right and how Dad had given him such a scrubbing at bath time that he'd skinned his neck. But Tessa jumped in first, with a rambling request to spend the night at Diane's and he was content to flop against his mother, inhaling lavender, perspiration and something half-remembered.

'So, can I go, Mum? *Please?*'

'Don't pester your mother, Tess.' Their father came into the room with something large, wrapped in brown paper.

Out of the corner of her eye, Tessa noticed that the white bundle on her grandmother's lap was moving but, determined to ignore it, she concentrated on the parcel. 'Is that for us, Dad?'

'Hold your horses. Aren't you two going to say hello to your new brother?' He placed the parcel on the floor, pushing it under the table with his foot.

11

'Don't rush them, Dick...' her mother's voice was barely audible.

Lewis stood up and sidled across to their grandmother but Tessa stayed where she was. 'What's the point of saying "hello" to a baby? He won't understand, will he?'

'Tessa!' Her father grabbed her bare arm, hauled her to her feet and pulled her across the room.

'Don't, Dick, please.'

'You're soft on her, Peggy. She's getting too old for this silly behaviour.' Squeezing both her arms, he shook her.

At school Tessa was forever protesting against accusations of misbehaviour – talking, passing notes, that sort of thing – but, having issued their verdict, the teachers never budged. Finding herself once again up against the injustice of an adult's demands, knowing that it was a waste of time trying to make her father understand, she shut her eyes and screamed, her voice sliding from one penetrating note to another in a blood-curdling yodel. 'Aaagh. Dad. Aaagh. You're hurting me.'

The baby joined in, letting out a high-pitched wail, his red hands jerking haphazardly. Gran got to her feet, jiggling the baby and making soothing noises but his crying continued, growing louder and more desperate. She glared at Tessa. 'See what you've done, madam?'

'You. Upstairs. Now.' Her father pushed her towards the door.

'Please, Dick. Don't...' Their mother half rose then seemed to surrender, sinking back on the sofa, her hand clamped over her mouth.

Tessa dashed upstairs and slammed her bedroom door, whilst the baby, seeming to sense that he was centre stage at last, continued his bawling and Peggy Swinburne, whose hand was no longer adequate to stifle her misery, began sobbing.

Unable to stand the noise, Lewis escaped into the garden

where he spent the rest of the afternoon pretending that he was on a desert island, the sole survivor from a crashed Spitfire.

Chapter 2

TESSA SPAT OUT THE TOOTHPASTE, watching the river of froth meander towards the plughole. 'Gordon. Yuck. What a disgusting name. Don't you think it's *bloody* disgusting, Lew?' Tessa found swearing exciting but the bad words – damn and blast – and the *really* bad words – bloody and bugger – didn't sound casual enough. She needed a lot more practice. 'I think we should make them change it to…' she wrinkled her nose then struck the side of the washbasin with her toothbrush 'Jim.' She was reading *Treasure Island* for the third time and was captivated by its hero.

It was nine days since their mother had brought Gordon home and Tessa was still refusing to get involved with, or show any interest in, her new brother. Lewis was less uncompromising and when Tessa abandoned him, going off to play with Diane or Susan, he often knelt on his parents' bed, peering into the cot and watching the strange little creature run through his repertoire of twitches. Lewis was a patient observer. He noticed how Gordon barely blinked his dark eyes and how he craned his head slowly from side to side, revealing folds of slack skin at the base of his neck. It reminded Lewis of Speedy. He also discovered that if he placed his index fingers against the silky-smooth palms, the baby clung to him, impossibly small fists gripping so tight that he could pull him up into a sitting position. During those intimate moments, Lewis decided that 'Pete' would be a much better name for his brother.

14

'How about 'Pete'?' Lewis ventured.

'Pete?' She shook her head. 'That'd be daft. Sweet Pete. Sweet Pea.' She wrinkled her nose. 'Sweet poo.'

Lewis, hurt by her dismissal of his suggestion yet eager to win her approval, took the game one step further, 'Smelly poo.'

'Smelly bum.'

Giggles escalated to shrieking laughter as they chorused, 'Smelly Gordon. Smelly Gordon.'

'This sounds fun. Can I join in?' Their mother stood in the doorway, eyebrows raised, a pile of folded nappies clutched to her chest.

'Lewis was telling me a joke.' Unsure how much her mother had heard, Tessa turned to Lewis for confirmation. 'Weren't you?'

'Yes … but I've forgotten it,' he mumbled.

'Well I hope you weren't being *mean* about anyone. It's cruel to say nasty things about people who can't answer back.'

Tessa, not caring for the way the conversation was heading, demanded, 'Can't we go somewhere, Mum? We're bored.'

'Why don't you play in the garden? It's much too nice to be indoors.'

'But what can we *do* in the garden? We've spent the whole holiday in the garden. We want to go to the pictures, don't we, Lewis? Why can't you take us?' Tessa knew that it was out of the question but it gave her satisfaction to put her mother on the spot and win another battle in her war against Gordon.

'Maybe we could go for a little walk this afternoon. To the park. Take Gordon on his first outing. You could help me push the pram.'

Tessa and Lewis's pram had been disposed of years ago, and their parents had bought the flamboyant vehicle now standing in the hall from a neighbour. A few weeks before the baby's arrival, their father had given it a complete overhaul. After it was duly oiled and polished, he demonstrated manoeuvring techniques – how to lean on the handle to raise the front wheels; how to apply the brake with a stab of the foot. Lewis thought it might be fun to push it along the pavement, fringed canopy dancing as the shiny black pram dipped on its strapped suspension.

'No, thanks,' Tessa answered.

With that, Gordon started a fretful grizzle and, without further discussion, their mother left them.

'What *shall* we do, then?' Lewis asked.

'Let's go to Cranwell Lodge.'

Lewis looked dubious. 'We'll have to tell Mum we're going out.'

'Why? She doesn't care *what* we do as long as we don't pester.'

They slipped out of the front gate, skipping along the pavement, pausing only to stroke a tabby cat, sprawled in the shade of one of the lime trees that punctuated Medway Avenue. They hurried on in silence, taking the second right into Cranwell Road, keeping up the pace, breathing heavily as the road rose steeply, lined on both sides with identical pebble-dashed semis. They toiled on up the hill until, beyond the last of the boring little houses, they came to the entrance of a detached villa, standing some way back from the road. Cranwell Lodge was inscribed in the rectangle of slate set in one of the brick piers. The rotting wooden gates hung open, revealing a paved drive, green with moss and creeping ivy, which, as it neared the house, was overhung with leggy bushes. It was a sombre place, the kind of place youngsters might scurry past, before a clawed hand reached from the foliage to clutch a tender throat.

The children slipped through the vegetation, following the overgrown path around to the back of the house where Tessa tapped boldly on the glazed upper panel of the door. They waited, ears inclined towards the grimy glass.

'She's singing.' Lewis drew away from the door as a voice, thin yet piercing, grew louder.

'It's "Oh Come All Ye Faithful",' Tessa grinned.

A figure, blurred by the frosted glass, appeared on the other side of the door and, still singing, reached first up then down, noisily drawing back the bolts before unlocking and opening it. The singer was a woman, perhaps seventy years old, wiry white hair cut short in uneven clumps. She wore a white blouse and a black skirt – standard old lady garb had it not been for the crimson satin dressing gown covering it and the matching velvet beret, dipped provocatively over one ear.

Their first meeting with Mrs Channing had been last summer when, against their mother's instructions, they'd wandered away from home in search of a slope down which to test drive a go-cart, recently acquired from a neighbour who was clearing an outhouse. They were cautious to begin with, starting their ride on the crude contraption a short way up the incline of Cranwell Road, taking it in turns to straddle the rough plank that formed the chassis. As they mastered the steering – a tug on the loop of rope which was connected to either side of the front axle – and brakes – the driver's heels, applied to the pavement – they grew more cocky until eventually they were careering down the hill, from top to bottom. Lewis was unlucky on his third run, when the front wheel caught the edge of a tilted paving slab, causing the axle to pivot and the wheel to ram into the plank, stopping the cart dead and throwing him off. In putting a hand out to save himself, he grazed his knuckles and twisted his wrist backwards. Tessa raced to help her brother, who was wailing, shock aggravating the actual damage. At that moment a taxi drew up and an old lady got out. Lewis had stopped crying at the sight of the woman, who cut an unusual figure, petite and fragile, in a floaty turquoise coat exactly the same colour as the feathers decorating her wide-brimmed straw hat. More striking than her clothes was the cage, containing a small white parrot, which the driver removed from the seat next to him and placed on the pavement. 'D'you need a hand with her, Miss?' the driver asked, pointing at the bird. 'No thank you, Mr Wilkins.' Then, as if she'd known them all their lives, she'd nodded towards them, smiling. 'The children will help me, won't you, dears?' Lewis, his injured left hand clamped under his right armpit, sniffed and said nothing but Tessa, sensing one of those moment when something remarkable was about to take place, nodded. Thus began the children's clandestine association with Mrs Channing and Blanche, the sulphur-crested cockatoo.

'Good morning, Swinburnes. This is an unexpected pleasure.' This had become the standard greeting whenever they turned up on her doorstep and her choice of collective name delighted them.

Lewis pointed out tactfully, 'It's quite a long time 'til Christmas.'

'Yes, my dear, but when one is as old as I am, there's no guarantee that one will be around next December. Do come in.'

They followed her through the scullery. Despite the soaring temperatures, the décor – clinical white tiles to a dado rail, then pale blue walls running up to a flaking white ceiling – gave the impression that the daylight was reflected off a carpet of snow. The faintest whiff of gas lingered in the austere room as she led them, all three singing … *Oh come let us adore Him … Oh come let us adore Him* … the crêpe soles of the children's sandals squeaking on the lino. They might have visited the house a dozen times since Lewis's mishap, but not once had they seen so much as a loaf of bread on the scrubbed table, a vegetable on the draining board or a pan simmering on the spindly-legged gas cooker.

By contrast, the breakfast room beyond, although spacious, was cosy. Swags of green velvet curtains excluded most of the daylight but the room was illuminated by table lamps stationed on the dark, bulbous furniture. Patterned rugs layered the floor like fallen leaves. The walls, covered with rust red wallpaper, were crowded with paintings and framed photographs of sailing boats and elephants and dreamy-eyed ladies and stern-faced men. There was a sofa and two armchairs, piled with cushions, and a floor-to-ceiling dresser cluttered with mismatched china. From the bay window, shafts of sunlight slid between the curtains and fell across the ruby red cloth covering the huge, round table. The mantelpiece was piled high with fascinating objects: a stuffed squirrel *not* in a glass case; a marble death-mask; a replica of the Taj Mahal; brass candlesticks and copper bowls – items the like of which the children had only seen in museums. Aladdin's cave or a Bedouin tent could not have been more engaging. Next to the fireplace, and without a doubt the star attraction, a white parrot with a yellow crest sidled back and forth along its perch, dipping its head and muttering to itself in gentle squawks.

'So, what have you got to tell us?' Mrs Channing stood next to the parrot, her words suggesting that the creature had an equal interest in whatever the children had to say.

'We've got a baby brother now,' Tessa sighed and stuck out her lower lip.

'And you don't think much of him.' The old lady spoke as if it were an established fact.

Tessa looked surprised. 'How d'you know that?'

'Well, for a start, you look as if you've lost a pound and found a penny. Besides, it's common knowledge that babies are a pain in the arse.'

The children stifled giggles, thrilled to hear such fruity language.

'Babies should be kept in the cellar until they are …' she put a gnarled finger to her chin as if performing a complex

19

calculation, '… three years old. That's when they start to become interesting.'

'Did *you* have any babies, Mrs Channing?' Lewis asked, imagining her slamming and locking a cellar door.

'No. No, I didn't. But I did have a brother. A younger brother. Harold.'

'The same as the one who got an arrow in his eye?' Tessa suggested.

'Yes, my dear.' She turned away, realigning the troupe of ebony elephants that paraded along the mantelpiece. 'He was killed in battle too, like King Harold. But not by an arrow. By Boer guns. At Ladysmith. He was twenty-two.' Her voice faded, as if the information was no longer meant for them.

The children stood in silence but their discomfort was almost immediately dispelled by the sound of enthusiastic nose-blowing from somewhere in the house. It continued, growing louder, until the door on the other side of the room opened and an elderly man, white handkerchief clutched to his nose, came in. Catching sight of the children, he gave his nose a final wipe and stuffed the handkerchief into his trouser pocket. 'Visitors. We have visitors.' He smiled, revealing impossibly white teeth.

Henry Zeal was a scaled down version of a man, barely a foot taller than nine-year-old Lewis. His ruddy face shone as though it had been polished then buffed with a duster and an overly large nose dominated it, rendering his deep-set grey eyes and near lipless mouth even less significant. An abundance of wavy grey hair topped him off, the waves running from side to side, like furrows in a ploughed field. But despite his physical disadvantages, he had the presence of a man twice his size and a full, bass-baritone voice, more fitting a Goliath than a Tom Thumb.

'Henry, these poor Swinburnes have suffered a great misfortune since we last saw them.'

Tessa was enchanted at Mrs Channing's and Mr Zeal's vocabulary. It reminded her of the time a group of actors came to the school to perform an adaptation of *David Copperfield*. She hadn't understood a lot of what they said but the sense was made perfectly clear by the way they delivered the lines. In fact it was just as if these two old people were putting on a show for her and Lewis and she wondered if they carried on in the same way once they were alone.

After a dramatic pause Mrs Channing continued. 'They have acquired a baby brother.'

Lewis, who seemed more able in this house than anywhere to speak for himself, filled out the details. 'We didn't … whatever-you-said … him. Mum did. He's called Gordon. He's okay, I suppose.'

'He's not,' Tessa snapped. 'Mum spends all her time fussing with him. She never takes us anywhere any more.'

Mr Zeal patted her hand, 'I'm sure it's just temporary, my dear, and everything will be back to normal before too long. But let's forget about Gordon for a while, shall we? Is it too early in the day to offer you both a glass of sherry?'

Tessa and Lewis giggled. They loved coming to this house where adults and children were treated as equals. And equality encouraged truthfulness. 'We're too young to drink sherry, aren't we, Lewis? I don't think we'd like it anyway. Dad let us have a sip of beer at Christmas and it was horrible.'

'Lemonade, then? One may be too young to drink sherry but one is *never* too old to drink lemonade.' Mr Zeal opened the cupboard at the base of the dresser and took out a bottle of lemonade and four cut glass tumblers similar to the ones that their mother kept locked in the glass-fronted cabinet and which *never* came out, not even at Christmas.

Once they had finished their drinks, the children turned their attention to Blanche, offering her sunflower seeds which she took from the palms of their hands, her black beak twisted to the side, transforming it from weapon to tool. Mrs Channing had taught them how to pet the bird, how to run the backs of their index fingers down her white breast and to listen for the burbling that signified contentment.

The children had managed to keep these visits to Cranwell Lodge and their friendship with Mrs Channing a secret. Even if their mother had heard rumours about an eccentric old lady, there was little likelihood that she would bump into her. Mrs Channing kept herself to herself, rarely leaving the house and when she did – to take Blanche to the vet or to see her bank manager – she went in Mr Wilkins's taxi. Groceries, meat and bread were delivered to the door and she had no involvement with the neighbours. Despite this, if they were to keep their visits a secret, the children dared not come too frequently or stay too long. As a result, these visits became an exquisite treat to be rationed like a box of chocolates.

The clock started to strike eleven. Tessa nudged her brother. 'We'd better go.'

Mr Zeal eased himself out of the armchair and delved into the pocket of his cardigan. 'Before you venture on your way, hold out your right hands.'

The children waited, savouring what they knew would come next.

The old man dropped a wrapped sweet onto each extended palm. 'From Morocco,' he said, as he always did.

They sauntered down the road, chewing the chocolate-covered toffees, which needed to be eaten before they reached home. Tessa, the faster eater, finished first. 'It was barley sugar last time, wasn't it?'

Lewis nodded.

'Those were from Morocco, too. D'you think he gets all his sweets from there?'

Lewis shrugged and mumbled, 'Dunno.' Then, swallowing, asked, 'Where is Morocco, anyway?'

'A long way away,' Tessa hedged. 'He must get them sent.'

'Probably in crates,' Lewis added.

Once back home, it was clear that their mother hadn't given them a second thought. The pram stood outside the back door, Gordon, barely visible beneath a mound of shawls and blankets, whimpering persistently.

'What's the matter with him, Mum?' Lewis asked, following her as she pegged nappies on the clothes line. He was getting used to the paraphernalia that had arrived with Gordon. It covered every surface, like debris after a bomb had exploded – nappies, bibs, safety pins, Vaseline, fancy cardigans and smocked romper suits, talcum powder, cotton wool. But he didn't think he would ever become accustomed to the grizzling that he knew would, without intervention, increase in intensity until the screaming baby was the only thing in the world.

His mother smiled. 'There's nothing wrong with him, Lewis. He's just a baby. All he can do is cry.'

'And wee and poo and puke,' he added, wanting to set the record straight, 'Like Tess said.'

His mother pushed his hair away from his forehead. 'Tessa's very stubborn. Once she says something she'll stick to it, whether it's right or wrong. And remember, she's not *always* right. You must make up your own mind.' Again and again her fingers ran through his hair, calming and attentive, and, looking up into her face, he willed her never to stop, but the baby's wail grew louder and she hurried to the pram. He followed, watching as she pulled back the covers and lifted Gordon, laying him gently on her left shoulder and stroking his back. 'There, there. Mummy's here. What's the matter? D'you want a cuddle? Do you?'

The baby soon stopped crying and Lewis noticed that his eyes were open and that he appeared to be peeping at him over his mother's shoulder as if to say, *She's mine.*

'I'm bored.' Tessa burst out of the house where she'd been looking for something to do. 'When's dinner ready, Mum? I'm starving.'

'I'll get something when I've fed Gordon and settled him for his nap.'

'That'll take *ages*. Me and Lewis need feeding, too. Why are we the ones who have to wait?'

Their mother swayed from side to side, the baby silent on her shoulder. 'You know what Dad said, Tessa. You two are supposed to be helping, not making things more difficult.'

'Just a jam sandwich to go on with?' suggested Lewis, inclined, as ever, to look for the middle way.

Lewis and Tessa took their sandwiches to the far corner of the garden, their favourite place to escape the baby-ness that had, during the previous week, permeated the house and transformed it into a foreign land. As they ate, they returned to the topic which now dominated their lives.

'See. I told you it would be like this, didn't I?' Tessa threw a clod of soil at a white butterfly that had settled on a ragged cabbage. 'We've got to do something.'

'Like what?'

Tessa sucked the end of her plait and then looped it under her nose. 'D'you like him?'

'How d'you mean?'

'D'you *like* him? D'you *like* it how it is now? Or d'you think everything was nicer before he was born?'

'Before.' Lewis came straight back with his verdict.

'Me, too. So we've got to *do* something.'

Lewis waited, confident that his sister had a plan.

'I've been thinking about it. What if we put a spell on him? Something to make him … to make it like it was … before.'

'We can't kill him,' Lewis said firmly.

'Not kill him. Just … send him back.'

'Back where?' He tried not to picture where Gordon had come from.

Tessa shrugged. 'Look. Why don't we just do a spell and see what happens? It probably won't work,' she conceded. Then added, 'Anyway, it'll be something to do.'

Lewis, feeling out of his depth, scrambled up into the flowering cherry that grew on the edge of the lawn, the bark on its trunk and lower branches polished to a rich red in several places, indicating the best foot and hand holds. Safely in the crown of the tree, he crouched, knees doubled up to his chin. In winter this made an excellent vantage point from which to study the houses and back gardens of Medway Avenue but now, peering between the leaves, he only saw fragmented sections of the same scene, as if it were a half-finished jigsaw puzzle and, when he looked up, the leaves stirring in the light breeze revealed shifting patches of sky, giving him the not unpleasant sensation that he, too, was moving.

'I've worked out what we've got to do.' Tessa stood at the base of the tree. 'We'll get started after dinner.'

Chapter 3

'I'VE MADE A LIST.' Tessa pulled a scrap of paper from the pocket of her navy shorts. The children were sitting cross-legged on the floor in her bedroom and, beyond the closed door, Gordon was crying. 'Plasticine. A dirty bib. Some of his hair – it doesn't have to be much. And...' she paused, 'a blob of poo. Gordon's poo, that is.'

Lewis closed his eyes and shook his head. 'I'm not touching poo. Can't we use something else?'

'No, we can't.'

What was the matter with Lewis? Wasn't it obvious that if the magic were to be successful they needed to use the right things – things that belonged to Gordon? People seemed to think that Lewis was brainy, and maybe he was as long as he had all day to work things out, but at the moment he was being completely dim.

'But you said the spell probably wouldn't work so I don't know why we're—'

'Because – we – haven't – got – anything – else – to – doooo.' She emphasised every word, effectively overruling his objection.

They sneaked around the house, locating a soiled bib and a ball of plasticine. The hair was trickier. Whilst Lewis asked his mother to write out a page of sums, Tessa sneaked the nail scissors from the manicure set that was kept in the middle drawer of her mother's dressing table. She tiptoed towards the cot, whispering the nonsense that people used as soon as they were within sight of a baby. 'There, there. Everything's fine. Fine. There.' It was a bit spooky when Gordon's intermittent crying stopped as, open-eyed and calm, he appeared to be looking at her. She lifted a few silky strands of dark hair from the nape of his neck, where it grew thickest, and snipped it with the scissors. He turned purposefully towards her touch, his parted lips in search of something, but she pulled away and, dropping the tuft of hair into an envelope she'd salvaged from the waste-paper basket, slipped out of the room.

The final item proved more straightforward than they could have hoped. When Gordon soiled a nappy, their mother removed it, folding it over, and set it to one side whilst she cleaned him up and pinned on a fresh one. Tessa made sure that she was with her mother on several nappy changes and eventually, when she went to find something in the bathroom, Tessa had the chance, with the aid of a wad of cotton wool, to collect a smear of poo from the soiled nappy. This she wrapped in a sheet of Izal toilet paper before placing it in an empty Smiths crisp packet. 'Like a pass-the-parcel,' she explained to Lewis later, thrilled by her own daring.

Lewis, relieved that his role in the plot had been so hygienic, smiled his admiration. 'When are we going to do the actual spell? Won't it look a bit funny if we start dancing around him, chanting or whatever we have to do?'

'We can do it without going anywhere near him. That's what all this is for.' Tessa held up the brown paper bag that now contained everything they needed to proceed. Getting hold of the spell items had been great fun in itself, like fulfilling a secret mission, and they agreed to leave it until the following day before carrying out the next phase of the plan.

Lewis settled at the kitchen table to do the sums, double-checking his calculations, muttering, 'Look at the sign,' before starting each one. Tessa sat opposite, cutting pictures and words from an old magazine then pasting them into a scrapbook. There was no purpose in her effort, no holiday homework to complete or Brownie badge in the offing – she was doing it because she liked cutting things out, liked the almond scent of the stiff paste. They concentrated on their projects, sporadically breaking into song, one starting and the other joining in. *'Maresy dotes... an dozy dotes... an liddle lambsy tivy'*, occasionally exchanging glances or kicking each other under the table.

Their mother was ironing in the dining room when the phone rang. The children stopped what they were doing, listening as she crossed the hall to answer it.

'Of course, Frank... Of course not... You'll have to take pot luck... See you later then.'

Tessa returned to the table. 'I think Uncle Frank's coming to tea.'

Lewis smiled. 'Good.'

They were playing hopscotch behind the garage when Frank Swinburne came whistling around the corner. 'You kiddos up to no good, as usual,' he grinned.

The children loved everything about Uncle Frank. He was one of the few people they knew – along with Mrs Channing and Mr Zeal – whose company lived up to expectations. He wasn't like other adults who promised 'I'll be there in a minute' but never came.

'Will you play hopscotch, Uncle Frank?' Lewis asked.

'Why else would I come to this hell hole? Don't you know I won medals for hopping when I was in the army?' He dipped his knees, catching each of them around the waist, lifting and swinging them round. When they signalled enough, squealing and screaming that they were going to be sick, he took his turn in their game, skidding the flat stone across the chalked grid, hopping from square to square, ensuring he made a bad job of it then feigning outrage at their amusement.

Peggy Swinburne came out, the baby a swaddled bundle clasped against her chest. 'What's all the noise about?' Her frown dissolved. 'Oh, hello, Frank. Dick's not home yet.'

'Hi, Peg. These two horrors are giving me a hard time.' He dropped to his knees, clutching his chest, then sprawled forward. 'You win. I'm a gonner. Aaaggghh.' He lay prone, eyes closed and legs twitching.

The children whooped with delight and their mother laughed. 'You're a daft beggar, Frank. You'll ruin your clothes.'

He jumped up, brushing chalk-dust from the knees of his pale trousers and the front of his short-sleeved shirt, and held his arms out, 'Let's have a gander at this new nephew of mine, then.' He took the baby in the crook of his left arm, loosening the sheet around the tiny head. 'Ugly little blighter, aren't you?'

Tessa couldn't square his unkind words with their tender delivery, or the way he raised the baby to his face, brushing his lips against the pink forehead. She looked to her mother, expecting her to look hurt by the insult, but she was smiling.

'We think he's ugly too,' Tessa crowed.

'Almost as ugly as you two.' He punched them both lightly on the shoulder.

'I think it's a joke,' Lewis whispered to his sister.

'I know. I'm not stupid.' In an instant, her adoration for her uncle turned to loathing. Did he really intend to treat this upstart as their equal?

'I'm a bit behind with the tea,' their mother announced. 'Could you hold Gordon while I get organised?'

'Why don't we have a picnic? Out here, in the garden.' Frank suggested. 'And we'll sort it out, won't we, kids? Give you time to settle this little fella down.'

This was more like it. 'Can we, Mum? Pleeease.' As their

uncle passed the baby back to their mother, Tessa immediately forgave him for his disloyalty.

Picnic preparations were well under way when the garage doors slammed, heralding Dick Swinburne's arrival. The children, who were tugging the plastic table-cloth, arguing over the best spot on the lawn to place it, abandoned their tussle and rushed to meet him.

'Dad. Dad—'

'We found a dead frog by the rhubarb—'

'Uncle Frank's hopeless at hopscotch—'

'He says Gordon's ugly.' This, gleefully, from Tessa.

'We're having a picnic tea, Dad.'

'Hang on, hang on.' Their father put down his well-worn brief case, hugged his children and nodded to his older brother. 'Hello, Frank.'

'How's tricks?' Frank asked.

'Fine, thanks. You?'

'Tickety-boo. Just took over a mate's book and doubled my commission. I'm thinking of changing my car. Peggy's looking well. And the nipper.'

'Yes. She's tired, of course, but it'll be easier when the kids are back at school.'

The two men sat on the steps leading up from the yard to the lawn talking about work and cars and cricket, while the children hovered hoping that each lull in the conversation signalled its conclusion. On and on they rumbled and Tessa closed her eyes, surprised how alike the men's voices sounded. They looked similar, too – brown hair, grey eyes, big ears and straight noses – but Uncle Frank's face seemed somehow gentler; more friendly. He always wore interesting clothes. Pale trousers and jazzy ties. Coloured socks. Not boring greys and browns like Dad. And, of course, he didn't limp.

Eventually the children could put up with hunger and inactivity no longer and went to see why their mother was taking so long.

After the picnic, Frank showed the children how, by blowing across a blade of grass clamped between their thumbs, they could generate a delightfully ear-splitting noise. Tessa struggled for a few minutes, refusing to take advice from anyone, then gave up altogether and began juggling with two tennis balls – something her brother couldn't do. Lewis persisted with the grass until he was able to produce the reedy sound at will.

Frank gave him the thumbs up. 'The lad's got talent.'

Delighted at gaining his uncle's approval, he marched around the lawn, blowing into his fist, drowning out the gentle evening sounds that floated across the gardens. But, after a couple of circuits, his father snapped, 'That'll do, Lewis. We've had quite enough of that racket.' He pointed to the open bedroom window. 'You'll wake Gordon.'

The grown-ups went on chatting and Lewis, near to tears at what he considered an unjust reprimand, retreated to the far corner of the garden. Here he pretended to be fascinated by a colony of ants as they went about their mysterious business, all the while wishing that his mother would come looking for him, to hug him and persuade him to rejoin the family group. But she didn't, leaving him feeling doubly abandoned. After a while the ants gained his attention and he pushed a twig down into the mound of frothy soil which marked the nest. Instantly, shiny dark-brown ants spilled out, scattering in all directions, many carrying a single egg the size of a grain of pudding rice.

'Ssshhh.' Tessa crept up behind him. 'Don't talk too loud. I think they've forgotten us and it's way past bedtime.'

'I *hate* him,' Lewis whispered.

'Who? Dad or Gordon?'

He thought for a moment. 'All of them.'

'What about me?'

He stared at her. What a silly question. Her 'What about me?'

31

was like asking what he felt about clouds or Saturdays or books. His sister *was* – and there was nothing more to be said.

A wail, quiet but powerful, seeped out of the bedroom window, like a factory hooter announcing that it was time to go home. Dick Swinburne glanced around and, spotting the children, pointed at his wristwatch. 'Come on, you two. Look at the time.'

'Ooohhh. Can't we have a bit longer, Dad? It's the holidays,' Tessa pleaded.

Frank jumped up, brushing grass off the seat of his trousers. 'I'm off now anyway. Got to see a man about a dog.' He grabbed the children gently by the earlobes and led them, giggling, towards the house where he said his goodbyes, shaking his brother's hand and kissing Peggy and the children on the cheek.

'See you soon, Frank,' Peggy said.

'Not if I see you first,' he countered, winking at the children, and the family stood on the doorstep, waving as he drove away, the novelty of the evening dissolving as he disappeared from view.

Tessa and Lewis undressed then went in search of their mother. She was sitting in her bedroom, giving Gordon his bottle, singing tenderly *'Lula-lula, lula-lula bye-bye…'* and smiling down into the baby's face, so absorbed that she didn't notice her other children, waiting in the doorway for her bedtime blessing.

'Where's the … stuff?' Lewis whispered after breakfast.

'Under the hedge, by the rhubarb.' Tessa checked that her mother was out of earshot. 'We'll do the next bit when she gives him his feed.'

During the course of the morning, Peggy Swinburne paid more attention to her older children than she had for weeks, apologising for the dreariness of their school holiday. 'Perhaps we can do something nice at the weekend, if the weather holds. Go to the beach, maybe. Dad'll be here to help…'

'Listen.' Tessa held her finger up. 'I think Gordon's crying, Mum.'

'My goodness, you've got sharp ears.'

They rescued the paper bag from its hiding place, removing the contents cautiously in case the magic had started without them, then, seeing everything was as it should be, they brushed the soil off a flat stone and laid the collection out.

'First we've got to make a baby.' Tessa rolled the plasticine between her palms, softening it. She subdivided it into six blobs and, after more rolling, pushed the blobs together to make a rudimentary human form.

'Is it supposed to be Gordon?' Lewis asked, critically.

'I haven't finished yet. Here, hold this.' Tessa handed the model to Lewis. Opening the envelope, she took out the snipping of hair and pushed it firmly into the clay skull. The next step was the one she had been dreading but, not wanting to lose Lewis's respect, she unwrapped the toilet paper.

'Aren't you going to put a nappy on him?' Lewis asked and in so doing provided her with the solution.

'Yes. With his poo in it.' She tore a rectangle from the corner of the toilet paper and folded it around the clay crotch, including the soiled cotton wool. Finally, she laid the effigy on the bib and rolled it up, securing it with the ties. 'There.' The parcel looked no more sinister than a folded face flannel.

'What do we do next?'

Tessa had worked out a broad plan but the details needed refining. 'We've got to send this,' she raised the parcel, 'away. We've got to get it as far away from the house as possible.'

Lewis looked doubtful.

'C'mon, Lew. We agreed, didn't we, that everything was much nicer before he came.'

'I'm not sure.'

'We're not going to hurt him or anything. Just send him…'

She had no idea where unwanted brothers went.

'We could leave the … thing … somewhere. For someone to find.' Lewis thought for a moment. 'Like in a phone box.'

Tessa kissed him and he flushed with pride. 'That's it. We'll leave it in the phone box. C'mon.' She was already walking towards the gate.

'What, we're going to do it now?'

'Why not? It won't take long and then it'll be done.'

The only phone box they could think of was on the far side – the out-of-bounds side – of the main road that marked the limit of their territory. Tessa took charge of the towelling bundle, safely concealed in the paper bag, and they walked briskly to the end of Medway Avenue then turned right, continuing along Buckingham Road until they reached the pedestrian crossing, almost opposite their target. The road was on several bus routes and local traffic used it to avoid going through the centre of the town. The noise and the rush of filthy air from the passing vehicles deterred even Tessa from breaking the rules laid down by their parents and they settled themselves on a garden wall. At last a young woman paused at the crossing and Tessa, having satisfied herself that the woman was a stranger – it was essential that word of this didn't get back to their mother – grabbed Lewis's hand and approached her. 'Could you cross us over, please?'

Safely on the other side, they raced to the empty phone box and pulled open the heavy door. Tessa placed the package on the black metal shelf, next to the handset, turning it this way and that, as if it were vital to have it in exactly the right position.

'What happens now?' Lewis asked.

Tessa stared at the bag then shrugged. 'I don't know. Nothing much if we stay here. Let's get back.'

They hurried home, on the way concocting an alibi for their absence. *We were playing outside the front gate when an old woman came past and asked us how to get to the library. She couldn't see very well so we took her as far as the main road. But we didn't go across.'* And, when it became clear that Peggy Swinburne hadn't missed them, they were disappointed not to have to make use of it.

After dinner they debated whether to go back to the phone box, to check on the package, but Diane Stoddy turned up, holding her ground on the doorstep until their mother invited her in.

'Tessa, why don't you show Diane your new theatre?' she suggested.

'Gordon brought it for us when he came home from the hospital,' Lewis explained.

'Mum and Dad bought it, stupid,' Tessa corrected her brother. 'Anyway, *we* had to do the hard part – glueing the thing together. Colouring the scenery. Cutting out the figures.'

'When Mum had *our* baby, I got a dolly,' Diane boasted. 'She opens and closes her eyes and says "Maa-Maa" when you sit her up.' She gave a mewling impersonation of the doll.

'"*Dolly*"?' Lewis half-laughed, half-snorted, wondering why his sister bothered with this silly girl who spoke like a three year-old and never had anything interesting to say.

They set up the little stage, wings and proscenium arch but when it came to breathing life into the tiny cardboard characters, Diane's presence somehow clogged their creative channels, like fluff on a gramophone needle, and the performance never came to anything.

'You can come to my house if you like,' Diane suggested, slipping her arm through Tessa's. 'Mum might let us take Linda out in the pushchair.'

Lewis was still tingling with excitement from the morning's exploit and he wanted to be alone with Tessa so that they could talk about it properly. He couldn't believe that she would abandon him for the company of silly Diane and her stupid baby sister.

But he needn't have worried.

'No thanks. Anyway, I can't. We've got to go and visit … a mad old lady in the loony bin. Haven't we, Lewis? She went mad because … because she was haunted by the ghost of … her brother … who she locked in the cellar. And who starved to death.'

Lewis nodded and grinned.

Chapter 4

THE PLACID AUGUST SKIES boiled into navy and indigo as the heat wave broke in a succession of spectacular thunderstorms. The first raindrops dried almost before they had chance to seep into the warm ground, giving off a musty smell, like curing concrete. Then, as the thunder cracked, the rain started in earnest, bouncing off the brick-hard soil and forming puddles on the parched lawn. It cascaded down the roof, overflowing the gutters and splashing on the back yard. Within minutes of a storm's passing, the sun reappeared and the heat built again, drawing curtains of steam from slate roofs and lapped garden fences, creating the illusion the rain had doused a fire but left it smouldering.

At first, the children found the storms thrilling, chasing upstairs to get a clearer view of the lightning and to count the seconds until the thunder cracked, sometimes shaking the house and causing them to shriek with terrified delight. But they soon tired of it. They were trapped in the house for hours on end. The temperature never dropped. Milk curdled and chocolate melted. At night it was impossible to find a cool inch of sheet and the air seemed low on oxygen. The whole family became tetchy through shortage of sleep. The baby failed to settle, day or night, and he developed an angry-looking rash.

'D'you think it's got anything to do with … you know?' Lewis whispered to Tessa after watching their mother dab Gordon's tiny torso with calamine lotion.

'Mum says it's a heat rash. We didn't ask for a heat rash, did we?' she dismissed his query.

At every opportunity, the children grumbled. 'We've had a horrid summer.' Or 'It's been *so* boring.' Or 'You haven't taken us anywhere.'

'Never mind,' Peggy Swinburne consoled, 'You'll be back in school next week. And then you'll have plenty to do.'

Tessa wasn't sure if her mother was making a joke and, although she felt obliged to protest, 'I don't want to go back. I hate school,' she was looking forward to the following Monday and the start of the new school year. She liked going to school and found the work easy, usually coming near the top of the class in weekly maths and spelling tests.

'I can't wait for *next* September, when I go to the grammar school,' Tessa sighed.

Lewis hesitated. 'I don't want you to go to another school, Tess. It'll be horrid without you.'

'Well, I've got to go. And that's that.'

Lewis blinked a couple of times and fiddled with a tyre on his Dinky car. Tessa suddenly lassoed him with her arms, squeezing him against her, planting a rough kiss on his cheek. 'I love you, Lewis.'

'Oh.' Lewis smiled. 'I love you, too.'

'I don't ever want you to die. Or love anyone more than me.'

'I never will, Tess. I promise.'

The new term began. Breakfast times were more hectic than they'd been before Gordon was born and, whilst their mother fussed with the baby, Tessa and Lewis were left to sort out their own clothes and remember whatever they needed to take to school that day.

Their father made it clear that he had no time to spend running around after them. 'I've got a job to go to. Goodness me. You're perfectly capable of getting your own breakfasts.'

Lewis held out the lopsided round of bread which he'd hacked off the loaf. 'I can't cut it straight, Dad.'

'Don't they teach you anything at that school?'

'They don't teach us bread cutting,' Tessa muttered.

'Don't be cheeky.' Her father flicked her upper arm with the back of his hand and yet another day began in a drama of incorrect dinner money, un-brushed hair and misplaced games kit.

As the weeks went by, the baby cried less, content to lie gurgling in his pram. His cheeks filled out and dimples puckered his tiny knuckles. He began to look like a real person. He learned to smile and the children amused him and themselves with games of peek-a-boo, pushing their faces towards him, mimicking his chuckle as his legs pedalled the air in excitement.

It was more difficult to get to Cranwell Lodge once school started back. Visits had to be short and were limited to weekends, when their absence from home was unlikely to be spotted. Mrs Channing never failed to ask how they were coping with the baby and, keen to entertain the old couple and maintain the impression that they were still opposed to the intruder, Tessa had *almost* let on about the spell. But, at that very moment, Blanche had nipped Lewis on his index finger, whereupon Mr Zeal had applied a large sticking plaster, given Blanche a stiff talking to and prescribed a double helping of Moroccan sweets – humbugs on this occasion. By the time the fuss died down, she'd had second thoughts about disclosing their secret with its embarrassing details of poo collecting.

The Swinburne family's routine flexed to accommodate its newest member and, by half-term, memories of life before Gordon were fading. He became less of a threatening presence and there were times when Tessa forgot to dislike him.

'You need new winter coats,' Peggy Swinburne announced one chilly November Saturday. 'Dad says he'll stay here with Gordon while we pop into town on the bus.'

As they were going out of the door, Dick Swinburne dug in his pocket and produced two shilling pieces, 'You're good kids. Extra pocket money this week. And Mum,' he gave Peggy a theatrical wink, 'why don't you treat them to cream cakes?'

The bus to the town centre stopped not far from the phone box where the children had left the paper bag. Whenever they passed, Tessa felt uneasy, half hoping that it had reappeared so that they could retrieve it. Once, when they were near the phone box keeping an eye on the pram while their mother was in the butcher's, she thought it *had* come back. But when she went to investigate, it turned out to be a bag from the bakery, a dab of jam and a sprinkle of sugar suggesting that it had contained a doughnut.

They didn't have long to wait for the bus. 'Let's go upstairs,' Tessa insisted. Following her, Lewis struggled up the twisting stairs and down the aisle to the front of the bus, hanging on to the backs of the seats whilst the bus swayed along.

Their mother joined them. 'Uncle Frank thinks I ought to learn to drive. He says he'll give me a few lessons. It'd make things a lot easier.'

Lewis had only recently realised – when a lady doctor driving a shiny black car had come to see his mother – that women *were* allowed to drive. He'd never seen any of his friends' mothers, or any of their female neighbours, behind the wheel. It was difficult to imagine his mother in the driving seat of their car, turning the jangly ignition keys and fiddling with that choke thing. His father had explained what the choke was for but its operation hinged on too many *if*s and *but*s for Lewis's liking. Then there were those three pedals that needed pressing – surely out of the question for his mother's dainty feet in her pretty shoes.

'I like coming on the bus, Mum.' He wanted to say something reassuring, to confirm that things were fine as they were.

She patted his shoulder. 'You're a good boy.'

'Couldn't Dad teach you?' Tessa asked.

'That might not be such a good idea.'

'You mean he'd shout at you if you made a mistake?'

'No, of course not. It's just that...'

'Uncle Frank's more fun?'

'No...'

'We think he's more fun, don't we?' Tessa looked to her brother for affirmation. 'He's always got time to play with us. Not like Dad.'

Peggy Swinburne frowned. 'That's not quite fair, Tessa. Of course Uncle Frank plays with you when he comes to the house. But that boils down to an hour or so every couple of weeks. Dad spends far more time with you than that. And before you tell me that Uncle Frank never tells you off, it's because you're not his responsibility. Your father and I want you to know how to behave properly. To be able to tell right from wrong.' Her voice softened. 'And he loves you both very much. Didn't he give you extra pocket money this morning?'

Pupils at the primary school did not have to wear a uniform, but it was expected that whatever they did wear was plain and sensible. Their mother enjoyed sewing and made most of their clothes but their coats and mackintoshes came from McKay's in Bridge Street. It was an old-fashioned, gloomy shop with ornate wooden counters running down either side. Behind the counters, labelled drawers with cupped brass handles lined the walls, reaching almost to the ceiling. The shop assistants used a step ladder when they needed to get to the uppermost drawers. Every footstep sounded on the bare, polished floorboards and the whole shop smelled of woollen jumpers and paraffin.

A neat man, dressed in a dark grey suit, tape measure draped around his neck, came forward to serve them. He was courteous enough as he brought out a succession of overcoats, occasionally muttering, 'This style's very popular, madam,' or 'Excellent value for money,' but his face remained deadpan. When Peggy Swinburne finally made up her mind – navy blue with a belt for Tessa, and an oversized grey duffle coat for Lewis – his mouth stretched in a mechanical smile and Lewis remembered the ventriloquist's dummy from last year's Christmas party that had haunted his dreams for so many nights.

Relieved to escape the creepiness of Mckay's, they hurried to WH Smith's where Tessa spent her pocket money on a set of coloured pencils. She already had plenty at home but seeing the twelve pencil rainbow in its flat box, sharpened and ready to go, she couldn't resist, then became impatient when Lewis, unable to decide between an *I-Spy Book of Cats* and a magnifying glass, eventually decided to save his shilling until their next shopping trip.

Their last stop was the Kardomah Café in the High Street. The children loved the fug of warm, coffee-scented air; the intimacy of the panelled booths; the waitresses in their starched white pinafores and caps who brought them selections of fancy cakes and never minded how long they took to choose. They were the only children amongst the groups of smartly-dressed women but, sitting next to their mother, they felt comfortable in this well-mannered world of chit-chat and bone china tea cups, watching the heavy revolving door with its polished brass handles, swishing round, depositing and removing customers like a giant carpet sweeper.

Tessa inspected the other customers. Many of them were wearing hats. Not sensible hats like the ones Mum and Gran wore in the winter, but unnecessary hats that perched on their heads at frivolous angles and required hatpins to keep them there. Mrs Channing had shown them how a hatpin worked and had let them push the elegant pin through the crown of her feathered hat, making a satisfying *pop* as it punctured the tightly-woven straw. They wore sparkly brooches on the lapels of their coats, silk scarves around their necks and, when they removed their gloves, their nails were shiny with nail varnish. She wished her mother's coat wasn't so drab; her nails so short; her hair so windswept.

Lewis, too, was fascinated by these women. They reminded him of the mannequins that displayed clothes behind the huge plate glass windows of the larger stores. He imagined that, were he to get close enough to touch one of them, she would be cold, her skin as solid and inflexible as an eggshell. He was sure, too, that she would give off a strong smell, like the hyacinths that his grandmother grew in a green bowl every spring and that filled her living room with sickly perfume. He edged closer to his mother, enjoying having her to themselves for a while and content to remain sitting there long after he had eaten his chocolate éclair and drunk his lemonade.

It was getting on for twelve-thirty when, carrying the wrapped parcels containing their new coats, they got off the bus. There were lots of people out and about in Medway Avenue, tidying front gardens, carting bags of weekend provisions back from the shops or simply making the most of a day off work. They stopped several times for Peggy Swinburne to chat with acquaintances. This was one thing the children disliked about expeditions with their mother. How was it possible to spend so long discussing nothing in particular? They shifted from one foot to the other, sighing and gazing longingly towards home, hoping that she would take the hint.

When they were within sight of the house, the children ran ahead, eager to show their father the results of the morning's shopping. They chased round to the back door but found it was locked. Then, returning to the front of the house, they pounded on the oak door with the heavy knocker. But no one came and they gave up, sitting on the doorstep until their mother arrived.

'Dad's out,' Tessa announced.

'That's odd.' Peggy Swinburne checked her watch then took the house keys from her bag and unlocked the front door, calling, 'Dick?'

'The pram's not here.' Lewis pointed at the space in the hall where the pram usually stood.

'Dad must have taken Gordon out for some fresh air. They're sure to be back soon,' she said, 'it's nearly dinner time and Gordon needs a bottle.'

While the children tried on their new coats, she began preparing lunch.

At half-past one, there was still no sign of their father and Gordon. The three of them sat down to cheese omelettes accompanied by wedges of bread and butter. Tessa could see from the way she kept glancing at her watch and getting up to peer out of the window that her mother was becoming uneasy. She attempted to reassure her. 'Dad's probably chatting to people in the street. Like you did.'

'Yes, but…' Peggy Swinburne shook her head, laying her knife and fork on the plate next to her half-eaten meal.

At five minutes to two, the telephone rang and, with no attempt to conceal her anxiety, their mother hurried into the hall to answer it.

'Something's really wrong,' Tessa whispered but they stayed where they were until a *clunk-ching* signalled the return of the heavy black handset to its cradle. There was a pause, followed by a low moan.

Lewis wanted nothing more than to stay in the kitchen, the haven where sometimes Mum let him roll out the trimmings from apple pies, twisting the crinkly-edged cutter in the pastry to make jam tarts for tea; or soaked foreign stamps off envelopes, drying them on blotting paper before sticking them in his album; or watched Mum beating eggs, the soft flesh on her arm wobbling, the whirring fork striking the side of the tilted china bowl.

'She's crying.' Tessa seemed uncertain what to do next but, in the end, they tiptoed out of the kitchen and along the hall.

Their mother was sitting on the stairs, crumpled up somehow, folded arms clamped across her chest. She was crying, quietly but fiercely, tears trickling down to her jawline. She didn't appear to notice her children, standing a few feet in front of her.

Lewis edged closer, reaching a hand out to touch her knee. 'Mum?'

His voice tugged her back from wherever she was and she dragged first one hand, then the other, across her eyes and under her nose then wiped them on her best skirt, as if it were no more than an old towel. 'Don't worry. I'm being silly.' She tried to smile but it didn't work and the tears started again.

'It's Dad, isn't it?'

In her mind's eye, Tessa watched her father crossing the main road, too impatient to do his road drill and failing to notice a van, or maybe a motorbike, bearing down on him. Hampered by the cumbersome pram and his limp, unable to sprint to the safety of the far pavement, the vehicle ploughed in to him.

'He's had an accident, hasn't he?'

'Is he dead?' Without waiting for an answer, Lewis started sobbing.

Peggy Swinburne held her arms out, inviting her children to hug her but still she didn't explain. As they huddled together in an awkward embrace, the telephone rang again, jangly and threatening. She released them immediately, snatching up the receiver. 'Have they found him? Please tell me they've found him.'

Found him? Could their father have been scooped up on the bonnet of the speeding car and whisked off down the road?

'I'm coming now... No... I'm coming.' The call finished, she took several deep breaths before leading the children back to the kitchen. 'There's been some sort of terrible mix-up.' She paused, shaking her head and pushing the hair away from her forehead.

'Tell us, Mum,' Lewis pleaded.

'That was Dad. He went out. To give Gordon some fresh air. And buy a newspaper.' The story came in short bursts, as though she could only manage a few words before needing to re-fill her lungs. 'He went into the newsagent's. Carson's. Left the pram outside the shop door. Right outside. Then, when he came out, the pram was there but Gordon had disappeared. Gone.' The last words came out with a rush and she held her hands up to her mouth, stifling a kind of squeaking noise that was coming from the back of her throat.

Tessa and Lewis stood motionless and silent, not knowing which was worse – losing their baby brother or seeing their mother crying.

Chapter 5

HALF AN HOUR LATER, Gran turned up in a taxi and the children knew that the situation was serious. She bustled in, took one look at their mother who was standing at the sink, eyes tight shut, hands clamped over her ears, and waved the children away. 'Off upstairs. No arguing.'

Relieved to escape their mother's embarrassing behaviour, they holed up in Tessa's bedroom, lying back-to-back on her single bed, spines touching. Lewis was the first to break the silence, his voice gruff. 'Will they find him?'

Tessa rolled on to her back and stared at the ceiling. 'Of course they will.'

'Where d'you think he is?'

'*I* don't know. Perhaps someone's taken him by mistake. Instead of their own baby.'

'But they wouldn't have left the pram—'

'Sshhh.' Tessa held up her hand. 'Listen.' The sound of weeping filtered up the stairs.

'Why isn't Dad here?' Sometimes Lewis asked questions, not because he expected Tessa to supply the answer but to organise his own thoughts.

'He's looking for him, stupid.' The words were harsh but her tone unsure.

The telephone rang and footsteps tapped down the hall. Although they couldn't catch what she was saying, it was clear,

47

from Gran's solemn tone, that their brother hadn't been found.

The children lay alongside each other, warm and disconnected from the unfolding crisis, and soon they fell asleep.

'Your mother's gone … out.' Doris Lloyd stood at the bedroom door. 'I've got biscuits in the kitchen.'

She seldom volunteered treats and as they sat at the table, drinking milk and eating custard creams, Tessa remembered that the last time Gran had made this much fuss of them was the previous spring, when she and Lewis had chickenpox. Come to think of it, there was an air of the sick room in the house today, as if they were all in quarantine, waiting to see whether a horrible disease was going to strike them down.

Tessa held her biscuit between thumb and middle finger and prised the upper layer off with her front teeth. Once she'd eaten it, she licked the sweet filling. 'Have they called the police, Gran?'

Doris appeared uncomfortable at the direct reference to the crisis, clearing her throat before replying. 'Yes. Just to be on the safe side.' Then, as if no more needed to be said, suggested, 'Why don't you go outside and play?'

Lewis, who had been studying the opaque skim that the milk had deposited on the inside of his empty glass, looked up. 'It's getting dark, Gran. We're not allowed to play outside in the dark.'

'Aren't you, dear?' Unprompted, Gran held out the plate of biscuits, saying nothing when Tessa took two.

Sensing that her grandmother's defences were down, Tessa pressed on with her interrogation. 'What *d'you* think's happened to Gordon, Gran?'

'There's been a mistake of some sort, I expect.' Then, under her breath, she added, 'Poor little mite.' She removed her glasses and dabbed her eyes with the hem of her apron.

This first hint that Gordon might be suffering – might be in danger – sent a recollection of his thin wail shooting through Tessa's memory. Eager to silence it she asked. 'Can we watch "Sugar and Spice"? We always watch it, don't we, Lewis?' Without waiting for a reply, they skipped off into the living room, stationing themselves on the sofa, facing the television set.

'Gran?' Some rules might be rewritten today, but Tessa was sure that the ones concerning the television – only grown-ups were allowed to touch it – would never be scrapped. Raising her voice, she directed her demand to the open door. 'Gran? It's nearly five o'clock. Can you switch it on for us?'

Their grandmother appeared, approaching the set as though it were a beached mine, primed and ready to blow them to smithereens. It was a Philco Table Model. The name had a homeliness to it, like that of a best friend and Lewis loved everything about it – the curve of its snot-coloured screen; the smell of warm dust that seeped out of the slatted board at the back; the ribbed plastic knobs – Volume and Contrast – with gold inserts.

Although Gran owned her own television, the children could see that she had no idea where to start with this one. Lewis, who had watched his father closely and memorised every step in the procedure, talked her through it, pointing at the relevant controls. 'Power plug in … and switch it on. Now switch the set on … that's it. It takes a while for the tube to warm up.'

Tessa smiled proudly at her brother's expertise and the three of them sat side by side, Tessa in the middle, watching the ghostly image sharpen. Bu there was something not quite right about watching their programme with Gran sitting alongside them. She *would* keep fidgeting and making stupid comments about the presenters – 'He could do with a decent haircut,' or 'What does she think she looks like?'

The telephone rang and Gran hurried to answer it. She was

back within minutes. 'That was your mother. You're to spend the night at my house. Why don't you pop upstairs and sort out what you'll need? And bear in mind we've got to take it on the bus, so don't pack the kitchen sink.'

Once upstairs, Lewis looked baffled. 'What *do* I need, Tess?'

Tessa reeled off a list. 'Toothbrush. Toothpaste. Pyjamas. Slippers. Dressing gown.'

'Books?'

'That's a good idea. And drawing paper and crayons. And a jigsaw. There's nothing to do at Gran's house.'

'Can I bring my Dinkies?' Lewis pictured himself toiling to the bus stop, dragging a sack containing his most precious belongings, but Gran appeared with two shopping bags, warning them to be sensible about what they took.

It felt no warmer inside Gran's house than it had in the street and a smell of cooked fish hung in the hallway.

'Take your coats off and hang them up. Then we'll have a bit of tea.'

The children shivered in the ill-lit dining room, standing close to the electric fire, the single glowing bar scorching the wool of their long grey socks. When tea materialised, Lewis noticed that everything about the meal was yellow and white – a boiled egg and thin rounds of bread and butter, followed by banana – one between the three of them – sliced into bowls of custard, all laid out on a white tablecloth. To take his mind off the custard skin that was lodged at the back of his throat, he made a mental list of other things that were yellow and edible. Tinned peaches. And pineapple. Cheese. Oranges were sort of yellow. No they weren't, they were orange. Tessa kicked him under the table, then stuck out her tongue, revealing a disc of discolouring banana surrounded by a sea of custard. He copied her and they kept this up, poking tongues out and pulling them back in until, unable to suppress their giggles, they spluttered custard over the tablecloth. Gran shook her head. 'How can you behave like that when your poor mother … and your poor little brother…?'

She made up the narrow beds in the spare room, slipping hot water bottles between the pilled, flannelette sheets. They undressed, Lewis turning away from her as he slipped off his underpants and struggled into his pyjama bottoms, tying the cord securely to ensure that the fly didn't gape. They washed in the cheerless bathroom, the yellowness there again in the pungent bar of Coal Tar soap, and were cleaning their teeth when there was an insistent *rat-a-tat* at the front door.

Gran raised a hand to her throat. 'Now who can that be?'

The visitor knocked again, more forcefully, and she went downstairs.

Defying her instruction to stay where they were, the children tiptoed out on to the landing, hanging over the banister in an attempt to hear what was going on in the hall below.

Lewis put his lips close to his sister's ear. 'Perhaps it's Mum and Dad.'

It wasn't their parents, it was Uncle Frank but, rather than rushing downstairs to greet him, something made them hang back.

Tessa and Lewis saw nothing strange in Frank Swinburne – their father's brother – visiting Doris Lloyd – their mother's mother. Their father had, on several occasions, tried to explain the relationships connecting their various aunts, uncles and cousins, drawing diagrams to show the Swinburne and the Lloyd family trees, but it was boring and complicated. A cousin was a cousin – why bother with tiresome details?

The conversation, in low tones, continued in the hall until their uncle's 'I'd better pop up and see them,' sent them scurrying back to their bedroom. They were engrossed in their library books when he tapped on the open door.

'Well, well, well. What have we here?' He bent to kiss them but seemed not to know how to continue.

Tessa went to his rescue. 'Have they found Gordon yet?'

'No, love. Not yet.'

'Where's Mum and Dad?' Lewis whispered, 'Why can't they come home?'

'Nobody's telling us anything,' Tessa complained.

Frank Swinburne sat on the edge of Lewis's bed, fiddling with his watch strap. 'You two are pretty sharp so there's no point in pretending things aren't serious. The baby's been missing for,' he looked at his watch, 'roughly eight hours. Since about midday. And everyone's starting to get a bit twitchy.'

Tessa had never seen their uncle anything but cheerful and, although it bothered her, it didn't prevent her from taking the opportunity to ask the question that her grandmother seemed intent on avoiding. 'What happened exactly, Uncle Frank? Gran won't tell us.'

Frank dragged the palm of his hand across his mouth. 'Okay. Dick – your dad, I should say – went to Carson's to buy a newspaper. When he got there he found that the pram was too big – too wide – to go through the shop doorway. So he left it parked outside, just for a few minutes, while he nipped in. There was a queue – the man in the shop says it's always busy on a Saturday morning – and he was a bit longer than he might have been. When he came out, the pram was precisely where he left it but,' he cleared his throat, 'Gordon had disappeared.'

Tessa was disappointed. Apart from the bit about the queue in the shop, this was more or less what Gran had told them. But there had to be more to it.

'Did Dad phone nine-nine-nine?' Lewis asked

'Not straight away. Your dad and the other people who were there went searching to see if they could spot him and to ask if anyone had seen anything suspicious.'

'Like what?' Tessa pressed.

This appeared to confound Frank. 'Well…'

'He couldn't have got out of the pram on his own, could he? He's a baby. He can't even crawl yet.'

'Well, if he'd been crying, someone might have picked him up. To comfort him, sort of thing.' Uncle Frank was clearly struggling.

'What, and forgot to put him back in the pram?' Tessa frowned.

'D'you want to hear the rest of it or not?' Frank Swinburne snapped, then shook his head, 'Sorry. Sorry. We're all at the end of our tethers. Anyway, that's when they called the police in and they took over. There's not much we can do now, apart from wait.'

'Where *are* Mum and Dad?' Lewis asked. 'Why did we have to come to Gran's?'

'To be honest, kids, your Mum and Dad are both pretty upset. They're at the police station so as to be on the spot if they're needed. It's best for you to stay here, so they know you're absolutely safe.'

'But we could help, couldn't we, Tess? We're excellent at looking for things.'

Their uncle gave a tired smile and planted a mock punch on Lewis's jaw. 'Tell you what, kiddo,' he pointed to the paper and pencils lying on the table between the beds, 'why don't you write them a letter? Cheer 'em up. Tell them you'll see them soon. How does that sound?' He stood up. 'While you're doing that, I'll nip down and have a word with your gran. Give me a shout when you've finished.'

The children sat in bed, wondering what they could write. They thought about including a selection of jokes or riddles but in the end decided simply to say that they loved and missed them both. Neither of them mentioned Gordon.

After Uncle Frank had gone and Gran had been up to switch off the light and wish them goodnight, they lay awake in the unfamiliar darkness. 'What's that?' Lewis asked, suddenly, but it was only a cat *yowling* in a back yard along the terrace.

In the end, it was Lewis who voiced the question that had been suspended between them from the moment they'd heard of Gordon's disappearance. 'Was it us?'

'Was *what* us?' Tessa asked knowing quite well what he was talking about.

'Did we do it? Did we make him disappear? Did the magic work?' His worries tumbled out.

'Be sensible. How could a lump of clay make a baby disappear?'

'I don't know. But something has.'

'Some*one* has,' Tessa corrected him. 'Some*one* took Gordon out of the pram.'

Lewis sat up, the hot water bottle slurping with his sudden movement. 'Why would anyone steal a baby? They're just a nuisance.'

Tessa flicked back the covers on Lewis's bed and wriggled in beside him. 'Were you listening, really listening I mean, when Uncle Frank told us how it happened?'

'Yes.' He thought he had been.

'Didn't you spot something … fishy?'

'What d'you mean?'

'Well, Uncle Frank said that Dad *went to buy a newspaper.*'

'So?'

'Dad has a newspaper delivered every morning, doesn't he? He already *had* a newspaper.'

Lewis flopped back on the pillow. 'Yes. But he might have read it quickly. And wanted another one.'

'He's never, *ever*, bought two papers, has he?' Tessa dug an elbow into her brother's ribcage. *'Has he?'*

'No.' He felt sick at the thought of his father telling a lie.

The following afternoon, the children collected their belongings together, ready to return home. This time Gran packed, too, and it was clear from the size of her suitcase and the selection of things she put in it – knitting, a hot water bottle, smelling salts, a photograph of her late husband – that she was planning to be away from home for several days.

As they reached the bus stop, it began to rain – a fine drizzle blown on a stiff breeze. When the bus turned up they travelled on the lower deck, sitting on the sideways-facing bench seat, their bags stowed in the cubbyhole beneath the steep stairs. An effective heating system, coupled with the close-packed bodies of the other passengers, drew the damp out of overcoats and mackintoshes, tainting the air with a wet dog smell. The threesome barely spoke as the bus ground its way across the dark town and, by the time they were trudging down Medway Avenue, they had ceased talking altogether.

Lewis was pleased to be leaving Gran's house but he wasn't sure he wanted to go home. What if his mother was still crying? What if his father was in one of his tempers? What if the police asked him how many newspapers his father read? Would his parents have got rid of all the baby things – cot, bibs, safety pins, little vests and jackets – yet? Then there was the pram that the baby snatcher hadn't taken. Might they be able to claim the wheels – really big wheels with fancy tyres – to make a second go cart? His nervousness increased when, on reaching the front door, Gran fussed with their coat collars and told them to stand up straight, as though they were going to be inspected by an army officer. Once she had them organised to her satisfaction, she pounded on the knocker.

Their father opened the door and when the children saw that, as usual, he was wearing his brown slippers and corduroy trousers, for a few seconds it was as if nothing had changed and it really had been a silly mistake after all. He pulled them to him, bending to kiss the crowns of their damp heads and, as they nuzzled their faces in his prickly jumper, they knew it was true. Tessa could contain herself no longer and started sobbing. Lewis joined in.

Their grandmother had been watching this display of emotion. 'Come on, you two. You've got to be brave for your mum and dad.'

'It's okay, Dot. It'll do them good to have a cry. Peggy's in bed if you want to go up. The doctor's given her something but she's not asleep.'

'Is there … any news?'

'Nothing.' His voice cracked.

'Well, you know what they say…' She trudged upstairs.

During the days that followed, the children discovered that school was the best place to be. When they were doing sums or learning spellings, or playing tag or marbles, everything was as it had always been. But, as soon as the end-of-school bell sounded, life went haywire. Their mother rarely left her bedroom and never got dressed. When they went upstairs to see her it was like visiting an invalid whom they shouldn't tire. She smiled vaguely and asked them questions about school, as if she'd never met them before. Sometimes she stopped in the middle of a sentence, forgetting or abandoning what she was about to say.

They weren't allowed to walk home on their own – something they'd been doing for years. Their father, or more often their grandmother, was stationed on the pavement opposite, ready to shepherd them down the road, grabbing their hands as if they were toddlers. And once they reached the house, they were forbidden to set foot out of the front gate without permission.

When Tessa demanded to know *why*, the explanation she received from Gran was a wary, 'You can't be too careful these days.'

Tessa noticed that, when she and Lewis passed neighbours in the street, they looked away or, at best, muttered a hasty, 'Hello,' before scurrying by. Neither Diane nor Susan invited her to tea after school. Lewis's friends didn't ask him to play football. Neither of them received invitations to the several birthday parties that took place.

Home became a place where people whispered and closed doors. Relatives whom they barely knew made brief visits, scarcely acknowledging them beyond an irritating 'Goodness, dear, haven't you grown?' The phone rang at all hours. Newspapers were pushed out of sight. Unsmiling men, whom the children supposed were plain clothed policemen, came and went. One woman, with fat legs and flat shoes, spent a great deal of time with their mother, but again the door was shut and the children had no idea what they talked about. Strangers hung about outside on the pavement, watching the house. The doctor called most days, patting them on the head or ruffling their hair before going up to their mother's room. Their father didn't seem to go to work any more.

There *was* one bright spot – Lewis was relegated to a camp-bed in Tessa's room so that his grandmother could use his. One night he slithered out of bed and pulled open the bottom drawer of the chest. He rummaged around beneath Tessa's clothes and brought out the purse, still bulging with their unspent holiday money. 'I've been thinking. When the kidnappers get in touch, we can give this to Dad, to put towards the ransom, can't we?'

'He's been gone for a whole week, Lewis. Kidnappers would have been in touch by now.' Tessa whispered. 'I don't think they'll ever find him.'

'That's horrible,' Lewis whimpered. 'I wish we hadn't—'

'Look, we've been over and over this. What we did was just a bit of fun.' She laughed but it came out more like a dry cough.

He was silent for a few seconds. 'Perhaps we *did* send him back, like we were trying to do. Think about it. Mum's not very well, is she? She never gets dressed and the doctor comes every day. Perhaps—'

'Don't be daft.'

Tessa clambered out of bed and began tickling Lewis. Soon they were screaming with laughter and failed to hear their grandmother plodding up the stairs.

'Another peep out of you two and one of you will be in with me.' Gran stood in the doorway, silhouetted against the landing light. 'Now off to sleep.'

They scrambled back under the covers, lying quiet and motionless until they heard her talking to their father downstairs. Tessa reached down towards the camp bed where her brother lay and they linked fingers.

Chapter 6

SWATHED IN COATS, HATS AND GLOVES to combat the winter chill, the children were in the garden, repairing their den. A couple of months earlier, their father had been clearing out the garage – something he did at the end of every summer – and they had persuaded him to let them have three sheets of hardboard, water stained and warped after years of storage. 'Okay. I don't suppose I'll be using them now,' he'd conceded. The construction, located well away from the house, was a simple affair, little more than flimsy 'walls' wedged upright between piles of bricks, with odd lengths of wood spanning from side to side to suggest a roof. Insubstantial though it was, it had become the focus for their most exciting games. Sometimes it was the stockade where the cavalry held out against the Apaches; sometimes a tent in the snowy wastes, shelter for intrepid explorers on their way to the South Pole; sometimes a bulletproof bunker where soldiers might hide from an invading army. The games were fun, but better still was the satisfaction of adapting the structure and adding new features. This morning they had commandeered an orange box, destined as kindling for the fire, and were sitting on it discussing the injustice of their curfew.

'I wish we could go to Cranwell Lodge,' Lewis said. 'We haven't been for ages.'

Tessa inspected the ends of her plaits. 'I don't see why we can't.'

'But they'll notice we're not here. They can see us from the window.' Lewis peeped round the hardboard wall and, as if to prove his point, their father appeared at the bedroom window, peering across the garden.

'Wave at him,' instructed Tessa.

They both emerged from the den, waving and smiling, and their father raised a hand in acknowledgement, then turned and moved away from the window.

'Okay. If he looks out again and *doesn't* see us, he'll think we're in here, out of sight. He's bound to stay upstairs with Mum because Gran's gone home to fetch some things.' She bent low and grabbed the sleeve of Lewis's coat. 'Come on. If we go right away, we've got at least half an hour before he even wonders where we are.'

They slunk down the garden, keeping close to the privet hedge and, once out of the gate, ran at full tilt along Medway Avenue and up Cranwell Road, breathless by the time they knocked on the back door of the old house.

Mr Zeal opened the door but, instead of the customary welcome, he stared at them, mumbling, 'Good gracious. My-oh-my. There's a thing,' until Tessa piped up, 'It's only us, Mr Zeal. Can we come in? Just for a minute.'

He stood aside, waving them through to the breakfast room where the beginnings of a fire crackled in the grate. Greenish-grey smoke from the coals snaked up the chimney but no heat came from it yet and the children's panting breath was visible in the shafts of light which filtered between the heavy curtains. 'I'm afraid you've caught us out,' he said, gathering a pile of newspapers and pushing them under one of the cushions on the sofa.

What on earth did he mean *'caught us out'*? Tessa glanced around. 'Where's Mrs Channing?' she asked.

'She's busy at the moment. Why don't you talk to Blanche and

I'll let her know you're here.'

'We can't stay long,' Lewis called as Mr Zeal disappeared into the hall.

After the efforts they'd made to escape from the garden, Tessa felt let down. This morning, Mr Zeal, chin stubbly and wearing a shapeless green cardigan, looked like any other old man. So far he'd said nothing in the slightest bit rude or interesting. There was no singing. No offers of sherry. Blanche was silent and uncooperative. The furniture looked shabby and, when she made her regular inspection of the ornaments on the mantelpiece, she noticed that they were covered in dust. Today everything about Cranwell Lodge seemed ordinary. Could that be what he'd meant – that he and Mrs Channing had been 'caught out' being ordinary?

'We ought to be going, Tess.' Lewis pulled his right earlobe.

'It'll be okay. We'll just wait and say hello to Mrs Channing.'

Tessa flopped on the sofa and the cushion slipped, exposing the headline on one of the newspapers that Mr Zeal had stuffed beneath it – *SEARCH CONTINUES FOR MISSING BABY*. Tessa held it up for her brother to read. 'Look at this, Lewis.'

The next newspaper she pulled out had been folded open. *NO TRACE OF SWINBURNE BABY* headed the page, accompanied by a picture of Gordon's empty pram. She examined the papers stowed under the cushion and each one was opened at an article concerning their missing brother.

Before they had a chance to discuss what this meant, voices sounded on the far side of the door. Tessa gathered up the papers, shoving them back in their hiding place, and the children were standing, side by side in front of the fire, when Mrs Channing and Mr Zeal came in.

'Good morning, Swinburnes. Allow me to apologise for not being here to greet you but I was at a rather intricate juncture in my ablutions.' At least Mrs Channing, clad in her shiny red dressing gown, hair contained in a sort of decorative net, was living up to expectations. 'How are you, my dears?' she asked in a breezy tone, without a trace of the pity they'd become used to hearing during the past week.

This surprised Tessa. It was obvious that she and Mr Zeal had been keeping up with the story and they *must* realise that the missing baby was the very one that she and Lewis had grumbled about during recent visits.

'It's been horrible—' Lewis started.

Before he could say any more, Tessa jumped in. 'It's been horrible weather, hasn't it? All cold and horrible.' She glared at her brother who looked confused by her interruption. 'Anyway. We'd better be going. Dinner'll be ready soon.'

Grabbing his arm, she pulled him towards the door.

'Hold your horses.' Mr Zeal went to the dresser drawer and took out a paper bag. 'These should keep you going.' He handed the bag to Tessa. She peeped inside then held it out for Lewis to see. The bag contained boiled sweets, each individually wrapped in clear cellophane – maybe ten or a dozen in all. On previous visits, Mr Zeal had produced the sweets from his trouser pocket and deposited them on the palms of their hands, with a flourish. Today he'd given them boring old boiled sweets in a crumpled bag.

'Thank you. Where do these come from, Mr Zeal?' Lewis asked.

The old man looked puzzled. 'The sweet shop in the market, as far as I recall.'

'Not from Morocco, then?'

'Aaahhh.' The old man smiled, his large white teeth looking out of place in his unshaven face. 'Only in a manner of speaking.'

'What was he on about?' Lewis asked as, sucking boiled sweets, they raced down Cranwell Road.

Tessa seemed not to have heard him. 'Did you notice how

they didn't say anything about Gordon? Even though they'd been reading about it in the paper? Don't you think that's—'

'Fishy?' Lewis liked this word, which he'd learned from his sister.

'Exactly.'

'Perhaps they thought talking about him would upset us.'

'Mmmm. I don't know.'

When they reached the house, the garden gate, which Lewis was positive he had latched, stood ajar. 'Someone's come,' he whispered.

They tiptoed between the house and the garage, scurried past the back door and on down the path to the safety of the den where they collapsed on the orange box, giggling with relief.

'I told you it would be all right,' Tessa grinned.

They hid the rest of the sweets under an inverted flower-pot before making their way back to the house. Four cups and saucers stood on a tray on the kitchen table. A faint whistling came from the kettle on the stove, warning that it was coming to the boil and, as the sound rose to a penetrating shriek, their father came in. 'So there you are.' He glared at them. 'And where have you two been?'

'Nowhere. Well, just in the Avenue.' Tessa pointed at the cups. 'Have we got visitors?'

'Don't try and change the subject, young lady. And you were not "just in the Avenue" because I watched you tearing off somewhere.' He poured the hot water from the kettle into the brown teapot. 'You know perfectly well what the rules are. We'll discuss this later. Take your coats off. And those muddy shoes. There's a gentlemen and a lady who want to talk to you.'

'But we've already talked to someone,' Tessa complained. 'We've already told them that we went to town and got winter coats.'

'I'm not asking you if you *want* to talk to them, I'm telling you that you're *going* to.'

It was the first time that they'd seen their mother out of bed and dressed since last Saturday afternoon, when they'd gone to Gran's. Sunk in an armchair, staring, unblinking, in the direction of the window, she looked not much bigger than a child. The pallor of her face was emphasized by the shadowy skin around her eyes. Her lank hair was scraped back and held in place by a couple of Tessa's hair slides. Tessa thought how old and ugly she looked.

The lady – Tessa recognised her as the one who spent a lot of time with her mother – and gentleman had been to the house several times before. Now they sat on the sofa, still wearing their overcoats, looking as if they might jump to attention at any minute.

'Hello,' the lady said, smiling. 'You must be Tessa. And you must be Lewis. My name's Miss Underwood and this,' she turned to the man, 'is Mr Hulbert.'

'Are you detectives?' Tessa asked politely.

'We are. And we're here because we want to find your baby brother,' the man took over, 'as I'm sure you do. That's right isn't it?'

This wasn't a man to argue with and she nodded enthusiastically. 'Yes.'

'Yes.' Lewis echoed.

'Good.' He beckoned them closer. 'No need to be shy. We'd just like to go over what happened. Make sure we've got it absolutely straight.'

Balancing the cup and saucer on the broad arm of the sofa, he pulled a small black notebook from the inside pocket of his coat and flipped it open. 'Now, tell us what you did last Saturday morning.'

From where she stood, a couple of feet in front of Mr Hulbert's knees, Tessa was unable to see her parents but she knew that they were listening very closely to every word she said. 'We went to town with Mum. On the bus.' She gave a factual account of everything that they'd done that morning – the purchase of the coats, spending her pocket money, the visit to the Kardomah.

'And when you got back home?' he coaxed.

'We had omelettes,' Lewis chimed in.

The policeman turned to him. 'Who had omelettes, son?'

'Me and Tessa and Mum.'

'Not your Dad?'

'No. He wasn't there. Mum was a bit worried—'

'That's right,' Tessa interrupted, 'And then Dad phoned to say that … well, to tell Mum what happened. Then we went to Gran's.' Tessa glanced at her mother who had swivelled in her seat, her face showing neither encouragement nor disapproval of what her children were saying.

'Tess and I have been thinking about it quite a lot and what we don't really understand is *why* Dad went to buy a paper. He has one delivered every morning,' Lewis chirped.

'I see.' Mr Hulbert smiled at Lewis, pencil poised over the little notebook. 'That's very clever of you to think of that. Is there anything else you … don't understand? Anything … unusual? Anything … out of the ordinary?'

The room was still, as if everyone in it were holding their breath. Tessa turned to catch a glimpse of her father's face. He was sitting on the arm of her mother's chair, his eyes shut, his head bent forward, fingertips raised to his forehead. She knew that her brother was trying to help the detectives and to demonstrate their skill at spotting 'fishy-ness' but it did seem disloyal to hint that their father was lying.

'The whole week's been a bit strange, actually. Lots of people we've never seen before keep coming to the house. Gran's staying here and she usually only does that at Christmas. And Lewis is sleeping on a camp bed in my room. He's never done that before.' Tessa's confidence grew as she painted the picture of their disrupted life. 'We have funny things to eat at the wrong times. We're not allowed to walk to school on our own. And we're not allowed to play out in the street.' She paused. Perhaps she should leave it there, without mentioning that her mother had taken to her bed and her father was permanently in a bad mood.

'So why were you sneaking out of the garden this morning?' her father asked wearily.

'We weren't sneaking. We were only—' she stopped.

Mr Hulbert cleared his throat. 'Thank you both. You've been very helpful.'

Tessa didn't trust this man with the fake smile who was pretending to be their friend, and asked eagerly, 'Can we go now?'

He nodded, adding as they reached the door, 'And don't forget, if you think of anything – anyone you've seen hanging about, or anyone behaving strangely – anything at all, come and tell me or Miss Underwood. We'll be popping in regularly.'

'I wish I hadn't said anything about the newspaper,' Lewis whispered when they were back in the kitchen. 'Dad'll be cross with me.'

Tessa scowled. 'Actually *I* was the one who spotted it so *I* should have been the one to tell.' But, seeing her brother's lip tremble, she relented. 'Dad's cross with both of us anyway, for going out, so we're both in trouble.'

For the first time in over a week, the family ate a meal together. Lewis didn't feel much like eating, even though it was his favourite – beans on toast. Their father prepared the food whilst his mother sat, stiff-backed, at the table, hands gripped together in her lap as if to keep them still. Her lips were curved in a faint smile but her eyes stared blankly at the wall behind his head. He wanted to throw his arms around her and kiss her but

66

was scared to, in case he discovered that what he was looking at was a ghostly likeness of his mother and that she, too, had left them. The food came but the silence continued, broken only by the chink of cutlery on the blue and white striped plates. Lewis speared glistening orange beans with his fork, impaling them on squares of soggy toast, wishing someone would say something, even if it were his father telling him off, but the silence went on and on and on, until he thought he was going to be sick.

In the end, his mother stood up, pushing away her plate, her food untouched. 'I think I'll have a little lie down,' she murmured and went upstairs.

Lewis could bear the weight of wrongdoing no longer. 'I'm sorry, Dad. I didn't mean to tell on you.'

'You've got nothing to be sorry for, Lewis.' His father's face softened. 'You were absolutely right to try and help the policemen. It was very clever of you, as Mr Hulbert said. But they've already asked me about all that and we've cleared the matter up. You see I was buying a *Football Argus* – County were playing in the Cup.' He reached out, touching the hands of both children, looking from one to the other. 'I'm really not cross with you but I do need to know where you two went this morning. I know for sure you weren't playing in the Avenue because I came looking for you.' He paused. 'Mum and I aren't trying to spoil things, you know. We just want to be sure that you're safe. We couldn't bear any harm to come to either of you.'

Lewis grabbed the warm, rough-skinned hand and Dad squeezed his in return. Still hanging on to it, he squirmed off the chair and snuggled into their father's chest, inhaling the smell of cigarette smoke and hair cream. Although he couldn't see her, he knew that Tessa was doing the same and that they were standing, one either side of their father, crying and hugging and being loved.

They went into the living room and, sitting on the wide

arms of their father's chair, Tessa explained everything from the beginning, describing how they had made friends with Mrs Channing and Mr Zeal and telling of their subsequent visits to Cranwell Lodge. 'Mrs Channing's ever so interesting,' she explained. 'She wears beautiful clothes and uses really complicated words—'

'And Mr Zeal's nice too. He gets sweets from Morocco—'

'They've got a white parrot—'

'We always refuse when they offer us sherry—'

'And Mrs Channing thinks babies are horrid—'

'And they should be locked in cellars—'

'And—'

'What did you say?' Dick Swinburne sat up and grabbed Tess's outstretched leg. 'Tell me what this … this Channing woman said about babies.'

'Ouch, Dad. You're hurting.' Tessa, alarmed by her father's reaction and his grip on her leg, played for time. She needed to keep a clear head if she were to avoid admitting that she and Lewis had started the whole thing by moaning about Gordon.

'Can you remember exactly what you told her about Gordon?' Dad had become stern and distant again. 'Come on, Tessa. This isn't a game.'

'Not much,' she said, 'we didn't tell her much. We just told her that we'd got a new baby brother. And then she said the stuff about the cellar.' She looked at Lewis, daring him to make one of his untimely contributions. 'But they've definitely been reading about him disappearing. We saw all the newspapers hidden under the cushion, didn't we, Lew?'

'Stay here. You are not to leave this room, d'you hear me? I've got to make a phone call.' Dick Swinburne went into the hall and, from the occasional snatches of overheard conversation, it was clear that he was telling someone about Mrs Channing and Mr Zeal.

'We shouldn't have told him,' Lewis whispered. 'It's got him angry again.'

Tessa shrugged. 'I wish they'd make their minds up. They keep on to us to tell the truth then, when we do, we get into trouble.'

'Who d'you think he's talking to?'

'That Hulbert man, I expect.'

Tessa was right. Within half an hour, Mr Hulbert and Miss Underwood returned and made the children go through the whole story several times, stopping them frequently to ask questions. 'What was the exact date of your first visit to Cranwell Lodge?' 'Were the man and the woman both there every time you went?' 'Did they ask you to do anything that you didn't want to do?' 'Did you ever see anything odd … unusual … peculiar … when you went there?'

This last question made the children smile. 'Of course we did,' said Tessa, '*Everything* was unusual. That's why we liked going to see them.'

Lewis nodded, 'And they were very kind to us.'

The days went by. The pram wasn't returned to the house and, little by little, the baby clothes and paraphernalia vanished too, until there was hardly any evidence that their brother had existed.

Mr Hulbert and Miss Underwood called occasionally but never stayed long and Tessa kept out of their way. She knew they must have gone to Cranwell Lodge with their black notebooks and stern voices, and she felt bad about that. Although they'd told the truth about what they'd seen and talked about there, it had made the old couple sound a bit … mad. Tessa was sure that Mrs Channing had only gone on about babies and cellars to make them laugh and cheer them up, in the same way that she'd offered them sherry and sung carols in July. There was no chance that she and Lewis would be visiting the old house for some time. Actually she wasn't sure that she wanted to go there again.

'Should we write to them?' Lewis asked. 'Just to say we hope they're okay and that we won't be able to come for a while?'

Tessa was taken with Lewis's idea but, seated with paper and pencil, they couldn't think what they wanted to say and ended up playing hangman instead.

Their father returned to work but Gran stayed on, taking the children to school and steering the household through each week. At weekends she returned to her own home. 'I'll get out of your way – I'm sure you could do with some time to yourselves,' she'd say as she hurried off to catch the bus.

Frank Swinburne popped in occasionally, bringing the children a bar of chocolate or a comic. Sometimes he took them out for a ride in his car or to the park. His jolliness was doubly welcome after Gran's *hush*-ing and *shush*-ing but, as soon as they got back home, the fun stopped and even Uncle Frank looked solemn.

Their mother spent a lot of time in bed. She was clearly ill because Tessa counted seven different bottles of tablets on her bedside table, and Gran was forever asking 'D'you fancy anything to eat, Peg?'

'When will Mum be better?' Lewis asked their father. When he'd had measles he'd been off school for three whole weeks.

'I'm not sure,' Dad answered. 'We have to be patient.'

'What's wrong with her exactly?' Tess probed.

He reached out and grasped their hands. 'Mum's very … sad. She's missing Gordon.' He cleared his throat and squeezed their fingers.

'The police are sure to find him soon, aren't they?' Lewis's voice wavered.

Their father pulled them to him and, although their heads

bumped together, they didn't complain.

Gran was strict but she was more approachable than she used to be. She taught them a terrific card game called *Newmarket* and joined in when they played *Ludo* or wanted help with the difficult bits of a jigsaw.

If their mother was asleep or resting, the children carried on as if she were out shopping or at the hairdresser's. It was easier than thinking of her alone and unhappy upstairs. Whenever she came down to join them for meals or to sit by the fire in the living room, they made a great fuss of her. 'Would you like a stool to put your feet on?' Tessa asked, eager to keep her with them. But her presence never felt permanent. She was like a bird ready to fly away at the first sign of danger.

Lewis who, since he had been a toddler, had relied on physical manifestations of his mother's affection, missed those moments spent snuggled against her while she read to him or they talked through the events of the day. Several times he manoeuvred himself to be next to her, waiting for her arm to reach around his shoulder or her hand to fondle the nape of his neck. But she seemed to have forgotten what he liked; how to be his Mum.

November slipped, grey and cold, into December. At school the children made gifts to take home and decorations for the classroom. A towering tree appeared in the corner of the school hall, the scent of pine resin almost masking the smell of stale milk and wet raincoats.

Their mother promised she'd come to the Christmas concert but, when Tessa and Lewis stood on the stage singing about shepherds and kings and angels, they saw only their father and grandmother sitting in the third row.

'Let's buy Mum something really special,' Tessa suggested. 'Bath salts and a box of chocolates with a satin bow. That'll make her feel better. Or we could ask her to make a Christmas list, like we do. We could buy one of the things off it. It would still be a surprise.'

But talking to their mother had become a tricky business. Dad or Gran were always around, a couple of guard dogs, keeping them at bay with 'That's enough, now' or 'Don't tire your mother.'

For the rest of the world Christmas arrived brimming with magic but none of it touched the Swinburne household. Christmas Day was a sombre affair. Their mother barely acknowledged the calendar that Lewis had spent hours making or the embroidered pin cushion Tessa had toiled over in sewing lessons. The *Cussons* soap and talcum powder set – three-and-eleven from Boots – didn't do the trick either. Even Uncle Frank's crackers, exploding with jokes and paper hats, failed to make her laugh.

'I know she's missing *him* but she's still got us,' Tessa whispered when they climbed into bed that night.

The year turned. It became increasingly clear that wherever Gordon John Swinburne had gone, he'd spirited their happiness away with him, just as the Pied Piper had spirited away the children of Hamelin.

II

1962

Chapter 7

THE BREEZE FROM THE OPEN WINDOW lifted several sheets of paper from the pile on the corner of the table, sending them drifting to the floor. Tessa, sitting on the upright chair in front of the table, painting the toenails of her right foot, glanced up, watching her revision notes slip through the air as she might watch autumn leaves falling from a tree. She twisted the chair round, extending her leg to examine her handiwork. Returning the brush to the bottle, she shook it vigorously before drawing her left foot up, bracing her heel on the seat of the chair and repeating the procedure. The iridescent pink varnish flooded off her nail and trickled between her toes. 'Fuck,' she whispered, wiping it off with a piece of cotton wool and trying again. Finally, satisfied with her efforts, she rested both feet on the table and turned her attention to her fingernails.

Why must they do exams in the summer? She closed her eyes and flopped her head back, turning her head from side to side, her hair tickling where it brushed her shoulders. Why must they do exams at all? It was as if clever people were punished for being clever. It wasn't fair. 'Thickos' left school at fifteen. They didn't have to sit in stifling bedrooms on sunny afternoons, plodding through Chaucer or *Richard II*. Her father's response echoed in her head as clearly as if he were standing in the room behind her. *No, young lady, the 'thickos' certainly aren't sitting in nice clean bedrooms. They're sweating away on building sites or in factories while you're keeping your hands soft and getting a decent education. Something your mother and I never had.* If she ever had children, she'd never force them to do exams. Or go to university.

University. Oh, God. When she'd filled in the entrance form last October, it had seemed more of a handwriting exercise than a commitment to a further three years of study. Recording her academic successes had been easy – nine 'O' level passes, like most of the other girls in her class at the grammar school. More difficult was listing 'Hobbies and Pastimes', something the careers mistress seemed to think could be the deciding factor. In a moment of compliance, she'd joined the youth club at the Baptist Church but stopped attending once she'd had her interviews. She couldn't remember discussing with anyone – teachers or parents – whether she even *wanted* to go to university but somehow here she was, with a place lined up at Exeter. What was the point in spending another three years doing exams and complying with childish rules and regulations if she intended to write best-selling thrillers and romances. No, she needed to experience life and love first-hand not via Wordsworth and Jane Austen.

A car door slammed and she went to the window, looking down into Salisbury Road, watching her father clamber out of the car. He'd removed his suit jacket and taken off his tie and she could tell from the slump of his shoulders as he limped up the front path, that he was tired. Hastily, she tossed the bottle of nail varnish into the drawer of her bedside table, gathered up the papers from the floor and, by the time she heard his footsteps on the stairs, she was bent over her text books.

'How's it going?' he asked pushing open the door.

'Okay.' She turned and smiled, curling her pink fingertips into the palms of her hands. 'Hot. Exhausting.'

'Well, it'll be worth it in the long run. When's your first

exam?'

'Next week. Tuesday afternoon.'

'You'll feel better once you get a couple under your belt.'

'I expect so.'

'Where's Lewis?'

'Doing his paper round, I suppose.'

'And Mum?'

'I'm not sure.' She gave her father a bright smile. 'Can you shut the door behind you, Dad? I can't work unless it's quiet.'

Although nothing could rival a good row, Tessa had to admit that conflict might not always be the best way forward. Her new tactic was acting. Since half-term, when members of the upper sixth form were allowed to revise at home, she had been playing the part of a girl working flat out for her 'A' level exams. It wasn't a difficult role. It boiled down to no more than keeping to her bedroom or, when she did go downstairs, making sure that she had a book in her hand or a folder under her arm. There were moments when she wondered whether it mightn't be as easy to do the wretched work. But then something, some little switch, flicked in her head and set her firmly back on course.

Alone again, she flopped on the bed, her thoughts meandering from the black pumps with the pointy toes that she'd seen in Dolcis to what she could wear to the dance on Saturday night and, inevitably, moving on to what she hoped might happen after the dance. Rolling on to her front, she reached across and opened the drawer of the bedside table. From beneath a folder containing writing paper and envelopes, she pulled out a black and white photograph showing three young men sitting on a park bench. The one in the middle stared, unsmiling, at the camera, his arms draped across the back of the bench, whilst those on either side turned toward him, laughing, as if he'd just made an incredibly funny remark. His hair looked dark in the picture but she knew that it was, in fact, dull red, like the pelt of a fox.

Having managed to get the seat behind him on the bus one day, she was also familiar with the way it dipped to a point at the back, between the tendons that ran down from the base of his skull. She knew that he smoked. And that he, Tony Rundle, was Mike Stoddy's best friend. At Tessa's request, Diane had pinched the photograph from her brother's wallet and now, lifting it to her lips, she kissed the stern face before quickly replacing it in the drawer, as though it might fade if exposed too long to daylight.

She could hear the murmur of her parents' voices, their low tones rumbling on, unrelieved. They had been married for twenty years. They'd always lived in this town – first in Medway Avenue and now in Salisbury Road – and her father had always worked for the Post Office. He hadn't fought in the war. He hadn't been abroad. Or to Scotland. Or north of Manchester, as far as she knew. Her mother suffered from 'nerves', whatever that meant. She didn't go out to work and she never went anywhere or did anything on her own. Nothing ever happened to them so what on earth did they have to *say* to each other? But it didn't stop them wittering on, always in the same pessimistic tone, as though it was their job to spot the failings of everyone and everything they came across. God, she wanted to scream. Every parent with a child between the age of twelve and eighteen should be locked in a cellar, where they could moan to their heart's content and let everyone else get on with their lives in peace. She was sure Mrs Channing would agree with her. Occasionally the old pair popped into her thoughts and she wished that she and Lewis had gone to visit them one last time, to make sure that they understood. Never mind. They were probably dead by now.

One of the major props in Tessa's subterfuge was the revision schedule pinned to the notice board in front of her table. Before she went downstairs, she filled in the space allocated to this afternoon's session. '2hrs-English. 1hr-History'. Not bad.

*

'D'you want me to test you?' Lewis asked. It was Saturday morning. Tessa was sprawled on her bed and he was lying on the floor next to it. 'Vocabulary? Quotations?'

He was bemused. Tessa had been unbearable in the run up to her 'O' Levels, panicking and crying, continually chanting equations and chunks from Shakespeare and irregular French verbs. And she had sailed through all nine exams. But this time, with more at stake and only three days to go, she was uncannily composed.

'No thanks.' Tessa dropped a sherbet lemon on to his chest.

He popped the sweet in his mouth and closed his eyes. He rolled it over and over with his tongue, enjoying the delicious bitterness and the way the rough sugar casing grazed the roof of his mouth. It would take at least ten minutes before it became smooth and thinned, eventually splitting and allowing the fizzing sherbet to erupt. Immobilising it between his cheek and his teeth, he asked, 'Aren't you nervous?'

'About the exams? No. Not really. Why? D'you think I should be?'

'It's just that I was reading somewhere that being scared improves performance. Sharpens our wits. It's a kind of chemical thing. And you seem a bit … I dunno … a bit too calm.' She didn't reply but, sensing that she was staring down at him from her elevated position, he opened his eyes. 'What?'

'Lewis? D'you remember when we were living in the other house and Gran was staying and you slept on the camp bed in my room?'

'Sort of. Why?'

She smiled. 'I loved it.'

'How can you say that? It was horrible. Mum crying. Dad being blamed for … you know, and Gran watching us like a hawk. And there were the neighbours, all steering clear. As if we had some infectious vanishing disease and if they came anywhere near us, their children would vanish, too.'

'But didn't you love it when the light was off and it was just us two, lying in the dark?' She sat up and swung her legs over the edge of the bed, resting her bare feet on his chest. 'I won't believe you even if you say you didn't.'

Without warning, she spat her sweet at him. It landed on his cheek and he grinned, tossing the sticky yellow remains in to the waste-paper basket. 'Now that's more like the Tessa Swinburne we know and love. I was starting to think there was something wrong with you.'

'Lewis…'

'What?' He raised his eyebrows. 'What?'

But she shook her head. 'Nothing. I'd better get on with some history.'

After the lively chaos of his sister's room, his own, with its pale green walls and neat bookshelves, was comfortingly dull. Tessa was constantly pestering him to 'liven it up a bit' and a few months ago, mainly to shut her up, he *had* put a few posters up but Elvis Presley and Brigitte Bardot gazing at him as he undressed for bed made him uncomfortable and he'd replaced them with the Periodic Table, a map of the world and an exploded drawing of a jet engine.

The buckles on his satchel jingled as he took out his textbooks and piled them on the desk. The stacked books, with their brown paper covers, gave him a kind of self-belief – a sense of knowing what was going on and what was expected of him. Now that he was in the sixth form, he had finished with all those waffly subjects – history, English, religious education – and he could get on with the stuff that mattered.

He was in the middle of calculus homework when Tessa summoned him. 'Can you come here for a sec?'

Without protest, he went.

'Lewis, you know a lot about this sort of thing.'

He was accustomed to the way his sister dived into a topic, expecting everyone to jump in after her. 'Do I?'

She stood in front of the mirror, backcombing her hair, shifting her gaze from her own reflection to his, and he was aware of the asymmetry of her familiar face, only noticeable when he saw her in the glass. He grinned.

She stopped pushing the comb through her hair, tangling it into a dark mop, and spun around. 'What are *you* laughing at?'

'Sorry. I'm sure it'll look fab. Once the birds have nested.'

'Pig. At least I've got a hair *style*, not just a hair *cut*. Anyway,' her frown vanished and her tone softened, 'I need you to back me up on something. It's a bit like the nerves thing you were telling me. Well, it isn't really but—'

'Tess, just tell me what you're on about.'

She clapped her hands together as if needing to make sure he was paying attention. 'If a person worked *all* morning and *all* afternoon, wouldn't they benefit from taking some time away from their books? To kind of revive their brains and…' She gave a beseeching smile. 'There's a dance at St Marks Hall tonight and I really, *really* need to go. Please help me persuade Mum and Dad.'

'I don't see what I can do—'

'Can't you come up with a sort of scientific-y reason why it'd be good for me to take the evening off? Because I honestly know it would. There must be *something*.'

Throughout their childhood, Tessa had been the one who came up with terrific ideas for schemes and adventures. She was clever and fearless, single-minded and resourceful, which made the instances when *she* deferred to *him,* particularly significant. Seeing her expectant face, he was determined to fulfil her confidence. 'There is something, actually…' he paused, 'but I don't suppose you'd be interested in what anyone with a mere hair *cut* has to say.'

'Lewis!' she screeched, hurling a hairbrush at his head.

'Okay, okay. I read in one of the science journals – *Scientific American*, I think – that there's been some research done on how physical activity can be beneficial to brain function. They proved that regular sessions of exercise improved the students' exam performance—'

'Brilliant.' She hugged him.

'Hang on a minute. The subjects were taking a five minute break every half an hour. Sprinting round a track – that sort of thing. They weren't working all day, then going out dancing all night.'

But Tessa wasn't listening. She turned back to the mirror and sprayed her tangled hair with something sickly-smelling then moulded the tangle into a helmet, the ends flicked up to form a kind of gutter. He glanced down at the exercise book lying on the bed. Written across the front in curlicued script, was 'The Woman Who Loved Too Much by Tessa Swinburne'.

By midday the temperature was in the eighties. It was airless inside the house and they took a snack lunch into the garden, spreading a tartan rug in the shade of the laurel hedge. Lewis could see that his mother was having one of her 'good days'. She had been working in the garden, reclaiming an overgrown rockery near the back door, and the sun had raised a crop of freckles on her thin arms. Were he to run a finger along the underside of her upper arm, where the skin was still creamy-white, it would feel even softer than the petals of the white rose that scrambled along the garden fence. The trouble was that he had no idea how she would react if he did. There were days when she was fine – laughing, full of energy, ready for anything – and others when she seemed unable to deal with the simplest things. Last week a butterfly had been scrabbling against the window, trying to escape, and Lewis had found her watching it and sobbing but doing nothing to help it.

They talked about Tessa's exams and their parents both expressed admiration for the hours of work she was putting in. For the umpteenth time they told her that it would pay off and how lucky she was to have the opportunities that had been denied them. His sister kept glancing at him, raising her eyebrows, eventually prompting, 'Sometimes my head feels clogged up like a blocked drain.'

Then he did as she had asked, even exaggerating a little to make it appear that the perfect treatment for her sluggish brain was to go to the Saturday night dance.

Chapter 8

TESSA PHONED HER FRIENDS, suggesting that they use Lewis's revelation about exercise as ammunition if their parents weren't keen on them going out so close to exam time. She didn't bother with Diane Stoddy. Tony Rundle would definitely be put off if she turned up with his friend's little sister in tow. When it came to it, Pamela Blackmore was the only one who sounded keen and the two girls arranged to meet at the bus stop.

Tessa planned what she would wear. She was disappointed that she'd been unable to afford the black pumps. They would have looked terrific with her green sheath dress, but they cost twenty-nine and eleven and she had less than a pound in the toffee tin she used as a money box. She'd begged Lewis to lend her the balance and he'd looked apologetic. 'I've got to buy a decent tennis racquet before the house tournament. A couple more weeks' paper round money and I'll have enough. Sorry, Tess.'

On Saturday afternoon, safe behind her bedroom door, she Veet-ed her legs and under her arms and re-varnished her nails, throwing open the window to get rid of the telltale smells. This done, she logged '1 hour – French verbs' on her chart.

'Who else is going?' her mother asked when she went downstairs to get a drink of squash. 'Diane? She's a nice girl.'

'No. Diane can't come. There'll be a crowd of us I expect but I'm going with Pamela. You remember Pam, don't you?'

'Is that the tall girl, with the blonde hair?'

'No, Mum.'

When they moved from Medway Avenue, Tessa and Lewis had continued to attend the same primary school but, perhaps because of the tragedy that made them for ever 'that odd family', few friends came to play at the house. Then when Tessa passed her eleven-plus exam, she'd started at the grammar school and acquired a host of new friends – Pamela and Caroline, Anne and Rosemary, Sarah and Gail. She introduced them to her parents at school concerts and speech days but, perhaps because they all wore navy gymslips and white blouses, her mother constantly muddled them up. Was it Caroline or Gail who wore glasses? Sarah or Anne who played the violin? She did, however, always remember Diane Stoddy – the little girl who had lived round the corner in that previous life.

Tessa envied her friends. She imagined them nattering with their mothers about boys and clothes and periods; having rows and loving reconciliations. She would have given anything to be able to tease her mother and share secrets. But she had seen the panic in her mother's eyes when a wrong word or a stray thought threw her off kilter, driving her into that distant, silent place. Her father maintained that it wasn't a matter of telling her to 'snap out of it' but Tessa couldn't help feeling that it was worth a try. The spells in hospital, the medication and the kid gloved approach weren't doing much good, so why not? Every now and then, when things started to go adrift, she wished that whoever had taken Gordon would come back for her mother and allow the rest of them to get on with their lives.

Tessa's inability to confide in her mother left her without an ally in matters like hairdos and make-up. Her father was a stickler when it came to his daughter's appearance. 'A touch of lipstick's fine,' he would say, 'but you don't need all that other rubbish. You're pretty enough as you are.'

Tessa *was* a striking girl. Her dark-lashed eyes, tanned skin and full lips needed no enhancement. Nevertheless, conforming to the fashion, she applied the palest pink lipstick then dabbed her lips with a powder puff to make them paler still. She smeared green eyeshadow – the magazines said that green brought out subtle tones in brown eyes – across her lids. She ringed her eyes with harsh black eyeliner, extending the lines away from the outer corners, curving and tapering them. Finally, she spat on the block of black mascara, scrubbing at it with the miniature brush, sweeping it through her lashes, again and again, until they were stiff and spiky.

Lewis loved to watch his sister performing her 'going out' ritual. It was always fascinating to watch an expert at work, be it a motor mechanic, an artist or a girl putting on make-up. He made excuses to come to her room *Did I leave my slide rule in here?* or *Can I borrow your coloured pencils?* then hung around, whilst she magicked her everyday self into one of those untouchable creatures whom he saw behind the counter in Boots. Many of his friends had sisters but they didn't talk about them much. When they did, it was obvious that they thought sisters were a waste of time and, whenever he came across these girls, he could see why. They were wishy-washy, always giggling and whispering. 'Your sister's a bit … I dunno … scary,' one of them remarked after Tessa told him that nail biting was a disgusting habit. Lewis had grinned his satisfaction. 'Yes, she is.'

'How do I look, Lewis?'

Tessa had transformed herself into a dark-haired Dusty Springfield in a tight-fitting green dress which was obviously the effect she was after. But as far as he was concerned, she was an intimidating stranger.

'You look fine.'

'Are my seams straight?' She swivelled round to show him the backs of her legs. 'What's the time?'

'Five-to-seven.'

'Do me a favour?' she wheedled. 'Pop and check where Dad is. He blows his top when he sees me wearing make-up.'

Their parents were in the kitchen, his mother arranging roses from the garden in a tall vase and his father at the sink, washing up. Lewis went to the bottom of the stairs and whistled softly, signalling the all-clear.

Tessa crept down, pausing briefly in the hall to shout 'I'm off now. Won't be late.' She smiled at her brother, whispering, 'Thanks. I'll do the same for you.'

He should tell her to take care, to stay with Pamela, not to break the ten-thirty curfew. 'Tess—' The door slammed and she was gone.

Lewis felt awkward when Tessa wasn't there to balance things up. Two parents – two children. That was how it should be. But in a few months, when Tessa left, the family equilibrium was going to change and attention would focus on him. He wasn't sure how he would deal with that, feeling, as he did, that he had been born to play a supporting role. He'd never felt resentful. On the contrary, he knew he was extraordinarily lucky to have a sister who made anything and everything interesting. Tessa was the Lone Ranger and he the faithful Tonto.

When he was aimless, as he was that evening, he would lie on his bed, staring up at the model aeroplanes suspended from the ceiling on cotton threads. Caught by the draught, they slowly revolved, opening the dreamy portal that allowed him to enter his alternative existence.

Tessa is on her way to the dance and, in the spare bedroom (which, of course, isn't spare at all), Gordon is shouting for him to come and help with an Airfix kit or a jigsaw. His brother is almost eight – in Mrs Benson's class at school – and he's reading Famous Five *and, because he's such a good reader for his age,* Biggles.

He's got brown hair and gangly legs. His bony knees are dirty with grass stains and two crinkly-edged incisors are pushing into the gap where his baby teeth used to be.

Throat aching, Lewis could go no further.

Tessa wasn't surprised that Pamela Blackmore was the only one to come out that evening. She was going to teacher training college and only needed to scrape two A Levels. Tessa liked her dizzy good humour, added to which she made Tessa feel exceptionally brainy.

Pam was waiting at the top of the road. 'I like your dress. *Trés chic.*'

Tessa had chosen the fabric herself – glazed cotton, the colour of Granny Smith apples – and *Vogue* pattern and her mother had made the dress as a present for her eighteenth birthday, a couple of months earlier. She had complied with Tessa's request to add a large, flat bow beneath the bustline, but refused to make the dress as tight-fitting as her daughter would have liked.

But seeing her friend in a pink short-sleeved sweater and straight grey skirt, Tessa knew that the dress had been a mistake. 'This? I've had it for ages,' she lied, as if age could make it look less formal, less like something she would wear to a wedding.

Her confidence waned further when they reached Saint Mark's Church Hall and she saw that the girls, collecting in gaggles of two or three on the pavement outside the squat building, were dressed like Pam, in straight skirts and demure blouses. Some of them were in the year below her at school, fancy-free on that particular Saturday night because the Lower Sixth's exams didn't start for a couple of weeks.

'C'mon. There's no point in standing out here,' Tessa said, leading the way up the steps and into the dingy building.

Despite the heat wave of the past weeks, a smell of damp carpets and disinfectant lingered in the foyer. They handed over their money to the young man sitting at a baize-covered table, in return for which he stamped the back of their right hands with a purple splodge.

They went through the double doors into the dimly-lit hall where a few people were starting to assemble. 'Is Geoffrey coming?' Pam asked.

Tessa had had a stream of boyfriends. From the third form onwards, a boyfriend was an essential commodity, a step in a pre-ordained progression. Menstruation, brassieres, high heels, leg and underarm depilation – but not necessarily in that order. Amongst her girlfriends, she would have been thought a failure if she didn't have, or be about to get, or have just split up with, a boyfriend. The pairing involved nothing more than an exchange of cards on Valentine's Day, intertwined names doodled on pencil cases, a great deal of French kissing at the cinema and 'heavy petting' at parties. Tessa was intrigued by sex and in no doubt that she would adore, and be very good at, *it*. She wasn't interested in 'saving herself for her husband' but she wanted the 'first time' to be with someone who knew what they were doing; someone who would make it unforgettable. One day, when she became a famous author and was writing her memoirs, she wanted the anecdote of her first sexual encounter to be one of the high spots in a thrilling story. She couldn't allow it to be with a ham-fisted schoolboy.

Her current boyfriend was an extremely tall boy called Geoffrey who was in the Upper Sixth at Lewis's school. She'd noticed him at the Christmas hop – one of the few occasions when the pupils of girls' and boys' grammar schools officially got together – and she was attracted to him because of his height. Having identified her target, Geoffrey didn't stand a chance.

'No.' It hadn't crossed Tessa's mind to invite him. 'He needs three As for Bristol so he's putting in twelve hours a day. What about Tim?'

'What about him?' Pam shrugged and giggled. 'We're free agents. *Femmes fatales.*'

Chairs lined both sides of the hall and, at the far end, there was a low stage with shabby red curtains at either side. Another shabby curtain, dusty black this time, formed a backdrop. A drum kit, white with sparkly blue insets, stood centre stage and power leads snaked across the bare boards. A boy Tessa recognised from somewhere – one of Lewis's crowd, maybe? – stood in the wings, playing records on a record deck linked to some kind of amplification system. The two girls, arms linked, made a few slow circuits, seeing and being seen as the hall filled up.

The Katz started playing at eight but an hour later there was still no sign of Tony Rundle or Mike Stoddy. Tessa wondered if Diane had misled her and that her brother and his friend weren't coming to the dance after all.

Another half-hour passed. Pam had gone outside 'for some fresh air' with a young man called Chris, who worked at the Co-Op Bank. Tessa had given in and was dancing with a nondescript boy – sweaty hands and reeking of unnecessary aftershave lotion – who had been trailing her all evening. The group wasn't up to much. They played deafening cover versions but at least it eliminated the need to converse with her partner, and she abandoned herself to the rough and ready beat.

She noticed Tony Rundle in the middle of *Blue Suede Shoes*, sauntering down the hall with Mike Stoddy, heading towards the stage. She took a few quick steps to her right, dancing into his path, making sure that his arm brushed her hip as he passed. Her mouth dried. She felt stirrings, agreeable yet not quite proper, where she imagined her bladder to be.

It was still warm and his mother had gone into the garden to dead-head the roses and water the plants in the rockery. Lewis couldn't settle to anything and followed her out. 'Need a hand, Mum?'

She was concentrating hard, dribbling water from the watering can into the pockets of soil between the huge stones.

'You can put the deckchairs away, if you like, Lewis.'

One parent – one child. Equilibrium again.

He folded the chairs and took them to the garden shed then gathered the weeds which his mother had spent her afternoon pulling up and now lay, in wilting heaps, along the path. 'Look, Mum.' Something dark and fluttery circled the garden. 'It's a bat.'

They stood together in silence as it disappeared into the shadows of the sombre laurels to reappear, silhouetted against the evening sky. Round and round it went, gaining then losing height, completing its erratic circuits. Then it was gone.

'I used to be terrified of bats. I thought they'd get tangled in my hair.' She shook her head. 'All the silly things we worry about. And then…'

Lewis put his arms around her thin shoulders and pulled her to him. 'I love you, Mum.'

She kissed his cheek and he felt her shudder. 'Brrrr. It's gone chilly.'

It was gloomy in the kitchen and, when they put the light on, evening instantly became night. His mother made three mugs of cocoa and they took them into the living room where his father was watching the news. Lewis tried to immerse himself in the item on the new Coventry Cathedral but his gaze kept straying to the mantelpiece where the hands of the clock crept towards Tessa's deadline.

Tessa kept dancing, edging down the dance floor until she was a few feet from the stage, alongside Mike Stoddy. Tony Rundle stood on the far side of him, hands in pockets, concentrating on the music. He was wearing a black leather jacket, a white tee-shirt and tight black trousers. The jacket was scuffed and worn around the cuffs and she was sure, were she to reach out and touch it, it would be warm and pliable. He was several inches taller than Mike and dipped his head now and again to shout something in his friend's ear.

The group finished the number and announced that they were taking a short break before their final set.

'Hi, Mike.' Her heart was hammering.

It was a second or two before recognition settled on Mike Stoddy's pleasant face. 'Oh, hi. It's Tina, isn't it?'

'Tessa.'

'Sorry. Tessa. Of course.' He nodded towards the stage. 'What d'you think of them?'

Tony Rundle stood within arm's reach and this might be her only chance. 'I think they're rubbish.' She raised her voice and leaned forward, directing her remark around Mike and towards him. 'What do you think?'

Tony Rundle appeared irritated by her intrusion. 'What do I think about what?'

'Tessa, here, thinks the group's rubbish,' Mike explained.

'And on what is *Tessa here* basing her judgement?' He stared at her, framing the question as though she were incapable of answering it herself.

His gaze scrambled her thoughts. 'Ummm … I don't know … just … a feeling, really.'

She saw herself through his eyes – a naïve schoolgirl, in a home-made green dress, no different from any of the other girls at a stupid teenage hop.

'Feelings are good,' he said at last. 'And I agree. They're rubbish.' He nodded towards the drum kit, 'I'm looking for a drummer for my own group but it won't be that one.' He checked his watch and she noticed the nicotine stains on his index and middle fingers, the mat of hair on the back of his hand. 'We're off to *The Bell*. We've got time for a pint or two. Coming?'

'Okay.' And, as easily as that she was with Tony Rundle.

The seedy pub, near the railway station, was a renowned haunt for hard-drinking men. It had none of the refinements – plush seats or fancy low lighting – of the pubs that Tessa occasionally went to with Geoffrey. In the saloon bar – barely bigger than their living room at home – the air was grey with cigarette smoke and fruity with the smell of beer. She appeared to be the only female in the hot, cramped bar, which she found both thrilling and intimidating.

'What'll you have?' Mike asked.

'Cider, please.' Her hand went to her bag. Did she have enough money? All she'd anticipated paying for was a dance ticket, a soft drink and the bus fare home.

'No. I'll get them.' Mike set off, elbowing his way to the bar, leaving her on her own with Tony.

Again, she could think of nothing witty or meaningful to say but Rundle seemed unconcerned by the silence between them, a silence accentuated by the clamour of the inebriated customers. The huge wall clock hanging over the fireplace, its face yellowed by years of seeping cigarette smoke, gave an inescapable warning that she would miss her curfew. God, it was so unfair. Rundle and Mike didn't have unreasonable fathers, waiting on the doorstep, stopwatch in hand. They had no examination hoops to jump through, no 'reputation' to protect. They could go where they liked and stay out all night if they wanted to.

'How come you know Mike, then?' Rundle asked. His eyes were khaki-coloured – nearer yellow than green – with thin eyebrows arching above them. It was a cruel face until he smiled.

'I'm at school with his sister.' If she didn't tell him, Mike would.

'Aaahhh. School.' He nodded as if that one word told him everything he needed to know about her.

Mike returned with the drinks. She took several gulps, attempting to counter her schoolgirl-ness. The cider smelled of rotting apples and its cloying taste assailed her taste buds. It was nauseating. Disgusting.

In the instant she acknowledged her repulsion, she also lost her nerve. She shoved her glass back into Mike's hand. 'Sorry. I've got to go.'

If she ran she could get the last bus and be no more than ten minutes late.

Chapter 9

When Lewis was thirteen, Uncle Frank had given him a second-hand bicycle for his birthday enabling him to do a morning paper round. In the beginning his parents were dead against it. He could see their point, but Carson's had been taken over by a local chain of newsagents and, with a change of name and modernised premises, it was almost possible to forget that it had been the scene of the tragedy. The pay was poor, but Lewis was careful with his money, unlike the other boys who bought sweets and crisps, their paltry earnings going straight back into the till. Last year, when he was sixteen, he'd doubled his income by taking on the evening round, too.

Even on icy mornings or gloomy afternoons, he enjoyed the job. He liked the camaraderie as the lads gathered in the shop, waiting whilst the manager, Mr Fisher, and his wife sorted the papers and magazines into rounds, pencilling house numbers and abbreviated street names in the top margins before loading them in the canvas satchels. He loved the smell of newsprint and the dramas captured in the day's bold headlines; the morning calm and the teatime bustle in the streets. He took pride in ensuring that the papers and periodicals went to the correct address, something the customers appreciated and expressed by giving him a generous tip at Christmas. 'We're going to miss you when you leave us, lad,' Mr Fisher muttered regularly.

A new address appeared on his evening delivery list.

Wellington House, Wellington Gardens. The detached house – solid and gracious – was set back from the road. He leaned his bike against the low redbrick wall and pulled out the *Evening Post* then walked down the path, rolling the paper ready to post it through the black iron letterbox. Before he had chance to do that, a girl appeared from the rear of the house and, involuntarily, he raised his hand to his chest.

'Sorry. Did I scare you?' she apologised.

'No. Yes.' He shook his head. 'At least you're not a dog.'

She raised her eyebrows. 'Well spotted.'

He blushed. 'What I mean is, dogs can be a bit of a problem. They don't only bite postmen, you know.'

The girl was dressed in khaki shorts and a yellow Aertex shirt, fair hair dragged back in an untidy ponytail, hands streaked with what appeared to be oil. Smudges of the same stuff covered her clothes.

'Are you any good with bicycles? I'm trying to fix my chain but I think I may need to take a link out.'

Lewis pushed the paper through the letterbox. 'I'll have a look, if you like.' How could someone wearing what seemed to be boy's clothes look so attractive?

'Thanks. I'm Kirsty by the way.' She trilled the 'r' enchantingly.

'Lewis,' he said, then, as if his parents' choice of name needed excusing, added, 'as in Carroll.'

He followed her into the back garden where a bicycle, reduced to its component parts, lay strewn across an extensive area of paving. She grinned, holding her hands out, palms up, as if she had performed a complex conjuring trick. 'See. I'm good at taking things to bits.'

Seeing that it might take some time to reassemble the machine, he promised to return once he had completed his round.

*

The evening paper round became the high spot of Lewis's day. Once he'd collected the papers, he rearranged them in his satchel so that Wellington Gardens came at the end of his route. If he started on time, and pushed on hard, he could spend fifteen minutes with Kirsty before he needed to head home for the evening meal.

Lewis learned that the Ross family were from Scotland but they had lived all over the country. 'Pa works for a bank. If you want to get on in banking, you have to go wherever they send you,' Kirsty explained.

'What about school? It can't be much fun, making friends then moving on and having to do it all again.'

She wrinkled her nose. 'It doesn't bother me. I rather like my own company.'

'But what about school work?'

'I'm quite clever,' she said, without a trace of arrogance. 'Pythagoras is the same everywhere. And Shakespeare. And the kings and queens of England.'

She was right. Facts were facts wherever you lived. He'd never thought of that. Neither had he ever met anyone who admitted to being 'quite clever' and he found it enchanting. Within one week – just five, fifteen-minute encounters – he established that Kirsty Ross was a few months older than he and went to the private school in the centre of the town. She had two brothers – hence the hand-me-down shorts and shirt. One was studying medicine in Edinburgh and the other – a Civil Servant – worked in London. Her A Level subjects were economics, history and maths and she hoped to study law.

Lewis said nothing to Tessa about Kirsty Ross. He wanted time to see how his new friendship would pan out. Although it felt like a betrayal, he persuaded himself that his sister already had enough on her mind and that it should wait until she'd finished her exams. In truth, he *was* quite concerned about her.

Each time she returned from an exam, he asked her what she'd thought of it; if the 'right' topics had come up; whether it was a fair paper. He expected her to enthuse or rant but her response was always a non-committal, 'not too bad' or 'okay'. His parents seemed happy to accept Tessa's new-found self-possession but to him it didn't ring true.

One evening, when she was washing her hair, he slipped into her bedroom. There had to be a clue or a sign, something to explain her uncharacteristically reasonable behaviour. He stood in the centre of the room. In the bathroom, Tessa was singing, her voice echo-y and sweet. *'Every day, it's a-getting closer...'* The tap was running and he pictured her leaning over the sink, rinsing the shampoo from her hair. Up in the roof the cold water tank hissed as it refilled. He pulled the bedside table drawer open a few inches, looping his index finger through the dull metal handle, as if employing a single finger was less deceitful than using a whole hand. Jewellery and cosmetics lay jumbled together at the front of the drawer. He eased it open a few more inches. Towards the back of the drawer, he could see the red leather cover of a fat diary. He took it out and – resolved to read no more than was necessary – he flicked through the year until he reached June.

Blessed with an excellent memory, having once learned something, Tessa retained it. Two years earlier, before she had recognised how pointless exams were, she had worked flat out for her O Levels, preparing reams of revision notes, then précising those notes into memory-jogging points. She'd chanted rhymes and mnemonics, made essay plans, memorised columns of irregular verbs. Her exam technique had been polished to perfection and now, seated again at the rickety exam desk in the school gymnasium, it was hard to shake off the years of training and subdue the impulse to succeed. This wasn't made any easier when, despite having done no revision at all during the previous three months, she was able to complete most of the French translation paper. Consoling herself that the other exams would be harder, she struggled to make convincing errors. Performing badly wasn't going to be as straightforward as she'd assumed.

Tessa had often felt let down by her mother's detachment from what was going on around her but in the current circumstances it was to her advantage. When she could no longer bear the tedium of her room, she read or wrote in the garden, confident that her mother would fail to work out that Dennis Wheatly was unlikely to feature on the A Level syllabus and that Chapter Seven of *The Woman Who Loved Too Much* had nothing to do with the Reform Bill of 1831. In contrast, her father was extremely observant, a skill honed, she imagined, by his years at the Post Office, where every stamp and paper clip had to be accounted for. On one occasion, he was two hours late coming home from work because a consignment of manilla envelopes had gone missing. Thus, when he was around, it was safer to keep well out of range of his eagle eye.

Although he hadn't mentioned anything, she suspected that Lewis was on to her. He stared at her when she was eating or doing her hair; he appeared in her room for no particular reason as if wanting to catch her out. He kept asking how her revision was going; what the exams were like. She felt rotten about deceiving him. Lewis had always been her truest friend and they'd never had secrets from each other. They'd pricked fingers and mingled blood; they'd sworn on bibles and drunk each other's spittle, making pact after pact that nothing would come between them. They'd clung to each other when her mother was too ill, their father too preoccupied, to bother with them. Lewis was loyal and funny and clever. He'd been the first to know, in an abridged version, when she'd started her periods and he'd confessed to her when he experienced his first wet dream. But it was too much to ask him to help her fail her exams; too embarrassing to explain how Tony Rundle made the intimate parts of her body ache and tingle.

Tessa feared that she had ruined her chances with Rundle but, a few days later, the phone rang. Her mother answered, half covering the mouthpiece with her hand as she shouted, 'Tessa. Someone for you. It doesn't sound like Geoffrey.'

'Who's this Geoffrey?' Rundle asked when she came to the phone.

'Oh. No one in particular.'

'Good. I was wondering what you were doing on Friday.'

She glanced towards the kitchen, checking that her mother wasn't listening. 'Why?'

'I'll be in The Bell from about eight o'clock on, if you fancy a drink.'

'Okay.'

'What's on tonight, then?' her father asked as they were eating their evening meal. Tessa smiled, aware that Lewis, who was sitting opposite, was watching her face.

'Nothing much. A few of us thought we'd go out. To sort of celebrate being half way through the exams. We're going to The Presto for a coffee. That's all.'

'Is Diane going?' her mother asked.

'Yes. Probably. I'm not sure.' Tessa tried not to catch Lewis's eye.

'Well, ten o'clock is plenty late enough for a Friday night. It's not safe for young girls to be in town when the pubs turn out.'

She hated her father, the way he blackmailed her with constant digs about safety and not worrying her mother. He'd been the one who lost the wretched baby after all – and therefore the one who'd driven their mother around the bend. *He* was the one who shouldn't have been allowed to go out.

'Okay, Dad.' She was tempted to add that she'd be staying out as long as she liked in a couple of months time – all night if she wanted to – but it was silly to start an argument now.

This time she dressed more casually – a navy blue skirt and a crisp white blouse – and clipped on pearl earrings, hoping to look older than her eighteen years. With no idea what an evening with Tony Rundle might entail, she raided her shoe fund, placing two half crowns in her purse.

Lewis heard Tessa crossing the hall and his father shouting, 'Ten o'clock,' as she opened the front door. He was in the kitchen, helping his mother with the dishes and she was telling him something about an appointment Gran had with the specialist the following week, but he was only half-listening.

'Don't worry, Mum,' he said, 'Gran's as tough as old boots.'

It had become a habit with all of them to reassure Peggy Swinburne whenever she showed any signs of agitation. Her pessimism filled the kitchen, infecting the very air, and he escaped as soon as he could, explaining that he wanted to get his weekend homework out of the way so that he could play tennis. 'If I buy that racquet tomorrow, I'll need to get used to it before I play a proper match.'

Before he took his books out, he slipped in to Tessa's room and removed her diary from the drawer. He felt less guilt this time. Her yarn about the coffee bar had been unconvincing and, if he were to help her, he first needed to find out what she was up to. The diary was a substantial one, with a full page for each day. Today's page was, as yet, empty except for 'Rundle. The Bell. 8pm' written beside the date. It didn't take a genius to work out where his sister was going and with whom.

Until now, Tessa's boyfriends had been pupils at Lewis's school or belonged to the Scout troupe he attended. They had all been friendly enough, no doubt hoping that he would put in a good word on their behalf. They might not have been so sanguine if they'd known that Tessa was sharing details of those inept courtships with him. 'Save you making the same mistakes. Not that anyone would fall for you, little brother.' Those days were over. Tessa had abandoned boys and was throwing herself at a man, apparently besotted with him, as were the rest of her silly friends. He appreciated that Rundle was handsome, in a moody, James Dean way, but it was common knowledge that he'd had a string of girls, and rumoured that he'd fathered a child when he was seventeen.

Lewis lay on his bed and stared at the model aeroplanes twisting on their cotton lines. The scientific aspect of human reproduction was awe-inspiring, but the urges that initiated it seemed disturbingly random. Wouldn't it be better for the human race if sexual gratification were to be separated from impregnation? His friends hinted at their sexual expertise but they never supplied any credible details. Lewis guessed that most of it was speculation – all to the good as he was sure that they were incapable of connecting their adolescent fantasies with the reality of parenthood.

His thoughts slid sideways, to Kirsty Ross. Although he'd only met her a few weeks ago, Lewis felt he'd known her for ever. Like Tessa, she was self-assured and held firm opinions but he was pretty sure she wouldn't bulldoze or bully in the way that his sister often did. Kirsty knew interesting snippets about everything – plants, the solar system, music, aeroplanes, cooking – but she never showed off, revealing her knowledge only at the appropriate moment. Not only was she intelligent and sympathetic but he liked the way her hair escaped from restraining clips to form a fuzzy halo around her head; her pale, clear eyes; her lips, tilting up at the corners, as though she were always on the point of laughing; her strong arms and unpainted fingernails. He wondered what it would be like to kiss her. Not the slithery, sloppy kissing that went on when they'd drunk cider and played postman's knock at Jenny Daniels's party last Christmas, but firm, dry kisses that would prove that he was more than another seventeen-year-old seeing how far he could get. Perhaps he *should* kiss her, before someone else did.

Tessa reached The Bell a few minutes before eight. A clamour of voices, punctuated by coarse laughter, came from the far side of the shabby door to the saloon bar. She glanced up and down the street, hoping to see Rundle.

'Fancy a drink, love?' The invitation came from a stocky, balding man, older than her father, who had crossed the road from the bus stop opposite.

'I'm waiting for someone, thanks.'

'Why don't I keep you company until the lucky man turns up?'

For a moment she regretted her tight skirt and thick mascara, but the smirk on the man's face transformed regret to rage and she glared at him. 'Why don't you fuck off, you grotty little pervert?'

'Slag,' he muttered and pushed through the swing doors.

Proud of the way she'd handled things, yet upset to have come across as 'that sort of girl', she hurried away from the pub. Hanging around outside The Bell was going to lead to trouble but if she went in she would have to face the disgusting man again.

Caught up in indecision, she failed to notice Rundle, walking towards her.

'Hi,' he said then, as though it were the most natural thing in the world, he kissed her on her lips. Throwing his arm around her shoulder, he claimed her and, squeezing her against him, swung her around and they headed towards the pub.

She did not relish a second encounter with the leering man, and the earthy smell of Rundle's leather jacket and the intimacy of his arm around her gave her confidence. 'Couldn't we go … somewhere else?'

He stopped and pulled her against him, kissing her hard, forcing his tongue between her lips. 'We could go back to mine, if you like.'

All she had intended to suggest was that they go to a different pub but, instantly and shockingly aroused by his kiss, she whispered, 'Okay.'

On the bus, he kept his arm around her, occasionally leaning to kiss her or nuzzle her neck. He asked a few questions – where she lived, what music she listened to – clearly expecting no more than a word or two in reply which was a relief because she was finding it increasingly difficult to think.

'You okay?' he asked, unlocking the front door. 'You look a bit – I dunno – shaky.'

She had always known it would happen this way – unexpected yet undeniable. It was a shame that Pamela and Diane Stoddy and Geoffrey and even the horrid man couldn't see her now.

She had no idea whether this stranger had hair on his chest or what size shoes he took and yet she was going to get into his bed and allow him to touch her most intimate places. She knew how to deal with boys like Geoffrey, how to make them do what she wanted and to stop them when they needed to be stopped, but Tony Rundle was a man and she wasn't so naïve as to imagine that she would be dictating terms.

She took a deep breath and smiled, 'I'm fine,' then followed him through the hall and up the lino-covered stairs.

She'd expected his room to be decorated with pictures of motorbikes and obscure bands but, apart from a mirror and a poster for a Picasso exhibition in Madrid, the white walls were bare. One corner was kitted out as a rudimentary kitchen with a sink and a couple of gas rings. The pale-wood furniture was plain and timeless. Books and records were arranged neatly on shelves next to a record player. The dark green bedspread, draped symmetrically over the single bed, matched the curtains.

'You're shivering.' He pointed to the raised hairs on her arms. 'Here.' He took off his jacket and draped it around her shoulders. 'Fancy a drink?'

If this were *it*, she needed to be more relaxed. 'Yes, please.'

He opened a small cupboard beneath the sink. 'I've got beer or whisky.'

The leather of his coat was warm and supple, giving her the odd sensation that she had grown another skin; that she was beginning the metamorphosis into the next phase of her life. 'Whisky, please.'

He poured whisky into two small tumblers. 'Anything with yours?'

She had never drunk whisky before and couldn't think what 'anything' might be. 'No thanks.'

The whisky smelled of mild herbs but it numbed her tongue and burned its way to her stomach. Within seconds the alcohol was setting her cheeks on fire and disconnecting her, making it progressively more difficult to concentrate on what was happening.

She stole a look at her watch. It was already nine o'clock. 'D'you have a telephone?' she asked.

'There's a phone box at the end of the street.' He raised an eyebrow. 'Got to phone Mummy and Daddy?'

She tried not to hear the sneer in his voice. 'Of course not. I just wanted to—'

'That's okay, then.' He took the glass from her hand and placed it on the table next to the bed. Brushing her cheek with the back of his hand, he whispered, 'You're a funny girl, aren't you? You're burning hot now. Perhaps you've got too many clothes on. Let's put that right, shall we?' Without waiting for her answer, he pushed the jacket off her shoulders and began to undress her, kissing her as he removed each item of clothing before folding it and placing it on the arm of the easy chair. Cardigan. Blouse. Skirt. It seemed to go on and on. Once or twice she attempted to help him undo a button or zip, but he brushed her hand away. She let him continue, feeling dirty yet excited, knowing she should ask why he still had all his clothes on, but unable to speak because he was kissing her and she was melting. Bra. Stockings. Wasn't this what she had wanted? Suspender belt. Knickers. He pushed her down on the bed and, still fully clothed, knelt over her. His face looked different now – soppy and sweaty and distorted.

She was glad that she was drunk. It was as well that her mind was floating away from her body whilst this panting stranger inspected her.

'Can I have another drink, please?' Her voice echoed in her head as though she were speaking from the bottom of a well.

He poured more whisky into her glass then began stripping his own clothes off, this time dropping them on the floor, hopping as he yanked first one leg, then the other out of his jeans.

Whenever she accidentally caught sight of Lewis without his clothes on it was funny and rather sweet. He looked much like he had as a child but with a fuzz of dark hair above his little dangling willy. Rundle's nakedness shocked her. His engorged penis protruded from a mat of thick, red curls. It seemed to defy gravity, pointing up and out at an impossible angle. She'd seen drawings scratched on the back of doors in public lavatories; discussed it at length with her friends. All the information had been there in the biology books but she hadn't believed it because it was so unbelievable.

He pushed his hips out and grinned as if proud of himself and wanting her to appreciate the 'thing'. It was so big and so ugly

Chapter 10

LEWIS PLOUGHED ON THROUGH HIS HOMEWORK but, as it neared the time when Tessa should come home, he found it impossible to keep his mind on his books. The television rumbled on in the living room below and he pictured his father getting up from his armchair to wind the clock on the mantelpiece. He could see him swinging open the convex glass, waiting for Big Ben to strike ten before nudging the minute hand backwards or forwards, revealing to the second how late Tessa might be.

His father called up the stairs. 'Lewis?'

'I'll be down in a minute.'

Tessa always expected him to back her up, rounding extravagant statements off with '…wasn't it, Lewis?' or 'I'm right aren't I, Lewis?', tangling him up in her schemes. It was getting a bit much. Before going down, he tossed Tessa's diary on her bed. If she knew he was on to her, she might think again before continuing on her reckless path.

The volume on the television had been turned down but his mother, hunched forward in her chair, arms folded tightly across her chest, was staring at the flickering screen as if trying to lip read. His father stood in the bay window, peering up and down the street. 'Your sister's twenty minutes late. It's not good enough. She knows how worried your mother gets.' He habitually used his wife's 'nerves' to short circuit debate and imply that his stringent rules were based on altruism. 'D'you know any of these girls that she's gone out with?'

Lewis shrugged. 'She goes round with a crowd.'

'Do we know where any of them live?' Dick Swinburne glanced between Lewis and his wife, his 'we' including her for the first time. She shook her head.

Lewis *did* know where several of Tessa's friends lived – he delivered newspapers to their homes – but disclosing this would enable his father to go knocking on doors, checking to see whether these girls, who had almost certainly not left the house that evening, were safe home. 'No, Dad. Sorry.'

Another ten minutes passed and Dick Swinburne took the car keys from his pocket. 'Something must have happened to her. You stay here and take care of your mother. I'm going to drive into town. To the coffee bar. If I don't find her, I'm phoning the police.'

'But Dad, it's only just ten-thirty—'

'The sooner we start looking, the more chance we have of finding her.'

The statement was absurdly melodramatic but Lewis could understand why his father felt he had to take action. When Gordon went missing, the question that came up time and time again was why had it taken him so long to contact the police.

Lewis wasn't a great advocate of what people called 'instinct', preferring to weigh up an argument and then make a considered decision. But, unable to see any other way to prevent his father from making a fool of himself, he had no time to ponder and was forced to tell the truth, a truth slightly distorted to avoid mentioning the diary.

'She never went to The Presto, Dad. I ... I overheard her telling ... friends that she was meeting a chap called Tony Rundle. In The Bell.' He felt sick at his own treachery.

His father shook his head. 'Christ.'

Lewis attempted to minimise the damage he had done. 'He's

quite a decent bloke, or so I've heard. He's Mike Stoddy's mate. Diane's brother. You know Diane Stoddy, don't you, Mum?'

His mother looked up, the light from the muted television flickering across her impassive face, and he thought she was going to say something but his father butted in. 'That's neither here nor there. She lied to us and I will not have it. The girl's in the middle of important exams and she's going to throw it all away. Anyway, what sort of lad asks a girl to meet him in a pub? A respectable boy would come and collect her. And see that she's home on time.'

As if jolted out of a trance, his mother stood up, brushed the creases out of her skirt and went into the kitchen. Her action seemed so purposeful that they followed, watching as she filled the kettle and set out three cups and saucers. 'I expect she's missed the bus or something.' Her voice was calm.

'Then why hasn't she phoned? Answer me that,' Dick Swinburne snapped.

'Perhaps she's lost her purse.' Her moderate reply showed no hint of agitation.

'How can you be so bloody cheerful? Don't you understand, woman? Your daughter is God knows where, with God knows who.'

Lewis had grown up believing that the slightest upset might push his mother over the edge, yet here was his father, yelling and suggesting that something unspeakable had happened. But his mother continued stirring her tea, the trace of a smile on her lips, and Lewis could only assume that the pink pills she swallowed every morning were doing the trick.

The door opened and the three of them turned to see Tessa standing half in, half out of the kitchen, her smudged makeup and dishevelled hair giving her a slightly out of focus appearance.

'Sorry I'm a bit late.'

Lewis felt as if he were floating, lifted by a surge of relief, and he wanted to hug her and apologise for the dreadful thing that she didn't yet know he had done.

'The front door's wide open. Anyone could walk in.' She yawned. 'I'm ready for bed.'

His father swung round, nudging the table and rattling the cups in their saucers. 'Come in here, young lady. Lewis, upstairs. Now.'

Lewis whispered, 'Sorry, Tess,' as he squeezed past her, his eyes averted, relieved to be dismissed yet feeling he should stay to give her his support. He took the stairs two at a time, dropping down to squat on the top step.

When he and Tessa were small, they loved to sneak out of bed and sit on the stairs, 'spying' on the grown-ups. In those days, visitors – Nan and Gramps, before they moved away; Uncle Frank and one of his friends; the couple from next door – dropped in on a Friday or Saturday evening and it was such fun to sit, side by side in their dressing gowns, listening to them laughing and gossiping over a game of whist. Their mother shuttled back and forth to the kitchen, with plates of sandwiches and cups of tea, pretending that she didn't see them on the stair, her collusion making the whole thing all the more special.

Beyond the kitchen door, his father was ranting, his words indiscernible but their meaning unambiguous. Lewis closed his eyes and rested his head on his knees. In a few months Tessa would leave home, would be living by her own rules, free to break them whenever she wanted to. Why couldn't his father see that dialogue was more effective than authoritarian rant? 'Softly, softly, catch-ee monkey,' as Uncle Frank would wisely, and graphically, put it.

Now it was Tessa's turn, her voice getting louder and more belligerent as it all came tumbling out. Once she got the bit between her teeth, she never knew when to stop. So many times he'd seen her reach the 'bugger it' point, when anything and anyone was fair game.

Lewis tiptoed into his sister's room and pushed the diary back in the drawer. She had enough on her plate without discovering that her brother had been poking around in her secrets.

He was sitting on the edge of his bed when his mother tapped the door and called gently. 'Are you okay, love?'

'Not really.'

She came in and sat next to him, putting an arm around his shoulder. She was hot, smelling earthy and sweet, like parsnips just pulled from the soil. His throat ached. 'I wish I hadn't told on her. But I was scared Dad would ring the police.' He tilted his head, resting it against hers. 'I can't stand it when they fight, Mum.'

'I can't either, love. But it's not easy, being a parent. Knowing where to draw the line. Dad wasn't always like this. Maybe you can't remember, but he used to be full of fun. Then … well … you know. It's the responsibility, I suppose. You'll understand one day.'

'Yes, but she's safe home. He's told her off. Why can't he leave it at that?'

'You know Tess. She won't let it go, either. She rubs him up the wrong way. They're too alike.' Suddenly his mother looked vague and panicky, as if the quarrel going on downstairs had breached the defences of the little pink pills.

'Do you realise what time it is? Your mother and I have been worried sick. And don't bother to give us a cock and bull story about friends and coffee bars. We know where you were.'

Tessa's heart was thudding but it seemed to be located somewhere in her throat. Voices sounded amplified and distorted, like they did in the public swimming baths. She stared at her feet. Her left shoe was scuffed across the toe where she'd caught it against a kerb stone. She must get some navy blue shoe polish and try and cover it up. Why was he going on and on like this? She was home in one piece – well – what more did he want? She kept looking down because, were their eyes to meet, he would know.

'I lost track of time. I thought it was better to run for the bus than waste time looking for a phone box,' she said, tempted to add that she was only home now because she'd forked out half a crown for a taxi.

'Who is this man, anyway? What's he after?' He came closer, lifting her chin with his forefinger so that she couldn't avoid his eyes. 'You're drunk, aren't you?'

'What if I am?' She gave him one last chance. 'Don't you remember what it's like to want – to *need* – to try new things, Dad?' She softened her voice, 'Look. I could have left school two years ago. I could be working in Woolworth's, then you wouldn't treat me like a child.'

'Whilst I'm paying for—'

'That's not fair, either. It's not the dark ages. You don't own me. You haven't bought the right to tell me what to do.'

'If you're living under my roof, you're my responsibility.' He jabbed the air with his index finger.

'Fine. That's easily solved. I'll move out.'

'Don't be ridiculous, Tessa. What about your exams?'

'Fuck the fucking exams. I'm not doing any more exams. Ever.' She rode the wave of recklessness. 'And I'll be gone by tomorrow evening.'

'Watch your language,' her father growled. 'And stop being so theatrical.' He paused. 'Where would you go, anyway?'

'I'll rent a room.' The wave rolled forward, gathering speed. 'I'll get a job and rent a room. Lots of people do that.'

'And what's that going to do to your mother?' Again, the blackmail.

'I don't know. I can't be expected to live my life for someone else. It's not fair.' She had to save herself. 'If you need to blame someone for the state Mum's in, perhaps you should think back to what started it.'

Her father closed his eyes and dragged the palms of his hands down his face. 'Look, we're both tired. Let's leave it at that, before we say things we don't mean.' He attempted a smile. 'Tessa…' He reached a hand out towards her and, on any other night but this, she might have taken it.

Chapter 11

LEWIS LAY IN BED, LISTENING. First, Tessa's footsteps stomping up the stairs, followed by the crash of her bedroom door. Next, the front door chain rattling into place and his father's irregular tread on the landing. Voices, murmuring and urgent, from his parents' room.

He rolled onto his front, jamming his folded arms beneath the pillow, closing his eyes to exclude the moonlight which penetrated the gingham curtains. And he went on an imaginary cycle ride, something he'd learned to do when sleep wouldn't come.

He rode to Kirsty's house and, hovering at first floor level, peeped in at her window. She was sleeping, her hair still loosely plaited, that delightful smile playing on her lips. He tapped on the glass and she opened her eyes, not appearing at all surprised to see him. They waved to each other then he dropped back on to his bicycle and rode on. He crossed Buckingham Road and turned down Medway Avenue. The lights were on and the curtains open at their old home and he braked briefly before deciding to give it a miss. He'd stopped on previous night rides, creeping in through the unlocked door, visiting the familiar rooms but never coming across any of the inhabitants. Dream cycling was effortless and he rolled on, up Cranwell Road to the very top, leaning his bike against the wall of Cranwell Lodge. The lights were on here, too, but the heavy curtains were drawn.

He pressed his eye against the pane, hoping to catch a glimpse of someone through the chink, but all he could see was a white parrot on a perch and a table heaped with sweets.

'Lewis'. Tessa's urgent whisper jolted him from half-sleep. 'Shove over.' She switched on the bedside lamp.

He wriggled to the far side of the narrow bed, making room for her to sit down. 'What's the time?'

'Midnight. I need to talk to you.'

He sat up, squinting against the light. His sister was still dressed. Her hairstyle had lost its symmetry and the make-up around her eyes was smudged. She looked as though she'd been in a fight. A trace of scent – What was it called? Something pretentious – clung around her, overlaid by the chemical smell of alcohol.

He waited, expecting her to berate him for informing on her but instead she said, 'Guess what, Lew?'

'What?'

'I'm leaving home. Tomorrow. No, today.'

He giggled. 'Don't be daft. What about—'

'Don't you start. Dad's been through the whole rigmarole. Mum. Exams. Getting drunk.' She sounded not the least upset.

'But … but he's right, isn't he? You *should* think about those things.' He was no longer sleepy. 'Anyway, what's the point of leaving now? You'll be going to university in a few months.'

'The point *is* I have no intention of going to go to poxy university. I don't want to spend another three years doing exams. Having to justify every little thing I do. Being dependent on him for money.'

Lewis tugged his ear lobe. 'Where will you go? How will you live?'

She shook her head and sighed. 'God, Lewis, you're starting to sound just like him. I'll get a job and live in a bedsit. Lots of girls are working by the time they're eighteen.'

'But you haven't got any qualifications.'

She raised her eyebrows. 'Actually, if you remember, I've got nine O Levels. Anyway, you don't need qualifications to work in a shop. Or a pub.' She clapped her hands. 'I'll work in the day and write in the small hours. This is the best thing that could have happened.' She fiddled with the tail of her watch strap. 'I may even go and live with Tony Rundle for a bit.' The light was behind her, making it difficult for him to see her expression.

'Rundle? How come? Has he asked you to?'

'Not exactly. But I'm sure he'd love me to.' Another pause. ''Specially after what happened tonight.' She spoke clearly and defiantly.

Dreading her answer, yet unable to stop himself from asking, Lewis said, 'What did happen?'

'Don't be dim, Lew. Isn't it obvious? Don't I look different?' She stood up as if to give him a better view. 'It's funny though. It wasn't at all—'

'La-la-la-la-la.' He rammed his fingers in his ears and squeezed his eyes shut, filling his head with noise. 'La-la-la-la. I don't want to hear. It's disgusting.'

He'd know it would happen one day and it was inevitable Tessa would tell him it had. Of course she was never going to be a virgin bride. She was too impatient for that. He'd been hoping it might be with one of her harmless boyfriends – Geoffrey or Mike, his predecessor. Or with a nice, straightforward student whom she'd meet at Exeter. But allowing a bastard like Rundle to do that to her... As soon as it got out – and it surely would – she'd be labelled as another of Rundle's tarts. It wasn't that he was a prude. He wanted to have sex with Kirsty, but not for a long time yet and only when they both agreed that it was right. It would be private and special. He wouldn't even tell Tessa.

He pulled the pillow around his head, clamping it against his ears, as if by doing so he could eradicate her sickening words.

At three o'clock, hunger drove Tessa down to the kitchen. She devoured a bowl of Sugar Puffs and two rounds of toast and jam. Whether she stayed or went, nothing in this kitchen would change and she took mental snapshots, fixing every detail in her memory. *Click.* The pans on the shelf above the gas cooker, arranged largest to smallest, from left to right. *Click.* The decorative plates tilted back on the dresser; the peg bag hanging on the back of the kitchen door. *Click.* The sickly spider plant on the window sill. She rinsed her bowl and plate and stacked them in the rack on the draining board. *Click.*

She slid the battered suitcase from the cupboard under the stairs and took it up to her bedroom. Opening it, she caught the hint of suntan lotion and pakamacs, trapped there since last summer when the family had spent a tedious fortnight in Weymouth. By the time she took a second sniff, the holiday had seeped away, leaving only the mustiness of the stained paper lining.

In the thick silence of the summer night, she sorted through her clothes, only now facing the fact that she needed some sort of escape plan. If she turned up on Gran's doorstep, she would be frogmarched straight back without the opportunity to tell her side of the story. Uncle Frank was a good sport and he would definitely put her up for a night or two, but he would nag her to patch things up and return home. Besides, he was probably 'on the road' as he put it. None of her friends' parents would welcome 'that Tessa Swinburne' – an insurgent who might contaminate their innocent daughters with her free will.

That left Tony Rundle.

Generally on Saturdays his mother made a cooked breakfast – bacon and eggs or beans on toast – but, when Lewis returned from his paper round, his father was alone in the kitchen, standing at the sink, a bowl of cornflakes in his hand. 'No doubt you've talked to your sister.'

'Yes.' Denial was pointless.

His father indicated the table and they sat down. 'I don't know what she told you, but I may have been a bit heavy-handed last night.' He looked exhausted, the sallowness of his face accentuated by stubble on his chin and upper lip. 'We both lost our tempers. Said things we didn't mean. Tessa's strung up about these exams. And I was worried because ... well, one day you'll understand. Neither of us was thinking straight.'

Lewis ran his fingertips back and forth across the embroidery on the scallop-edged tablecloth. Hundreds and hundreds of silky stitches – orange, yellow and green – traced out bunches of marigolds in the corners and a circular garland in the centre. Gran had presented it to his mother a few Christmases ago, proudly flipping it over to show that the stitching was as neat on the back as the front. It seemed ridiculous for an old person to waste their remaining days doing something so futile.

'She's threatening to leave home.' He paused. 'Is that what she told you?'

'Yes.' Lewis realised that his father was waiting for him to expand on this. 'She's pretty determined.'

Dick Swinburne dropped his head and massaged his temples. 'I don't like involving you in this, Lewis, but I was hoping ... your mother and I were hoping ... that you might talk some sense into her. She'll listen to you.'

'She's made up her mind, Dad.' Tessa was going, Lewis was sure of that, nevertheless, seeing his father's stricken face, he tried to soften his assertion. 'Perhaps she needs to get away for a couple of days, to think it over. She'll probably see that she's being hasty.'

His father shook his head. 'If your sister leaves this house today, she won't be back. Who'd blame her? Who'd want to live with a deranged mother and a crippled father?' It sounded pathetically self-indulgent and Lewis might have laughed had his father not begun to cry, dry sobs, like a chesty cough, wracking his body.

Lewis stood up and backed towards the door. 'I'll talk to her now.'

Tessa was rummaging through the drawer of her bedside table. 'I suppose you've been sent to drum some sense into me.' The contents of her wardrobe were heaped on the bed. Shoes, bags and books covered the floor. 'Can I borrow your rucksack, Lewis? And, dearest, loveliest brother of mine,' she jumped over the clutter, grabbing him in an exaggerated hug, 'd'you have any cash? I'll pay you back as soon as I've got a job. Cross my heart.'

He wriggled out of her embrace and studied the room. Her desk had been cleared of text books and the exam schedule was rolled up and jammed in the waste-paper basket. 'Dad's crying in the kitchen. It's horrible. He's asked me to stop you going.'

'And how d'you intend to do that? Brute force?' She poked her tongue out as if this were nothing more than a squabble.

Had she forgotten their pacts of loyalty, solemnly sworn and sealed with blood? Had she forgotten the days and weeks and months when their parents were out of their minds and they were everything to each other? 'Please don't leave, Tess.'

'It's okay for you. You're happy sitting in your room, making model aeroplanes—'

'That's not fair.'

'Well you are,' she snapped then wrinkling her nose added softly, 'I'm not saying there's anything wrong with that. We can't all be the same, can we?' She took his hand and kissed the back of it. 'I'd be going in September anyway. You've always known that. So what's the difference?'

There was all the difference in the world. He'd daydreamed

119

of visiting her at university; sitting in smoky rooms with her student friends, discussing things that mattered; getting a taste of the life he might soon be leading. But, if she slammed her way out of their lives, his parents would pretend that she had never existed. He'd seen how easily that happened.

The curtains billowed out from the open window then sank back, as if sighing in resigned acceptance.

'You can have my racquet money, if you like.' He couldn't bear to think of her begging Rundle for money.

'Thanks, Lewis.' She kissed him noisily on the cheek. 'Cheer up. It's the start of my brilliant adventure. I'm going to be a famous writer. I'll make my fortune and buy a huge house and you can come and live with me.'

For a moment he was utterly happy.

Before Tessa reached the top of the road, the pressed tin handle of the suitcase had cut into her fingers and, in swapping her load from one hand to the other, she had scraped her left shin. On the way to the bus stop she passed two neighbours, walking their dogs, both of whom enquired after her parents whilst taking in every detail of the bulging rucksack and the arm-wrenching case. It wouldn't be long before the story of her leaving percolated through the neighbourhood. She found the prospect elating.

Tony Rundle might be dubious about sharing not only his bed but also his kitchen and bathroom with a girl whom he had met only twice, so it was vital that he liked what he saw when he opened the door to her. With this in mind she had selected a full cotton skirt with a stiff petticoat and a low-necked blouse which her father had once said was 'unsuitable for a girl her age'. If she survived the first few minutes, she was confident she could charm Rundle into submission.

During the night, there had been plenty of time to reflect on what had happened. The 'first time' was supposed to be special but her recollection of it was indistinct, as if it were an out of focus film. The first part had been okay but what followed was ugly and crude. None of her friends had 'gone all the way' although they all bragged that they had come pretty close. She'd assumed that the truth about sexual intercourse – what it felt, sounded and looked like – fell somewhere between the flowery vagueness of romantic fiction and the bald facts set out on page eighty-three of the biology textbook. She'd dreamed that the act would be a combination of shared endeavour and gratification, all enveloped in some kind of spiritual enlightenment. How naïve. Nothing had been shared. Rundle had rammed his way inside her and *he* might have gained satisfaction from the whole business but she hadn't. On the plus side, it had been uncomfortable rather than painful, not unlike the discomfort she'd experienced when she'd slipped off the saddle of Lewis's bike and straddled the cross-bar. Rather a small plus.

'You got home okay then.' Tony Rundle was staring at the case and the rucksack. He was wearing the tee shirt and jeans he'd had on last night, his hair was uncombed and his eyelids puffed with sleep.

'Yes, thanks.' Tessa gave what she hoped was an enticing smile. 'Can I come in?'

'Sure.' He stepped back, leaving her to push her bags into the room. 'Going away?'

'Yes. No. I'm leaving home, actually.'

'Oh, yeah.' Unsmiling, he closed the door.

'Dad found out about … last night. About … you know.' She blushed, embarrassed by the reference to what had occurred yet determined to arouse his guilty sympathy. 'He's thrown me out. So I was wondering…'

He held up his hands, like a policeman stopping the traffic, and shook his head. 'Uh-uh.'

She pressed on. 'It would only be for a week or so. Until I can find a job and a room.'

'The answer is no.'

His unconsidered reply affronted her. She wanted to slap his face and tell him that he was arrogant and that his feet smelled but she reined in her fury, pouting and adopting a little girl voice. 'I won't get in your way. Honestly. You'll hardly know I'm here.'

'It's nothing personal. I never let girls stay here. End of story.'

She could contain herself no longer. 'Prick. You owe it to me.'

'How come?'

'You got me drunk and … took advantage of me.' She glared at him.

'And that entitles you to move in?' He shook his head in mock amazement. 'If it worked like that, I'd have a dozen girls cluttering up the place.'

Frustration, rage and exhaustion swept over her and she was unable to hold back the tears. 'Bastard,' she howled. 'I can't believe I wasted my virginity on a creep like you.' She folded her arms around her head as if to protect herself from any more blows.

'Okay, okay. I didn't realise. Honest, I didn't.' He chewed his lip. 'Look, how's this? You can stay until Monday. But then you'll have to sort something out.'

Chapter 12

LEWIS PUSHED OPEN THE DOOR, set to retreat if Tessa shrieked or threw a shoe at his head. But she had gone, her abandoned clothes covering the bed and the floor like seaweed dumped on the beach after a storm. He tiptoed in and closed the door. Stepping over the mess, he made his way across the room, and sat on the upright chair, still and silent, as if he were in a holy place waiting for a miracle to happen.

Had his parents been in here since she left? Surely not or it wouldn't still be in this mess. His mother fretted if anything was out of place and was forever hanging coats in wardrobes, pushing socks and underwear into drawers, replacing books on shelves. A few weeks earlier he'd asked her, gently, not to tidy his books away when he was in the middle of homework. 'I'm sorry, dear,' she'd apologised, as if unaware that she was doing it.

Tessa's Fair Isle jumper, patterned with green, blue and white zigzags, poked out of an open drawer, one sleeve dangling as if it were trying to make a break for freedom, too. He took it out, burying his nose in the scratchy wool, disappointed that no hint of her smell lingered in the intricate rows. When someone died there was a funeral and their possessions were disposed of, but if someone simply disappeared – what happened then? During wars and natural disasters, people went missing all the time but, once in a while, years later, one of them reappeared. Did they expect to find their belongings, if not exactly where they'd left them then, at any rate, safely stored somewhere? He had no idea what had happened to Gordon's things. Was his mother keeping them safe, just in case? There were lots of cardboard boxes in the attic and they could well be packed in one of those. But what would have been the point? Were Gordon ever to turn up, rattles, bibs and little vests would be of no earthly use to him.

Lewis had been trying to keep Tessa's confession locked in a soundproof box at the back of his mind. But the essence of his sister dominated the room, trapped in her abandoned clothes and etched in the mirror on the wardrobe door. And this essence – this force – eased the lid off the box, and her words seeped out again. *Especially after what happened tonight.* It was impossible not to picture what had gone on and he felt ashamed of himself for doing so. But, worse than that, he was disappointed in Tessa.

He folded the jumper and put it away. Dresses, skirts and slacks went back on their hangers. Books on the desk. Dressing gown on the hook on the back of the door. Finally he collected her discarded shoes – sandals, tennis shoes, slippers, pumps – pairing them and placing them, side by side, in the bottom of the wardrobe. The tidied bedroom eradicated some of the violence of her leaving.

He took refuge in his room. His parents would want him to track Tessa down and talk her into returning; they would cross-question him, trying to wheedle out any secrets that she might have confided in him. They would watch him like hawks; they would demand to know where he was going and with whom; they would smother him with attention. They would expect too much of him. He understood why they would behave like that. They had just lost another child.

Opening his maths books, he immersed himself in the comforting formulae. Immutable and reliable, here was something that would never let him down. But despite the alphas and betas, the x's and y's, he couldn't stop thinking about Tessa.

'Lewis?' His father's voice came from the other side of the door, tentative and polite, as though he were talking to an invalid. 'Lewis?'

'In here, Dad. I'm doing my homework.'

Dick Swinburne had discarded the old shirt and trousers he generally wore at weekends, replacing them with grey flannels, a pale blue shirt and striped tie and, despite the heat, a blazer with mock military buttons. His forehead shone with perspiration. 'Could you stick around? Keep your mother company? I'm going out for a while.'

'Are you going to look for Tessa?'

'Yes.'

'Where is Mum?'

'Downstairs. I think she should take a tablet and lie down but she wants to stay near the phone.'

'Dad?'

'Yes?'

'...'

'What, son?'

Lewis didn't have the heart to tell him that he was wasting his time and that Tessa had no intention of being found. 'You look very smart.'

His mother was sitting in the kitchen, flicking over the pages of *Woman's Own*, her eyes skimming the pages like an apprehensive patient in the dentist's waiting room.

'Fancy a cup of tea, Mum?'

'That's kind of you, love. Yes, please. You're a very thoughtful boy, Lewis. Thank you.' Her gratitude was pitiful and he felt rotten.

This whole business was stupid. With his parents – strictly

speaking, his father, because his mother never seemed quite present – everything in the world was either right or wrong. There was never any 'perhaps' or 'maybe', no blurred edges or room for negotiation. Tessa could be a pain in the neck but teenagers were notoriously difficult, weren't they? There were countless films and books and songs on the theme, so how could the phenomenon have taken his parents by surprise? What they could do with was a crowd of friends. They could all sit around grumbling about the problems they were having with their delinquent children. They'd soon see, then, that the odd broken curfew wasn't so terrible. But they didn't have friends any more. The only regular visitors – not counting people like the insurance man or the man who read the gas meter – were Gran and Uncle Frank. Distant cousins and obscure relatives, 'connected by marriage', whatever that meant, occasionally dropped in to report on a death or deliver a Christmas card, but they were invariably on their way somewhere and never had time to stay long.

Gran came every Friday to help his mother with the weekend shopping and she usually stayed for tea. She seemed smaller and paler than she used to be, but no less pessimistic. Tessa was convinced that Gran was losing her marbles and, indeed, sometimes she didn't seem too sure who he was. Only last week she'd called him Michael and asked him where he lived.

Uncle Frank, too, had lost his appeal. Now that he could no longer amuse them with rough and tumble games and corny jokes, he seemed not to have a clue how to talk to them. He still liked to hold the floor but he tended to repeat the same old tales and he'd been quite sharp with Tessa when she'd teased him about it. 'You should have more respect for your elders and betters,' he'd growled and it was clear that, for once, he wasn't joking.

The phone rang. His mother flinched and rose a few inches

off her chair then, as though she'd thought better of it, asked, 'Could you answer it, love?'

Lewis lifted the receiver. *Beep*-ing followed by c*lunk*-ing indicated that the call was from a public phone box. He grinned. 'Tess?' But it was his doubles partner, demanding to know why he had missed tennis practice.

Dick Swinburne returned, irritable after an unproductive search, and Lewis, pretending that the phone call had been from Mr Fisher, asking him to do an extra paper round, was able to make his getaway.

It was a perfect day, the breeze barely stirring the bunting on the garage forecourt and, as he spun along on his bicycle, his spirits lifted and the world regained its steadiness. He rode aimlessly, wondering how to occupy the hour before he genuinely was needed at the shop, contemplating calling on Kirsty before his scheduled visit with the evening paper. It would be a tremendous relief to tell her everything that had happened and to have her opinion on the mess they were in. But he daren't do that. The Ross family were faultless. Mr and Mrs Ross treated Kirsty like an adult, asking for, and taking heed of, her views on all family matters. They'd lived in the town only a few months, yet already they had a host of interesting friends – proof that they were sociable and fun. Douglas and Gavin Ross, both brainy and successful young men, made frequent visits home, clearly enjoying their parents' company. To top it all, every member of the Ross family was remarkably good-looking – Kirsty had shown him a photograph of them at a recent family wedding.

In turn, of course, she wanted to know everything about the Swinburne family. He explained about the accident which had caused his father to be classified unfit for military service; how his mother was gentle and loved gardening but wasn't very strong; that his sister was bright and creative and funny. He omitted to mention that his baby brother had disappeared without trace; that his mother had, on two occasions, been an in-patient at the local mental hospital and was now scared to go anywhere on her own; that, over the past eight years, his father had hardened into an unapproachable, unhappy man who preached that the world was a dangerous place. Now he could add to the dismal record that his schoolgirl sister had had sexual intercourse with the local Casanova, dropped out of school and run away from home. Why would a Ross want to associate with a Swinburne?

He followed the dreamy cycle route he had taken the previous night. The phone box where he and Tessa had abandoned the plasticine baby was still there on Buckingham Road, red and solid, as permanent as a war memorial. Leaning his bike against the railings he pulled open the door. The interior smelled of stale cigarettes and disinfectant and there was a puddle of liquid – he didn't like to think what it might be – in one corner. The metal shelf next to the phone had been defaced with initials and slogans gouged into the black paint in angular lettering. It was an ugly and unhappy place. On the shelf, in the precise spot where he and Tessa had abandoned the paper bag, there was a cigarette carton, empty apart from a few flakes of tobacco and the silver paper which had wrapped the cigarettes. Someone had pencilled a telephone number on the fold over tab of the carton and, for a fanciful second, Lewis wondered whether it might be important.

Looking up he noticed that a woman was waiting to use the phone. Realising how stupid he must appear to an observer as he stood there without making a call, he dropped some pennies in the slot and dialled the number on the carton. He felt panic and excitement flutter in his stomach. What would he say to whoever answered the phone? He wished Tessa were with him. She was brilliant at this sort of thing. The phone rang and rang but no one picked it up and Lewis, half relieved, half disappointed, pressed the 'B' button and his coins were returned to him, down the metal chute.

Strictly speaking, in taking this cycle ride, he was breaking the promise he had made to his father eight years earlier. 'You children are not to wander off. I don't want you going anywhere near the old house. Or that weird couple. It would only start tongues wagging and get your mother in a state.' Once or twice, in the beginning, Tessa had suggested they go back to search for clues but when Lewis had refused to go with her, she seemed happy to let it go. That was all so long ago now and Lewis felt excitement not guilt as he resumed his journey.

On a summer's day like today, Medway Avenue – the branches of the plane trees touching overhead – used to be a long green tunnel stretching as far as a child's eye could see. But many of the trees had been taken down and the few that remained severely pruned. The Avenue had lost its grandeur and Lewis, whose recollections of his life there had been framed by arching branches, felt that he had been duped.

As he passed number seventy-four he freewheeled, standing on the pedals and raising himself off the saddle. There had been many alterations to the house and he saw that it looked nothing like it did in his dreams. Its once green window frames were now harsh white and the old front door – varnished oak, solid and steadfast – had been replaced by something modern with a glass panel at the top. Flower beds no longer lined the path leading up to the door. His mother had been so proud of those beds and she could identify every variety of rose that grew in them. 'Peace', 'Golden Showers', 'Ballerina', 'Prosperity'. Names that evoked a benevolent world. The clipped privet hedge had been replaced by a low wooden fence and the whole front garden was grassed over. It looked like the home of people who didn't have time.

He wished Tessa were at his side. It wasn't right to be time-travelling – because that's what it felt like – without her. Then, remembering how readily she had ditched him and gone chasing off after Rundle, he carried on down Medway Avenue and turned right. Head down, he toiled up Cranwell Road, not sure what he wanted to see when he reached the top. If the garden of Cranwell Lodge had been cleared and the house 'done up' it would surely mean that Mrs Channing and Mr Zeal had gone and, along with them, the opportunity for atonement.

But, like the phone box, Cranwell Lodge was still there, gloomy and fascinating. Peering through tangled briars and overgrown shrubs, it occurred to Lewis that nature, once left to its own devices, reached a kind of end point where it imploded and sustained itself and that, were everyone in the world to let their gardens go untended, there would be no dire consequences for life on earth.

Wedging his bike between the low front wall and the sickly hedge, he pushed through the foliage. He had been mistaken – the house *had* changed. The paint on the front door had lost its sheen and it was impossible to tell whether it had once been green or brown; several of the leaded lights in the hall window were cracked; the remnants of a coir doormat lay on the doorstep, half buried under a layer of compacted leaves which must have lain there since the previous autumn, or the one before.

He knocked the front door. The ride up the hill had made him sweat but, standing there in the heavy shade, he shivered. His bladder felt tight and he wished he'd gone to the lavatory before he left home. 'No one there,' he whispered, then felt foolish at having spoken his thoughts out loud.

He was debating whether to risk peeing behind the laurel bush when he heard a quaver-y, 'Who is it? What do you want?' from the far side of the door.

There was still time to walk away but it would be wrong,

unkind, first to scare Mrs Channing – he was sure it was her voice – and then increase her anxiety by disappearing. He leaned close to the door, 'Don't worry, Mrs Channing. It's Lewis Swinburne. From a long time ago. My sister and I used to visit you. I was just passing.' He was reluctant to shout the additional piece of information, the thing which would unquestionably jog her memory.

She spared him that. 'Did they ever find your brother?'

'No. No, they didn't.'

The door opened a few inches and, although he could only see a narrow slice of her through the gap – white hair, searching blue eyes, some sort of kimono, red slippers – she was unmistakable.

'The door is sticking,' she said. 'Can you give it a shove from your side?'

Lewis pushed hard and managed to get the door half open. Looking down he saw the cause of the problem. The mosaic floor tiles were raised in places, as though they had been pushed up from below.

'And where *is* your sister?' Mrs Channing asked as she led him through to the back room.

'Ummm, I'm not sure.' The old lady raised her eyebrows and Lewis pre-empting any sharp observation carried on, 'She's out with a friend.'

'Please make yourself comfortable.' Mrs Channing indicated the armchair next to the fireplace. 'If you'll excuse me for one moment.' She left and he heard her footsteps going slowly up the stairs.

To be sitting, once more, in this room filled him with a sense of achievement. He'd thought that he would never see it again, but here he was. At first glance it was as he had remembered – exotic and opulent, crammed with captivating objects – but, as he focused on the details, he became conscious that there were changes.

Blanche no longer surveyed the room, haughty and beady-eyed, and a cane-seated chair occupied the spot next to the fireplace where her perch had been. There used to be four black elephants, with removable ivory tusks, on the mantelpiece. Now there were only three. Dust had turned their backs grey and the smallest had lost a tusk. The knick-knacks – three wise monkeys in brass, a silver bell, a posy of flowers carved from soapstone, a peacock's feather – had disappeared from the dresser shelves, replaced by the pieces of a rather ordinary dinner service. The walls that had been patchworked with paintings of camel trains and Indian dhows were bare apart from two insipid watercolours of indeterminate flowers.

Lewis listened for returning footsteps and, hearing nothing, he peered at the floor beneath the cane chair, scrutinising the stained floorboards, seeing no trace of feathers, millet seed or sunflower husks, only dust and the pale grey corpses of woodlice, like empty suits of armour. He tiptoed across to the dresser, eased open the right-hand drawer and peeped in. It was empty but he ran his hand around it in case a toffee or a Minto lurked in a dark corner. Nothing.

By the time Mrs Channing returned, he was back in the armchair. 'Did you have a good look around?' she asked.

He blushed.

'I've always held that curiosity is a virtue and greatly undervalued. Creativity and curiosity. Forget all that faith, hope and charity humbug.'

Reassured by this statement, he admitted, 'I did, actually. It's the same, but different, somehow. I'm not sure whether I've remembered it wrong—'

'*Wrongly*. Or *incorrectly*. Adverb not adjective.' Her tone was gentle and her smile bright and she looked, to Lewis, like a little bird, a brilliantly coloured bird from the rainforest or a tropical island.

'Can I let you in on a secret? Memories are always correct. It's what's going on before our eyes that we misinterpret.' She winked. 'Now, I expect there are several things you would like to know but are too polite to mention. Shall I start you off? Yes, poor Blanche is dead. I came down one morning and she was dangling from her perch by her leg chain. Stiff as a board. We debated having her stuffed but, as I never liked the wretched parrot, it seemed an unnecessary expense.'

'What did you do with her?'

'We put her in the dustbin.'

Lewis couldn't help laughing. 'That's a terrible thing to do.'

'Not at all. We might have buried her in the garden, I suppose, but it would have amounted to the same thing. She would still have ended up in a hole in the ground.'

Lewis settled back in the chair. 'You said 'we'. Did you mean you and Mr Zeal?'

'I did.'

'Is he…?'

'Yes.' She stood at the big circular table, tidying the envelopes and newspapers piled on it. 'Last year. November the seventeenth. A week before his eightieth birthday.'

'I'm really sorry. I didn't mean to…' Lewis had never before been required to offer sympathy for a death and he could think of nothing to say. 'It's horrid.'

'It is. Horrid and irreversible and inevitable.'

Lewis left what he considered to be a decent interval before asking. 'Who was he exactly? Tessa thought he was a lodger.'

She shook her head. 'Henry wasn't a lodger. He was my cousin. Our mothers were sisters. We were born within a year of each other. I am, correction, I *was* the older. And we spent a great deal of time together during our childhood, mainly because my mother was incapable of looking after me. But that's a story for another day. Anyway, when my husband abandoned me, Henry

Chapter 13

IT WAS AS IF THE MENTAL AND PHYSICAL ELEMENTS constituting Tessa Swinburne were becoming disengaged; her will no longer controlled her actions. She was behaving like a puppet, manipulated by Rundle the puppet master. It was pathetic. Had she been able to escape from the stuffy room for a while she might have snapped back into herself but he had disappeared without leaving her a set of keys. When she opened the window to check whether it was a possible means of exit and re-entry, she was confronted by a row of vicious railings topping the front wall six or seven feet below, a gruesome accident in the making.

Looking for something to read, she examined Rundle's bookshelves but the books were all science fiction or travel writing and nothing appealed to her. He had a terrific record collection but his record player was complicated-looking and she was afraid to touch it. Eventually she spotted a pack of playing cards on the kitchen windowsill and laid out a game of patience but, even when she cheated, she couldn't make it come out. Besides, she had enough puzzles to solve. Lewis. Her mother. Whatever was going on between her and Rundle. Money. Somewhere to live. And back to Lewis again. She must speak to him. She could waylay him on his paper round or better still, catch him at the newsagent's when he collected his papers.

Tessa was surprised to see the *Weekly Gazette*, a newspaper she considered to be reading matter for old fogies, folded neatly on the table next to the bed. As usual it was full of 'news' about cats stuck up trees, increased car parking charges and local councillors opening youth centres. The only interesting pages were what Gran referred to as 'the small ads'.

Her grandmother spent hours trawling through this section of the paper, searching the 'For Sale' columns for bargains that she had no intention of buying. When they were younger, whilst Gran was tutting at the price of things she didn't want, she and Lewis read the 'Pets' section, on the lookout for a replacement for the short-lived Pete. When they spotted a likely candidate, the stock reply would inevitably come back from their father, 'Dogs are a tie. They stop you going anywhere.' 'But we never go anywhere, anyway,' she would complain, 'and Mum would love a pet to keep her company. Wouldn't you, Mum?' It hadn't worked.

Rundle had ringed a couple of items under the section headed 'Music'. 'Alto saxophone – suit beginner.' and 'Full set of drums – owner emigrating.' Satisfied that she had discovered his reason for buying the newspaper, she was on the point of discarding it when she spotted 'Situations Vacant'. Folding the page back, she worked her way down the list. 'Car Mechanic.' No. 'Insurance salesman – commission basis.' No. 'Dental Nurse – training given.' Yuck. 'Nanny, to help with girl (4) boy (3) through summer holidays. Live in.' Live in. How difficult could it be to look after two children? She could put up with anything for a month or so, until she found something more worthwhile. It was the perfect temporary solution.

She found a ballpoint pen and copied the telephone number on to the back of her hand. Slipping the catch on the door to Tony's room, she ran downstairs, doing the same with the street door. Hell, she would only be gone for a matter of minutes and she could keep an eye on the front door from the phone box.

She inserted her pennies in the slot and dialled the number.

'Hello. I'm phoning about the job advertised in yesterday's *Gazette*. Has it gone?' She tried to speak slowly and to deepen her voice so that she sounded less like a schoolgirl who didn't know one end of a child from the other.

'No. No, it hasn't.' The woman's voice was husky and interesting and Tessa detected the hint of an Irish accent. 'Could you hang on for a sec? I'll close the door.' The sound of children screeching and laughing was suddenly muffled. 'That's better. Little hooligans.' She laughed. 'God forbid I'm putting you off. They're little darlings, honest they are. So, would you be able to start right away?'

'Shouldn't you interview me? Ask me questions?'

'There's no point in doing that if you can't start next week. We're going away, you see. To Cornwall. And I'd need you to come with us.'

'Well, I could start on Monday if you think I'm suitable.' The whole business was ridiculous but it was also thrilling. 'You really should ask me a few things, you know.'

'You're right, of course. Okay. Ummm. Are you a child murderer? Or molester?'

Tessa giggled. 'No. Of course not.' The woman was clearly mad.

'Perfect credentials.' There was a crash and a howl in the background. 'Oh, God. Will you listen to that? I've got to go. Come on Monday. Please.'

'But where shall I come. And what's your name?'

The woman gave her an address on the outskirts of the town. 'I'm Liza. Liza Flynn. See you on Monday, whoever you are.' And the phone went down before Tessa had a chance to tell her.

The sensible thing was to go home. If she apologised, she would get a lecture from her father and lots of tears from her mother, then the whole business would blow over and they would have all Sunday to get back to normal. That's what the Diane Stoddys, the virgins of this world, would do.

When she thought about her parents – her father dogmatic and unimaginative, erecting high walls around the family to isolate them from some unspecified awfulness and her mother, trapped inside, pale and quivery like a nervous poodle – she wanted to cry. So she put them right to the back of her mind.

Lewis was a different matter. She'd taken his money and left without saying goodbye. He could be a pain in the bum but her going, especially like this, would wound him as badly as an amputation and the thought distressed her. Still, it was probably best to make a clean break. This way he would be distraught for a couple of days and then he'd sort of slip his feelings into neutral gear – he was good at that – and carry on. She'd contact him the moment she'd found a proper job and a place to live.

She was in bed when Rundle returned, well into the early hours of Sunday morning. He stank of beer and cigarette smoke. 'I've found him.' He poured two glasses of whisky and thrust one at her. 'Let's drink to it.'

'Found who?'

'A drummer. He's going to sit in with us next week. See how it works.' He undressed quickly, sliding under the sheets next to her and running his hand up between her legs.

Lewis was in a state of high excitement. He had been back to Cranwell Lodge. The police investigation – the thing that had for so long made a visit unthinkable – had not been mentioned but Mrs Channing would not have welcomed him so warmly had she borne a grudge. He'd solved the mystery – or partially solved it – of Mr Zeal but, from her tone of voice, he guessed that there was a great deal more to discover. And he'd promised to return next weekend.

Setting out on his Saturday evening paper round, he wondered what to tell Kirsty. He was embarrassed by the circumstances surrounding Tessa's departure. How could he explain without it sounding as though his sister were depraved? It would be safer not to mention it at all but, were the whole matter to come out later, Kirsty would be hurt and disappointed in him.

When he got to the Ross's house, Kirsty was sitting on the front wall, waiting for him to appear round the corner. She was wearing a dark skirt, a white lacy blouse and delicate pink slip-on shoes. Her hair hung in one neat plait threaded through with pink ribbon.

She grimaced and jumped off the wall. 'Do I look a complete freak?'

'No. You look…' He wasn't sure what he wanted to say. 'You look not like you.'

'I *feel* not like me. We're going out with some new friends of my parents – to a posh restaurant – and Mum said she was sick of me looking like second-hand Rose. Or rather second-hand Robert.'

'But I like the way you dress.'

'Thanks, Lewis. Dad wants to impress these people for some reason – work I suppose – so I'm going along with it. It's bound to be deadly dull but the food might be okay. And apparently they've got a son about our age so at least I'll have someone to talk to.'

A son about our age. Her words pounded into his guts like cannon balls.

'Oh.' He looked down, avoiding her eyes, then stamped on a caterpillar which was undulating its way across the pavement. 'Don't let me keep you from your new friend.'

Kirsty stood squarely in front of him, her face serious, and placed her hands on his shoulders. 'I don't know what's wrong but there's no need to take it out on an innocent caterpillar.'

Without considering that it was broad daylight or that they

were standing in full view of the Ross's house, he lunged forward and kissed her on the lips. It was over so quickly that, as she ran up the path towards the house, all he could remember was the smell of freshly washed hair. It was only when he was half way home that he noticed the undelivered newspaper in the bottom of his bag.

Uncle Frank and his father were in the garden, sitting on the wall outside the back door. He didn't feel up to his Uncle's bonhomie, or his father's pessimism, and, leaning his bicycle against the side wall of the house, he eased the front door key out of his pocket, hoping that he could sneak in without being spotted. He was unlucky.

'Here he is. The man himself.' Frank Swinburne stood up.

'Hi, Uncle Frank. Can't stop. Need a pee.' Lewis jiggled about reinforcing the reason for his haste.

Tea that evening was a dismal affair. The four of them sat in the kitchen, Frank Swinburne taking Tessa's place at the table. There was no sign of a hot meal and they made do with jam sandwiches and slices of Swiss roll, whilst Uncle Frank told them an involved tale about a pack of dogs that had chased his car. Lewis noticed that his mother's mouth was fixed in an unvarying smile, the food untouched on her plate, whilst his father laughed too loudly at his brother's tired jokes.

'And how's my favourite nephew?' Uncle Frank asked when he had run out of anecdotes.

'Fine thanks.'

'Not working too hard, I hope. You know what they say.'

Lewis concentrated on unravelling his slice of Swiss roll, wondering whether, given its circumference, there was a mathematical equation to calculate its uncoiled length.

'That sister of yours has flown the coop, I hear. A week or two in a bedsit – no hot water or cold milk – and she'll be back.' He nudged his saucer towards his sister-in-law who, unbidden, refilled his cup. 'Ta, Peg.'

Lewis gripped the edge of the tablecloth, imagining what it would feel like to yank it up and send cups, teapot and cake, the whole cosy lot, hurtling through the air.

'See you around, then,' Rundle muttered as he stood on the landing watching her struggle down the stairs with her bags.

'Maybe.'

She closed the door firmly behind her.

When the bus came it was packed with passengers on their way to work. Tessa found a seat next to a young woman barely older than she was. The woman's hair was fixed in a tight Hepburn pleat and Tessa could smell the lacquer that was holding it in place. She wore a cotton frock and a white cardigan and she was fiddling with an engagement ring, its tiny diamond appearing the more insignificant for its elaborate setting. A secretary or a filing clerk? Something boring like that.

Tessa looked around her. Rundle was better-looking than any of the men sitting on the lower deck of the bus. Friday night might not have been the stuff of schoolgirl dreams but, after a couple more 'goes' over the weekend she felt she was getting the hang of sexual intercourse. Rundle had been if not gentler then more patient, guiding her through it. Last night she'd reached her first orgasm. It had been wonderful but what surprised her was how it took a grip of her, driving her spiralling into herself. It was nothing at all to do with the giving and sharing that she'd imagined it would be, but more two people set on gaining their own satisfaction.

She'd found out other things, too. How to drink her coffee black; that it was possible to wash knickers using a bar of soap; how to cry silently in the dark. And that sex was messy and need have nothing to do with love.

The lacquered girl smiled. ''Scuse me.'

Tessa stood up to let her pass, watching as she stepped down from the platform of the bus and tottered down the pavement towards her dull life.

When she wrote her memoirs, her deflowering by bad lad Rundle and her subsequent exodus from Salisbury Road would make an infinitely more dramatic tale than if she'd lost her virginity to the likes of Geoffrey.

The address Liza Flynn had given Tessa took her to an area of the town that she had never visited. The houses here had obviously been built for people of wealth and standing, many of them were detached with wide driveways and large gardens; mature trees towered above elaborate tiled roofs and, in some of the front gardens, classical figures kept watch over ornamental ponds. Tessa pictured Edwardian women in feathered hats and men twiddling waxed moustaches strolling along the wide pavements but the woman who answered her knock didn't look in the least old-fashioned.

Liza Flynn was alarmingly beautiful. She had grey eyes, a perfectly straight nose and her blue-black hair, no more than an inch long, covered her head like a furry cap. At first sight, she had an exceptionally high forehead but, when Tessa had time to study it more closely, she saw that the hair had been shaved to an even hairline. She wore a short, white shift dress which showed off her tanned arms and legs. The fabric of the dress was sheer and it was apparent that she was wearing nothing beneath it.

The children, Valmai and Connor, were beautiful too, dark-haired and energetic, like two little imps. As soon as they saw Tessa they grabbed her hands, dragging her into the garden to show her the row of mud pies they were assembling along the path. Aware that Liza was watching and that these first few moments with the children were vital to her escape plan, she did her best to appear enchanted with the precocious pair.

'You're a natural,' Liza assured Tessa, rescuing her from the muddy clutches of her charges.

They sat in the garden and Tessa gave Liza a sketchy version of her recent history, saying that she had fallen out with her parents over trivialities but not mentioning her weekend with Tony Rundle.

Liza explained that the children's father, Jay, had come in to some money when his grandfather died. 'He was a sweet old man but I must admit he did us a favour by dropping dead. We were renting a few rooms down near the docks – painters don't make a great deal of money, you know – so when his will was read, and we heard that he'd left Jay this house, it was a miracle. I don't think the neighbours are particularly delighted, but I have the feeling we won't be here for long. It's all a bit too grown up for my liking.'

'Your husband's a painter? As in artist?'

'Yes. But Jay Costello isn't my husband. None of that *petit bourgeois* rubbish for us. C'mon. I'll show you your room.'

Liza filled her in on the family's plans. They were off to St Ives in a few days time, to join a crowd of painters who were renting a large house for the whole of the summer. 'I used to earn quite a few commissions. But it's impossible to get anything done with these two.' She nodded at the children, bouncing and screaming on the bed. 'I need some help with the kids so that I can paint. That's the idea, anyway. But I'll be happy to laze in the sun. It's years since we had a proper holiday.'

They left Tessa to unpack and catch her breath. She sat on the bed, kicking off her shoes and inspecting the room. It was twice the size of her bedroom at home and it had a double bed covered with a fringed cotton bedspread, smelling of dye, decorated with intricate geometric patterns. One enormous canvas – splashes of yellow and grey superimposed with crude black outlines of what might be hands or spiders – dominated the wall facing her, uneasy against the floral wallpaper. A spherical paper lampshade covered the overhead light. A mirror in the shape of a splash of water hung above the mahogany chest of drawers. A rainbow rug on the floor next to the bed, mocked the sober beige carpet.

It was too good to be true. Four days ago she had been a schoolgirl in the middle of her examinations but here she was, sexually experienced, with a job, a room of her own and the promise of wild adventures with this fascinating family. She would mingle with artists, free-lovers, atheists, musicians, drinkers and drug takers. Her life, which had stalled eight years ago, could resume in earnest.

When she left home she had packed clothes that she guessed Tony Rundle would like his girl to wear. One glance around her new home told her that she would have to rethink her wardrobe. Jeans, shirts, tee shirts – that was the sort of thing she would need. Nothing too girl-y. Plenty of black and white. And she'd have to do something more interesting with her hair.

'Could you keep an eye on the kids, Tess?' Liza asked when she came downstairs, 'I've got to sort out the packing.'

Valmai and Connor were undisciplined and demanding. Their mother let them have chunks of cheese or bowls of cereal or biscuits whenever they asked. 'We eat when we're hungry, so why shouldn't they?' she said. It wasn't simply a matter of keeping an eye on the children while they got on with their games. They insisted that she join in, playing up if her attention wandered. They'd been allowed to run wild and were incapable of concentrating on anything for more than two minutes. Exhausted, she racked her brains for games that she and Lewis had played when they were that age but they didn't want to play hide-and-seek or shop, preferring to strip their clothes off and roll around the lawn.

When the children eventually ran out of steam, she and Liza

cajoled them into bed. 'I'll get an early night, if you don't mind,' Tessa said, longing for the solitude of her room.

'Good idea. The kids will be rarin' to go again by seven.'

Tessa brushed her teeth. She'd stick it out until after the trip to Cornwall but when they came back, if the children were completely unbearable, she would look for something else.

She was crossing the landing when the door opposite hers opened and a man emerged.

'Hello,' he said. 'Do I know you?'

He was slight and blonde, his skin pale, as though he never went out in the sun, and to her, were it not for his paint-spattered shirt, he looked nothing at all like an artist. 'No. I'm Tessa. I'm… I don't really know what I am.'

'Not many of us do, Tessa. Some days I think I'm a painter but, who knows, I might be fooling myself. Anyway, whatever you are, I'm pleased to meet you.'

Chapter 14

TESSA MADE A LIST OF EVERYTHING SHE NEEDED and at four o'clock the following afternoon, when Liza took the children to visit a friend, she was outside the newsagent's waiting for Lewis. Hidden by the post box, she watched as he balanced his bicycle against the shop wall and went in to collect his papers. Tessa had taken her brother's unconditional support for granted but seeing him, carrying on calmly as though nothing had happened, made her less certain.

'Lewis,' she called when he came out of the shop with his bag.

'Tess. Where've you been? Dad's doing his nut. And Mum's going round like a sleepwalker.'

'What about you? Obviously my disappearance hasn't affected you at all.'

'Oh yeah. I'm having the time of my life.' He hesitated. 'Where are you staying? With Rundle?'

'God, no. He's such a moron.' She hunched up her shoulders. 'Guess what? I've got a job. With a way-out family. He's an artist—'

'And what are you doing for him? Nude modelling?'

Tessa frowned. 'Don't be horrid, Lew. If you must know, I'm helping look after their kids.'

He shook his head. 'You might at least have phoned to let us know you were okay. Mum hasn't eaten anything since you left.'

'That's exactly what I'm doing now, isn't it? Telling you I'm fine. Actually I'm going to Cornwall with them tomorrow. For the whole summer. It's going to be fantastic.'

'Oh.' He pulled at his ear lobe.

She took the list from her pocket. 'Could you do me the hugest favour? Could you sneak these things out of my room tonight? Leave them behind the bush in the front garden? I'll nip back first thing in the morning to collect them.'

'That's so cowardly. Why don't you come home, tell Mum and Dad what you're doing, and collect the things yourself? That's what a grown-up would do.'

Her brother's cheeks flushed and Tessa knew that he was near to tears. She put her arm through his. 'You know I'd only end up having another row with them and they'd get even more upset. It's best if I keep out of their way for a while.' She stroked his arm. 'I promise I'll write home every week. Let them know where I am and what I'm doing.'

He shrugged off her arm and took a pace back. 'Come home, Tessa. Not for Mum and Dad, but for me. I don't like it without you.'

Tessa loved Lewis, she really did, but it wasn't as if his life depended on her returning whereas hers definitely depended on leaving. There would be occasions in the future when he really needed her and then, obviously, she would come but, at the moment, he was miffed that she'd had the courage to make the break.

She hugged him and thrust the list into his hand. 'Please, Lewis. You'll be fine.'

The previous evening, when Lewis had turned into Wellington Drive, he'd been taken aback to see Kirsty sitting on the wall as usual. His surprise was followed by bewilderment when she made no reference to what had happened between them on Saturday. They chatted about Wimbledon and end of term exams, and he began to doubt whether he had ever kissed her at all.

This evening she jumped down from her perch and came to meet him. 'You're late,' she said. 'And you look a bit … fed up. D'you want to talk about it?'

'About what?' he asked cautiously.

'About whatever you like.'

'I'm not sure—'

'Lewis!' she laughed, 'You're hopeless.'

'Am I?' Suddenly he felt light-hearted.

'Why are you playing so hard to get? At this rate we're never going to get anywhere.' She stood on tiptoe and kissed him, a gentle lingering kiss on his lips. 'There. And in case you're wondering, I'm not doing anything next Saturday evening.'

He zigzagged through the park on his bike, taking his time, reluctant to return to the gloom that hung around Salisbury Road. He felt so, *so* alive and it occurred to him that, in the three days since Tessa had left, everything had changed. Up until then he'd seen her as his shelter; his protector. Maybe he'd got it wrong. Had she, in fact, been holding him back? Look how easy it had been for him to re-connect with Mrs Channing. Tessa had always made out that the old lady must hate them but she'd seemed delighted to see him. And, oddly enough, it was the sadness in his face, sadness that Tessa was leaving, that had pushed Kirsty into kissing him. Perhaps everything would be better if she did go away – for a while, anyway.

When his parents went to bed, Lewis left it an hour before creeping along the landing to Tessa's room. It didn't take long to locate the items on her list – he'd put most of them away only a few days earlier – and he stuffed them in the canvas duffle bag that he used when he went to Scout camp. The next bit was trickier. He took a cushion from the living room and, clamping it over the latch, he muffled the metal on metal noise as he slid the chain off and opened the front door.

Safe outside, he pushed the duffle bag under the hydrangea bush, as Tessa had instructed. It was a still, clear night and he sat on the garden wall, its smooth bricks warm after a day of unbroken sunshine. The neighbouring houses were mostly in darkness, a low light showing here and there, and he remembered how, when he was five or six and terrified of the wolves that lived under his bed, his mother used to leave his bedroom door open and the landing light on.

He found an old exercise book in a kitchen drawer and settled down to write to Tessa. When she'd turned up at the shop, she'd been so full of herself that he'd not had a chance to tell her about Cranwell Lodge and, determined to let her know that she wasn't the only one who had adventures, he described his visit and Mrs Channing's insistence that he return soon. But he was embarking on an even more momentous adventure and he doodled on the corner of the paper, debating whether to write about Kirsty Ross and the two kisses, in the end deciding to wait until he understood it better himself.

Dawn was breaking when he went back outside, untied the cord of the duffle bag and slipped the letter on top of Tessa's clothes.

Tessa had been concerned that she would oversleep and fail to collect her things before her father was up and about. But she needn't have worried. Valmai and Connor arrived on her bed at six o'clock. She'd already okay-ed it with Liza to absent herself for a couple of hours and, once she'd given the children bowls of cereal and told them to wake their mother if they needed anything, she returned to Salisbury Road.

Standing on the concrete path, she looked up at the house that she'd left what seemed like a hundred years ago. The curtains were closed and the fanlight of the room above the front door – her parents' bedroom – was ajar. She pictured them, side by side in the double bed, six inches separating them, no more than fifteen feet away from her. She focussed her thoughts on where she guessed her mother's head lay. *Mum, all you have to do is come to the window now and ask me to come back.* She waited, giving fate two minutes to intervene; two minutes to alter the course of her life. The curtains remained shut.

Two bottles of milk stood on the doorstep, waiting for her mother to take them in when she came down to make breakfast. They wouldn't need as much milk now. Tomorrow or the day after, her mother would write a note – 'One and a half pints a day in future, please.' – in her neat, childlike handwriting then roll it into a tube and push it into an empty milk bottle.

The duffle bag was exactly where she'd asked Lewis to leave it. It was already ten-to-seven and, up there, her father would be snuffling and yawning, starting to wake up. She dragged the bag out and, as she walked away, it occurred to her that it might not take so very long for her mother, her father and Lewis to regroup and form a harmonious trio.

Tess discovered that she wasn't the first 'nanny' whom Liza had employed and that her two predecessors had lasted four days and two weeks respectively. It was easy to see why. The Costello children were opportunistic creatures, ready to take advantage of her the minute her guard was down. In Valmai, she detected many of her own traits – boldness, imagination and impatience – and to see sister and brother, caught up in their world of schemes and secrets, stirred memories. It also flagged up warnings so she formulated a simple but rigid system of penalties (no sweets or bedtime stories) and rewards (lots of sweets and bedtime stories). 'Do whatever it takes,' Liza said, clearly desperate not to lose her.

The holiday house was on the outskirts of St Ives, overlooking Porthmeor beach and the Island, beyond. Tessa had never seen anything as splendid as the curling breakers chasing out of the turquoise sea, pounding the near-white sand. Every night the muffled crash of the waves lulled her to sleep.

The Costelloes' friends were easy-going, and a stream of intriguing people – painters, musicians, writers – came and went. Often she found herself picking her way around sleeping bags, their occupants having turned up unannounced and made themselves comfortable in any available corner.

Jay Costello, though quiet and undemonstrative, was clearly the leader of the enclave. He rarely joined in the rowdy discussions about what they should eat or where they should go but Tessa noticed that, when the hubbub subsided, everyone looked to him for the final decision. Sometimes, when she was gathering shells with the children or drying their wriggling brown bodies after they had been swimming, she found that he was watching her and she would look up, holding his gaze, enjoying feeling her heart race.

She got on well with Liza who was chatty and disorganised but Tessa was convinced she wasn't as scatterbrained as she would have people think. Nobody expected much of Liza, which meant that she was free to spend time sunbathing or reading, and being legendary for her bad cooking she escaped kitchen duty. Very smart indeed.

'How's the painting going?' Tessa asked, knowing that Liza's satchel of paints and pastels lay untouched on the bedroom floor.

Liza put a finger to her lips. 'Don't snitch on me, Tess. I'm having such a lovely time.' She fumbled in her bag and handed Tessa two pound notes. 'Here. I forgot to give you this week's pay.'

The days sped by and, determined never to forget her

first summer of freedom, Tessa bought a notebook, bound in dark blue linen patterned with butterflies, and began keeping a journal. Intending it to be more impressionistic than a conventional diary, she scribbled descriptions of the people who stayed at the house or whom she met on the beach, reporting conversations and thoughts and any other snippets that caught her fancy. Sometimes, when she found an unusual wildflower or interesting shell, she sketched it in the margin of the book. One evening, the children finally asleep, she was sitting on the bench in the garden, writing her entry for the day, when Jay Costello came out of the house carrying a mug of coffee.

'What is Tessa Swinburne up to, I wonder?' He spoke into the cool evening air as if he hadn't noticed that she was there.

'Nothing.' She closed the book and laid her hand on the cover. 'Thinking. Writing.'

'Aaahhh. So our Tessa is a writer. I guess there's more to her than meets the eye.' He raised his eyebrows and smiled making her feel breathless and unsettled. 'Am I interrupting?'

'No.' She shuffled along the bench and he sat beside her, his thigh almost touching hers.

'Fancy a slurp of coffee?'

He offered her the mug. It was the first time that she had ever shared a cup with anyone – not counting Lewis of course – and it struck her that, sitting alongside a charming man, sipping from the same mug, was more sensual, more satisfying, than anything she'd done with Tony Rundle.

It was three weeks before she remembered her promise to Lewis and, to make up for her failure, she wrote two postcards, sending them on the same day but from different postboxes, as though that would put things right.

Lewis couldn't disclose the part he'd played in Tessa's leaving but somehow he had to let his parents know that she was okay.

He pretended that she'd phoned when they were in the garden. 'She says she's fine. She's got a job with a nice family. Looking after their children. They were just leaving to go on holiday and she was in a rush. Oh, and she promises to keep in touch.' He was tempted to add *she sends her love and wants you to know that she's sorry* but he'd already told enough fibs.

Lewis's anger increased with every postal delivery. He'd fulfilled his side of their bargain now all Tessa had to do was write – such a tiny effort to make in return for deserting him. She had been so quick to give her word and he wondered whether she even remembered doing it; ever intended keeping it.

Then two picture postcards arrived on the same day.

Dear Mum, Dad and Lewis,
I'm fine and enjoying my new job. St Ives is interesting
and we've had good weather so far.
Love, Tessa x

Dear All,
The family I'm working for are thinking of visiting
Ireland. They want me to go too. It sounds fun.
I'll keep in touch. x T

After keeping them on pins for weeks, she'd come up with a few banal words that conveyed nothing. It upset Lewis to see his mother, reading and re-reading the cards, scanning the bright pictures, searching for a hidden message, a promise that wasn't there.

Lewis turned to Kirsty for the companionship that Tessa had provided. She often went with him on his evening paper round and sometimes she was outside her house at seven, bleary eyed, to catch him as he delivered the morning paper. At weekends they played tennis or meandered along the canal tow path. Now and then, but not often because neither of them liked being indoors if the weather was good, they went to the cinema. There were times when they talked and others when they were silent together. They didn't argue. Kirsty never tried to make him do anything he didn't want to do. By the time term ended, she'd accepted his invitation to become his girlfriend.

Kirsty introduced him to her parents. It was all very relaxed and soon he was a regular visitor. Mrs Ross evidently enjoyed having a house full of people and, if he called when Kirsty was out, she invited him to wait, offering him a cup of tea or a cold drink, chatting to him as she pottered on with whatever she was doing. Mr Ross was equally hospitable and, once in a while, asked for Lewis's help when a chore he was engaged in – lopping a tree or moving furniture – called for a second pair of hands. Lewis soon felt more comfortable in their house than in his own home.

He told Kirsty the whole story – Gordon, his mother, Tessa, everything.

'I knew all that, you idiot,' she smiled. 'You can't keep secrets like that around here.'

Kirsty put no pressure on Lewis to meet Peggy and Dick Swinburne. His parents knew he was seeing a girl but they skirted around it. 'She must be quite special, whoever she is,' his father taunted, watching Lewis combing his hair before he went out, and he wished that they would be honest and ask him, outright.

The new school term began and Lewis, now in the Upper Sixth, had decisions to make. His maths master wanted him to try for Cambridge and gave him extra tuition, twice a week, during the lunch hour. 'Give it a go, Swinburne,' he said. 'You'll kick yourself if you don't.'

But Lewis wasn't sure. He could probably cope with the work

but, from what he'd heard, the majority of Cambridge students were from posh backgrounds and he might end up feeling pretty isolated. Besides, he didn't much like the idea of being separated from Kirsty.

'I don't see why we can't go to the same university,' he said.

'Be sensible,' she replied gently, 'We're only eighteen. Neither of us can know how we'll feel next year or the year after. We must pick the course that's right for us.'

'Are you saying that what's between us isn't the real thing?'

'No. I'm saying that if this *is* the "real thing", whatever that means, it will survive. And there are trains and buses and weekends and holidays. We'll probably see more of each other than we do now. You're the mathematician. Work it out.'

Reluctantly Lewis filled in the forms for Cambridge whilst Kirsty chose York.

They worked hard at school, spending whatever spare time they had together. They held hands when they walked by the canal and, when they sat in the darkness of the cinema or whenever they parted, they kissed. After a while, and with Kirsty's encouragement and guidance, Lewis mastered the knack of undoing the hooks on her bra. Each time he cupped her soft breasts and felt her nipples harden to his touch, he wanted to weep with pride and awe.

They heard from Tessa once in a while – a postcard from Ireland, then a couple of scrawled notes postmarked Bristol and Gloucester, but with no address. As far as Lewis could gather, the children she had been looking after were now at school and consequently the family no longer needed her so she had been finding temporary work in offices and shops.

The Saturday before Christmas, when Lewis and his father were out collecting a Christmas tree from the market, Peggy Swinburne received a phone call from Tessa. 'She just rang to wish us merry Christmas. And to say that she was fine. I asked

Chapter 15

A TAXI PULLED UP OUTSIDE THE FRONT DOOR.

'She's here,' whispered Lewis.

His father, struggling to adjust his slippery black tie, joined him and they peered through a gap in the closed curtains. 'Thank God for that. It would have finished your mother if she'd missed it. Is my tie okay?' He lifted his chin so that Lewis could inspect the knot.

'Perfect.'

There was a jaunty knock on the front door and Lewis took a deep breath. It was improper, shocking even, to feel so excited on the day of his grandmother's funeral but Tessa was at the door and he'd seen her only half a dozen times in the past five years.

'Hello, Lewis.' She stood on the threshold, her breath a vapour cloud in the February air.

Laughing, he pulled her inside and they clung together, her cheek icy against his, the insubstantial fabric of her coat, cold to his touch. 'You're freezing. Come and sit by the fire and I'll get you a cuppa.'

'Haven't you got anything stronger?' she asked, shivering. 'How's Mum?'

'She's as well as can be expected considering that her mother – your grandmother – died last Thursday.' Dick Swinburne was standing with his back to a small, smoky fire. 'Good of you to come.'

'You don't have to explain who Gran was, Dad.' She crossed the room and brushed her lips against her father's cheek. 'And you knew I would come.'

How long has she been in the house, Lewis wondered. Thirty seconds? And they were already squaring up for a fight. 'Mum's upstairs. She might appreciate a hand. We'll be leaving in an hour or so.'

The funeral service was uninspired and impersonal, not surprising as Doris Lloyd wasn't a churchgoer. There weren't many mourners. The Lloyd side of the family had dwindled and Doris had few friends, fewer still who were prepared to turn out on a bleak winter afternoon. The sparse congregation did their best with the hymns whilst Peggy Swinburne, pinched and colourless, leaned on her husband's arm, a handkerchief clamped against her face. Earlier that morning he and his father had coaxed her to take the stronger pills prescribed by the doctor to 'get her through the day'. To an onlooker, she might appear calm but Lewis, who was next to her, could feel her whole body quivering; he could see her gloved fingers pulling at the button on her coat.

Tessa stood on the far side of their parents. Her face looked thinner, her nose more prominent. She wore her hair loose. It just grazed her shoulders and the long fringe that obscured her eyebrows made her look like every other girl he passed in the street. Her fingers were nicotine-stained. She wore too many rings and her nails needed a trim. She didn't appear at all like a young woman who was having the time of her life.

Lewis stared at the coffin, the dark wood too shiny, the handles too bright, trying to remember what his grandmother looked like, to recall her voice. But all he saw was a wizened body, curled up under a blanket on a high, metal-framed hospital bed, and a locker stacked with oranges and barley sugar sweets that she would never eat.

After the service, a handful of men – Lewis, Dick and Frank Swinburne, a cousin and a neighbour – were going to the cemetery whilst the women returned to the house.

Tessa whispered to Lewis that she had never witnessed a coffin being lowered in to the ground. 'I quite fancy doing the "earth-to-earth" bit.'

He sighed. 'You can't leave Mum on her own. Just for once, couldn't you put someone else's needs first?'

'Okay. Okay.' Tessa picked a thread of cotton off his coat. 'So where's this mysterious girlfriend of yours? What's her name? Christine? Katie? I was hoping to meet her at last. Perhaps you're ashamed of her – or maybe me?'

He might have said that he was hardly to blame that they hadn't met. Tessa's visits were few and far between, and she certainly didn't encourage people to visit her.

'Of course I'm not. And her name's Kirsty, as you well know. She wanted to come but she couldn't take time off work.'

This wasn't true. She had offered to come but Lewis had dissuaded her. Today wasn't the day for his relationship to be subjected to Tessa's scrutiny and, besides, his parents, though civil to Kirsty, never seemed comfortable in her company.

They stood outside the church, waiting while their father fussed about who was to travel in which car.

'What did that vicar say? "Doris Lloyd led a full and happy life."' Tessa gave a mirthless laugh.

'I'd settle for that,' Lewis said.

'Really? You'd better get a move on then.'

'What d'you mean?'

'Well look at yourself. You're twenty-three years old and you still live with your parents. Christ, you even teach in the same school you went to. What d'you want out of life?' She shook her head. 'What happened, Lewis? Why didn't you go to Cambridge? You were brilliant at maths.'

'I got a first. Some people might consider that to be—'

'Yes, but from a second-rate dump all of twenty miles away. You didn't even leave home to do that.'

Tessa's criticism contained a deal of truth. But it was truth recognised in hindsight. When he'd made his choices they'd seemed logical and for the best. Cambridge, with its ornate architecture and aura of privilege, grew less and less attractive as the moment for his leaving drew closer. He'd discussed it with Kirsty for whom change was the norm. But he wasn't used to change. He liked constancy; stability. Kirsty had listened then said that he had to make his own mind up. He'd talked about it to his mother, keeping the conversation light, trying to give the impression that it was all the same to him whether he went to Cambridge or not. Her quiet 'I'll miss you but I'll manage. I'll be all right,' made it clear that she wasn't sure she would be. What tipped the balance was nothing to do with family or class. It was his friendship with Mrs Channing and his love for Cranwell Lodge.

'It wasn't that straightforward, Tessa. I wasn't as sold on Cambridge as everyone else seemed to be. To tell you the truth, I felt bad about buggering off to the other side of the country, leaving Mum and Dad here without anyone to keep an eye out for them. You'll find this hard to understand, I expect, but I like this town. I feel I belong here. Lots of the blokes I was at school with are still around if I fancy a pint or a game of tennis.'

Tessa shrugged. 'Well, as long as you've got someone to play tennis with, everything's hunky-dory.'

Before he could reply, she pointed to the car waiting to take the men to the cemetery. 'Off you go. Dad's getting fidgety.'

'How are you doing, Mum?' Lewis asked when he and the men

got back to the house. 'You look a bit brighter.'

Livid patches glowed in the centre of Peggy Swinburne's pale cheeks and her eyes sparkled, giving her a feverish look.

It's all a bit unreal. I feel like I'm floating. I expect it's the pills … and this.' She lifted a half-empty glass of Bristol Cream sherry. 'It's lovely to see Tessa, isn't it? It's kind of her to come. I expect she's busy.'

Kind? Busy?

The lights were on. It wasn't yet five o'clock but it was dark. On Wednesdays Lewis ran the after school chess club but this evening a fellow teacher was deputising for him. He imagined the muffled *plonk* as the boys dropped the carved pieces into their baize-lined boxes before sliding the lids shut and returning them and the well-worn chessboards to the cupboard. Not so long ago – four or five years – he had been one of those boys. His thoughts slipped back to Tessa's 'What d'you want out of life?' but, to be honest, he had no idea what he wanted other than to be nine years old again.

Tessa stood in the kitchen doorway, beckoning, and he followed her upstairs into his bedroom.

'I'm sure they can spare you for a few minutes.' She flopped on his bed. 'I could recognise this house from its smell alone, although I couldn't tell you what it smells of. I suppose the rugs and the curtains get impregnated with everything that's ever been cooked and polished and painted. *L'essence de la maison. L'odeur de l'enfance.* Quite pleasant if used sparingly, but nauseating in large doses.'

'Have you been drinking?' He shook his head. 'Sorry. That was a bit Dad-like.'

'I have, as a matter of fact.' She fumbled a quarter bottle of vodka out of her handbag and unscrewed the cap. 'Want a slug?'

He didn't but he took a swig anyway. 'When are you going

162

back?'

'Not sure. Depends.'

'On?'

'You, little brother. You.'

'How?'

She raised her forearm, palm towards him. 'How. Pale-face heap po-faced.'

'Tessa. For Christ's sake stop arsing about.'

She sat up straight and hooked her hair back behind her ears. 'I'll stay tonight as long as you take tomorrow off. I'll skive off work if you'll do the same.'

'I can't—'

'Of course you can. What's all the fuss about? A few snotty little boys missing a double period of quadratic equations. Big deal.'

'I've never—'

'Well it's high time you did. And I promise you the world will go on turning. I'll give you three minutes to decide then I'm leaving for the station.' She pulled her sleeve back and stared at her watch.

If she stayed, the four of them could be together this evening, watching television or simply talking. She'd be there in the morning when they had breakfast. They would be a family again, if only fleetingly.

He nodded. 'It's a deal.'

'Tessa's going to stay tonight. Go back tomorrow afternoon. That's nice, isn't it, Dick?' Peggy Swinburne was clearing the dirty crockery. The mourners had gone – with the exception of Frank.

Lewis watched his father's expressionless face. 'Yes.'

'You shouldn't be doing that, Peg. Not today,' Frank said but he remained seated.

Lewis motioned to his sister and they took over at the sink whilst the others went to sit by the fire.

'What was it like? At the end?' she asked.

He knew what she was talking about. 'Pathetic. Pointless.'

'Nobody's mentioned her. Isn't that weird? I thought we'd all be reminiscing about what a *wonderful woman* she was. How we'll never forget her.' She rolled her eyes heavenwards. 'But nobody's said a word about her since we left the church. Doris Lloyd – who was that? It's bizarre.'

'Did you expect anything different? This family never discusses anything important,' he said.

'How long did it take you to work that one out?'

They joined the others in the chilly sitting room. His mother perched on the edge of the sofa, repeatedly massaging her knees through the fabric of her pleated skirt, whilst his father placed a few lumps of coal on the fire. Uncle Frank was reading the evening paper. Lewis wondered if they'd all been struck dumb whilst he and Tessa were in the kitchen.

'It's difficult to believe that we'll never see Gran again, isn't it?' Tessa tossed it into the room as if it were no more important than an observation on the weather.

It was typical of Tessa – childlike and theatrical – yet Lewis couldn't believe that his sister would choose this moment to indulge herself. He sensed, rather than saw, his father and Uncle Frank freeze as he watched his mother's face, expecting it to crumple.

But instead she gave a regretful smile. 'Yes. It's going to be hard. I wouldn't have survived without her when … through those terrible days. I shall miss her dreadfully.'

'Lewis, d'you remember how she used to make us drink cold cabbage water? She said it was good for the brain.' Tessa looked at him for confirmation. 'God, it was disgusting.'

Suddenly, as though his memory had been restored, he could

see his grandmother, standing in her little kitchen, wrapped in her faded pinafore.

He laughed. 'Yes. And how she had us undoing knots in bits of string so she could use them again?'

'And how she tipped the tea leaves on the garden to stop the slugs'

'And let us polish those things that kept the stair carpet in place.'

'Stair rods?' their mother suggested.

They all joined in with recollections, even their father, reconstructing Doris Lloyd, breathing life back into her and, for a while, calming Peggy Swinburne's restless hands.

As the evening wore on, the lie Lewis was intending to tell niggled. Keen to get it sorted out, he telephoned the deputy headmaster who, on hearing that Lewis was needed at home, 'to comfort my mother', sent his deepest condolences and said that he fully understood. It crossed Lewis's mind that his readiness to consent could have something to do with the Swinburne family's history, the details of which were doubtlessly well known within the staff room.

Tessa grinned. 'There – you see – wasn't I right? Now. What shall we do tomorrow?'

'Aren't you going to spend it with Mum?'

'I suppose so. But not all day. Can't we escape for a couple of hours? She paused. 'Shall I tell you what I'd really like to do?'

'I shudder to think.'

'I'd like to go to Cranwell Lodge.'

This was the last thing that Lewis had anticipated.

He'd been visiting Cranwell Lodge ever since the day that Tessa left. At first he'd wondered whether, without Mr Zeal and Blanche to keep her on her toes, Mrs Channing might lose her edge, but not a bit of it. When he reappeared in her life, the old lady – then, he calculated, in her early eighties – seemed to gain a second wind and stepping through the back door of Cranwell Lodge was, as ever, like a trip to the theatre without knowing, or caring, which play was to be performed. Their conversations ricocheted from topic to topic, like the shiny balls in a pinball machine. Her vocabulary was astounding. She eschewed clichés – bread and butter to his unimaginative parents – modifying them to suit her purpose. 'A washed pot never boils,' she confided as she measured milk for their customary Ovaltine into a grubby saucepan. 'Cleanliness is next to uselessness.' She made outrageous assertions, employing them as firelighters to set discussions ablaze. Arguments were, in her words, 'As good as an iron tonic without the side effect of constipation.'

Cranwell Lodge was not ideal accommodation for a lone octogenarian. The house was draughty, shabby and far too big, but Mrs Channing made it clear that she had no intention of moving. 'Don't tell me I'd be better off in a "nice little bungalow" or I'll banish you from my presence. I've always gone upstairs to bed and I will continue to do so.'

The garden had, since Mr Zeal's death, got completely out of hand. The paths were impassable; ivy snaked up the walls, obliterating several of the windows; tree branches groaned in high winds. Lewis knew nothing about gardening but he threw himself into the task, hacking and trimming, digging out bramble roots and burning debris. The shrubs and trees thrived on his inexpert pruning and, by the second season, although it wouldn't have come up to his mother's standards, the garden had been reclaimed.

When Tessa had phoned a few weeks earlier, off his guard and tired, he'd contrasted their grandmother's deterioration with Mrs Channing's chirpy good health, thus letting the Cranwell Lodge cat out of its bag. Until that moment his visits there had been a secret he shared with no one, not even Kirsty. He'd attempted to play the whole thing down but Tessa always could tell when he was flannelling and he ended up telling her everything. 'Wasn't Mrs C furious that we'd told the police about the baby-in-the-cellar conversation?' Tessa had asked.

'No. She thought it was hilarious. I expect they gave that Hulbert chap a hard time, mind you. She said he was pretty disappointed when he discovered that they didn't have a cellar. And to clinch it, they had a rock solid alibi for that whole weekend. Their boiler had packed in and they'd been staying in a hotel while it was being replaced.'

Lewis raised his eyebrows. 'You want to go to Cranwell Lodge? Isn't that a rather prosaic outing for someone from the metropolis?'

'You tell me. I've a sneaky feeling that these visits to Cranwell Lodge are what's keeping you in this Godforsaken town.'

He glanced away. 'Now you're being downright silly.'

'Let's go tomorrow and then I can judge for myself.'

Chapter 16

TESSA CLOSED THE DOOR AND FLICKED ON THE LIGHT. Furniture, curtains, wallpaper, rug next to the bed – all the same. She dragged her finger across the surface of the bedside table, expecting to find five years accumulation of dust deposited on it, but her skin remained clean. Her mother came in to clean the room, yet she had moved nothing, not even the bedside lamp. Tessa opened the wardrobe. There were her clothes, or more accurately the ones which Lewis hadn't stuffed into the duffle bag. And on the hangers at the far end, her school uniform. Whilst she had been going from bedsit to bedsit, lover to lover, this room had been holding its breath, lying in wait for her. She shivered.

Undressing quickly, she took her dressing gown from the hook on the back of the door, slipped it on, and got into bed. The sheets were cold and she drew her feet up, enveloping them in the hem of the dressing gown. Her head throbbed. It was hours since she'd had a cigarette. Earlier that afternoon she'd tried to open the window, thinking to lean out and puff the telltale smoke away, but the winter rain must have caused the frame to swell and it wouldn't budge. She reached for her handbag and took out the vodka bottle, shaking it to confirm that it was empty, but raising the bottle to her lips anyway, tipping it to get the last drops.

She'd considered sending a wreath and making some excuse

– work or holiday – but she had been fond of her grandmother. Gran had done her best for them when their mother suffered her first breakdown. Tessa wanted to acknowledge that, and also to ensure that the *real* Gran, not a fictitious paragon framed by some vicar's imagination, got a mention before she was consigned to family history.

It was a while since she'd seen Lewis – last summer, in fact, when he'd come to London to watch a chess tournament and they'd had a meal together near Paddington. She loved being with him but it was risky. His face, his hands, the way he spoke; his cautious response to events; his interest in the physical world; his naïve faith in the system. Lewis the man was Lewis the boy and he still had the ability to breach the defences she'd spent years building around her heart.

She wondered if her mother was asleep. What must it feel like when one's mother dies? Death, drawing a thick black line across the page, signalled the instant when nothing more can be said even if there is more to say. Her parents, in their own way, had tried to look after her. They simply hadn't been much good at it. One day, when she was successful and had justified the upheaval surrounding her leaving, she might feel able to let them all back in to her life.

Jay had sulked when she'd phoned to let him know that she wouldn't be back until the following evening. But she could hardly be blamed if her grandmother's funeral clashed with one of his sporadic visits to London. Then, when he'd put the pressure on, saying that he might not be free the following night, she'd told him that she'd take that chance. It was easy to be resolute when she couldn't see his face or smell his musky sweat.

She slept fitfully, waking when her father blew his nose, signalling the start of his morning ritual. She stayed where she was, beneath the tangle of blankets, picturing what was going on. Underwear, socks, vest and trousers on. Bathroom to wash and shave. Back to the bedroom for shirt, tie and shoes. Downstairs. Kitchen for a breakfast of cereal, toast and tea. Comb his hair. Jacket on. Out of the front door immediately after the news headlines.

Tessa went downstairs at ten-to-eight – enough time to say her goodbyes but not enough to start a fight.

'Your mother's not been sleeping well but she's dropped off now.' He was pouring a cup of tea and she noticed a blob of white foam beneath his ear lobe.

'D'you still wet shave, Dad?'

He sighed. 'Go on. Tell me I'm a dinosaur.'

When she was five or six, she used to sit on the edge of the bath, watching as he whipped up shaving foam with the stubby brush and lathered his face, waiting for the moment when he dragged the razor down his cheeks, revealing tracts of smooth skin beneath the froth. Best of all, she loved the way he distorted his mouth, pulling it this way and that, stretching the skin so that he could get at the bit under his nose and the depression below his lower lip. At the weekend, when he wasn't in a rush, he sometimes removed the razor blade and let her pull the empty razor across her own soapy face.

'Not at all. It's … nice. It's … very masculine.'

'It's good to know I can do something right.'

He put his suit jacket on and she reached out to wipe the shaving soap from his face. 'Bye, Dad.'

'Goodbye, Tessa. See you…'

He turned and she was sure he was going to add something but he raised his index finger to his forehead in an odd little salute and he was gone.

'Does Dad know you're skiving?' Tessa asked Lewis when he came down for breakfast.

'I told him I'm not feeling well.'

She yawned and stretched her arms above her head. 'It's sad.

A grown man scared of his father.'

'I am *not* scared of him. But I'm the one who has to live here. It's too bloody exhausting to be in a constant state of confrontation.'

She grinned. 'Just keeping you on your toes. Fancy bacon and eggs? Or will we be flogged for having a fry up on a week day?'

Peggy Swinburne, still in her nightdress and dressing gown, appeared in the kitchen. 'Something smells good.'

Tessa put extra bacon in the frying pan and took a third egg from the carton.

Her mother looked thinner and greyer than when she'd last seen her a few weeks ago. Tessa had chanced to telephone and, hearing how ill Doris Lloyd was, had made a brief visit, going straight from the station to the hospital. Her mother was already there and had pressed her to go back to the house but, although Tessa had her toothbrush and a change of underwear in her bag, she'd chickened out, saying that she needed to be at work first thing next morning.

They tucked into breakfast, teasing Lewis for burning the toast and not putting enough tea in the pot.

Tessa screwed her face up. 'It's like dishwater.'

'You're lucky I'm here to make your wretched tea,' Lewis countered. 'I shouldn't be.'

Their mother set down her knife and fork and patted their hands. 'Maybe not, but it's lovely to have you both here. It'll do me more good than all those pills.'

The morning wore on and Tessa became twitchy. Yesterday the focus of attention had been the funeral but, now that it was over, she feared that the spotlight might be re-directed at her.

Peggy Swinburne disappeared for a while and returned clutching a battered shoe box. 'I thought we might go through these. I ought to explain who they all are.'

The box contained the family photographs which only came

out when a significant event took place. Tessa's craving for a cigarette made the prospect of a couple of hours with sepia-tinted relatives inconceivable. 'I was thinking I might pop to the shops, Mum. Make myself useful. Get some food in for you.'

'Why don't we all go?' Lewis intervened. 'Mum can do the shopping and we can haul it home.'

Peggy Swinburne looked anxious. 'Gran and I shop on a Friday ... used to shop, I mean.' She pressed her fingertips against her mouth.

It took some time but they eventually convinced her that it would do her good to get out of the house.

'Let's go now,' Tessa said, 'While she's asleep. We won't be more than an hour. I'll come back here for a cup of tea and get the six-fifteen train. I'll be gone before Dad gets home. We parted amicably and I'd rather quit while I'm ahead. Come on.'

'You'll freeze in that thin coat. Here, borrow this.' Lewis draped his old donkey jacket around her shoulders and they left the house.

Her bicycle was still in the shed and in surprisingly good condition considering its years of inactivity. Lewis found an old towel and wiped the worst of the grime off the saddle and handlebars, pumped up the tyres and they set off. She trailed behind her brother, glancing at their old home as they rode down Medway Avenue but the biting wind caused her eyes to water fiercely and she could hardly make it out through the blur of tears.

Cranwell Lodge, leafless shrubs clustering around the old house like skeletons of creatures that had perished whilst in the act of protecting it, looked forbidding in the murky afternoon. They left their cycles by the gate and Lewis led the way to the back of the house, past piles of roof slates stacked against the wall, the Belfast sink at the top of the steps up to the garden, the pulley for a long-perished clothes line fixed to the brickwork near the door. A crow that had been hunched on the chimney stack let out a hoarse cry and swooped away.

'Shit.' Tessa jumped, grabbing Lewis's sleeve.

He took a key from his pocket then paused. 'Perhaps I'd better knock. She won't be expecting me and I don't want to frighten her.'

'You've got your own key?' Tessa raised her eyebrows.

'Yes. It seemed sensible for someone to have one.'

'It's more serious than I thought, then.'

'What is?'

'Your relationship with her.'

'My relationship? You make it sound as if she's my girlfriend or something.'

'No, Lewis. Your girlfriend is Kirsty what's-it – remember? – that girl you don't want me to meet.'

He rapped on the door and they waited in silence. An indistinct form appeared beyond the glass. The bolts rattled and Mrs Channing opened the door.

'It's only me,' Lewis said. 'I've brought my sister to see you.'

'How can it be "only me" if there are two of you?' Her voice was thin and high pitched, her words perfectly articulated.

Tessa moved close to her brother as if this might meld them together and thus disprove the old lady's caustic observation.

'Hello, Mrs Channing. Lewis is playing hooky this afternoon. We were hoping we could hide here for a while.'

'Your brother isn't the only one who has been playing truant, I believe.' The old lady fixed her with a steady stare. 'You'd better come in.'

'That's put me in my place,' Tessa whispered as they followed Mrs Channing through the austere kitchen.

The room beyond was, as Lewis had promised, essentially unchanged but it was no longer the magic cavern that it had been to her ten-year-old self. The stains on the rugs, the tatty fringe on the lampshades and the discoloured wallpaper might have been there in nineteen fifty-four but what child notices shortcomings in housekeeping? Mrs Channing, although unmistakable, was a desiccated version of the person Tessa remembered. Her white hair stood away from her head like a puff of dandelion seeds, so sparse that it failed to conceal her baby-pink scalp; her colourless face, wrinkles running in all directions, resembled crazed pottery; translucent skin stretched taut over the bulbous joints of her skinny hands. Everything else was hidden beneath a blue satin dressing gown, badly in need of washing.

They drank stale sherry. Tessa noticed how Lewis, when asked to fetch the glasses and a packet of Marie biscuits, went straight to them, without needing directions. He stoked the fire without being told – an intimate and assertive act. He was at home here.

'How fortunate that you came today.' Mrs Channing raised her index finger. 'I need a hand to move some more boxes.'

Lewis stood up but Tessa hesitated, unsure if she were included.

'You, too, young woman. No doubt you're curious to see what lies beyond that door.' The old lady pointed to the door leading into the hall.

The hall was startlingly cold, as was the high-ceilinged room which led off it. A wooden dining table, straight-sided with semicircular ends, dominated the room. Eight chairs with studded leather backs encircled it. Two cardboard boxes and a collection of china sat on the table, surrounded by a sea of crumpled newspaper. Thirty or forty similar boxes, stacked two or three high, extended along the wall opposite the generous bay window.

'Now take those,' Mrs Channing pointed at the two boxes, 'and put them with the others over there. Gently, mind. *Gently.*'

'Are you moving?' Tessa asked as she and Lewis edged crab-wise across the room, carrying the boxes between them.

'No. I'm being realistic. When I die, which can't be too distant an event, I want whoever has the unenviable task of disposing of my worldly goods to have an inkling of their history and their value. See.' She indicated a white label pasted on the side of one of the boxes. Written in neat, ornate script was a summary of its contents. 'Dinner Service: 1911: Wedding present: Never used.'

Tessa shook her head. 'But you must know who that's going to be. You must have written a will.' It was the pitiless remark a child might make, but the old lady had been abrupt with her and it was unlikely that they would meet again.

'I don't, as a matter of fact.' Her face was expressionless. 'Lewis, come with me. I need your opinion on the bathroom tap. It's dripping.'

Tessa felt put out. Why had Lewis kept his involvement with the old lady from her? Whenever she thought about her brother, she pictured him at school, standing in front of a blackboard, or in the living room watching telly with her mother, or mooning around with his invisible girlfriend. She hadn't dreamed that he was popping up here to Cranwell Lodge, making himself at home.

Snubbed and deserted, she crept across the hall and opened the door to the room opposite. It was a sitting room – high-ceilinged and even bigger than the dining room. Two button-backed sofas and several matching armchairs were grouped around a flamboyant fireplace. Several pieces of furniture – a desk, various tables, a sideboard, a cabinet – were dotted around the walls. A glass chandelier, looking too heavy for the slender chains supporting it, hung from the centre of the ceiling. Woven rugs, intricately patterned in dark reds, deep blues and rusty bronzes, covered the woodblock floor. But the mantelpiece, the glass-fronted cabinet and the sideboard, in fact everywhere that she might expect there to be ornaments and knick-knacks, were bare. The walls, too, were devoid of pictures, rectangles of un-faded wallpaper all that indicated their earlier presence. Mrs Channing had been very busy indeed.

Voices rumbled on upstairs and Tessa walked around the room, willing the ghosts of the past to speak with her, to tell her what had gone on, thirty, forty, fifty years ago, in this now lifeless room. But she was disappointed. Pausing at a compact, upright desk, she flapped the leaf down, delighted to find that its contents were still in place. Writing paper and envelopes. A bottle of black ink. A wooden ruler. Scissors. A fountain pen – mottled green with a gold clip and lever, rather masculine in scale and design, the very sort a writer might use. She imagined it, wrapped in yellowing newspaper and tossed in a cardboard box. Such a waste. She slipped it into her handbag and replaced the leaf.

Opening the drawer beneath, she revealed a cache of leather-bound books. Diaries. The desk drawer was filled with diaries. She pictured the exotic bric-a-brac that had once cluttered the breakfast room and which was now consigned to the cardboard boxes. The old lady had clearly led an intriguing life. Lewis and she were as thick as thieves but even if he were privy to the details of Mrs Channing's past he hadn't let on. It would be typical of him to promise not to tell and then to *keep* his word.

She took a diary from the top of the pile and flicked through it. Its flimsy pages were crammed with minute writing, illegible without a magnifying glass. If Lewis couldn't or wouldn't tell her she would find out for herself.

A floorboard creaked overhead and she took a handful of the little books, stuffing them deep in the pocket of her borrowed coat. Mrs Channing might be a stickler for good grammar but anyone who put a dead parrot out with the weekly rubbish wasn't averse to breaking the rules. She had probably done far more outrageous things in her long lifetime than reading someone else's diary. Tessa would fathom out how to get the diaries back into Cranwell Lodge once she'd studied them. Lewis might even be persuaded to help if she could coax him down off his high horse.

'Lewis, we should be going,' she shouted up the stairs, keen to escape with her booty.

When they got back, their mother was waking from her nap. She told them that she'd slept soundly and was feeling better. The box of photographs sat stubbornly in the centre of the table and Tessa, accepting that this would be the least challenging, if not the most appealing, way to occupy what remained of the afternoon, sat next to her mother nodding at the convoluted family roll call whilst wondering where Jay Costello might be at that very minute.

At five o'clock she went upstairs. Shutting herself in her bedroom, she lifted the foot of the bed, dragged it through ninety degrees then pushed it hard up against the wall. Next, she put the table, which she had once used as a desk, next to the bed, with the chest of drawers alongside it and the lamp on top of that. The wardrobe was too heavy to move and had to stay where it was but she took a sheet off the bed, spread it on the floor and piled all her clothes and shoes on it, drawing in the corners and tying them together to form an outsized bundle. She tipped the contents of the bedside drawer into a pillowcase, tying the top quickly, denying herself the chance to revisit the moment when she had severed her connection with her life here. Finally, on the scrap of wallpaper which had lined the drawer she wrote, *'LEWIS. Please see that the pillowcase goes straight in the bin. This lot can go to the rag man'* and pinned it to the bundle.

Lewis took her to the station. The London train was delayed by twenty minutes and they were glad to forsake the draughty platform for the sanctuary of the station buffet.

'So what's this job you're doing at the moment, Tessa?'

How typical of Lewis to save his cross-examination until the last minute.

'It's with Ward & Cox, the publishers. In the editorial department.'

'Is it permanent?'

'I did a couple of weeks there as a temp and then this job came up.' She was unsure where his questioning was leading. 'I'm general dogsbody at the moment – typing, filing, running errands. But they're a fun crowd and I'm learning useful stuff about the book trade.'

He nodded then continued, 'Have you ever considered doing some exams? Getting a few qualifications?'

'Lewis, I know you mean well but I'm not one of your pupils. I don't need careers advice. Let's talk about something else, shall we?'

'Like what?'

'News. Scandal. Gossip.'

He tugged his ear lobe. 'Actually there *is* something. I meant to keep the paper but what with everything… It was about that bloke you used to know. Tony Rundle.'

It was a long time since she'd thought about Rundle and she was surprised how the mention of his name caused her stomach to lurch. 'He was a real bastard.'

'Mmmm. Well now he's a real rock'n'roll star, too. According to the article, his band had a record in the charts. At number thirty-seven, I think it was.'

'Big deal.' She took a sip from her mug of tea. 'What's the band called? Or the song?'

Lewis couldn't remember but promised to keep any further cuttings he came across. 'Now.' He folded his arms and lent forward, clearly relishing what he was preparing to divulge.

'What d'you call something that comes from Morocco?'

'What are you on about?'

'Answer the question. *What do you call something that comes from Morocco?*'

She shrugged. 'Moroccan, I suppose. But I don't see—'

'Yes, Moroccan. Or,' he paused theatrically, 'Moorish. More-ish.'

She raised her hand to her mouth. 'Oh, God. How could we have been so slow?'

'Come on, Tess. "Moorish" isn't exactly an adjective in common usage amongst ten-year-olds, is it? Another thing. Mr Zeal wasn't her lodger. He was her cousin. I'm not sure how, or why, they ended up together in that big house.'

Mr Zeal with his wavy hair and his fussy manner flashed into Tessa's mind. 'D'you think he was a queer? There was something very … cloying … about him.'

The station announcer apologised that the London train was delayed by a further ten minutes.

'It looks like I'm stuck here.' Tessa regretted her quip as a look of hope crossed Lewis's face.

'Perhaps I can come up to London for a weekend soon,' he said. 'Observe you in your natural habitat.'

Tessa pictured her second-floor bedsit in Camden Town; single bed with saggy mattress; gas fire and the clothes airer permanently stationed in front of it; brown carpet and flimsy chest of drawers, its top scorched by careless cigarettes. By the time she paid her rent and fares to work, ate one decent meal a day and made sure that her clothes were clean, there was nothing left for theatre visits or concerts or meals in Italian restaurants or stylish clothes.

'That'd be fun. But why not leave it until the better weather? Easter or Whitsun.'

The train arrived and they went out on to the platform. They

179

hugged, mumbling 'take care' and 'look after yourself'. Lewis helped her onto the train, making sure the door was properly shut.

As the train pulled away, Tessa pushed the window down and leaned out, watching Lewis, hands stuffed in his overcoat pockets, get smaller and smaller until he was indistinguishable from the other figures on the platform.

Chapter 17

IT WAS HOT IN THE TRAIN and the misted windows obscured the lights of towns and villages as the train sped on. Tessa leaned her head back against the prickly upholstery and closed her eyes.

So that was it. Gran was gone ... puff. In Tessa's mental snapshots of the family, Gran was always there in her 'pinny' making sure everyone had a cup of tea. How could a person – a life force – be there one second and not the next? It was too brutal.

The shadowy phantom of Gordon stirred. He, too, had been there one moment then gone. When their mother brought him home, Tessa had seen him as a human cuckoo chick, edging her and Lewis out of their comfy nest. Was he a planned baby or a 'mistake'? A mistake might be forgiven, whereas a conscious decision to alter the family set-up – well... It was odd how little she remembered – *really* remembered – of life before he was born. Christmases and seaside holidays, birthdays and outings to the pantomime, yes, but the ordinary days, dozens and dozens of them, what had they been like?

'Tickets, please.'

The guard came through the carriage and, opening her handbag to find her ticket, she saw the diaries. The volumes differed slightly in size, none of them larger than six inches by four. Each was bound in leather – dark red, green or navy blue – with gold-edged pages, and two of them had miniature pencils concealed in their spines. The dates, embossed on the covers, revealed that the earliest was 1904 and the latest, 1916. She fanned them out on her lap, staring at the scuffed leather. It wasn't as if she were prying into a current life – that would be inexcusable. No. Whatever was recorded in the little books had taken place sixty years ago and was more or less ancient history. What harm could reading them possibly do?

Jay Costello was waiting in her room. Overcoat on, he was sitting on the floor, leaning against the bed, reading the *Evening Standard*.

He looked up from the paper and smiled. 'Hi. You look tired. Was it grim?' He nodded towards the half bottle of vodka and two packets of cigarettes on the table. 'Help yourself.'

'It was okay. Better than I thought.' She poured generous measures of vodka into two glasses. 'I'm glad I stayed the night.'

'I'm not. But you're here now.'

Jay was no good for her, coming and going like he did, making other men she met seem lacklustre in comparison. From the beginning, he'd made no promises, given her no false expectations, but his honesty didn't make matters any better because her failure to end the affair implied that she accepted his terms. Guilt might have pushed her into finishing it but Jay and Liza had 'an open marriage'. 'He's a great lover, isn't he?' Liza had said the first time she saw them coming out of Tessa's room together. And, to make sure Tessa understood the rules of the game, she gave her the low-down on his several other current lovers.

Jay never banged on about what she ought to do with her life, unlike other men she met, who, after a few dates, started to chip away, telling her that she was too bright, too clever, to be drifting in and out of mediocre jobs. Lewis was as bad. They all wanted to improve her whilst Jay seemed happy with her as she was. Recently, however, it had occurred to her that his reasons might not be completely altruistic. After all, it suited him to have her trapped in dead end jobs, never meeting anyone more interesting that the doorman or the office junior and therefore grateful for his intermittent attentions.

After they had made love, Jay told her about his meeting with the owner of a Bond Street gallery – his reason for being in London.

'He's talking about putting on a show of my stuff. Sounds pretty keen. That'd be terrific. The cash from the sale of the house is long gone. And,' he kissed her forehead, 'it would mean that I'd be spending the summer in London, setting it up.'

'Wonderful.' She *was* pleased for him. He was a good painter and he deserved recognition but she couldn't suppress a niggle of envy of his success.

Tessa had skimmed through a couple of the diaries on the train. Each page had held a surprising amount of information but the poor illumination in the carriage and the feint pencil script had made it difficult to decipher the entries. It wasn't until the weekend, after Jay had returned to Ireland, that she found time to study them properly. She laid them out, seven in all, in chronological sequence. 1904, 1905, 1908, 1910, 1911, 1915, 1916. Lewis had said that Mrs Channing was almost ninety. So she must have been – what? – in her mid-twenties in 1904, the very age that Tessa was now.

Reading them was as tantalising as hearing one side of a telephone conversation. There were references to the weather and to family birthdays, the sort of thing Tessa noted in her own diary, but much was unexplained, people and places referred to by initial letters. Understandable. Mrs Channing hadn't intended them to be read by anyone else. *Can't bear it. A. sleeping in guest room. Doctor says nothing's amiss.* Tessa became intrigued and frustrated in equal parts. The cryptic phrases were like the points in a dot-to-dot puzzle. For a picture to be revealed, she would need to join them up.

Lewis spent the Easter weekend in Manchester, with Kirsty. They went to the cinema, the City Art Gallery, read the papers, cooked for each other and went for a long walk. Their lovemaking was as satisfying as ever. They talked and laughed and did the things that they always did. But once or twice Kirsty seemed distracted, losing the thread of what she was telling him.

With a week before school started back, Lewis decided to go to Cranwell Lodge. Mrs Channing needed more gummed labels for her boxes and, after a morning at school working on lesson plans for the coming term, he raided the stockroom, picking up a selection of pens, envelopes and paper along with the labels.

'It's only me,' he called, letting himself in through the back door.

The house was silent.

'Hello?' he called again as he went into the breakfast room, expecting to find her sitting in her armchair, tackling the crossword.

The remains of yesterday's fire lay, grey and cold, in the grate but there was no sign of her. He returned to the kitchen. An unwashed bowl stood on the draining board, porridge caked on the inside of it, like pebble-dash on the wall of a house.

Had she gone out? Her grocery shopping was delivered weekly and, because she had been a good customer for so many years, the soft-hearted grocer also brought her regular order – a chop, a slice or two of liver, some sausages – from the butcher. She kept a well-provisioned larder and boasted that she could manage for a month '…as long as I don't tire of oxtail soup or sardines...' were there to be a bad snowfall, like the one a few Christmases ago. Whenever she needed to visit the bank or go to the hairdresser, she went by taxi, but these were infrequent occurrences requiring pre-planning, and she invariably mentioned things like that to Lewis.

He found her in the bathroom lying, fully clothed and face-down, on the black and white chequered linoleum. It was obvious that she was dead and while it was too late be classed an emergency, not knowing what else to do, he dialled nine-nine-nine.

The doctor thought that she had probably been dead for two or three days, although the Coroner would have to verify that. The police asked lots of questions. What time had he found her? What brought him to the house that particular day? They seemed unable to understand why, as he wasn't related to 'the deceased', he was in possession of the keys to her house. When he explained that he and Mrs Channing had been friends, they listened stony-faced, their disbelief apparent in their, 'You are twenty-three, sir, and you say the deceased was ... eighty-nine?' They took down his details – name, address, occupation, when he had last seen her alive. The dead pan manner in which they delivered the questions made him fear that he might, unwittingly, have broken the law, a fear irrationally reinforced by the bag of stolen stationery still lying on the table. After an hour or so, they told him he was free to leave, adding that they would need to talk to him again. He was sure they would, because it couldn't be long before the penny dropped and they dug out the files from fourteen years ago.

He cycled slowly home, delaying the moment of getting there. He would have to come clean with his parents and admit that, for the past five years, he had been slinking off – that's how his father would see it – to visit Mrs Channing. In their eyes, Mrs C was in some way linked with Gordon's disappearance, although it had been proved otherwise. Lewis wouldn't expect them to understand why visiting her had become so important to him. When he was at Cranwell Lodge, he became a more interesting person. He couldn't understand why but he did and, for the first time since finding her in the bathroom, he reflected on what he had lost, and somewhere between Cranwell Lodge and home, he sat on a garden wall and wept.

Dick Swinburne made a great song and dance about his son's covert association with Mrs Channing. 'How could you, Lewis? After all that went on there.' Nothing had 'gone on' there but Lewis could see how, once the police arrived asking more questions as they surely would, their stolid insensitivity and persistence would dredge the whole business up. It was bound to because his own head was already swirling with thoughts of his brother.

Gordon wasn't dead because, for fourteen years, Lewis had been keeping him alive. At first he'd created a parallel existence for the Swinburne family, a life in which his father returned from the shops with the baby and the newspaper, and the five of them lived in idyllic harmony. But, as time went on, Lewis could no longer square this whimsical account with his credo. Science, not science fiction, provided the blueprint for life on earth, forcing him to come up with an explanation that complied with the laws of chemistry and physics.

Gordon was fine. The woman who had taken him from his pram on that November day in 1954 was beautiful, kind, rich and well-educated. Her soldier husband had been absent, on service in Cyprus, or Malta, when their son was born. Unfortunately that baby had died and, temporarily deranged, she had snatched a replacement. Gordon – although he would have been re-named something like Christopher or Jeremy – was fourteen now and at public school. He was a good all-rounder, excelling at maths and sport. He could ride a horse and sail a dinghy and play the cello.

And he bore a startling resemblance to Lewis. Christopher had a younger brother. Perhaps a sister, too. The family home was in Devon, or the Cotswolds, and they lived in sunny tranquillity. Yes, he was fine.

He wasn't sure that Tessa would like the idea of Gordon's new life. Her goal had, or so it seemed, been to loathe their father and the catastrophe only really satisfied that need if Gordon had 'gone to a better place', and not as in Devon or the Cotswolds. So for fear that with a few ugly sentences she would annihilate Christopher aka Gordon, he kept his hopeful conviction to himself. Neither was the topic mentioned by his parents, who seldom spoke about the past or anything connected with it. Bereaved families found consolation in recalling happier days, when the family circle had been complete, but the Swinburne circle had been irreparably fractured and looking back would be like asking them to take comfort from a car crash.

The post-mortem revealed that Mrs Channing had suffered a massive stroke and would have died instantly. Lewis was glad. It was a relief to know that she had not lain on the bathroom floor for hours, cold and frightened, waiting to die. The police informed him that they had tracked down and notified her next of kin – a second cousin who lived not far from Ipswich. This was no more than a formality as Mrs Channing had taken steps to ensure that no one should turn up and railroad the final proceedings. She had set her affairs in immaculate order, down to the details of her funeral. *Humanist. No flowers. No mourners – not even Lewis Swinburne.* And where her ashes were to be scattered: *in the River Wye, near Symonds Yat – I've always liked the sound of that name.*

Three weeks after Mrs Channing's death, Lewis came home to find a letter waiting for him. The unnecessarily large envelope was franked 'Richardson, Rolf and Newman', the town's most prominent firm of solicitors. The letter inside requested that he contact them.

'Any idea what it's about?' he asked the secretary who answered his phone call but, as he anticipated, she was unable to help him.

To be truthful, the communication didn't come as a complete surprise. Once or twice, Mrs Channing had hinted that she intended leaving him something as a remembrance of Cranwell Lodge. There was, of course, no question of his ever forgetting the place but he liked to think that she might bequeath him the ebony elephants or the walking stick with the handle carved in the shape of a snake's head or the painting of the Indian dhow floating on the purple ocean.

But, when Mr Newman gave Lewis a copy of her will to read, it wasn't the elephants or the stick or the picture. Mrs Channing had left Lewis the house. She had left him Cranwell Lodge and its contents.

'There is, however, one very unusual condition.' Mr Newman's voice was deliberate and rather too loud, as if he wanted to ensure that his words penetrated even the thickest skull. 'The house is yours on condition that you occupy it for the next ten years. Thereafter it is yours to do with as you see fit. This condition will be overseen by a board of trustees appointed by my late client.'

'And if I don't want to?' Lewis's question sounded petulant, the terminology inexact.

'If you "don't want to" or if you live there for one single day short of ten years, the property and its contents will be sold and the sum realised donated to a charity.'

'Which one?' Lewis didn't see Mrs Channing as a philanthropist and he was intrigued to hear which charity she'd chosen.

Mr Newman flicked over the pages of the document and adjusted his spectacles, and it occurred to Lewis that the man was probably the leading light in some amateur dramatic society. 'The International Society for the Welfare of Parrots.'

Lewis pictured Blanche, put out with rubbish one Thursday morning, and he laughed.

The terms of the will allowed Lewis one month in which to make up his mind. For the first week he kept the revelation to himself. If he decided to refuse the proposition, there would be no need ever to tell anyone. Throughout the week, the dilemma consumed him and, as he veered from acceptance to refusal and back again, he became increasingly furious with his would-be benefactor. How dare she, and why had she, put him in such an invidious position? It wasn't a decision that could be made rationally, by making lists of pros and cons. If he tried to think of it as a money-making scheme, his investment was ten years of his life. Faustian, that's what it was.

He rewound to the day before Mr Newman read the will. What had been his life plan? What had he been striving towards? There was no point in deceiving himself – he had no vision, no goal for the future. A few elements were there, ill-defined and drifting, killing time until fate anchored them or blew them away. Kirsty. And his parents – mainly because no one else had included them in their plan. Teaching. Children of his own. Tessa stood there too, in perfect focus.

'Are you all right?' his mother asked. 'Nothing wrong at school? You haven't fallen out with Kirsty, have you? You seem to be in a world of your own these days.'

They were in the kitchen, waiting for Dick Swinburne to get back from work. Lewis watched her, methodically setting out the cutlery and putting three plates to warm on the rack over the cooker, wishing that, together, they could examine a future where he married Kirsty and moved to Manchester, visiting them in the school holidays or at Christmas. A future where she and his father 'managed' without him. For all he knew it could be the making of all of them.

*

Lewis went to Manchester to talk to Kirsty.

'What a grotesque thing to do,' she said. 'Why would an old woman want to play games with a young man's life? It's bizarre.'

For days Lewis had been trying to solve this puzzle. Mrs Channing, although frequently caustic, was not malevolent. She must have thought that forcing him to make this choice would be in some way beneficial. Might she have done it as a way of compelling him to face his future, of jolting him off his comfortable fence?

It was clear from Kirsty's tone that she assumed he would reject the proposition. 'What I don't understand is why you never told me about her or her wretched house. It was obviously a huge thing in your life.' She paused. 'It makes me wonder if I really know you at all.'

'It wasn't really a "huge thing" as you put it. I used to call in now and again, like anyone might call in on an elderly neighbour.'

Her sceptical gaze stopped him from perjuring himself further and he tried another approach. 'It's a fantastic old house. Sort of magic.' He stared at a swirl of undissolved instant coffee, floating on the surface of his drink. 'You'd love it. Of course it needs—'

'Stop. Before you go any further, you should hear what I have to say. I've been offered a promotion. A real step up the career ladder. It's a fantastic opportunity but it would mean moving to the firm's Newcastle office.'

Now he understood. 'Was this on the cards at Easter? I knew you were distracted but I didn't say anything.'

She raised her eyebrows, reminding him that he was in no position to demand justification for her keeping her secret. 'Maybe we don't really know each other at all.'

*

Two months later, with Tessa's encouragement, his parents' misgivings and Kirsty's regretful farewell ringing in his ears, Lewis took possession of Cranwell Lodge.

IV

1976

Chapter 18

TESSA POURED A GLASS OF WINE and stared at the blank sheet of paper protruding from her typewriter. The phone rang and she jumped, knocking over her glass. 'Shit.' She righted it, but it was too late to prevent a rivulet of white wine running across the table and reaching the stack of paper at the side of her typewriter. 'Fuck.'

The caller was Lewis, asking what time she would be arriving on Saturday. *Saturday.* She glanced at the calendar, pinned above her desk. 'Home' was undeniably written there in her own handwriting. 'I can't see me getting there before mid-afternoon. And I'll have to come back on Sunday, after lunch. I've got something on in the evening.'

Lewis arranged to pick her up from the station adding 'It hardly seems worth your coming.'

'One of those things, I'm afraid,' she said.

Were Tessa to star in the film of her life, here the camera would home in on her hands, pounding away on the typewriter, whizzing the carriage back at the *tring* of the tinny bell before wrenching page after page from the rollers, scrunching them up and lobbing them towards the overflowing waste-paper basket. A sweeping shot across the floor would reveal dozens of discarded pages and the audience would understand – *here was a writer in full spate.* But Tessa's waste-paper basket was empty and the floor un-littered.

Writing the first book had been a breeze. She had completed it in six months, whilst holding down a full-time job. When it was published, the newspapers had loved the whole thing – not only the novel itself but also the circumstances surrounding its publication. She had given numerous interviews explaining how she had infiltrated her manuscript into the pile waiting on the editor's desk; how she – the anonymous office girl – had been given the job of typing the letter to Tess Swinburne, congratulating her on her work and making an offer for *The House on the Hill*. The book had remained near the top of the best-seller list for weeks and, on the strength of its success and the generous advance offered for a second novel, she had given up her job.

The second book had taken over two years to complete and had been a flop. By that time she was renting a tiny flat of her own. The privacy and agreeable surroundings, the pleasant view across Hampstead back gardens, seemed to dissipate her creativity. It was as though, spared the discomforts of the rush hour and the hurly-burly of the office, her imagination had withered.

She had adapted the first book – a tale of an unconsummated marriage, homosexuality and incest, set in the years running up to the First World War – from Mrs Channing's diaries. The diaries' sketchy entries had hinted at disappointment and humiliation but there were few concrete facts. Tessa had managed to 'join the dots', coming up with a melodramatic version of what might have taken place. Working at Ward & Cox had taught her that readers couldn't get enough sex and scandal. So she'd made sure to incorporate plenty of both.

The critics panned the follow-up, saying that it was lacklustre, with unconvincing characters and a formulaic storyline. 'Not a patch on Swinburne's debut novel.' To have any hope of redeeming her reputation, her next book would have to be a knockout.

Confronting the blank page and contemplating failure became demoralising and so she dreamed up 'essential' tasks. She painted her bedroom chocolate brown, hoping to alleviate her insomnia; she spent whole afternoons searching for a book that she was sure, or almost sure, she owned and which she suddenly *had* to re-read; she washed dust off the leaves of houseplants; she cooked elaborate meals, then found she had no appetite.

By midday, Tessa ached with boredom. A walk, that's what she needed. Or, better still, something worthy yet diverting. A visit to the British Museum or the National Gallery.

She caught the number twenty-four bus and climbed to the upper deck, enjoying the tacit camaraderie of her fellow travellers as they made their stop-start progress towards Trafalgar Square. The bus approached the British Museum but there was too much spring in the air to spend the afternoon with mummies and shards of pottery and she remained seated, finally getting off halfway down Charing Cross Road. Unable to resist, she went into Foyles, following the signs that led to the fiction department. There were three copies of *The House on the Hill* nestling amongst the 'S's' on the endless shelves, but no sign of *Master and Servant*.

Perhaps she was no more than a 'one-hit wonder'. It had been a shock when her last bank statement revealed how little remained in her savings account. If she failed to come up with a winning idea within, say, the next three months she would have to look for a job.

A poster, fixed to the railings outside the National Portrait Gallery caught her attention. It was advertising *Hope*, the current exhibition by a celebrated photographer, darling of the Sunday supplements. It might be worth a quick look – faces were always fascinating – and she could take advantage of the 'Ladies' in the basement.

Startling images, some in colour, some black and white, extended across the off-white walls. The photographer, famous enough to command a string of eminent sitters, had instead directed his lens at hopeful unknowns who had, so far, failed to make it to the top of their chosen fields. Delighted to have happened across such an absorbing show, she moved from picture to picture, inspecting the defiant faces, admiring their self-belief.

She was in the second room when she spotted Tony Rundle scowling at her from one of the pictures. Positive yet disbelieving, she checked the caption. *The Mighty Handful; Bristol 1974.* Yes, she was sure that was the name of Rundle's band. A couple of years ago they had won the local heat of a national talent contest and Lewis had sent her a cutting from the *Gazette*. She calculated that Rundle must be in his mid-thirties now, but his face hadn't altered. The same sneer; the same khaki-coloured eyes beneath those rather effeminate eyebrows. He was wearing his trademark black leather jacket, glowering at the camera, guitar slung low across his hips. She glanced around the gallery, suppressing the impulse to tell everyone that the moody guitarist on the left of the picture had been her first lover.

'What time's the London train due in?' Although Lewis already knew, he double-checked with the man on the gate.

'Ten minutes, sir. Platform two. Up the steps and over the bridge.'

He bought a platform ticket and crossed the footbridge, peering down the tracks for the first sign of the train. Tessa's visits were never plain sailing, but whenever she stepped down from the train his spirits soared, as if he had received a shot of a drug that gave his plod-along routine a boost of perilous excitement.

Dick and Peggy Swinburne assumed that, on her infrequent visits home, Tessa would spend every available minute with them. It was also taken for granted that Lewis would come to Salisbury Road to see his sister, bringing his wife and daughter with him. These gatherings were an ordeal for all of them, leaving his mother exhausted for days. Added to that, Andrea and Tessa didn't get on. 'She turns up once in a blue moon then expects us to drop everything. And she never says a word of thanks for all you do for your parents. It must be wonderful to sit in London, being the Famous Writer, no time to spare for anyone but with everyone at your beck and call.'

Lewis appreciated his wife's position but, even so, he wished she could be more charitable. He explained that Tessa was ... well, just Tessa, but his indulgence intensified Andrea's resentment and lined him up as the secondary target of her attack. 'Hitler was just Hitler, but that doesn't excuse his behaviour.'

'How's life at the Bates Motel?' Tessa asked as, arms linked, they walked back to the car. 'Never mind. Another three years and you can take the money and run. I only hope it was worth doing time for.'

'C'mon, Tess. That's a bit harsh. You were pretty keen for me to take it on if I remember rightly.'

'Yes, but only because I saw it as one small step for Lewis Swinburne. Once you'd cut the apron strings, I assumed you'd wriggle out of that ten-year malarkey, sell the place and get the hell out. A clever lawyer would have found a loophole.'

Tessa wasn't the first to suggest this. After he and Andrea became engaged, she had, in a more subtle way, talked about the same thing. But something – possibly the alarming prospect of self-determination – had prevented Lewis from following it up. In the end, he found it simpler to intimate that the conditions of the will had been tested and found watertight.

'Look, *someone* has to be around for Mum and Dad.' Lewis didn't believe this any more but trotting it out had become a habit, useful ammunition against accusations of inertia. 'If I've got to live in this town, I'd rather live at Cranwell Lodge than anywhere else.' He squeezed her shoulder. 'Let's not go over it again. Tell me about you. How's number three shaping up? Got a title yet?'

'Yes. I'm going to call it *Hope*. It's going pretty well.'

He was glad. The reviews of *Master and Servant* had knocked her back and he was relieved that she'd scraped herself off the floor and started another book.

He was also nervous.

Before he was halfway through the first chapter of *The House on the Hill* he'd realised that it was Mrs Channing's story. The old lady hadn't revealed much of her history to him but she'd made references to her time in India and the Far East, hinted at an unsatisfactory marriage and regret at her childlessness. It was all there in Tessa's novel. But his sister had taken each thread and spun it into prurient melodrama, liberally seasoning it with wife beatings, affairs and incest. The character that was so obviously Mr Zeal was the protagonist's bisexual younger brother. There was even a pet monkey called Bianca. 'Where did you get all that stuff from?' he'd asked Tessa. 'I pinched a handful of diaries. And don't look so po-faced. The rest ended up on a bonfire didn't they?' That wasn't the point but Lewis had let it go. At least Mrs Channing hadn't been alive to read it. All he could do now was cross his fingers and hope that this new one was fiction – better fiction than the last – and that Tessa hadn't found another life to plunder.

'That's good news. Am I allowed to ask what it's about?'

She clamped her lips together and shook her head.

Lewis dropped Tessa off at Salisbury Road and went home.

Andrea was in the breakfast room, helping Sarah with a jigsaw puzzle. His wife looked tired, her face grey and her eyelids puffy.

'Look, Daddy.' His daughter pointed proudly at the puzzle. 'It's Humpty Dumpty. And it's got twenty pieces. Mummy only helped a bit.'

'Very good,' he said, stroking her hair, feeling the fragile skull beneath the fine, blonde curls.

Throughout Andrea's first pregnancy, he had been convinced that their child would look like Tessa or him. It seemed unthinkable that his family's dark hair and eyes would not triumph over Andrea's auburn hair and freckled skin. Four years ago, when the nurse came smiling into the waiting room, inviting him to meet his new daughter, he had followed her, fully expecting to see a shock-haired, noisy, squirming bundle. Sarah lay awake but tranquil in her mother's arms. 'Isn't she beautiful? Our daughter,' Andrea whispered, offering him the baby, and Lewis had found it incomprehensible that the bald scrap of life, swaddled in the white sheet, had anything to do with him.

He fed, changed and winded Sarah. He wheeled the pram around the neighbourhood and patted her back through colicky evenings. As she developed into a toddler, he pushed the swing, suffered Walt Disney films, sang nursery rhymes and read bedtime stories. People said that he was a 'natural'. This was all pretty weird considering that, from that first sighting, Lewis had been encased in an insulating membrane that somehow made it impossible for him to connect with her. It wasn't a comfortable sensation. He'd gone as far as making an appointment with the doctor to discuss it, but he'd cancelled at the last minute, scared of what he might learn about himself.

'How are you, love?' he asked his wife. 'Did you manage to put your feet up?'

'I'm okay. Feeling a bit like Nellie the elephant.' She patted the bump concealed beneath the folds of her roomy dress and turned to Sarah, who was clasping the final two pieces of the puzzle. 'We had a little lie down, didn't we, darling?' Grimacing, she puffed out her cheeks and exhaled noisily. 'Only a few more weeks.'

It seemed to Lewis that Andrea had been pregnant for the last five years. Sarah had been born eleven months after their marriage. It was a straightforward pregnancy and delivery but the two that followed had resulted in miscarriages at three and four months. The doctors assured them that there was no reason to think that the current pregnancy would not be successful, all the same it had been an anxious time, a time of restraint and caution, and this unborn child had already dominated their lives to such an extent that Lewis sometimes wished that they had called it a day after Sarah.

'Tessa seems well.' If he didn't mention her soon the omission would lurk between them, coiled like a rattlesnake, waiting to rear up and strike. 'I thought we might pop down, later.'

'We won't be able to stay for long. I don't want Sarah going to bed late.'

He might have argued that it was Saturday and that a late night, once in a while, would do no harm, but instead he stalled. 'I'll ring them in a minute. See what their plans are. Fancy a cuppa and a chocolate biscuit?'

Lewis stood in the kitchen, waiting for the kettle to boil. It was no longer the inhospitable scullery that it had been in Mrs Channing's day, but a home-y place, with plenty of useful cupboards and wipe-clean work tops. His daughter's gaudy paintings covered the cork pin-up board and houseplants decorated the windowsill. The three of them ate their meals here and, on warm days, they left the back door open so that Sarah could potter in and out of the garden.

It had taken several years to renovate the house and sort

out the garden. His father had offered to help but, when the sugar soap and sandpaper were broken out, it became clear that Dick Swinburne saw himself purely in an advisory roll. Once he realised how long it was going to take, Lewis borrowed a lump sum from the bank and employed a firm of painters and decorators. That part of it had been straightforward. The contents of the house, including Mrs Channing's boxes, all of which under the terms of the will became his, presented him with a more difficult problem. Once the solicitors had extracted the essential documents from the mounds of private letters and papers, Lewis had incinerated the rest. He was doubtlessly destroying things of great interest but he felt it was the proper thing to do. He hung on to a few of the knick-knacks that had fascinated him as a child – the miniature replica of the Taj Mahal, the puzzle-box with the secret compartment, the elephants, of course – offering the furniture and everything else that remained, to the second cousin, relieved when a pantechnicon arrived and hauled the lot off to Ipswich.

When he rang Salisbury Road, Tessa answered, pleading in a low voice, 'Help. Get me out of here. I'm going crazy,'

'You've only been there an hour,' Lewis said.

'Exactly.'

'What d'you want me to do?'

'Nothing. I've done it already. I told them that you asked me to babysit this evening. So that you and Andrea could go out for a couple of hours. A sort of final fling before the baby. I'll be with you by seven-thirty.'

'Do you ever tell the truth?' He couldn't help admiring her ingenuity.

'That's what writers are supposed to do, isn't it? Make up stories?'

'Won't they complain if you desert them?'

'They can't because I invited them to come too. Naturally,

thank God, they declined. So, technically speaking, *they* abandoned *me*.'

'Does that mean I can book a table for two, somewhere?' he asked.

'Now you're talking. I prefer Indian if there's a choice.' She paused. 'Only joking, Lew. Maybe we could get a takeaway. And I promise I won't upset Andrea.'

Tessa's mother was impatient to show her the pile of clothes she had already knitted for the baby. 'White and lemon. It'll do for a girl or a boy. Lewis says they don't mind which it is, as long as it's all right. It would be lovely if it were a little boy, though. One of each.' She looped the tiny matinee jackets over her forearm, stroking the fine wool as if she were calming a fretful animal.

'They're lovely, Mum.' Talk of babies and childbirth unsettled her. And she couldn't imagine what it must do to her mother.

Jay had put no pressure on her to have the abortion, but she had been only twenty-two, neither ready to become a mother, nor selfless enough to bear a child for another woman. After the operation she was euphoric with relief. Then suddenly she'd plummeted into what the doctors said – rather insensitively she thought – was a form of post-natal depression induced by the fluctuation in hormone levels. For months she was low, wanting to do nothing but sleep or cry. Jay had sent money to help with the rent and food bills when she couldn't work. Pills got her through.

On the second occasion, unsure which of several lovers might have fathered the child and needing to finish the second book, there was no question of having the baby. Not wanting to risk another episode of 'post-natal depression', she had talked the doctor into prescribing something straight away and, despite feeling a bit 'down' she'd managed to carry on.

Looking back she wondered if the doctor's explanation had

been correct. She'd seen how losing a baby had driven her mother mad with grief. Might her own illness have, in fact, been a form of grieving? After all, she'd 'lost' an unborn child. *Two* unborn children.

Lewis opened the door, Sarah clinging to his leg as though she were afraid of being swept away by a flood. Tessa still had trouble believing that her brother was a father. Each time she saw him with his daughter, she had to adjust to the notion all over again.

It was equally difficult to think of him as a husband. When Lewis and that Kirsty girl – the one whom Tessa never met – split up, he hadn't seemed too disturbed. They had never discussed the ins and outs of it, but she imagined it was one of those schoolboy romances that had run its course. About the time of the split, the school where Lewis taught became co-educational and, the next thing Tessa knew, he was engaged to Andrea Something-or-another, the geography teacher inherited from the girls' school. Andrea was pleasant enough. Pleasant. And reliable. And dogged. And all the other attributes that Tessa equated with geography. She was okay-looking, for those who went for freckly, redheads with watery blue eyes. And she and Tessa had loathed each other on sight.

'I need a drink. An hour with Mum and Dad and I'm ready to explode.' As she came in she tripped on the doormat. 'Fuck.'

Lewis frowned, pointing towards his daughter who untangled herself from her father and ran down the hall towards the breakfast room.

'Sorry. Have I blotted my copybook already?'

Andrea's arrival let her off the hook. 'Hello, Tessa. It's ages since we've seen you. New haircut. Very trendy.'

Tessa smiled, groping for a compliment to return. Andrea always looked pale but today her face was pasty, her freckles standing out like splatters of mud. She wore an unflattering maternity dress, the Alice in Wonderland styling – prim white collar and puffed sleeves – looking, to Tessa's eyes, bizarre if not obscene on such a distorted body. 'Thanks. And how are you? Remind me. When's the baby due?'

This was all it took to set Andrea off, slogging through tedious details, as if nothing in the world could be more fascinating than the birth of her child. Tessa fixed her face in a sympathetic smile and tuned out.

A fleeting look around the breakfast room reassured her that Lewis hadn't been tempted to replicate Mrs Channing's eclectic décor. The furnishings were from Habitat or somewhere similar. Wooden-framed chairs with washable cushion covers stood around a pale, clean-lined table; paper lampshades hung where there had once been elaborate glass shades; bright prints – Monet, Van Gogh, Lautrec – decorated the cheery yellow walls; fitted carpet running up to white woodwork replaced threadbare rugs on squeaking floorboards. Bright and hygienic and modern. Tessa was glad. The old people and their world had faded away leaving only her and Lewis to remember the magic that they had woven amongst the over-stuffed furniture and dusty knick-knacks.

Catching Lewis's eye, she glanced towards the corner and smiled, knowing that he, too, was encouraging Blanche's contented murmurings to drown out the monotony of Andrea's voice.

Chapter 19

'I'LL BE FINE ON MY BIKE,' Tessa insisted.

Andrea was plumping the cushions on the sofa, a hint that she should leave.

'But you haven't got lights,' Lewis countered. 'And you're tipsy. I'll drive you back.'

'True. On both counts.' Having made the gesture, she felt able to accept Lewis's offer and with it the opportunity to have him to herself.

'You go on up, love,' Lewis suggested to his wife. 'You look whacked.'

Tessa kissed Andrea and pointed at the ungainly bulge. 'Good luck with… Hope it all goes well.'

Tessa was struck by the immaculate state of Lewis's car. Blanket neatly folded on the back seat, sunglasses located in a clip on the dashboard, map book and driving gloves in the pocket on the door. Not a toy, sweet wrapper or discarded apple core to be seen. The vehicle could have belonged to an elderly widower.

'Is this how you thought it would be?' Tessa asked as he started the car.

'Is *what* how I thought it would be?'

'This.' She circled her hand in the air, indicating the inside of the car, the semi-detached houses outside and the world beyond. 'Everything. Work. Marriage. Fatherhood. Everything.'

He drove on in silence, as though she hadn't spoken.

Swivelling in her seat, she faced him. 'Stop.'

'What?'

'Stop the car. If you're going to keep up this *everything in the garden's lovely* charade, I'll walk the rest of the way.' She reached down, grabbing the door handle and opening the door several inches.

Lewis pulled in to the kerb. 'Go on then.' He stared ahead, turning to look at her only when she had shut the door again. He sighed. 'Why d'you do this? You breeze in, trot out a load of hurtful statements then breeze out again. D'you get a kick out of upsetting everyone?'

Tessa grinned. 'Backbone detected in suburban man. Three cheers.'

'It's not funny.' He spoke quietly and calmly. 'Anyway, is your life so perfect? You live in a pokey little flat, lurching from one sad fuck to the next. You refuse to take on any sort of responsibility. You're selfish and inconsiderate. You kid yourself that you're a writer when what you actually did was steal an old lady's life and sensationalise it. Is this how *you* thought it would be?'

Tessa got out of the car and started running along Medway Avenue. Behind her the car door slammed and she heard Lewis calling her name, running after her. She slowed.

'Sorry, Tess. I lost it. I didn't mean—'

'Oh, I think you did. That was quite some speech. You must have been working on it for years.'

Had her brother's tirade been directed at anyone else, she would have been delighted to discover him capable of such vehemence, but his outburst wounded her.

Someone opened a front door and milk bottles clinked on the step. Distracted by the noise, Tessa and Lewis turned to see where it was coming from.

'God. Look, it's our old house,' Tessa whispered.

They froze, still and silent, until the door closed and the hall light went out.

'Come on.' Tessa tugged the sleeve of her brother's jacket, pulling him towards the driveway.

To avoid the light cast by the street lamps, she kept in the dense shadow of the boundary hedge, tiptoeing up the drive, in no doubt that Lewis would follow. A wrought iron gate now replaced the old wooden one between the garage and the side wall of the house. Running her hand across its cold curlicues, she found the latch.

'Let's hope they don't have a dog,' she murmured, pausing to see whether the scrape of the latch had alerted anyone in the house. But no lights came on, no dog barked.

They slipped through the gate and into the past, the moonlight revealing the stone steps leading up from the backyard to the lawn; the cherry tree, its branches silhouetted against the night sky; the privet hedges dividing the back garden from the ones on either side. They were standing close to where their den had been and, peering into the shadows, Tessa saw two happy children playing at make-believe.

She caught Lewis's hand and squeezed it. 'You can feel us, can't you?'

'Tessa, please. Let's get out of here before we're arrested.' He tried to pull her away.

'Don't be such a wimp,' she said, 'this is … important.' A breeze blew across her neck and she shivered. 'I need to pee.'

'Tessa,' Lewis groaned.

'It's okay. No one's watching. I'll go behind the garage.'

She pulled her tights and pants down and squatted, steadying herself with a hand against the garage wall. 'It's only what cats do.'

'What?'

'Cats. They mark their territory with pee.'

She finished and stood up, tidying her clothes. 'Your turn.'

She heard his stifled laugh. 'You can't be serious.'

'Please. You must. It will make this place forever ours.' She pointed towards the dark form of the cherry tree. 'Over there. Under your tree.'

She expected him to argue but he didn't and, as he walked towards the tree, she was shaken to realise the power she had over him and consequently the responsibility she had for him.

'I can't believe I did that,' Lewis said when they were back in the car.

She leaned across and kissed his cheek. 'But I bet you're glad you did.'

'You talk such bullshit,' he laughed.

Tessa wound down the window and lit a cigarette. 'So, are you ready to answer my question? You've had plenty of time to think about it.'

'Which one is that?'

'Don't play silly buggers with me.'

He drew in a deep breath. 'No. I don't know what I thought it would be like – but not like this.'

'Me, neither.' She offered the cigarette to him but he shook his head. 'I only come back to see you. You must know that. It's hard to believe that Peggy and Richard Swinburne are anything to do with me. I don't even feel pity for them any more. Christ, I'm a cow. But I'm an honest cow.' She took a deep drag on the cigarette, blowing the smoke expertly out of the car window then cleared her throat. 'D'you think about him at all?'

This time he did not plead ignorance. 'Yes. I think about him most days. It's a nasty habit I've slipped into.'

'D'you think he's dead?'

'Probably.' He paused. 'But I kid myself that he's living a great life somewhere – the life I'd like to have lived, I suppose.'

Lewis was clasping the steering wheel of the stationary car, as if by doing so he was keeping the world on course.

Tessa laid her hand on his forearm. 'Blimey. That's a bit heavy.'

'Things don't get much heavier than having your baby brother snatched away. Do *you* think about him?'

'Of course I do. Maybe not every day. But sometimes I see a lad in the street or in a bar, who looks a bit like you, a bit like *us*, and I ... wonder.' She flicked the cigarette butt out of the window, its tip still glowing as it rolled across the pavement. 'Once, years ago, when my first book came out, I was doing a signing at W H Smith's in the Strand, and a blonde woman, middle-aged, smartly dressed, came up to the table. She had a boy with her – fifteen or sixteen I suppose – and, I don't know, the age was right and there was something about him – his eyes, his smile – made me think, that's got to be him. He looked very happy.'

'What did you do?'

'I signed the woman's book.'

Lewis glanced at his watch. 'I really ought to—'

'Please, Lewis, just a bit longer. We never get to talk.' She clapped her hands. 'I know, drive us somewhere.'

'Where?' His very question signified acquiescence.

It was in her power to save them both. They could abandon everything, here and now, and together they could drive through the night to ... anywhere. Lewis was such an old woman, worried about breaking rules and desperate to be liked. But he was the only person in the world upon whom she could count. Even Jay, in the end, had turned out to be a bastard. Despite all that 'open relationship' crap, not long after the pregnancy he'd converted to monogamy and, the last time she heard, he and Liza had moved somewhere exotic – Tunisia? Turkey? – and had produced two more children. Perhaps Lewis wasn't ready to be saved. He would need to admit that he was shackled hand, foot and soul before he stood a chance of making his heroic escape.

'I don't know. Yes, I do. Gran's house.'

They drove across town and over the bridge that spanned the muddy river, darkness concealing the shabbiness of the wharf buildings along the waterfront. The Saturday evening picture-goers were coming out of the Odeon, some of them hurrying to the pub across the road for a drink before 'last orders'. Others swelled the queue at the bus stop. They drove on. Past the chip shop. Past the inelegant stone church. Past the launderette. As children, they had made this journey dozens of times, in their father's car or on the top deck of the bus. And, as they turned into the narrow street, Tessa yearned to find Gran in the draughty little house, waiting to feed them boiled eggs and scold them for talking with their mouths full.

'What exactly are we doing here?' Lewis asked as they drew up outside the familiar house. 'And I don't mean that in a metaphysical sense.'

Their grandmother's house was in darkness. Whoever now occupied it was in bed or enjoying a Saturday night out. 'I don't know. It was either come here or the school – we never went anywhere else.'

Lewis laughed. 'Rubbish. You're so choosy with your memories. We went to loads of places.'

'Okay. Where else did we go?'

'We went to the seaside—'

'Well you aren't up for driving to Weymouth tonight, are you?'

'I'm surprised you'd let a little thing like that deter you. Okay. Let's think. We used to go to Uncle Frank's—'

'Yes, but not often. In any case, he never lived in the same place for more than five minutes. What's he doing now? I've lost track. Is he still "in ladies underwear", or whatever it was he used to flog?'

'Insurance. And you know it. Yep. He turns up now and again. He's got a bedsit somewhere near the hospital.'

Tessa fiddled with the handle on the glove compartment. 'Has it ever struck you that Uncle Frank's … a bit … weird? That dodgy job. Living alone in a bedsit when you're fifty-something.' She paused. 'D'you think there was something … I don't know … something iffy going on. Between him and Mum.'

'For Christ sake, Tessa—'

'Don't you remember how chirpy she was whenever he was around? He was such a show-off. I thought it was for our benefit but maybe… Dad used to be so bad-tempered when Uncle Frank got us laughing. Perhaps it was because he was jealous.'

'Whilst you've been doing all this *thinking*, have you ever thought what Dad's had to deal with in his life? What if you'd been crippled when you were fourteen? How would you feel if one day you'd been playing football, the next parked on the sidelines? If a girl went out with him, he must have wondered if it was out of pity. The mortification of watching his brother go off to the war whilst he was stuck in an office full of girls and old men. Then, just when things were looking up and he'd regained some self-respect, the Gordon thing. We can't even begin to imagine what he went through – is still going through. Every time he looks at Mum he must—'

'I know all that. But what about Mum and Uncle Frank?' Tessa persisted.

'You're sick.'

Neither of them spoke on the way back to Salisbury Road but when they were pulling up outside, Tessa reminded her brother that she had, as far as their parents were concerned, been babysitting that evening.

'Will I see you tomorrow?' she asked, getting out of the car.

'I'm not sure what we're doing.' His voice was cool.

'I'll take that as a yes then, shall I?' She slammed the door.

'Did Lewis bring you home?' her father asked when they were eating breakfast.

'Yes. We had a good chat. Caught up a bit.'

'That's nice,' her mother smiled.

Tessa noticed how enthusiastically she was tucking in to her cooked breakfast. She looked fuller in the face and less apprehensive. She wasn't constantly fiddling with the cutlery or picking crumbs off the cloth.

'You look really well, Mum.'

'Thank you, dear. I'm feeling well. The new baby has put a smile on all our faces.'

And they were off again, into the mind-numbing province of shawls and pushchairs.

Tessa and her mother were in the garden when Lewis and Sarah arrived. 'Andrea's taking it easy,' he explained and went into the house to make coffee.

Tessa expected there would be intimacy – cuddles, jokes, indulgences – between grandmother and granddaughter but it soon became obvious that no such bond existed. Her mother addressed the child as though they were teacher and pupil on the first day of a new school year. 'Do you like my roses? Would you like one to take home for Mummy? You must be careful – they've got very sharp thorns.' The little girl looked anxious and kept her distance.

When she and Lewis were that age, long before Gordon was born, when they pleaded 'what can we do, Mum?' she always came up with something interesting. Old sheets and bamboo canes to make a wigwam; a treasure hunt: *Bring me a round pebble and a red flower and a feather. Quick as you can*; *Newspaper and flour-and-water paste for papier mâché puppet heads*; *Let's make the longest daisy chain in the world. I'll help.* Their mother had been so approachable, so full of fun then.

Or was that the mother she wished she'd had?

Lewis watched from the kitchen window. Every now and again Sarah turned to stare mournfully at him, a silent plea for rescue. She was a mixture of timidity and tenacity that he supposed she had inherited from him, and he wondered if he would find it easier to empathise were she a boy. Tessa and his mother were talking, ignoring the child, and he nodded and waved, willing his daughter to do something charming or amusing to grab their attention.

He'd not slept well. Andrea had been restless and at three o'clock he had taken himself off to the spare room, but he could not forget his conversation with Tessa. He couldn't deny that her observations were accurate. His mother *had* always seemed – what was the word Tessa had used? – chirpy, that was it, when Uncle Frank was around. But he was repelled by her suggestion that his mother harboured 'feelings' for her husband's brother.

Despite the open windows, the kitchen was hot and beginning to fill with the sickly smell of roasting lamb. The table was set for three – cutlery, tumblers and cruet set at the ready. Similar Sunday meat and two veg rituals were gathering momentum in kitchens all over the town, all over the country. Even now, Andrea would be putting a small chunk of dead animal in the oven at Cranwell Lodge. Lewis sighed.

'Did you have a good night?' His father came in from the shed to wash his hands at the kitchen sink. 'Where did you go in the end?'

'That new Italian place. Near the bridge.' How easy it was to slip into dishonesty.

His mother waved. 'Is there a film in the camera, Dick? We should take a snap now we're all together.'

Lewis should have been offended that the 'all' did not include Andrea but he understood that his mother still considered the four of them to be her family.

His father produced the camera that only came out on holidays and special occasions. The project set off a ripple of high spirits as they debated where they should stand and who should take the photograph.

'We could take several – rotate the photographer. Or is that too radical?' Tessa laughed.

And that's what they did, Dick Swinburne, Lewis and finally Tessa each taking their turn with the camera. Then they milled around in the garden. Tessa, evidently determined to show how good she was with children, tossed a tennis ball to Sarah, failing to appreciate a four-year-old's inability to anticipate the trajectory of a moving object and also failing to spot her niece's misery as, time after time, her small hands came together too late and the ball rebounded off her narrow chest. Lewis willed his daughter to pick it up and hurl it at Tessa's head, to stamp and scream, to say it wasn't fair. But, like an automaton, she retrieved the ball, threw it feebly back and waited for the next humiliation.

'How's Uncle Frank?' Tessa faked concentration on the game. 'D'you see much of him these days?'

'He calls in, once in a while.' Their father's reply was uninformative and their mother, bending down, pulling weeds from the rockery, had her face turned away.

Tessa persisted. 'Uncle Frank used to be so great with us when we were young. It's a shame he didn't have kids of his own.'

'We probably put him off for life.' Lewis severed the thread, unprepared to let Tessa tug it again. 'C'mon, Sarah. Say goodbye to Auntie Tessa. And Granny and Granddad.'

'Spoilsport,' Tessa muttered.

'When might we see you again?' Lewis asked as they walked to the gate.

'When it's most inconvenient. When you least expect it. When

I need something.' She laughed. 'I'm sure you've all worked that out by now.'

'Why d'you insist on casting yourself in the role of black sheep? You can't go on playing the naughty schoolgirl forever. You're thirty-one. We don't *mind* what you do. We don't much *care* what you do—'

'In that case why did you bother to ask when you'd be seeing me again?' She smiled triumphantly.

'You're so childish,' he snapped. 'I hear better arguments every day in the playground. And I asked because it's the polite thing to do. Manners. Ever heard of them? They sort of prevent the world descending into anarchy.'

'You're a boring fart, Lewis. All these years I've been holding my breath, waiting for you to turn in to a proper man. But you're never going to are you? Now toddle off home to your little wifey. Go on. Go and populate the world with dozens of dreary kids. Although I can't imagine you ever get aroused enough to—'

Lewis stepped forward and slapped his sister across her left cheek.

Chapter 20

BEFORE THEY LEFT FOR THE STATION, Tessa checked the local telephone directory. Rundle was an uncommon name, nevertheless she was disappointed not to find a single entry. She flicked on to the S's. *Saunders. Searle. Smith. Stoddy.* There. *T. J. Stoddy, 8 Winchester Crescent.* Diane's parents were still at the same address and, seeing the words, black and unalterable on the page, she was back in the prosaic semi that smelled of lavender polish and the Stoddy's fat spaniel, the house where she and Diane had failed to establish a lasting friendship. The next entry was *M. J. Stoddy.* Could that be Mike? She made a note of both numbers.

She told her parents just to drop her off at the station and go back home but they wouldn't hear of it, making a great performance of their farewells as though she were emigrating to the other side of the world. She hugged her mother and father, promising that she would return before too long.

'You'll want to see the baby as soon as it arrives, won't you?' Her mother's question was as near as she ever got to an instruction.

They made desultory conversation, Tessa keeping an eye on the huge hands of the station clock as they crept towards the moment when she was at last able to say 'I'd better go and check which platform it goes from. Thanks for a lovely weekend.'

As she entered the station, she turned and they were still there, standing by the car, arms raised in salute, like two cardboard figures from the toy theatre that Gordon had brought with him.

Lunch, during which her father probed crudely into her financial situation while her mother loaded her plate with food, had been an ordeal. And her exchange with Lewis had been unpleasant. She smarted not from his stinging slap but from his sharp words filled with barbed truth. Her visits generally started off well then the devil, or some such malevolent force, took possession of her and she found herself compelled to jerk them all out of their complacency; to apply her own brand of electro-shock therapy, powerful enough to jump-start the living dead. Her parents were beyond help so she'd directed her efforts at Lewis. All she wanted him to do was to make an honest appraisal of his situation. Then, if he was genuinely happy in his rut, so be it.

At each station, another band of London-bound travellers got on the train, returning to the anonymity of the city. Tessa watched them shuffling along the aisle, looking for seats. Had he, or she, spent pleasant days in the bosom of their family or had they, too, been setting loose evangelising devils to stir up the provinces?

She closed her eyes, picturing the collective guts of the passengers, churning away, digesting gobbets of lamb and beef and pork; gallons of gravy and custard and rice pudding. Were they, simultaneously, digesting hurtful remarks, painful revelations, unwanted information? Births. Deaths. Marriages. Divorces. Rapes. Murders. If the train crashed and they were all killed, would the world be better or worse for their mass passing?

The sun slanted in, warming the carriage and, as the train swayed along, her thoughts swirled lazily around the events of the weekend, inevitably arriving at the Gordon conversation. So Lewis, too, entertained the possibility that their brother was alive. Her thoughts meandered on. Had she and Gordon ever passed in the street? Or sat in the same cinema? What if he were on this train? Perhaps she should slip the guard a pound note and ask him to make an announcement on the intercom. *Will the young man who was snatched from a pram twenty years ago, please make himself known to the dark-haired woman in Coach E.*

'Are you all right?' The question came from the man sitting opposite.

'What?' She sat up and opened her eyes, feeling something trickle down her cheek. 'God. Sorry. Yes. I'm fine thanks.'

She swiped her cheek with the back of her hand. How long had she been crying?

'Here.' The man offered her a leather-covered hip flask. 'Brandy. Essential before tangling with … whatever demons await.'

If she accepted, he might think she was a pushover and, if she didn't, a prissy puritan. Before she could make up her mind which one to be, he leaned forward. 'I've been racking my brains. I think we might have met before.' He grinned. 'Not very original I know, but I think we have.'

She took a proper look at him. A little older than she was. Thirty-five? Clean but unkempt brown hair. Grey eyes. Full-lipped. The individual elements were nothing out of the ordinary but assembled they produced a wholesome, pleasant but unfamiliar face.

'About ten years ago. Or perhaps a bit more. In Cornwall. You were staying with Jay and Liza.'

'I was,' she said. 'Summer nineteen sixty-two. I was eighteen. You've got a better memory than I have.' She took a sip from the flask. 'I'm afraid I can't—'

'Well you wouldn't. I spent most of the time asleep or out of my skull on that Albanian white that Jay was peddling.' He closed his eyes and slumped in his seat, tongue lolling. 'Recognise me now?'

She laughed. 'Of course.'

'Dan Coates.' He held out his hand.

'Tessa Swinburne.' They shook hands and she noted that, although his hands were clean, there was a deposit of dirt beneath his fingernails.

The train crawled through the graffiti-ed suburbs towards Paddington and, as it pulled into the station, she was sorry that the journey was coming to an end.

It wasn't until their third date, when Tessa was starting to think that he didn't fancy her after all, that Dan Coates kissed her. And another month before they became lovers.

He was a sculptor, quite well thought of in his field. To supplement his irregular income – 'Only a handful of sculptors make a living wage' – he taught a couple of sessions a week at the Slade School of Art. In his early twenties, Tessa learned, he had married a painter who was a lot older than he and who, after a year, had left him for another woman. 'So, you see, I no longer take anything for granted.'

Tessa did not want to fall in love. It didn't fit in with her plan to write another bestseller, save Lewis from himself and make sure that Tony Rundle got his comeuppance. These objectives required her to be hard-nosed. Feelings of love, generosity and tolerance might divert her or weaken her resolve. She suggested that they should stop seeing each other but he laughed and asked, 'Why?'

Tessa found it easy to make men friends. In cafés, shops, on trains, walking down the street – the signals they gave out were easy to read. Female friends were more difficult. Thinking back to her school days, she couldn't recall one single girl whom she'd admired. The Diane Stoddys and Pam Blackmores had been okay when she needed someone with whom to go to dances or the cinema, but none of them had any gumption, none had been

220

on her wavelength.

When Liza Flynn no longer needed her to look after Valmai and Connor, she'd ended up in London where she invested in *Learn to Touch Type in one Week* and signed on with a temping agency. She liked working in different parts of the city, glimpsing different worlds. The lack of responsibility suited her. If she made a mess of something, she'd moved on before the mistake came to light. The majority of employees in offices were women, some of them good fun, but as she rarely worked in one place for more than a couple of weeks, they were never became more than acquaintances. Eventually, she'd landed up at Ward & Cox. During her time there, she made several real friends, in particular Charlotte Jamieson, a diminutive redhead who worked in the Rights Department. Charlotte was an ex-Cheltenham Ladies College girl, who drank like a navvy and smoked roll-ups. She was witty, urbane and shamelessly rich.

'I'm disappointed, darling,' she said when Tessa told her about Dan Coates. 'We can't have you mooning around with some artsy-fartsy no-hoper. Fuck him if you must but if you're starting to daydream about white dresses and all that nonsense I'll have to dig out my little black book and find you a nice rich boy.'

'But I don't need—'

'What you *don't* need is to subjugate your life to some second-rate artist.'

'He's not second-rate.'

Charlotte sighed. 'Oh. God. You're going to tell me that he's a genius and you're not worthy to wash his socks. It's nineteen seventy-six, Tessa. You should be at the barricades not the kitchen sink.'

Charlotte was inclined to exaggerate; nevertheless her remarks reinforced the warning voice nagging away at the back of Tessa's mind. But the thing with Dan wasn't serious so where was the harm?

One Friday evening, two days before the baby was due, Andrea bathed Sarah, put her to bed and went in to labour. Lewis had assumed he would be at school when this happened and that he would have to abandon his class to make the dramatic dash home. But even in childbirth Andrea was her usual efficient self. The whole weekend lay ahead – plenty of time to set support systems in place. No fuss. No drama.

He telephoned his parents and they were at Cranwell Lodge within twenty minutes, clutching a holdall containing their overnight things, ready to 'hold the fort'.

Between contractions, Andrea made a list of what Sarah liked for breakfast and the clothes she should wear next day. 'You could take her to the park. Or the library. Her books are on the table next to her bed.'

Listening to his wife and watching her calm determination, it occurred to him that she expected very little of him other than to be the taxi driver.

Andrea lay in the back of the car, moaning occasionally and making odd animal sounds and he could see her, in the rear-view mirror, her hands covering her face. The loci of their lives were about to be inexorably re-plotted and he wished that he could say something to set everything right between them, to erase the blots and false starts, but he sensed that she was excluding him, withdrawing, taking herself to the place where she needed to be. He concentrated on the one thing he'd been required to do – drive carefully.

The sun was setting, casting long soft shadows across the hospital car park as they walked through the revolving doors into the muffled staleness of the maternity unit. They went through the admission procedure, the nurses making encouraging noises whenever a contraction caused Andrea to gasp and close her eyes. It seemed to go on and on and he wondered whether a mother had ever been turned away, doubled up in agony, because her date of birth or address failed to tally with a list.

A nurse took Andrea's suitcase from him. 'Leave her with us, Mr Swinburne. You can go home if you like. We'll ring you when there's some news.'

'I'll wait, if that's okay.' He knew that was what Andrea expected him to say and his decision was ratified by her grateful smile.

'Fine. We'll get her settled then you can come and keep her company.'

The doctors had agreed that, if there were no complications, he could be present at the birth. 'They've put a note on my file,' Andrea explained. She ought to have discussed it with him first. The prospect of the blood and the slime, the real possibility that he might faint or vomit, alarmed him and he hoped that, when it came to it, he would be banished.

A nurse directed him to a featureless room with *eau de nil* walls and strip lighting. Spindly plastic chairs – pillar box red, electric blue and raw green – lined the walls, as though a 'bit of colour' was all it took to distract anyone who waited there from the pain and danger that surrounded childbirth. Having expressed the desire to stay, he had committed himself to this dismal place and, grateful that he had it to himself, he studied the floor, imagining the feet that had paced away endless hours, depositing the scuff marks on the grey vinyl tiles. The wall clock had stopped at four fifty-three and, unbidden, Uncle Frank's words came joking across the years. *At least it'll be right twice a day.* Lewis, then seven or eight years old, was reluctant to admit that he didn't understand and joined in the family laughter.

Dismissing the magazines piled on the incongruously domestic coffee table, he went to the window, peering into the semi-darkness, trying to find something – anything – to divert him, but the window overlooked a gated yard containing enormous lidded refuse bins and there was nothing to see.

After half an hour, he retraced his route to the reception desk where yet another nurse assured him, 'I'll fetch you as soon as they've finished the routine checks. Won't be long.' On his way back to the waiting room, he spotted the public phones. Digging in his pocket, he took out a handful of coins and it was only when he lifted the receiver that he realised that, although he knew the individual digits that made up Tessa's phone number, he wasn't sure of the sequence. As a mathematician, he understood how useless that was.

At eleven-thirty, he was dozing, his hand shielding his eyes from the relentless fluorescent light, when a nurse popped her head around the door. 'You can come and see her now. She's doing fine. I don't think it'll be too long.'

'How long is not too long?' he asked.

'Oh … you know,' was all she would say.

Andrea, clad in a hospital gown, was lying on a bed in a windowless room, propped against a pile of crumpled pillows. Her face glistened with sweat and her hair was damp. The powerful ceiling lights leached the colour from her skin and gave the scene an overexposed quality.

'How's it going?' He kissed her, her cheek clammy to his lips.

'Not too bad.' She gripped his hand. 'They've just given me a pethadine injection.' She pointed towards a metal dish on the locker just beyond her reach. 'Could you pass me that? I feel a bit queasy.'

It took all his willpower not to gag as his wife first heaved then vomited into the dish.

'Sorry,' she apologised and he felt ashamed. He was to blame for her swollen body and for the pain that she was suffering, yet all he wanted her to do was get on with it so that he could go home.

The nurse came with an ear trumpet device which she pressed

hard into the mound of Andrea's belly. Then, ear against it, she peered at the watch pinned, like a medal, to her starched apron. Her lips moved silently as she counted off the baby's heartbeats.

'That's fine,' she said, patting Andrea's hand. 'Keep up the good work.' And she disappeared again.

Time was lurching forward in fits and starts. He glanced at his watch at what he would have estimated to be regular intervals only to find that sometimes two minutes had passed, other times, fifteen. Andrea fidgeted and dozed, crying out when a contraction reached its climax. They hardly spoke and he knew it was because she was utterly focused on the awesomely barbaric process in which she was engaged.

At six-twenty she asked, 'Can you fetch someone, Lewis? The pain's pretty bad.'

He went into the corridor, momentarily unable to remember whether to turn left or right. He was dithering when a doctor – the first he'd seen since they entered the hospital – came around the corner and he explained that his wife needed to be checked.

'She's in there.' He pointed to the door. 'Could you tell her I'll be back in a minute? I need to take a leak.'

It was already light and it occurred to Lewis that emerging as he had from the warm, windowless room into the bright morning was not dissimilar to the journey that his child was about to take. *His child*. Perhaps, when he saw this baby, this sense of detachment would evaporate and be replaced by whatever was needed to turn him into a successful husband and father.

After the night's isolation, it was good to rejoin the world. After he'd been to the lavatory and swished his face with cold water, he followed the smell of cooking bacon to the cafeteria. A cheerful atmosphere filled the place, a sense of relief that another dreary night had passed. He collected a cup of tea and a slice of toast from the self-service counter, downed them quickly then went out into the car park and inhaled the chilly morning air.

Andrea was twisted to one side, a bundle resting in the crook of her arm. One nurse was gathering up bloodied sheets, a second writing something in a ledger and, seeing him, they both stopped what they were doing and stared at him as though he were a trespasser.

Andrea kept her eyes on the bundle.

'It's a girl,' she announced, her voice quavering. 'Not that you could give a damn.' She looked up. 'Where were you? What was so vital that you missed the birth of our baby?' She started to weep.

Andrea wasn't clever like Kirsty Ross, whose intellect and objectivity had left him feeling vulnerable, she was honest, diligent and conventional. She'd made him feel that he was in charge and he'd married her because he'd thought he could cope with her. But he'd failed to spot the steely determination which, once she'd identified her goals: husband, house, family, kept her tenaciously on course. These weren't such terrible ambitions but Tessa's *Is this how you thought it would be?* had exhumed the disappointment that he'd buried after Sarah was born.

'I'm so sorry, love,' he said.

But he wasn't. He was relieved not to have been there at that moment of ultimate commitment, which would have been tantamount to signing up for life.

'I was feeling faint. You had enough to worry about without my passing out.'

She stopped crying and patted the bed. 'Poor Lewis. Sit next to me and hold your new daughter.'

Chapter 21

TESSA HAD NOT YET INSPECTED HER NEW NIECE. She wasn't ready to face those conversations about whose nose the child had; how many hours it slept; whether it had a wet nappy or needed winding. Then, out of the blue, Andrea and the children decamped to Stafford leaving Lewis at Cranwell Lodge. Delighted though Tessa was to be let off the hook, it didn't make sense that her brother was spending the long school holiday on his own.

Tessa had been successful in separating her family from her London life. Before his marriage Lewis had come up for the odd weekend, but she made sure to keep him on the move, sightseeing or going to galleries, never at rest long enough to get a close look at her world. Therefore when he'd asked if he might spend a few days with her, the prospect of exposing her life to his forensic examination unnerved her. He was prepared to come whenever it suited her and she could find no reason to put him off. On the plus side, they hadn't seen each other since their spat several months earlier and she suspected that he wanted to patch things up. She did, too, and their reconciliation would stand a better chance if they were well away from factors that invariably precipitated a falling out.

Determined to prove to Lewis that he had a completely wrong picture of the way she lived, she tidied her bookshelves, shoved clothes into drawers and dumped piles of yellowing newspapers in the dustbin. She made umpteen trips to the launderette, bought cornflakes, bread, butter and milk and made sure there were coins for the gas meter. She changed the sheets on her bed and put clean towels in the bathroom. While she was engaged in these mindless chores, she pondered whether Lewis and Dan Coates should meet.

Tessa hugged Lewis. 'Welcome to my – how did you put it? – "grotty little flat".' She led him through to the living room and pointed to the sofa. 'That's where you'll be sleeping. It's quite comfy, so I'm told.'

'Before I forget…' Lewis unzipped his holdall and gave her something wrapped in several layers of greaseproof paper and tied with string. 'From Mum. It's one of her meat pies. Apparently you can't get food in London.'

'Has she never heard of Sweeney Todd?'

'Don't,' he shuddered. 'You used to tell me that story every time I went to the barber. I was pooing my pants by the time I sat in the chair.'

They drank coffee. Tessa asked after Andrea and the children. 'So what possessed you to call this one Jane?' She shook her head. 'Sarah and Jane. Hardly trailblazing.'

'We let Sarah choose. Andrea thought it would be good to get her involved. It's not easy when a sibling arrives. We know that, don't we?' He drained his mug.

Lewis worked his way along the bookshelf, checking the titles of Tessa's books. He did the same with her record collection. 'It's funny. I used to know every book you had. And every record. Now,' he pulled out a book at random, '*One Day in the Life of Ivan Denisovic.* I'd never have guessed you'd read Solzhenitsyn.' He held up a record, 'Or listened to Leonard Cohen.'

She frowned. 'Lewis, what *are* you on about?'

'There was a time when I knew everything about you and now

I know nothing about you.'

'What tripe. I don't have a clue what books you read when you were a kid, or what you read now. But that's got nothing to do with *knowing* you.'

'When you meet someone for the first time, I bet you take one look at their bookshelf and make an instant judgement. I bet you say to yourself *this person reads such-and-such, therefore they must be … whatever.*'

Tessa hurled a cushion at her brother's head. 'Or *this person talks a lot of drivel.*'

A typewriter stood on the table, concealed beneath its fitted cover. Lewis pointed to it. 'How's the book going?'

'Okay, I think. D'you mind if we don't talk about it? I'm a bit superstitious.'

Instead they discussed the heatwave. It hadn't rained for weeks and the soaring temperatures were breaking all kinds of records.

'They're threatening to cut off the water and erect standpipes,' Lewis said. 'It'll be tough if Andrea can't use the washing machine. The baby gets through half a dozen nappies a day.'

Tessa yawned. 'Shall we go for a walk? There might be a breeze up on the Heath.'

'You're the boss.'

It was late afternoon but, although the sun was sinking behind the rooftops, it seemed no cooler than it had at midday.

'Feel the pavement,' Lewis said. 'It's soaking up the heat then pushing it out, like a gigantic storage heater.'

Tessa crouched, laying the back of her hand on the grimy slabs as if she were a doctor feeling the forehead of a patient. 'I never thought of it like that.' She stood up and linked her arm through his. 'You are such a strange mixture, Lewis. You know all that difficult stuff – maths, physics, astronomy – and I'm sure you're a wonderful teacher, but you're clueless when it comes to ordinary things.'

'Ordinary things? What, for instance?'

'Well … like fashion. And music.' She let go of his arm and positioned herself in front of him. 'Look at you. Your hair's too short. Your clothes are too baggy. You look middle-aged. And you act middle-aged. You're only thirty and you're married with two kids.'

'I don't quite see how that makes me "clueless".'

She clapped her hands. 'See. You're even clueless about your clueless-ness.'

They bought Ninety-nines from a Mr Whippy van, and walked on, licking the melting ice cream before it dribbled down the cone. There was surprisingly little traffic yet petrol fumes, pungent and metallic, tainted the air. The few pedestrians that they passed seemed to be sleepwalking, as if they had been hypnotised by the heat.

They turned down a side street. At the end of it a narrow footpath, bounded on either side by high garden walls, led through to the Heath. A summer of tramping feet had worn away the grass and the compacted soil was cracked from the drought. Shouting and laughter echoed from the direction of the open air swimming pool, out of sight beyond the plane trees. Climbing slowly up the path, they reached the vantage point of Parliament Hill. Turning, they looked out across the city which sprawled as far as the eye could see, beneath the bleached sky.

'So spit it out. What's going on?' Tessa kept her eyes averted. He would find it easier to open up if she weren't looking at him.

He exhaled slowly, blowing out his cheeks. 'I wish I knew.'

'When's Andrea coming back? She *is* coming back?'

'I have absolutely no idea. We have polite telephone conversations. "How's Sarah?" "Fine." "How's Jane?" "Fine." "How are you feeling?" "Not too bad." It's as if we're strangers.'

A child ran past, trailing a kite behind him, the multicoloured construction scuffing along the ground, failing to lift off in the still air.

Lewis pointed at it. 'My life feels like that. A lot of effort for something that's never going to succeed.'

Tessa, unused to seeing her brother so despondent, tried to cheer him up. 'It's probably a touch of the baby blues. And, anyway, it's natural for her to want to spend time with her mother.'

He shook his head. 'It's not that. It's me. I've been behaving like a shit. But I can't seem to snap out of it.'

She gave an unconvincing laugh. 'We can't have that. Shitty is what I do. You're Mister Nice Guy.'

'Not any more.'

She didn't press him, knowing that the whole story would emerge during the course of his visit, and they headed across the Heath towards the bus stop.

They spent Saturday morning in the Science Museum which bored Tessa to tears and failed to engage Lewis. After lunch in the crowded cafeteria, Tessa searched out a public phone and rang Dan Coates.

'My brother's turned up,' she said, making it sound as though Lewis had arrived on her doorstep like an unsolicited parcel. 'I thought we might go out this evening. D'you want to come?'

She'd been in several minds about introducing the two men. There were too many skeletons struggling to get out of too many cupboards, but desire to dispel Lewis's melancholy overcame her reservations. At the last minute, to leaven the mix, she invited her friend Charlotte Jamieson to join them.

Had Lewis been feeling less dejected, he might have enjoyed his sister's solicitude. He guessed he was cutting a pathetic figure because she was treating him like someone with a terminal illness. However this hadn't stopped her from cross-questioning him – albeit more warily than she usually did – and he had every intention of telling her the ins and outs of it. But it wasn't easy to get started.

Solitude at Cranwell Lodge, coupled with an effort to maintain a façade of normality, was wearing him down. He'd explained to everyone who showed a bemused interest that there were jobs to be done around the house, and that it would be safer if Andrea and the children were well away from hammers, chisels and toxic paint fumes. To back up his story, he'd repainted the kitchen and creosoted the garden fence but physical activity couldn't stop him thinking and the more he thought, the more bleak his circumstances appeared.

'Who are these people we're meeting?' Lewis asked as they were leaving Tessa's flat.

'Charlotte Jamieson. Lotte. I used to work with her at Ward & Cox. Very rich. Very intelligent. Very … argumentative. And Dan Coates. He's a sculptor. I've known him for years.'

'Let me guess. Very good looking? Very sexy? Very … boyfriend?'

'Must you categorise everything? It's so unnecessary.'

'I disagree. I find it clarifies things. Saves a lot of time. Saves getting crossed wires. If you won't tell me, I may have to ask this Dan Coates which category he fits in to.'

'Don't try and be clever, Lewis. It doesn't suit you.' She poked her tongue out. 'Okay, if we're going to play that game, which category does *Lewis Swinburne* fall in to? Failing husband? Unwilling father?'

They had stopped outside a pub and he nodded towards the open door. 'Have we got time for a drink?'

It was unbearably hot in the bar, the air saturated with cigarette smoke. Following the signs *To the Beer Garden*, they ended up in a shabby yard where there were a couple of dilapidated wooden tables and they sat opposite each other amongst the dustbins, pigeon droppings and crates of empty bottles.

Tessa reached across the table and caught his hand. 'If you want to tell me I promise I won't say "I told you so".'

'You did, though. Tell me so, I mean.'

Tessa nodded for him to continue.

'Look at me. I've got a nice wife, two nice kids, a nice home and a nice job. So why am I being such a shit?'

Tessa frowned. 'Why would anyone equate "nice" with desirable? It's a synonym for mediocre if you ask me.'

'That's a bit harsh.'

'And a bit true.'

Lewis pressed the tips of his fingers against his closed eyes. 'Maybe I'm not cut out for marriage and fatherhood.' Orange and green patterns swirled on the backs of his eyelids.

'Or maybe you've landed yourself with the wrong wife and the wrong children.'

'Maybe. Knowing – admitting – is one thing, working out what to do is quite another. I can't just walk away from them, can I?'

'Andrea's the one who's done the walking. Perhaps she feels the same way as you do.'

He sighed. 'I think she'll come back on condition I promise to play the part of devoted husband and father.'

'And you're not prepared to do that?'

Lewis ran his fingers down the sides of his cold beer glass, moisture condensing on his hot skin. 'I don't know.'

Tessa was silent for a moment. 'No matter what you promise, you won't be able to go on, year after year, playing a part. You'll go round the bend. And anyway, you've never been any good at pretending.' She paused. 'Are you missing them at all?'

'Not really. It's a bit quiet at times…'

'So turn the radio on,' she said gently.

By the time they reached the restaurant, Lewis felt light-headed, a sensation that he attributed more to relief than the beer he'd consumed. Roman Catholics must feel similarly intoxicated coming away from the confessional, the only conditions for their forgiveness a few prayers and an undertaking not to repeat the offence. He had got it off his chest and been forgiven although Tessa wasn't the one he had offended against.

Tessa led the way to the rear of the restaurant, where a man sat at a table reading a paperback book. 'Sorry we're late,' she said.

The man stood up, inserting a bus ticket between the pages to mark his place, and Lewis saw that the book was *The Outsider*. So Coates was the sort of man who read Camus. A promising start.

'Only twenty minutes. Not bad for you, Tessa.'

The men introduced themselves and shook hands.

'I don't suppose Tessa's ever mentioned me. I suspect she compartmentalises her life. There are probably hundreds of us out there, locked away in soundproof boxes, ignorant of each others' existence.'

Lewis already liked Dan Coates.

He wasn't so sure about Charlotte Jamieson who, pleading the inadequacies of public transport, didn't show up until they were drinking coffee. She was, as Tessa warned, poised, intelligent and argumentative. It was difficult to imagine her losing control, but were she to do so it would be something to behold.

By the time they left the restaurant, Lewis, full of food and drained after his heart-to-heart with Tessa, would have been happy to go back to the flat but the others weren't ready to call it a day and they ended up in a jazz cellar, somewhere off Leicester Square. The sparse audience, concentrating in reverential silence, was a spectacle in its own right – middle-aged men with goatee beards and pony tails, young women with Nefertiti eyes, dressed from head to toe in black. Each number lasted for ten minutes or more, the musicians – drums, saxophone, trumpet and string bass – improvising, in turn taking up the intricate, meandering thread of the music. The visceral sounds stirred Lewis and he soon saw that what might be labelled 'discords' were, in fact, sophisticated harmonies, way, way beyond the simplistic rhythms of popular music.

The club turned out at midnight and, when they climbed the steps to the pavement, there were still crowds of people milling around, making the most of the breeze that bowled Saturday night litter, like tumbleweed, down the dusty streets.

When they reached the flat, Lewis was exhausted but too keyed up to sleep. His mind raced with the evening's events – conversations, extraordinary music and the touch of Charlotte's hand on the inside of his thigh. Sprawled on Tessa's sofa, he felt that he had, without knowing how or why, crossed an invisible border and strayed into an alien land.

'Would it be okay if I stayed another night?' Lewis asked next morning. 'I won't get in your way.'

'Fine. Anything particular you want to do?'

He tugged sheepishly at his ear. 'Actually, Lotte's invited me to a drinks party this evening.'

'That's odd. She didn't mention anything to me about a party.'

He cleared his throat. 'She thought you might be glad to get me out of the way, so you could spend some time with Dan. I don't want to bugger up your whole weekend.'

Tessa had to hand it to Charlotte who had, right under her nose, lured Lewis into her trap. He might be a grown man but he was inexperienced in the hunting methods of the predatory female, and particularly vulnerable at the moment. She ought to warn him that he was in moral if not mortal danger. But it might first be prudent to establish the facts.

Once she'd dispatched Lewis to get milk and the Sunday papers, she rang Lotte. 'What's all this about a party? You wouldn't have designs on my brother, would you?' She kept her tone breezy.

Lotte fobbed her off in an equally casual manner, saying that Lewis was a 'sweetie' but a little unsophisticated for her. 'He was telling me that he's a bit down at present. I thought a party might give him a lift.'

Lotte's parties – orgiastic affairs involving unlimited alcohol and shameless sex, shrouded in a fug of marihuana – were legend. If she set her sights on Lewis he wouldn't stand a chance.

Chapter 22

A COUPLE OF WEEKS LATER, Lewis returned to London. This time he spent two nights in Lotte Jamieson's king-sized bed.

He told his parents and Andrea that he had tickets for the Proms, but he had no choice but to come clean with Tessa.

His sister frowned, 'I hope you know what you're getting into.'

'Isn't this what you've been egging me on to do? Break a few rules. Live a little.'

What had happened was straightforward. He had been seduced by a woman who revelled in sex and was happy to share her delight with him. And that's all it was – sex without the least pretence of love.

After Sarah's birth, Andrea treated sex as a marital duty, giving no indication whether their lovemaking, which at the beginning of their relationship she had appeared to enjoy, any longer gave her pleasure. She initiated sex only when she wanted to conceive. Once Jane arrived, she couldn't escape fast enough, taking with her the two children she had so obviously set her heart on. He could almost convince himself that Andrea had pushed him into Lotte's bed. He made a pact with himself. If he wasn't brave enough to walk out of his 'nice' life, he would give Lotte up. In any case, once the novelty of corrupting a provincial lad wore off, he would undoubtedly get his marching orders. He was prepared for that. Then, whenever his squeaky clean existence as family man and deputy head of the Maths Department became unbearable, he would have those exquisite hours spent between Lotte's satin sheets as a consoling memory.

Before he left London, he called to see Tessa, not sure whether she would berate or congratulate him for his adultery.

She did neither, and, having made him a cup of instant coffee, returned to her desk saying, 'I can't stop to chat. I've got to get on with this,' her detachment smarting more than Lotte's dismissive, 'See you around, sweetie.'

At odd times – on his way to the library or cleaning the car or cooking his Boy Scout meals – Kirsty Ross popped into his thoughts. When they'd parted she'd moved to Newcastle, but she never failed to send Christmas and birthday cards. After his marriage, the messages in the cards became less personal and he appreciated her sensitivity. It was good to know that she was doing well; that she owned her own house and had a 'lovely boyfriend'. He wasn't sure why she kept in touch or why his heart raced at the sight of her handwriting. Neither was he sure why he kept all her cards in a manila folder at the back of his locker in the staffroom.

Tessa calculated that, at the current rate of progress, she would finish writing the book before Christmas. After her struggle with the previous novel, this one was a doddle and the days flew productively by. It was a blessing that her work was engrossing because other aspects of her life were less than satisfactory.

Dan Coates, in his unobtrusive yet persistent fashion, was becoming a fixture. Only four years older than she, there were times when he seemed like a tolerant parent, standing within arms reach, patiently waiting whilst his child mastered a new two wheeler. But, he was also a tender lover – the first to convince her that lovemaking had something to do with love. And it had been when Dan showed up that she began writing again.

Why did the thing between Lewis and Lotte bother her so much? Hadn't she constantly tried to spice up his turgid life? Okay, Lotte would soon tire of her brother's gauche charms but, if Lewis had acquired a taste for adultery, there were unlimited numbers of Lotte Jamiesons abroad in the world. But what if she'd made a dreadful mistake? What if he would be happier living his tidy, monogamous life and leaving her to walk on the wild side?

Determined to reassert her own 'wild side', she phoned Mike Stoddy, pretending that she wanted to get in touch with Diane about a school reunion. He said that he remembered her coming to the house and that they had all been following her writing career with interest, although he hadn't got around to reading the books. As they were saying goodbye, and as though it was the least important thing on her mind, she told him about seeing the photograph of Rundle in the exhibition.

'It would be great to go along to a gig. You don't happen to know where he's living these days, do you?'

'I do, as a matter of fact. He's down in Brighton. Hang on, it's here in my diary.' He reeled off a telephone number.

There was nothing to be gained by delaying. She dialled, imagining Rundle rousing from post-coital sleep and trekking from the furthest corner of a rock'n'roll mansion. But wherever he was, and whatever he was doing, he didn't answer. Edgy and disappointed, she phoned Dan and tried to start an argument, her bad humour aggravated by his refusal to rise to the bait.

It was three days and a dozen unanswered calls before Rundle picked up the phone. 'Yeah? Who is this?'

Four words after thirteen years and already her heart was racing. 'I'm not sure if you'll remember me. It's Tessa. Tessa Swinburne. From … a long time ago.'

'Aaaah. Tessa Swinburne. From a long, long time ago. You're quite the celebrity now, so Mike Stoddy tells me.'

239

Stupid, stupid, stupid. Naturally Stoddy had tipped off his mate that she was asking after him.

She mumbled something about the photograph. 'I wondered how things were going. With your band, I mean.'

'I didn't realise you were into music.' Was he mocking her? 'Actually we've packed it in. A couple of months ago. It was costing us more than we were earning. Equipment. Transport. Drugs. It'd be funny if it weren't so pathetic. Enough of my tale of woe. Where are you living these days?'

'London. Hampstead.'

'Nice.' He paused. 'Are you going to give me your phone number?'

It was her turn to hesitate. 'I'm not sure whether—'

'Tess, sweet Tess. You started this, don't forget. If my memory serves me well, you're a bit of a one for starting things.' He laughed – a gentle, intriguing laugh. 'Look. Why don't I say that I'll be … where? … at the bottom of Nelson's Column on Thursday afternoon. Three o'clock. It would be nice to bump into you.'

The gallery that represented Dan was putting on an exhibition of his recent work and he was assembling a guest list for the private view. 'I thought we'd ask Jay and Liza,' he said as he and Tessa were on their way to the pub.

'Weren't they living somewhere outlandish?'

'Not *that* outlandish.' He fished an envelope out of his pocket. 'Seville, in fact. I got this today. That's what made me think of them.'

Liza had written the letter. It was short and barely legible but it seemed that they were all – all *six* of them – having a right old time and Jay's work was starting to sell. *'Connor wants to be a bullfighter!'*

Dan jotted down names. 'Jay and Liza. Your brother, of

course. And what about Lotte? Or do we want to knock that on the head?'

The 'we' – redolent of permanence – made Tessa nervous.

'It's your party, Dan.' She sipped her drink and watched a lad pummelling the pinball machine near the door.

Two days had passed since she'd spoken to Rundle. His suggestion that they meet, and the implications of her decision, preoccupied her. From hour to hour she changed her mind. *Go. Don't go.* Her intention had been to get her own back – she wasn't too clear what for – and the effective way to hurt Rundle was not to show up. But then she'd heard his voice, and the whole thing became less clear-cut.

She went to meet him wearing a cream smock, its neckline low but not revealing, a leather belt gathering it at the waist. Beneath it, a gypsy skirt in reds and oranges, the wide hem swirling around her ankles. She left her hair loose – it made her look younger that way. The overall effect was, she hoped, modesty with feral undertones.

For once, the Underground was running perfectly. Fearful of arriving before him, she got out at Leicester Square and went into a shop selling tacky souvenirs, browsing aimlessly until it was well past three o'clock. In the end, concerned that the staff might think her a shoplifter, she bought a domed snowstorm containing a replica of Nelson's Column.

It was August and Trafalgar Square was like a beach, a holiday buzz uniting the sea of landlocked beachcombers. Although the fountains had been switched off because of the drought, old and young alike perched on the perimeter walls, dangling hot feet in the phantom water. Tourists bought grain from street vendors, squealing as wild-eyed pigeons homed in on outstretched hands. Another blurred snapshot for the album. Ice cream. Rucksacks. Maps. Sunhats. So many people. What if she failed to recognise

Rundle or missed him in the crowd?

She need not have worried. Flared jeans, pale blue tee shirt, denim jacket over his arm, there he was, standing between the lion's stony paws.

'Hello.' He smiled, standing quite still, making no move to kiss or even touch her hand. 'I wasn't sure you'd come.'

'I wasn't sure myself until an hour ago.'

He probably knew that this wasn't true, but mumbled niceties were a useful way to negotiate the initial awkwardness.

'Well I'm glad you did.'

He was more handsome than she remembered. His reddish hair was longer but neatly cut, and he was carrying more weight. That furtive look had disappeared and his smile – had she ever seen him smile? – was engaging. *A proper man,* that's what Gran would have called him.

'I brought you a present.' He took a paper bag from his jacket pocket and offered it to her.

Inside was a small stick of rainbow-coloured rock and, through the twisted cellophane she could make out the crude red letters running through it. BRIGHTON.

'I was going to eat it myself if you hadn't turned up. Easier to digest than a bunch of flowers. And, of course, I thought you'd appreciate the literary reference.' He grinned. 'I didn't actually think of that until just now. Anyway, what d'you fancy doing? I thought we ought to take a look at the photograph as it's responsible for bringing us together.'

Looking at the picture again, this time with Rundle at her side, she wondered if, by contacting him, she had tampered with fate. But that couldn't be right, could it? The whole point of fate was that whatever happened was *meant* to happen. Fate had tampered with her, more like.

The afternoon was proving to be not at all what she'd expected. Rundle was treating her with courtesy and it was as if they were on first a date. He talked a bit about the break up of his group; how they'd never been focused; how they'd spent too much time drinking and arguing.

'I was pretty pissed off when we folded but, if I'm honest, we were never going to make it.'

Over tea in the basement café, he told her that he was working as a car mechanic, a trade learned whilst doing National Service.

'I hated the army,' he said. 'All that bullshit. But it taught me a skill so I suppose it wasn't a total waste of time.'

The news that he had been in the army came as a surprise to her. He must have just been discharged when they'd met and it explained why he had been so fussy about his room and his possessions.

The cafeteria closed at five and the staff shooed the customers out on to the pavement. Everyone seemed to be hurrying somewhere, to know exactly where they had to be. Before Tessa could ask Rundle what he wanted to do next, he looked at his watch. 'My train leaves at six, so I'd better get a move on.'

'Oh.'

'It's a shame but I've got to get back.' He kissed her cheek and squeezed her shoulder – the first time that they had touched. 'Why don't you come down to Brighton sometime? Get some sea air. You've got my number, haven't you? Of course you have.' He grinned, raised his hand and was soon lost in the rush hour crowds.

As the Underground rumbled northwards, all she could think about was Rundle. Her plan was to captivate him then, once she had him in the palm of her hand, to reject him. She was prepared to do whatever it took. She had tidied the flat and changed the sheets; told Dan that she had a meeting with someone from Ward & Cox and would ring him the following day. Now Rundle had wrong-footed her with his conversion from selfish egotist to considerate companion. Correction. His *apparent* conversion. It was possible that he, too, had an undisclosed agenda. But, as it stood, unless she chose to contact him, the game was over.

The school holiday dragged on. In the beginning, Lewis's parents kept asking, 'When will Andrea and the kiddies be back?' Now, after four weeks, they rarely mentioned her.

Lewis took to dropping in on his mother for 'elevenses' or a sandwich lunch. Approaching sixty now, Peggy Swinburne's hair had turned almost white. She was too thin – she always had been – but, tanned after a summer spent in her beloved garden, Lewis had rarely seen her looking healthier.

It hadn't rained for weeks. Grass in gardens and parks was scorched and crunchy. Trees were already shedding their leaves. Newspapers and television encouraged people to *save water – bath with a friend*; to put a brick in the lavatory cistern; to ensure that cigarettes were extinguished before discarding them. His father disconnected sections of the cast iron downpipe and directed their bathwater, via more pipes and funnels, into an old water tank that he had stationed outside the back door.

'It was like this in the war,' his mother said nostalgically. 'We all did our bit. Made little sacrifices.'

A new routine emerged. Coffee with his mother; afternoons listening to his growing collection of jazz records or brushing up on scholarship-level maths; evenings listening to the radio whilst he worked on his most recent Airfix model. He was expanding his cooking repertoire. He discovered that ironing could be very gratifying and that the fewer rooms he used, the fewer needed tidying.

Andrea phoned often, reporting that the girls were well; that she was well; that her parents were well. Lewis responded in kind. How agreeable it was to have a long distance family who were all so well and so … absent.

Each evening he crossed the day off the calendar, watching the row of oblique strokes marching towards the beginning of term and the arrival of a fresh battalion of pupils. But this particular academic year had added significance. Sarah was due to start at the local primary school on the first Monday in September.

With only five days to spare, Andrea summoned him to collect them, giving him one day to tidy away his bachelor life. The half-finished model of the Ark Royal went in the shed. Coltrane, Jimmy Smith and Miles Davis were relegated to the remotest corner of the bookshelf. He cleaned the grease off the cooker, changed the bedclothes and emptied the waste-paper baskets. He popped into school to check the new timetable and replaced Kirsty's letters in his locker. Charlotte Jamieson could remain where she was, lounging between the satin sheets of his memory, a reminder that once, just once, he had broken the rules.

Chapter 23

ON HER RETURN, Andrea was unwilling to discuss her absence. She was regularly in bed by nine o'clock, pleading exhaustion. The children soaked up all her energy. The nights were short and fractured, the baby still demanding a night feed and Sarah waking soon after dawn. Lewis left for work early and returned late. He spent his evenings marking books or preparing lessons and, in order not to disturb Andrea, he slept in the spare room. He knew that they should have the matter out but *what you don't know won't hurt you, Boyo* as Uncle Frank might say. And Lewis didn't want anyone to be hurt.

Sarah had developed a limpet-like attachment to Andrea, making sure her mother was always within arm's reach whilst keeping a wary eye on her father, as though expecting him to make a sudden lunge and prise them apart. Starting school aggravated her timidity and there were tears every morning as the moment of parting approached. The arrival of a sibling often resulted in this sort of behaviour, according to *Dr Spock*.

The baby remained an unfathomable, demanding presence who cried whenever Lewis picked her up. Biology proposed that it was in the interest of the male of the species to protect and nurture his offspring but, if this were so, he was an exception to that rule. It wasn't that he disliked children – but so many of them were more appealing than his own.

A card arrived, inviting them to Dan Coates's private view.

Checking the calendar, Lewis saw that it fell within the autumn half-term break.

'What d'you think?' he asked his wife.

She reminded him that they had two small children. 'I can't imagine why they've invited both of us. They must know I can't leave the girls. But there's nothing to stop you going.'

He left a decent interval before replying, 'Sure? It seems a bit mean, abandoning you, but I'd like to see Dan's stuff and it would be a chance to catch up with Tessa.'

Andrea gave him a level stare. 'That's agreed then.'

The book was rattling along. Tessa was three parts finished and her contacts at Ward & Cox were enthusiastic, hinting that, with the right publicity, it would be a sure-fire best-seller.

'What's this one about?' Lewis asked when he phoned to accept Dan's invitation.

'Oh, the usual. Sex. Death. Deceit.' She paused to allow her generalisation to hit its target. 'It's a pity Andrea can't make it. You're welcome to stay here, if you don't fancy the milk train.' She paused again. 'Unless you've got other plans.'

Tessa had recently bumped in to Charlotte Jamieson. It was the first time they'd spoken since Lewis's second visit to London. Lotte had inquired, 'How's that adorable brother of yours? He's so … unspoilt. A veritable libido reviver.' Tessa had forced a smile but said nothing about Lewis's forthcoming trip to London. Futile really, attempting to keep her 'unspoilt' brother out of Lotte's clutches, especially if he was determined to scramble back into her bed.

Attempting to keep Rundle out of her own head was also futile. She didn't bother trying. A secret passion was undeniably nourishing and the tingle of anticipation ripened into an exquisite itch, begging to be scratched red raw. She held off until she could bear it no longer and twenty days after their meeting, she dialled his number. It was a Wednesday afternoon. He was sure to be at the garage – or wherever he worked – and she imagined the *trrring … trrring* fracturing the silence of an orderly room in a quiet Brighton street; pressed shirts and polished shoes in a wardrobe; a bottle of whisky in a cupboard under a sink; a pack of condoms on a bedside table.

She phoned a couple of times the next day, and the next, knowing that it was only a matter of time.

Dan was surrounded by clients and art dealers. Occasionally he beckoned Tessa to his side, introducing her, draping his arm across her shoulder. Not much liking the sensation of being claimed, she went in search of Lewis. Her brother had phoned, asking what he should wear. 'Anything you like,' she'd replied, 'but, Lewis, please don't try too hard. Boring will be fine.'

He'd been one of the first to arrive, looking handsome in jeans and white granddad shirt. Now he was chatting to Jay and Liza, the three of them sipping wine and laughing like old friends. Jay in black, as usual, his amused reticence giving him the air of a guru who was privy to the secrets of the universe. Liza, wide hems of her orange velvet trousers flopping over sandalled feet, breasts barely perceptible under brown satin shirt, playing high priestess. Androgynous yet sexy. Tessa glanced back and saw Dan smiling indulgently at her. She shivered. Too much of her past in one suffocating room.

Jay raised his hand and crossed the room. 'Don't panic. Your brother has nothing but admiration for his beautiful, clever sister.'

'Lewis *is* very loyal.' She accepted the cigarette that he offered.

'Congratulations on the books, by the way. I meant to drop you a line but…' he shrugged and smiled apologetically. 'That summer, in Cornwall, you were always scribbling in your

248

notebook. We should have spotted that we had a writer in our midst.'

She had no idea if he was taking the piss.

They talked about his work and the family's travels. 'It's been good. Good for all of us. But we're thinking it's maybe time to come back here. At least for a few years. We've brought the kids with us this time. Valmai and Connor are old enough to have a say in the decision.'

This time? 'D'you come to London often, then?'

'A couple of times a year.' He must have detected surprise in her question. 'Mainly to keep my gallery sweet. And to catch a few exhibitions.'

How totally he had discarded her.

He cleared his throat. 'Tess ... I'm not proud of the way—'

'No worries. Honestly. These things happen.' She made it sound as though the abortion had been no more than a forgotten birthday card. 'Anyway, what sort of a mother would I have made? Twenty-two. No proper job. No family around.' She grabbed a glass of wine – her fourth or fifth – from the passing waiter. 'It was a long time ago.'

'That's incredibly generous of you.' He touched her cheek and she wanted to slap his self-righteous face. 'Dan's a great guy. And he's crazy about you.'

Lewis was over at the window, his forehead touching the glass, peering down the dark Soho street, watching taxis slow at the corner then speed off again.

Tessa tapped his shoulder. 'Expecting anyone?'

He looked sheepish.

'Lewis, if you can manage to juggle your "nice" family life and a nymphomaniac mistress, you have my respect and my blessing.'

He turned to face her. 'Does it bother you, my meeting your London friends?'

'Not now that I have something to hold over you.' She smiled. 'I bet they've been giving you the third degree.'

'About you? Oddly enough, they haven't.' He grinned. 'They seem more interested in telling me about themselves.'

'Sounds about right.' She fiddled with the buttons on his shirt. 'What if Lotte doesn't show up? Will you go to her flat?'

He shook his head. 'I do have a modicum of pride, you know.'

Suddenly she wanted to sort it out for him, to prove that this was her world and that she had some influence in it. 'I'll phone her, shall I?'

There was a phone box further down the street, on the opposite side. It stank of urine; a wrapper, chips visible through the greasy paper, lay discarded on the shelf next to the phone. Lewis pointed at it and grimaced but said nothing.

There was no reply when Tessa dialled the number.

'What a cow,' she whispered, grabbing Lewis in a hug.

They stayed in the kiosk, reading the cards which Claudette and Mitzi, Raquel and Brigitte had wedged behind the cracked mirror, advertising their therapeutic services, until someone tapped impatiently on the glass.

It was starting to rain and they hurried towards the brightness of the gallery windows. 'What shall we do now, baby bruv?'

'Shouldn't you go back?'

'Probably,' Tessa grinned. 'Why don't you sneak in and get our things, then we'll find something more interesting to do?'

'You're the boss.'

She stood in a shop doorway, out of the driving drizzle, whilst Lewis completed his mission.

Dan was infuriatingly sanguine. 'I spotted Lewis leaving with his bag and your jacket. I don't blame you for mitching off. It was horribly pseudy, wasn't it? Where did you end up?'

'At that jazz club.'

'Good?'

'Fantastic.' Lewis had been rapt but she'd been too drunk to remember much about it. 'Then we came back here. He'll be on the train home now.'

'Jay and Liza want us to get together before they go back to Spain. It'd be nice to meet their kids. Of course you looked after the older two, didn't you?'

'"Looked after them" is overstating it a bit. They were completely feral. I didn't have a clue what I was doing. I was just there to stop them killing each other. Did Jay tell you that they might be coming back to London?'

'Yes. And I assume he told you that they got married last year?'

'Oh.' She felt foolish, as if she'd failed to notice that she'd put her shoes on the wrong feet. 'I wonder what happened to all that "we're free-loving-free-thinking-property-is-theft-don't-fence-us-in" crap they used to ram down our throats?'

He slipped his hand around her waist. 'It's not a criminal offence to change, Tess. *You* wouldn't want to be forever labelled as that bolshie, neurotic Tessa Swinburne, would you?'

'Better than being an arse-licking, chauvinistic bastard,' she snapped.

It was dark at four-thirty. Even with the fires lit, the dining and sitting rooms felt damp and draughty. Sarah had a perpetual cold, trails of green snot permanently dangling from her nose. She passed it to the baby who, unable to breathe, coughed and grizzled all night.

'I'm worried she'll vomit and choke. And Sarah keeps waking for a drink,' Andrea explained, taking both children in to bed with her.

Lewis moved his clothes into the spare room.

'I suppose you'll be spending Christmas Day at home,' his mother probed when he called on his way back from school one evening.

'I expect so.'

He and Andrea hadn't discussed it but since Sarah's arrival they'd spent Christmases at Cranwell Lodge, his parents joining them for 'dinner' and returning home in the evening.

'And what about Tessa? Have you spoken to her? We wondered if she'll be coming home.'

Home. He was sure that Tessa no longer thought of Salisbury Road as home.

'You'll have to ask her yourself, Mum,' he muttered.

The first Christmas cards arrived, amongst them one from Kirsty Ross.

Season's Greetings! Hope you are all well and looking forward to the festivities. My bit of news – I've moved to Bristol, to run the office here. It would be lovely if we could all get together sometime in the New Year.

She had printed her new address and phone number under the message.

Andrea was watching as he read the card and he made an effort to sound casual when he said, 'That's nice. We should take her up on it.'

'Yes. Who knows when we might need a good solicitor?'

Mantelpieces and shelves became festooned with Christmas cards and, when there were enough to conceal its loss, Lewis purloined the one from Kirsty, hiding it in his briefcase, oddly comforted to have it with him.

They continued to avoid the issue of Christmas Day arrangements until, finally, it was Sarah who brought the matter to a head. It was breakfast time and she was composing her letter to Father Christmas when she demanded, 'But Mummy how will he know to bring my presents to Stafford?'

Lewis put down his cup. 'Yes, Mummy. How *will* he know?'

Andrea looked flustered. 'Don't worry, Sarah. We'll write Nana's address on the top of the letter. He'll find you.'

'So when were you proposing to tell me that we're spending Christmas with your parents?' Lewis asked when Sarah went in to the breakfast room to make another paper chain.

'I'll be taking the girls, Lewis.' Andrea, her face expressionless, held his gaze. 'I'm sure you won't have any trouble finding someone to spend Christmas with.'

He let her insinuation go unchallenged. 'And the New Year?'

'I'm not sure.' She took a deep breath. 'Look. This isn't working out, is it?'

'You obviously *are* sure then, aren't you?'

She sighed. 'Can I just say what I have to say?'

'Carry on. I'll be interested to hear it.'

'I don't want to get into blame. It's no one's fault. Or rather we're both at fault for letting it drag on so long.' She paused and he nodded, signalling that she should continue. 'We liked each other and we assumed that we could rub along; that having children would somehow transform us into a proper family. The trouble is we had very different upbringings, and hence very different expectations.' She frowned as if double-checking that there were no flaws in her argument. 'We didn't take that into account.'

It started raining, the wind whipping the treetops and driving the raindrops on to the window pane behind Andrea's head. *Are you saying I should have found a wife whose baby brother had disappeared, whose mother had lost her mind and whose father had no soul?* He nodded again, wanting it to be over.

'We made a mistake, Lewis. That's all. And I think it best if we separate.'

An image of curdled milk flashed into his head. They were

on a sandy beach. Tenby? Oxwich? Tessa, who could swim, was teasing him because he still relied on an inflatable rubber ring. Their mother was unpacking the stripy canvas beachbag: metal sandwich box; Thermos and plastic cups; milk in a corked medicine bottle – because *tea tastes funny if the milk goes in the flask*. But the milk had 'separated' in the hot car, spoiling their picnic and their day.

'Lewis?' Andrea prompted, her expression moderating into concern, 'This can't have come as a shock.'

Shock? No. In fact he didn't feel anything, as if he were a bystander and this little drama had nothing to do with him. Arms extended, like a mother volunteering comfort to an unhappy child, she moved towards him. They hugged, her touch unleashing a tidal wave of relief, and he started to cry. It was as if a doctor had told him that his test results were negative; that the illness wasn't going to kill them. Misinterpreting his tears, she muttered soothing noises and stroked his back, weeping herself.

In the breakfast room, Sarah was singing 'Away in a Manger'.

During break the following morning, Lewis rang Tessa from the phone box outside the school gates.

'Has she got someone else?' was his sister's first question.

'You might at least pretend you're sorry.'

'Well has she?'

During a night of sleepless reflection, he hadn't even considered this. She *had* grown up in Stafford and it was entirely possible that ex-boyfriends were still living in the area.

'Not as far as I know.'

'She hasn't found out about Lotte?'

'I don't think so.'

'What *do* you know, Lewis? You're entitled to ask a few

questions when your wife tells you she's leaving. And what about the children? You'll be forking out maintenance money so you want to be sure—'

'Stop it. Please. This only happened last night. I haven't had time to think it through.'

'Sorry.' She paused. 'Well I wouldn't be surprised if there were another bloke. Andrea doesn't strike me as the sort to go it alone.'

'Maybe you're right. It doesn't change things though. I suppose I'd better tell Mum and Dad. They keep asking me what we're doing for Christmas. "Getting divorced" ought to shut them up.'

'Poor Lewis.'

'And don't imagine you can escape. Mum thinks you're going to come down here.' He paused. 'Anyway, what *are* you doing? You're very welcome—'

'Uh-uh. Otherwise engaged, I'm afraid.'

He waited, hoping that she would invite him to spend Christmas in London, but instead she talked about a problem she was having with her neighbours.

Tessa's book, re-named *Lost*, was published in the spring to initial mild acclaim followed by increasing interest once the newspapers had put two and two together.

Lewis telephoned demanding, 'What on earth possessed you?'

'Have you actually read the book?' she asked.

'Of course I have.'

'And?'

'How does it go? Frail woman has an affair with her charming brother-in-law. She bears a child. His child. Bitter, crippled husband finds out and murders the baby. How am I doing?'

'We don't know for sure he murders the baby.'

'No, we don't. But, surprise, surprise, it disappears from its pram, never to be seen again. For Christ sake, you can't alter a few names and assume no one will spot the parallels. You can't keep cashing in on people's lives. I'm surprised there isn't a phone box somewhere in it. Or are you saving that up for the next one?' He was shouting now.

Tessa held back the tears. Why was he being so unkind? 'I can't help it if everyone jumps to the wrong conclusions.'

'You're not stupid, Tessa. You must have known the papers would get hold of it. Well, congratulations. It's inspired publicity. Can you imagine what this is doing to Mum and Dad? Oh, and by the way, they had to get their phone number changed because the press was pestering them. But I won't give you the number because they wouldn't want to speak to you.'

Tessa wished she could see Lewis's face, better to gauge how to pull him back on her side. 'Please don't give me such a hard time. You don't understand the pressure I was under to come up with a really strong story. And you have to admit it is. It's already gone to a third print run.'

'Bully for you,' Lewis snapped, and the line went dead.

A letter, her father's laboured handwriting instantly recognisable on the envelope, arrived two days later.

Tessa,
What did we do to make you hate us? You have crucified us. Your mother is ill again and it is due to your filthy book. We are no longer your parents.

It was signed *Richard Swinburne* – the signature of a stranger.

She felt sick. But after several glasses of whisky, the stomach-churning diminished. So what? She was better off without them lurking in the background, forever criticising, dragging her down. In fact, a clean break was best all round.

Lewis refused to take her calls and returned her letters, unopened. No matter how many drinks she had, she could find no bright side to his disapproval. During the 'thing' with Lotte, they had become close again. Jazz, Moroccan food, adultery – it had been fun seeing him embrace new experiences. They'd been through sticky patches before, barely speaking for a year when he married Andrea. It might take a while but it would be all right. Lewis could manage without Andrea but he couldn't survive for long without Tessa.

Drink was her first thing she reached for when it all got too much, with Rundle a close second. Whisky and Rundle – doubly effective when taken together. She sneaked off to Brighton with increasing regularity. If Dan asked where she was going, she invented another book signing.

From the moment that she'd agreed to meet Rundle that afternoon, there had been no doubt that they would become lovers. Love? No. It was lust. Taking without giving, selfish and not quite 'nice'.

'You and me are two of a kind, Tess,' Rundle whispered as they lay, spent, on the floor of his room, passing the whisky bottle between them. Had her body not been tingling with the aftershock, she might have asked what he meant by that.

Chapter 24

LEWIS STOOD AT THE SINK, filling the kettle. Snow blanketed the back garden and the rooftops beyond, stifling every hint of colour and filling the kitchen with an eerie luminosity. His father was moving around in the bathroom directly overhead. He heard the flush hissing; water from the washbasin gurgling down the plughole; his father's uneven tread as he came down the stairs. He shivered. February the tenth, nineteen seventy-eight.

'Tea, Dad? Or something stronger?' It was not yet noon but normal rules could be overlooked today. He pushed a packet of shortbread biscuits across the table. 'You should eat something.'

Dick Swinburne took a biscuit then, as if he had forgotten what biscuits were for, he set it gently on the table. 'Did you get through to Frank?'

'Yes. He's coming over as soon as he can get his car started. Anyone else I should contact?'

'I've been thinking about that. There's a cousin somewhere up North ... Macclesfield or Wrexham...'

'Tessa?' Lewis suggested tentatively.

His father stared out of the window.

In fact Lewis had phoned Tessa as soon as the hospital confirmed that Peggy Swinburne was dead. That was in the early hours of the morning – *this* morning. His sister had clearly been drinking because, when he told her, she accused him of joking.

Too distraught to persevere, he'd hung up. A few hours later, he'd slipped away and rung again. 'Had she been ill?' she asked. The truce between them was flimsy and it was the first time they'd spoken since New Year. 'No. She's been a lot better recently, more relaxed. So much so, they've been letting her home for weekends. When Dad's around to keep an eye on her.' 'So she was at home when it happened?' Tessa had sounded surprised. 'Oh God, she didn't—' 'We don't have any details yet. I'll let you know the minute there's anything to report.' She'd offered to come immediately and then he'd had to come clean and confess that their father had no idea that he was calling her.

Lewis cleared his throat. 'We'll have to tell her sooner or later, Dad. She's got a right to know.'

'She gave up her rights when she wrote that filthy book.'

Before long there would be a plethora of things to occupy them but, for the time being, Lewis and his father were sidelined whilst the medical profession and the law deliberated how and why Margaret Anne Swinburne had died.

Father and son sat opposite each other, avoiding eye contact, as if they had seen something that they shouldn't and were too embarrassed to talk about it. Lewis wished that he'd put a cloth on the table. His mother used a tablecloth even when he popped in for a quick cup of coffee. He'd remarked, once, that there was no need; that she was making unnecessary washing for herself. 'What else have I got to do with my time?' There was no trace of irony or resentment in her reply. 'I think a cloth makes it feel like a tea party, don't you?' And, as if to prove her point, she'd gone to the cupboard and brought out a packet of chocolate teacakes, usually saved for special occasions.

The wind was in the north-east. Now and again it whipped the snow off the laden branches, creating miniature avalanches. It rattled the letter box and found its way under the doors. There had been no sign of snow the previous night when Lewis had left Cranwell Lodge, summoned by his father's desperate phone call. He'd pulled on yesterday's clothes and grabbed his old anorak. Now he drew the shabby coat around him but it failed to combat the arctic draughts. The feeble electric heaters made no impression on the temperature. The house was a giant cold store.

'Warm enough, Dad?' Lewis's breath condensed in the air, mocking his enquiry.

His father was wearing grey flannel trousers, a cardigan and a black tie, as if being warm and comfortable would be disrespectful. His eyes were dark-ringed, his cheeks waxen; a scrap of bloodied toilet paper drew attention to the razor nick below his left ear.

Lewis tried again. 'Shall I light a fire in the living room?' Fires. Cups of tea. Phone calls. Anything but what had taken place upstairs.

His father raised the biscuit to his lips and then returned it, untouched, to the table. 'We don't usually light the fire until after tea.'

We. Lewis ached for what lay ahead for this man.

Frank Swinburne turned up, stomping the snow off his shoes, making a great to-do about the lack of bread in his local shop and the tricky driving conditions.

Fuck your breakfast. Fuck the Council's failure to grit the by-pass. Fuck the forecast for more heavy snow. My mother is dead.

Lewis zipped up his jacket. 'I might go home for an hour or so. Sort a few things out. If that's okay with you.'

His father appeared not to have heard but Frank nodded. 'I'll hang on here until you get back.'

When Lewis stepped out of the front door, it seemed wholly fitting that, overnight, the world had been transformed in to an unrecognisable place.

*

Tessa tipped a measure of whisky into her coffee. She was hazy about what had happened in the night. Lewis's phone calls certainly hadn't been a dream. What precisely had he said? *Mum went to bed early and when Dad went up, he found her unconscious. She died before they could get her to the hospital.* Was that it?

She shook her head. *No.* That couldn't be right. Her mother was only sixty-something – nowhere near her three-score-and-ten. And she would have told them if there was anything wrong with her. She wouldn't sneak away like that, without giving them a chance to prepare themselves. That would be an act of appalling selfishness.

Tessa removed two letters from her desk drawer. Taking them, and the bottle of whisky, into her bedroom, she climbed back into her unmade bed, the mound of blankets still holding traces of warmth from the night. She leaned against the pillows and swigged from the bottle. The sky was overcast, sullen with threatening snow, and she switched on the bedside lamp, holding the sheets of pale blue notepaper up to the light, revealing a semi-transparent watermark. Basildon Bond.

The stationery, in a fancy box, had been a belated birthday gift for her mother. Tessa had been making a flying visit home and had picked it up at the station. It was nothing special, but her mother had been delighted. She'd been particularly taken with the envelopes, lined with royal blue tissue and tied in two bundles, each secured with satin ribbon. 'I'll keep it for best.' Her mother's parsimony and gratitude were exasperating. 'Don't be daft, Mum, I'll get you some more when you've used it all. What are "best" letters anyway?' That was a couple of years ago but she would wager a hundred pounds that the box was still in the top left-hand drawer of the sideboard, and that no more than half a dozen sheets had gone from the pad.

Following the furore over the book, Tessa had negotiated

an uneasy peace with Lewis. They'd written to each other and spoken on the phone several times and she was confident that, in time, they would get back on their old footing. But her father had not budged an inch.

Then, two months ago, the first envelope had arrived, tissue paper rustling beneath her finger as she'd eased open the flap.

17th December 1977

Dear Tessa,
I just wanted to wish you a very happy Christmas and to send you my love. You are never far from my thoughts.
A new year would be the perfect time for us all to make a fresh start. I'm praying that your father will reconsider but he's a proud man and it is not easy for him to back down. I keep reminding myself that he's doing this to protect me. All I want is for us all to get back to normal.
Take care. Love from Mum
P.S. Dad must never know that I have written to you.

There was no address at the top of the page but Tessa had heard, from Lewis, that their mother was, once again, a patient in the local psychiatric hospital. Letter writing would unquestionably be easier away from her husband's surveillance but what had prompted her to write? The clue lay in the first sentence. Christmas – when the past, lurking in every carol and strand of tinsel, threatened to spring out and deliver a below-the-belt blow.

Tessa had wanted to shake her mother, to yell at her *stand up to him*. He'd brainwashed her, and everyone who knew her, into believing that she was incompetent, systematically camouflaging his cruelty with attentiveness.

She'd envisaged her mother, tiptoeing along drab hospital corridors, apologising to the doctors for taking their time; to the nurses for putting them to any trouble. Prompted by this thought, she'd sent her parents a Christmas card – a non-committal card, depicting a robin on a snowy log. She'd addressed it to both of them and signed it simply 'Tessa'.

The second letter had turned up two weeks ago.

24ᵗʰ January 1978

Dearest Tess,
I have done all I can but your father will not change his mind. Lewis tells me you two are in touch again. You were always close and I know that, whatever happens, you will support each other. It's a great comfort to me. Good luck with your writing. You were such a clever little girl. I am so sorry for everything. This isn't how I wanted it to end.
Ever and always
your loving Mother xx

On re-reading, this message, delivered in her mother's girlish handwriting, was unambiguous. Tessa had chosen to read it as an acceptance of separation but it was clearly a leave-taking. Until today there had been the possibility – no matter how slight – that the Swinburne family, all five, might be reunited. But now it could never happen because they would be at least one short.

Tessa began to cry. How dare her mother give up on them? What right did she have to decide that it had ended? She took several gulps of whisky and flopped back against the pillows, closing her eyes, waiting for the alcohol to take effect. Turning on to her side, she drew her knees up to her chin and pulled the blankets over her head.

The council had already gritted Medway Avenue but, if it kept on snowing, Cranwell Road would soon become impassable. It was the steepest hill for miles and children had turned up from all over, equipped with toboggans, tin trays, plastic sheeting – anything that would slide – hell-bent on transforming Cranwell Road into the Cresta Run. The whole place echoed with shrill voices and the sound of shovels scraping on garden paths.

Lewis left his car at the bottom of the hill. On his precarious ascent he passed a growing battalion of snowmen and was caught in the barrage of snowballs between opposing armies of children. When he reached the top he saw his neighbour, clearing a path through the snow on the pavement. The family hadn't long moved in and they seemed pleasant enough but, apart from occasional comments on the weather and the vagaries of the dustbin collection service, Lewis hadn't had much to do with them.

The man stopped work and leaned on the handle of his spade, wiping his nose with the back of a gloved hand. His breath condensed and dissipated as, open mouthed, he gasped, 'I'm obviously … nowhere near as fit … as I thought I was.'

This man – *Dave? Yes, Dave* – was the first person, apart from family and hospital staff, that Lewis had spoken to since his mother's death. It seemed inconceivable that he bore no tell-tale mark, no scar, no stain to indicate that he had been struck by tragedy. It was up to him to say something but how could he broach the subject to this stranger, nice bloke though he might be, whose only concern was six inches of fresh, clean snow?

Lewis pointed to the trench running through the snow. 'You're putting me to shame.'

After the cutting wind, the house, even without a fire, felt pleasantly warm. He changed into corduroy trousers, woolly socks and a thick sweater, then made himself a mug of drinking chocolate and a jam sandwich.

Slumped on the sofa in the breakfast room, fatigue swept over him and he dipped into sleep. *Newton's First Law of Motion.* His head jerked forward and he roused then dipped again. *A body remains in a state of rest until an external force acts upon it.* Jerk then dip. *Body. Would that be everybody? At rest.* Jerk. *Rest in peace.* Awake. Dip. *Peace. Police.* Jerk. Dip. *Force.*

The doorbell woke him. For a second, the world was at peace then his haphazard thoughts consolidated into a wrecking ball, smashing him into consciousness with jagged recollection.

Dave stood in the porch, a spade in either hand, offering to help clear the pavement outside the house. Lewis guessed that he was keen to strengthen the neighbourly connection and the weather conditions offered the perfect opportunity.

'It won't take long and, if you haven't already eaten, you're more than welcome to join us for a bite. Casserole. Nothing fancy.'

Afterwards, Lewis realised that he couldn't have been thinking straight. Exhaustion, probably. And shock. But, at the time, getting togged up against the smarting cold, engaging in honest labour and looking forward to a hot meal shared with new friends seemed not such an inexcusable way to spend this exceptional day.

Chapter 25

'I'll come with you,' Dan offered.

'No. God, no.' He was driving Tessa mad, fussing as though she were an invalid. 'It's not as if you ever met her.'

Why did he put up with her? No matter how consistently she let him down, how offhand and bad-tempered she was, he came back for more. It seemed that taming her had become a matter of honour to him, a self-imposed mission. He was the white-hatted cowboy, determined to break the wild mustang.

'No, but I thought you might like a—'

'A what? A chaperone? A bodyguard?'

'Sshhh. Sshhh.' He kissed her mouth and stroked the nape of her neck. 'When this is over, we'll go away. Find some sun. Get you mended.'

The requirement for a post-mortem, combined with a backlog of burials following an influenza outbreak, meant that it was ten days before Peggy Swinburne's funeral went ahead. Lewis phoned frequently to keep her abreast of events.

'Is it grim there?' she asked.

'Not grim exactly. I feel … unsettled. Like I'm sickening for something. Waiting for the spots to appear. Will I or won't I succumb.' He sighed. 'Does that make sense?'

'None whatsoever.' She waited a second before asking, 'D'*you* think Mum killed herself?'

When he didn't reply she prompted, 'Lewis?'

'It's pointless to speculate. We'll only get ourselves in a state and we'll know the answer soon enough.'

'You're talking to *me*, remember, not giving a statement to the press. Aren't we already "in a state"? I'm asking you what you *think*?'

But he wouldn't be drawn.

'Should I come down?'

She half-wanted him to say *Yes, jump on the next train, I can't manage without you. And I forgive you for writing the book.* But he told her again that there was nothing to be done and really no need for her to come before the funeral.

'It's best if I keep out of the way, is that what you're trying to say? You're probably right. Dad phoned me, by the way. I suppose you had a finger in that.'

'What did he say?'

'Nothing much. It was terribly civilised. I had the feeling that Uncle Frank was hovering nearby, making sure Dad didn't have a go at me. Oh, and he told me how wonderful you were. Lewis, the rock.'

Tessa had known that she and her father would have to speak sooner or later, and, although she didn't look on it as a victory, she was relieved that he'd been the one to crack. During the brief conversation, they had both been on their guard, keeping the exchange factual, avoiding the unanswered question that was hanging over them all.

'How's he coping? I suppose he's got used to fending for himself over the past couple of months.'

'He's managing. I offered to stay there, or for him to come up here, but he refused. He says he's eating and sleeping okay. He's moved in to your room by the way. I expect he can't face—'

'*My* room? You still call it that.' Her voice softened. 'Anyway, how are you?'

'Oh … you know. The Head said I needn't go back to work until after the funeral but, to be honest, I feel better if I have something to do. Mind you, that's got its own drawbacks. Everyone's either steering clear or offering to make me cups of sweet tea.'

'Yes, Dan's been force-feeding me Typhoo.'

'So you two are still …?'

'Apparently. I've no idea why. We're not at all suited.'

'Could it be that he loves you?'

'No. Impossible. Anyway, love's a conspiracy to sell diamond rings and big white dresses. Any fool knows that.'

Lewis laughed. 'God, I've missed you.'

When Tessa told Rundle that her mother was dead, and it was possible that she had killed herself, he poured them each a double whisky and raised his glass. 'Here's to free will and self-determination.'

Any suggestion that theirs could be a casual friendship had been dispelled on her first visit to Brighton. After a perfunctory glance at the sea and a drink in Rundle's 'local' they had ended up in his bed. The following week he'd come to London but Tessa was on pins the whole time, anxious in case Dan turned up or one of her neighbours spotted him leaving her flat to catch the early morning train home.

Their liaison was based on sex. To pretend otherwise would have been absurd. Rundle fascinated her. Startlingly good-looking, in her eyes at least, he was intelligent and well-informed, yet he seemed happy to work as a garage hand, and it occurred to her that he must be reserving his *true* self for something other than his job. If he had friends, she never met them. She once asked whether he kept in touch with Mike Stoddy, or anyone else from the old days. 'Why would I do that?' was his reply.

Dan was a considerate lover. Competent would be a fair

description. Tessa was the one who orchestrated their love-making. But Rundle – he liked her using his surname. 'Like Mellors,' he grinned – needed no instruction. Their bodies spoke directly to each other, and not always politely. Whilst Dan *gave*, Rundle *took*. Sometimes it was necessary to conceal a bruise on her thigh or a weal at her wrist.

Rundle didn't talk much and when he did it was about a film he'd seen or a book he was reading. His observations were acute and incisive but it was as if his sphere of interest was limited to a fraction of what went on in the world. He shunned nostalgia, saying that the past no longer existed; that dwelling on it, or in it, dulled the senses. He was unyielding in this. Tessa wondered if, as a child, something unspeakable had happened to him and that looking back was, for him, a dangerous business. As for the future, he said that thinking about it was a waste of brainpower; guessing what lay ahead was as senseless as betting on a horse. 'Look how often the favourite loses.' Once or twice, hoping that his resolve had been loosened by alcohol or marijuana, she tried to tease out his history, but she never got anywhere.

The wind swung back to the south-west. By the end of the week only filthy slush and the smut-flecked remains of snowmen proved that it had snowed. For Lewis, its immaculate loveliness had been a distraction during which the town had come to an enchanting standstill. The problems of travel; of keeping the house warm; of procuring vital supplies had dissolved with the melting snow and there was nothing left to divert him from the funeral and whatever lay beyond.

Andrea said she would come to the service. He knew she would. She'd always been one to do the right thing and, despite their separation, Peggy Swinburne had been her mother-in-law and the girls' grandmother.

Whenever he went to visit his daughters, they were on their

guard, treating him like a benevolent uncle who brought them toys when it wasn't their birthday. He was welcome at any time – that had never been disputed – but Andrea wasn't keen on his having the girls to stay at Cranwell Lodge. 'I'm not sure you could cope. Jane's still a baby. And Sarah's only just settling at her new school. I wouldn't want anything to disturb that. It'll be different when they're a bit older.' He didn't argue. He made the tiresome journey every few weeks. Occasionally he'd taken his parents. When was the last time they'd all gone? It must have been a matter of days before his mother was admitted to hospital. It had been a gruelling trip and they were all frazzled by the time they got home but, in the light of events, he was glad that he'd made the effort.

'I could bring the children down on the train. Just stay one night,' Andrea suggested. 'It might be a comfort for you. And your father. Mum's going to look after them when I come for the funeral.'

Children about the place *might* be comforting but, when Lewis thought it through, it seemed a hazardous step. He was vulnerable at present. Yesterday he'd passed a dead cat in the gutter, sodden fur sleek against its lean body, tongue protruding between sharp white teeth, and before he knew it he was crying. Any show of tenderness by Andrea could scupper him altogether. He daren't risk it, not now that he and Kirsty were back together.

Within a few days of Andrea's leaving Kirsty Ross's Christmas card had arrived, complete with invitation. *'Come to Bristol for tea – I'm always around at weekends. We could go to the zoo. It would be lovely to meet you all.'*

Lewis had phoned straight away, explaining his situation. 'I'm so sorry, Lewis.' Then, with the candour that was so particular to her, she'd asked, 'It wasn't anything to do with me, was it?' He'd reassured her, saying that things hadn't been right between him and his wife for years, and that it really wasn't such a catastrophe. Not long after, he'd invited Kirsty to go with him to an orchestral concert in Colston Hall. It had seemed a level-headed, grown-up way to go about things. They met in a pub and, within minutes of being together, they had given their tickets to the young couple standing next to them, preferring to spend the evening in a second-rate Italian restaurant on Whiteladies Road, eating bad food and getting to know each other again.

On the morning of the funeral, Tessa caught an early train from Paddington. On arrival she hung about in the station buffet concerned that, were she to get to Salisbury Road too soon, she and her father would have time to fall out. This was bound to happen at some point during her visit but it would be better if it were after the service. The nicotine-yellowed cafeteria, echoing with garbled announcements from the platform beyond its steamed up windows, became her temporary sanctuary. Food. Warmth. Anonymity. It was tempting to stay here for the rest of the day, harming no one and coming to no harm. Who would guess, or even care, that the skinny young woman in black, covertly lacing her coffee with something from a screw-topped bottle, was about to attend her mother's funeral?

When she reached the house, her father was courteous. He kissed her cheek and hugged her but his embrace was mechanical. 'Tessa. Thanks for coming.'

Thanks for coming?

'Where's Lewis?' she asked.

'Getting the coal in, I think.'

'Anything I can do, Dad?'

'No. It's all under control. Ready for the off.'

So bright and bloody breezy, but she knew why. Her father had transformed himself in to an automaton, primed to spew out stock phrases and perform commonplace tasks. It was his only chance of getting through the day.

Her mother's absence was manifest in what was missing that morning. There were no fairy cakes cooling on the tarnished wire rack in the kitchen; no freshly ironed clothes heaped on the corner of the table, waiting to be taken upstairs; no bunch of mint in the brown jug on the windowsill. And the whole place *smelled* wrong. Again it was a *lack* that struck her – no hint of lavender furniture polish or the cheap eau de cologne that her mother dabbed on her hanky; no traces of last night's meal in the air; no smell of bleach in the bathroom.

Tessa pushed the living room door ajar and peeped in. Her mother's armchair was empty, the velvet cushions set at a neat angle, without trace of indentation.

Lewis appeared, dumping the brass coal scuttle next to the grate and holding out his arms.

'It's so good to see you,' he whispered.

The smell of his skin and his words of greeting released her tears. 'Shit. I was doing okay until I saw you.'

He handed her a white handkerchief, soft from years of washing. 'You look thin. And pale.'

'It's the bereaved daughter look. Very "in" at the moment.' She tilted her head back, still clinging to him. 'And if we're going to get personal, you're going grey.'

'Are you surprised?' Then he touched the bruise near the corner of her right eye. 'How did you get that?'

She drew away, dragging her hair forward, concealing the yellowing bruise, not answering his question. 'It'll be okay for me to stay at Cranwell Lodge tonight, won't it? I can't cope with Dad and this house at the moment.' She paused. 'That sounds selfish but he'll have to get used to being alone sooner or later, won't he?'

'That's fine. I think Dad's going to Uncle Frank's for a couple of nights.'

'What about Andrea?' The last thing Tessa wanted was to share Lewis with her sister-in-law.

'She's up at the house now, sorting through a few things. She's going to come back for a cuppa after the service then catch a train home.' Lewis seemed keen to change the subject. 'You should have something to eat. We don't want you passing out.'

'I wouldn't mind a brandy. Or is that too outrageous?'

They raided the sideboard and found the dregs of a bottle of brandy left from a Christmas past.

Lewis watched as Tessa downed the neat spirit. 'I don't know how you can drink that stuff.' He tugged his ear. 'It was a relief to get the post-mortem results.'

'A relief for whom?' she asked.

Lewis shot her a quizzical glance. 'All of us, of course.'

'I can understand why Dad's relieved. It lets him off the hook, doesn't it? No blame, no shame.'

'You sound as though you'd be happier if she *had* killed herself.'

'I think I would.'

'Christ, Tessa, that's a dreadful thing to say.'

'She was an unhappy woman who never asserted herself. Or rather she was never *allowed* to assert herself. I was crossing my fingers that, for once in her life, she'd taken matters in to her own hands. Decided that enough was enough and got the hell out.'

He shook his head. 'You're sick.'

'And you're sentimental,' she countered.

Members of the immediate family had been instructed to assemble at the house before following the hearse in the hired limousines. Andrea arrived first, stationing herself at Lewis's side, setting out cups and saucers on the kitchen table, resolutely establishing her right to be there whilst simultaneously drawing

275

attention to Tessa's laziness. She was polite but disapproving and Tessa was glad she no longer had to bother with her.

Frank Swinburne turned up next, with a couple whom she didn't recognise. It turned out that the man was her mother's cousin, from Oswestry. 'I haven't seen Peg since we were young'uns. She was a real scream. Played the piano accordion. And she was a lovely dancer.'

A picture of her mother, fox trotting around the room, weighty accordion strapped to her chest, sprang up before her.

'He must have come to the wrong funeral,' she whispered to her brother and she began to giggle, clamping her hand over her mouth, turning away so that her father and the others couldn't see.

Lewis caught her arm, steering her out of the kitchen and in to the living room. He shut the door.

'What is the matter with you?' he demanded. 'You might have the decency to pretend, at least for one day, that you care.'

'Pretend? Is that what you want me to do? Don't you see, that's what's ruined this family. Pretending. Baby gone missing? Let's pretend he never existed. Mother round the bend? Put a brave face on it. Daughter gone off the rails? Sshhh. Let's not mention it. Now *you've* started. Wife and children left you? Keep a stiff upper lip. But, at all costs, never tell anyone what you *feel*.'

Lewis slapped her across the cheek then, before she had time to register shock or pain, he was holding her. 'Sorry. That was unforgivable.'

'No, it's okay. It's exactly my point. You *should* go with your instincts.' She stood on tiptoe and kissed his chin. 'It bloody hurt, though.'

Lewis drew in a deep breath then exhaled slowly. 'Dad was being truthful when he told you precisely what he thought about your book. And that didn't solve anything, did it?'

Trust Lewis to identify the flaw in her argument.

'Only because he wasn't prepared to listen to *my* side of it. He's a bigot. He lives in a one-sided world. And, if you must know, I couldn't help laughing because you have to admit that the idea of Mum playing an accordion is hilarious. A shame we didn't hear about it when she was alive. We could all have laughed together.'

The hearse, sleek and menacing, drew up outside the house. Tessa squeezed her brother's hand. 'Come on. Let's get this over with.'

Chapter 26

BY THE TIME THEY LEFT THE HOUSE, the roofs and pavements were slick from a steady drizzle, and the pewter sky seemed no more than chimney-height above the ground.

The funeral service was a dreary affair, devoid of passion. The vicar had called at the house, earlier in the week, to discuss it with Lewis and his father. He had never met Peggy Swinburne although, several times during their conversation, he mentioned 'the sad events of the past'. They had attempted to paint a picture of her as wife and mother but, when it came to it, the vicar did no more than string together a litany of clichés in a one-size-fits-all ceremony. It was so unspecific that Lewis wondered whether the man had prepared something else but lost his nerve at the last minute. If that were the case, he should have tried harder to convey a life tarnished by sorrow. Wasn't it his obligation, not only to proclaim his God's triumphs but also to come clean about His failures?

Lewis and Tessa stood either side of their father, Lewis nearest the aisle, within three paces of the coffin which rested on a trestle arrangement in front of the altar. As a child he'd dreamed of having 'X-ray eyes', giving him the ability to see through solid surfaces. Today he was glad that his gaze could not penetrate the shiny box. Nevertheless he could not help picturing his mother, lying in the suffocating darkness, dressed in the powder blue suit – her 'best' – which he had delivered to the undertaker a few days ago.

There had been pitifully few people to notify of her death. No bunch of old friends, no workmates, no holiday acquaintances. Occasionally she had reminisced about school days, mentioning a Joan or Helen who had been sporty or gone on to greater things but, checking through the sparse entries in her address book, it was clear that none of them kept in touch. He was surprised, therefore, to see that there were perhaps thirty people in the congregation. Neighbours and work colleagues – both his and his father's – had turned out on that dismal afternoon to support the survivors rather than to mourn the dead. Not a *vast* crowd but enough voices to carry the hymns, enough eyes to fill with tears as the coffin passed back down the aisle on its final journey.

Most of the faces were familiar, with one notable exception. An elderly man, maybe in his seventies, was sitting towards the rear of the church. When the service was over and they were milling aimlessly on the pavement, the man stood separate from the rest, motionless and watchful. Wearing a dark grey overcoat, he had a military bearing, his black brogues shining like two enormous lumps of coal, and, for a second, Lewis wondered whether his mother did, after all, have *one* friend of her very own.

'Who's that?' he whispered to Tessa, nodding towards the man.

She shrugged.

Lewis went across to him and held out his hand. 'Good of you to come, Mr…?'

The man, unsmiling, took Lewis's hand and shook it emphatically. 'Hulbert. Brian Hulbert.'

Twenty-odd years on, the ex-detective was still a bulky figure and he hadn't lost that air of guarded vigilance and reticent mistrust which had permeated the house whenever he turned up. But he was no longer the sinister ogre that he had seemed to a small boy.

Hulbert, seeing Lewis's ill-concealed surprise, explained, 'I always read the obituaries in the local paper, sir, and when I saw the announcement I felt I had to come. Pay my respects.' He shook his head. 'It was a tragedy. A real tragedy. My failure to find your brother is the biggest regret of my career with the Force.'

All the time he was speaking, his eyes scanned the dispersing congregation and Lewis knew that the man was, even then, hoping to catch a glimpse of something that would shed light on the mystery. Lewis wasn't sure if he believed the bit about 'paying respects'. He wouldn't have labelled Hulbert as the respectful type – more a remorseless blunt instrument, battering away to achieve a result. He was *absolutely* sure, though, that Hulbert was the last person that his father would want to see today and he positioned himself so as to obscure Dick Swinburne's view of the interloper.

Before he could think of a way to get rid of the man, Tessa joined them and he was forced to make the introduction. He watched her face, knowing that she must be feeling as disturbed as he was and admiring her skill in concealing it.

'I've been following your career with interest, Miss Swinburne. Even as a child you had a very vivid imagination. I'm not in the least surprised that you've turned into a writer. To be honest, I don't generally read novels. I always say that truth is stranger than fiction, but I must admit your latest book caused me to re-examine my opinion. Fascinating … quite fascinating.'

There was an uneasy silence whilst they absorbed the implications of Hulbert's compliment.

Then Tessa gave a scornful laugh. 'Don't forget *Lost* is filed in the fiction section of the library, Mr Hulbert. I wouldn't go reading too much into it if I were you. Anyway, didn't you say you were retired?'

Hulbert bared his dentures in the parody of a smile. 'Point taken, Miss.'

'Are you going to come back to the house, Mr Hulbert? Join us for a cup of tea and a ham sandwich? Catch up on … things?'

Lewis recognised the sarcasm in his sister's voice but there was nothing he could do to stop her and she continued, 'It would be a chance to interrogate the witnesses again. Take a few more statements. Cast a few more aspersions.'

Hulbert raised his eyebrows, 'No need, Miss. *Someone…*' he stared at Tessa, 'has already cast plenty of aspersions.'

Lewis laid a hand on his sister's arm, determined to avoid the nastiness which threatened to develop. 'Sorry, Mr Hulbert. We're all a bit strung up.'

'No need to apologise, sir,' he spoke slowly and with a suggestion of condescension, 'it's perfectly understandable.'

As the cars pulled away Lewis turned to watch Hulbert standing impassively outside the church.

Even the lacklustre vicar could do nothing to diminish the enormity of the graveside ritual. Tessa had seen dozens of coffins lowered into dozens of graves in dozens of films. *Ashes to ashes.* She'd heard those words quoted, sung and misappropriated, but she had never really, *really* seen or heard. Coming home and witnessing the effects of her mother's death, watching her father's brave agony and her brother's bewilderment, had been draining enough but, by the time they laid Peggy Swinburne to rest beneath the sticky red clay, Tessa felt battered. Her mother's body – the blue-grey eyes, the cheek with the black mole, her restless fingers, her heart – was about to be dumped in a hole in the ground. Left to rot. It was appalling.

Every now and again her father drew in a deep breath and pulled his shoulders back, shutting his eyes then opening them wide as if, this time, he would wake up. The grass was sodden, the ground uneven, and he almost lost his footing. Pain flicked across his face as he took his full weight on his bad leg and Tessa edged closer to him, slipping her arm through his, finding unforeseen consolation in his fleeting smile.

When it was done, eagerness to escape the desolation of the cemetery overrode any reluctance to desert her mother. The three of them, along with Frank Swinburne, travelled back to the house together, the luxurious upholstery of the car's interior encasing them in its mournful cocoon, isolating them from the outside world.

They sat in the breakfast room at Cranwell Lodge, firelight sending shadows scurrying across the walls.

'I see you've changed the furniture,' Tess said.

'Yes. Andrea's taken a lot of stuff and I've been picking up a few odds and ends at house sales.' He patted the arm of the battered leather sofa and nodded to an antique dresser where another dresser had once stood.

They sat gazing into the fire, the only sounds the ticking of the clock on the mantelpiece and the crack of burning logs.

Tessa was the first to speak. 'That was pretty grisly.'

'Did you think it wouldn't be?' Her brother's question held no criticism, merely curiosity.

'I hadn't thought about it much. The actual burial, I mean. Then, when they lowered the coffin into the grave I felt this huge surge of … not love … pity, sympathy, empathy for Dad.'

'That's good, isn't it?'

'I don't know about "good". It's bloody confusing. I've made it my lifelong duty to dislike him, so I don't know where that leaves me.'

'There are lots of people you can transfer your dislike to. Cliff Richard. Edward Heath. The man who lives over the road. All worthy of your loathing.'

'I'll go for Noel Edmonds, if that's okay with you.'

The logs cracked and settled, sending sparks spiralling up the chimney.

'I think I'll call in at Uncle Frank's on my way to the station. See Dad. I'll probably feel different about him in the cold light of day.'

'You're going back tomorrow, then?'

'Yes.' There was nothing, no meetings or signings or work in progress, summoning her back to London but escaping from this place had become a habit. Besides she needed to examine the shift in her feelings towards her father – best done at a distance.

Whilst her brother was in the kitchen, preparing mugs of drinking chocolate, Tessa wondered what his life must be like, alone in this house. He probably spent most of his weekends with Kirsty Ross, and more time at school than was necessary. Even so, that left a significant number of solitary hours. And now there would be another man – her father – rattling around in another ghost-filled house, washing his own socks and plumping undisturbed cushions.

Lewis returned with a tray.

'Andrea looked well,' Tessa said, hoping Lewis would reveal how the land lay between him and his wife.

'Yes.' He raised his eyebrows. 'It's not your style to be oblique.'

She laughed. 'You're right. I must be going through one of my rare diplomatic phases. So. D'you want to tell me what's going on? I'm beginning to suspect that my brother is a bit of a one for the ladies. Lotte sends love and condolences, by the way.' She hadn't, but a reminder of his indiscretion might loosen his tongue.

'Andrea wants a divorce,' he said.

'Do you?'

'I suppose so.'

'Suppose so? Surely you want to marry Kirsty.'

'We haven't got that far yet.'

She snorted. 'Heaven forbid you should rush in to anything. After all, you've only known the woman for … what …?'

'Sixteen years.'

They sipped drinking chocolate, its sweetness and the firelight softening the edges of that harsh day.

'How did you – *why* did you – decide to accept this house? Didn't you love her?' Tessa asked.

Lewis stared into the flames and she thought he wasn't going to answer. Finally he gave a deep sigh and closed his eyes, resting his head against the back of the sofa. 'I did. Do. But nothing seemed clear-cut at the time.'

'You were very young.'

'Mmmm.' He cleared his throat. 'Actually I tossed a coin.'

Tessa laughed. 'What?'

'If you remember, I had one month to make my decision. To be fair, Dad didn't say much apart from the killer: "Your mother would love it if you lived nearby." But I couldn't ignore them. Mum had just come through a really bad patch. Dad was having trouble with his hip. He couldn't mow the lawn or doing anything off a ladder—'

'There are such things as gardeners and odd-job men,' she whispered. 'And what did Kirsty have to say?'

'Nothing. Only that the choice had to be completely mine or I would spend the rest of my life blaming her.'

'What? Instead of blaming yourself? But if she loved you …'

'Kirsty's love involves opening the cage not closing it.'

'Piffle,' Tessa snorted. 'Love is about doing everything in your power – playing dirty if you have to – to hang on to the one you love.'

He reached out with his foot and gently kicked hers. 'That's the Tessa Swinburne version of love.'

'Mmmm. So what about this coin tossing malarkey? You are having me on?'

'Not at all. You see, each and every time you toss a coin, there's an equal chance of it coming down heads or tails. Theoretically I could toss a coin a hundred, a thousand, a million times and it could be heads every throw.'

'That's ridiculous.'

'No. It's the theory of probability. So I said to myself, I'll toss this half-crown – we were pre-decimalisation then – ten times, once for each year that I have to live in Cranwell Lodge. Ten heads on the trot and I'll choose the house.'

'And?'

'Ten heads. Eleven actually.' He took a hanky from his trouser pocket and blew his nose. 'I've tried the same thing dozens of times since and the most I've got is seven.'

Tessa contemplated her brother's revelation, still uncertain if he was making the whole thing up. 'Well I'm delighted to hear that your life's been decided by sound mathematical theory. I'd hate to think you'd sold your soul to the Devil or anything as unscientific as that.'

Lewis rested his hands on his knees and leaned forward. 'Yes. Mathematics, and the assumption – incorrect as it turned out – that Kirsty would chuck up the Newcastle job and come back here. I was pretty pissed off with her for a while.'

'You would be. And that's when Andrea came along.'

'Yep. You've got it.'

'Blimey.'

She leaned against him. 'It'll be a doddle from here on, Lewis. You've done your ten years' penance. Divorce Andrea, sell the house and disappear into the sunset. Or Bristol if that's where happiness lies. Dad'll manage. And no more lame ducks – literally or metaphorically.'

Lewis crouched to put a shovelful of coal on the fire then placed a couple of logs on top of the smouldering pile. It was getting on for midnight but neither of them made a move to go to bed. Tessa slid off the sofa to sit, knees drawn up, on the hearth rug, her face prickling with the heat, her back cold from the draught.

'Got anything to drink?'

'No.' He answered too quickly.

She sighed. 'You've got to stop trying to save me from myself.'

Pushing herself up, she went to the dresser, opening the doors to the lower cupboards. The bottles stashed inside caught the dancing firelight. While he was out of the room, looking for clean glasses, she opened the right-hand dresser drawer. It was too dark to see what it held and she ran her hand over its contents, disappointed to find metallic objects, cold to the touch. Screwdriver, pliers, hammer.

They sipped whisky and grew sleepy, talking about their mother, dredging up and assembling memories of her, realising what disparate mothers theirs had been. Lewis's, gentle and sensitive, thoughtful and accepting; Tessa's, vague and exasperating, timid and dull.

'I wonder how Dad would describe *his* Peggy Swinburne.' Lewis spoke softly, staring into the fire.

And then, at the very close of that day, they got around to Gordon.

'I had some stupid idea he might show up. Come wandering out of the past. There was a bloke sitting at the back. Gingery hair—'

'That was Dave Brown, my neighbour,' Lewis interjected.

She closed her eyes, seeing a tiny lock of non-coloured hair at the nape of a silky-soft neck. The smell of baby – talcum powder and vomit – snagged her memory. 'D'you still think he's alive?'

'If he is, I don't want to know. It would be unbearable to think that Mum had missed him.'

Tessa woke sometime in the night. She was lying on a sofa, an eiderdown tucked around her. The fire was still alight, dull embers glowing red amongst the spent coals, a wire guard in front of it to prevent stray sparks. Her head felt fuzzy, and it took several seconds to think where she was, and why.

Chapter 27

SHE REMEMBERED HEARING LEWIS WHISPER, 'I'm off now,' then burrowing back under the eiderdown. Next time she roused, the quilt had slipped and her feet were icy. She dressed quickly, her clothes damp on her skin. Grabbing a coat from the back of the kitchen door, she pulled it around her, shivering while she waited for the kettle to boil. It was shocking, considering that it had been the day of her mother's funeral, but she'd slept more soundly than she had for months.

The house smelled sulphurous from last night's coal fire. She had never been alone here and, although surrounded by evidence of Lewis – slippers, discarded newspapers, his annotations on the calendar – she felt edgy without him, half expecting Mrs Channing's ghost to spring out of a wardrobe. Strong coffee helped overcome her uneasiness and, clutching her mug, she tiptoed from room to room, spying on her brother's life.

Lewis had it in him to be a monk or, at best, a lighthouse keeper and, true to form, he had chosen to sleep in the smallest bedroom. But when Kirsty stayed did they cling to each other in this spartan cell, making neat, mathematical love? *One and one make two*. There wasn't enough space for anything more expansive.

She crossed the landing to the bedroom that he'd once shared with Andrea. This was now a workroom – a large table near the window, littered with tools and bits of balsa wood, tubes of glue and an anglepoise lamp.

It wasn't all that hard to understand why Andrea had gone, but it was a mystery why level-headed Miss Ross had come back to take another shot at it.

The taxi dropped Tessa at Frank Swinburne's address. Flat-roofed, surrounded by municipal-style planting, the three-storey block was a place where people without much money or imagination would live. She located the stairway leading to Flat Fifteen, on the top floor. Before ringing the bell, she dragged her fingers through her hair and made sure her coat was neatly buttoned.

Her uncle came to the door. Frank Swinburne was two years his brother's senior but looked younger. Whilst her father's hair had thinned at the crown and was entirely grey, Frank's hair was suspiciously brown, springing vigorously from a precise side parting. He always looked smart and full of vim, as if he were permanently on his way to a party. He wore snazzy shirts with sharp creases down the sleeves; his shoes shone and he smelled of tangy aftershave. There was something of the bright-eyed fox about him.

Although he'd always lived in the town, he'd had numerous different addresses. As a child, visiting him in this place and that, she'd reasoned that his job as a travelling something-or-another required that his home, too, be peripatetic. By the time she was old enough to ask, his appeal had evaporated and there were more interesting things to occupy her.

After Cranwell Lodge, the flat felt cramped and the ceilings oppressively low. The uncoordinated furnishings contrasted starkly with the dapper man. Two chintz-covered armchairs; a splay-legged coffee table, its stained surface evidence of careless use; a contemporary sofa, upholstered in mid-blue Dralon, a tartan blanket draped across its back; a metal standard lamp with a fringed shade; prints of anonymous landscapes haphazardly ranged across cream walls. It was as startling as undressing a smartly-dressed woman only to reveal grubby, mismatching underwear.

Her father was sitting on the sofa, staring at the swirling pattern on the carpet, his hands clasping his knees, arms braced. He jumped up when he saw her. They hugged – a proper hug this time.

'Did you sleep, Dad? You must have been exhausted.'

'I did, believe it or not. I think Frank must have slipped something in my tea.'

Frank hovered like an overprotective nurse. 'Have you had breakfast, Tess? Most important meal of the day. How does it go? Breakfast like a king, lunch like a prince, dine like a pauper.'

'Yes, thanks,' she lied. 'I'm on my way to the station and I just popped in to see Dad.' She willed her uncle to leave them alone together but he stood his ground, wittering on, until she was forced to say, 'I wouldn't mind a coffee, if it's not too much trouble.'

Once he was gone, she asked her father gently, 'Anything you want me to do Dad? Any sorting? I can catch a later train.'

He patted the back of her hand, 'Thanks, love, but it's a bit soon to think about that. Best to let things settle.'

Love. How long, if ever, since he'd called her that?

'Well, I can come back any time and give you a hand.'

He nodded and shut his eyes, his mouth clamped in an awkward grimace as he held back his tears. She wanted to talk about her mother; to find out if at least the last day of her life had been a happy one. But Frank was back in a flash with a tray of coffee and biscuits, putting an end to their intimacy.

Before leaving, she went to the bathroom. Like the rest of the place it was serviceable but not much more. The towels were threadbare, the bath, clean but basic, the mirror above the washbasin, spattered with toothpaste. Her uncle was clearly not out to impress visitors. Way back when they were kids, he used to bring women, whom she'd assumed were his girlfriends, to family get-togethers – but he never brought the same woman twice. After Gordon, there had been no more family parties and, although he called regularly at the house, he was always alone. It was odd that such a trim, gregarious man should end up on his own, living in rented accommodation.

The phone rang and, through the flimsy wall, she could hear her uncle's voice rumbling on. The laundry basket – pale blue rattan, flicked with gold paint, just like the one Gran used to have – caught her eye. She lifted the lid. Shirt. Fawn socks. Aertex vest. And pushed down the side, a magazine. She pulled it out, amused that a man of sixty-odd, living alone, felt compelled to hide his smutty magazines from his brother.

It took a second or two to register that the picture on the cover was that of a young man, scantily clad in a tight, white vest, a leather pouch barely concealing his genitals.

Lewis didn't know what to make of Tessa's reconciliation with their father. It was Tessa all over, though – instant judgements, melodrama, everything black or white. Whatever had caused it, it was an opportunity for them – his father, Tessa and him – to start again. But, for it to stand a chance of lasting, they must be as honest with each other as he and Kirsty had been.

Lewis had tried to explain to Kirsty why he'd thought that marriage to Andrea would work. He confessed to lack of affection for his daughters – although he still failed to understand it – and to his fling with Lotte Jamieson.

Kirsty had listened, calm, and non-judgemental. 'Maybe you should talk to someone about your feelings for your daughters,' was her only comment.

Kirsty had had two lovers. The first had left her to become

a priest and the second, whom Lewis liked the sound of, had been killed in a road accident. After that she'd thrown herself resolutely into her career. No children. No flings. No lurking skeletons.

His mother's death had made it easier to decide what he should do and his conversation with Tessa had helped. He would, as she advised, sell the house, move to Bristol and, as soon as his divorce came through, marry Kirsty.

But when the time came, he could not bring himself to part with Cranwell Lodge.

'I know it's not rational,' he apologised.

'It wasn't last time, either,' Kirsty replied without bitterness.

They agreed that, rather than leave it empty, vulnerable to squatters and vandalism, they would find a tenant. There were always doctors or lecturers or bank managers like Kirsty's father who needed short-term accommodation. The rent would come in useful but, more importantly, someone would be on the spot, keeping an eye on the house.

Lewis wondered how his father would take the news. It was a bitter truth but he was going to have to face up to life as a widower. At least his job would structure his days and provide social contact. He had plenty of friends – look at the crowd of workmates who turned out for the funeral. Retirement was still four or five years away and by then he would have established a coping strategy.

If Lewis were ever to make the break, it must be now.

The blank sheet in Tessa's typewriter became progressively more intimidating. Her agent and publisher were pushing and she couldn't keep them at bay for much longer. Anxiety bred anxiety and the only time she could put it out of her mind was when she was drunk or with Rundle. When the 'thing' with Rundle started, it had been an adjunct to her London life; a dalliance. He was her 'stick of Brighton rock' – his words. Now he had become the first thing she thought of on waking; the last before she fell asleep. It was an unhealthy state of affairs and she should walk away, yet he made every atom in her body squirm with pleasure. Returning on the train, she would already be counting the hours until she could return.

Lewis and Kirsty came to London for a weekend. Tessa's flat wasn't big enough to entertain guests so they booked in to a small hotel near the British Museum. She quite liked Kirsty – or didn't dislike her – and knew she should be pleased that her brother seemed, finally, to have found the right woman. But seeing them together, so wholesome and respectable, grated.

Lewis invited her and Dan to join them at the theatre. 'Let's have a night on the town. Theatre. Meal. Jazz club. The whole shoot.'

Dan was enthusiastic. 'C'mon, Tess. You don't want to let Lewis down, do you?'

The play – the new Pinter – was worthy but Tessa failed to lose herself in the desolate tale and her attention wandered.

Did Dan ever suspect that she was seeing someone else? He never quizzed her on what she'd been doing or why she'd not been at home to answer his phone call. He did, however, ask how she'd come by the bruises. Usually a vague 'I walked into an open door' or 'I stumbled on the stairs' covered it but, noticing one particularly fierce bruise on her thigh, he'd insisted that she go to the GP. 'Get yourself checked out, Tess, All these falls …'

They had slipped in to the habit of seeing each other a couple of times a week, occasionally meeting up with Dan's arty friends or the Costelloes who were now ensconced in London. Every few months Dan asked her to marry him, or at least move in with him. At first her refusals had wounded him and he'd spent hours trying to make her change her mind. But these days his proposal and her rebuff were no more noteworthy than call and response between vicar and congregation.

'I was thinking,' said Lewis as they climbed the steps from the jazz club, 'Why don't the four of us grab a week away? We could find some sun. Spain or the South of France. I'm off for two weeks at Easter.' He looked at Tessa. 'Come on. It's been a pretty dismal six months.'

They settled for Nice. Jay contacted a painter friend who had a flat there which he rented out at a reasonable price. At the last minute, he and Liza decided to join them. With Duffy and Cezanne present in every vista and the scent of orange blossom in the air, they spent a week in a charming apartment a few yards from the Mediterranean.

Tessa was fascinated to see that, away from home, her brother became less hidebound. His conversation was witty and his French more than passable. Kirsty evidently took a hand in choosing his clothes and, with suntanned face and hair a little longer than he normally wore it, he looked rather dashing. They all got along well, particularly Lewis and Dan. Inevitably, after a few glasses of rough red wine, there was a little harmless flirting – Dan with Kirsty, Liza with Lewis, Jay with everyone.

'You look wonderful,' Dan said, watching Tessa as she dried herself after a bath. 'I know the "all pals together" thing isn't your scene, but I have to say you're looking very … relaxed. And so beautiful.'

She crossed the room to where he was sitting sketching and leaned forward, her bare breasts skimming his lips. 'To be honest, I didn't want to come. But I'm glad I did. It's fun.'

'What have I been telling you?' He sucked one nipple then the other. 'A little peace and contentment isn't such a bad thing. Life doesn't have to be one long struggle.'

'Maybe not,' she admitted.

One afternoon, while the others strolled along the *Boulevard des Anglais*, Tessa and Jay – she pretending she needed to sleep, he that he wanted to sketch the harbour – made love, for old time's sake.

All in all, it was delightful and, briefly, Rundle's hold slackened.

Lewis's final reservations about moving to Bristol were swept away by his father's reaction. 'Good idea. You need to broaden your experience. It'll stand you in good stead when you apply for a headship.'

Lewis admired his father's stoicism. Dick Swinburne never said much about how he was feeling but, then again, Lewis never had the courage to ask. A question like that might trigger a response which neither of them could deal with. It did occur to him that his father might consider this period of his life to be a penance for that one unforgivable mistake; a delayed sentence imposed by an overseeing authority; a means of redemption.

He visited his father often but was anxious to avoid the pitfalls of rigid routine, remembering how the weekly visits to his grandmother eventually became a depressing chore. And Frank wasn't far away, if he was desperate for company.

Lewis had seen his uncle several times since Tessa's disclosure. How had he not picked up on it? *Perhaps we never see the people closest to us for what they are.* He wished he were able to discuss it with his father, to ask when he'd first twigged that his brother was a homosexual and how it had affected their relationship; to ask whether his mother had known, or was even aware that such a phenomenon existed. Lewis had gleaned the rudiments of sex from biology books and dogs in the park, the spicier details fleshed out in the changing rooms after games lessons. As for homosexuality – the first he'd heard about it was when he was propositioned by a man in the public lavatories next to the bus station. He hadn't had a clue what was going on but something told him to shift like a bat out of hell. And the same instinct stopped him from telling his parents what had happened. Even now, he and his father skirted around anything 'intimate' as though it were quicksand. One false step and you were a goner.

Chapter 28

Each time Tessa moved her hand, a needle of fire shot up to her elbow. Even after several drinks the pain was no better.

'Get it checked out at the hospital,' Rundle muttered. 'I'm sure you can concoct a plausible story for how you did it.'

'Fuck you.'

She struggled back to London concerned that were she to visit a doctor in Brighton it would create a papertrail that might cause her embarrassment. By the following morning, it was evident that her hand was more than bruised.

The doctor at the Whittington diagnosed a torn ligament at the base of her thumb. 'I'll strap it up for you. Less cumbersome than plaster. Keep it elevated. Reduce the swelling. It'll be uncomfortable for a week or two.' He prescribed painkillers and warned her to avoid alcohol.

The simplest actions – fastening the hooks on her bra, signing a cheque, holding a cup – became a challenge. She used her left hand wherever she could but it made her brain ache. She screamed with frustration at her own clumsiness and wept with rage that she had allowed the Rundle thing to get out of hand. On top of everything else, why was Dan in Toronto now, the only time she'd ever needed him?

Dropping two painkillers on her tongue, she washed them down with a glass of whisky.

*

She told Lewis about her hand. He was sympathetic, but it was plainly only after clearing it with Kirsty that he phoned back, inviting her to come to Bristol. Andrea had never been more than a tolerated gatecrasher and she'd seemed prepared to accept the role provided that they kept up the 'happy family' charade. But Kirsty was a different animal and Tessa realised that she was going to have to share her brother because it wouldn't be a good idea to make him choose between them.

This would be a lot easier if she and Kirsty were friends but Tessa wasn't good at friendship. At primary school she couldn't be bothered with the girls who simpered around the playground playing 'house' or 'shop', as though they didn't get enough of those things in real life. She'd tried to persuade the boys to let her join in with them, offering to be a Red Indian or a Jerry in order to get a foot in the door. But their male prejudices were already firmly in place and their slogan – *girls are stupid* – set in stone.

Gossip regarding the Gordon affair had followed her to grammar school where a whispering campaign branded her as an unsuitable friend and the whole Swinburne family as 'iffy'. When she left home, a string of faithless lovers and a host of false friends took advantage of her body, her transitory fame and her short-lived prosperity. She'd erected a barrier around herself to protect what remained of the spirited girl with the bright ideas from false friendships. Lewis had always been on hand, willing to be the sister she never had, the friend she always craved and the only brother she ever wanted. But now she really would have to share him.

'Tell me again. How did you do it?' Lewis asked when they collected Tessa from the railway station.

'The bus pulled away suddenly. I grabbed the rail. I must have bent my thumb back.' She avoided Kirsty's shrewd gaze. 'It was stupid. But that's the definition of an accident, I suppose.'

'Shall I help you wash your hair?' Kirsty asked.

Tessa wasn't sure she wanted those no-nonsense hands detecting the shape of her skull beneath her scalp; this stranger smelling her wet hair and seeing the pale skin on the nape of her neck. 'It's okay—'

'I'd like to.'

'Really?'

'Yes. I dreamed of being a hairdresser when I was a child. My brothers used to let me wash their hair and set it in rollers. Backcomb it, even. Gavin was the spitting image of George Harrison.'

Tessa snorted with laughter. 'You're making it up.'

Kirsty kept a straight face for a few seconds before raising her hands in capitulation. 'You're right. I *am* making it up.'

From their first encounter, Tessa had seen Kirsty Ross as a beautiful Nordic princess – cool, wise and flawless – which made her untruth all the more startling.

'So why *did* you offer?' Tessa asked.

'I thought it might help break the ice. Women divulge all kinds of things to their hairdresser. Hairdressers and taxi drivers – they're the ones who hear the nation's secrets.'

'You think I have secrets?'

'Yes, I do.'

'If I did, it would take more than a shampoo and blow-dry to dislodge them.'

Kirsty combed her wet hair, easing the tangles. 'You have beautiful hair.' She tugged at her own, held back from her face by two tortoiseshell combs. 'Mine's so fine. Like baby hair.'

'Aaahhh, but it's blonde. And that gives you a huge advantage.'

'In what way?'

'Oh ... men open doors for you and pull out your chair in a

restaurant ... and aren't villainesses always dark-haired? Mrs Danvers. The mad woman in *Jane Eyre* ... what's her name?'

'Bertha Mason. I would have thought you'd punch anyone who touched your chair. And hang on,' Kirsty stopped combing, 'what about Snow White? And Scarlett O'Hara? They both had the blackest of black hair.'

'Yes, and one was a dwarf-lover, the other a scheming opportunist.'

Kirsty put the comb down and sat next to Tessa on the bed. 'My guess is that you enjoy playing the villain.'

Tessa frowned. 'That's a funny thing to say.'

'I think you find it easier to shock than to please; to destroy than create. And you're right, it is. It's also an effective way of gaining attention. I encounter a lot of people in my work who think the same way.' Kirsty spoke dispassionately, as though she were in a case conference, reporting on an absent third party.

'You must be right, then,' Tessa snapped.

Outside the window, Bristol sprawled, dipping away towards the city centre. Tight rows of terraced houses, long-shadowed in the winter sun, clambered up the contours, defying the terrain. Here and there, tiny parks and the gardens of grand houses loosened the mix, like currants in a bun.

When she and Lewis were children, Bristol Zoo had been a favourite destination for Sunday school trips and family outings. More than anything in the world, Tessa had wanted to ride on the back of Rosie, the zoo's famous elephant. She'd desired it so fiercely it made her dizzy and she wished the lion would escape from its flimsy enclosure and devour her father when, as he always did, he refused to fork out the sixpence for a ticket. Then she'd sulk for the rest of the visit, willing Rosie's smug passengers to fall and break their necks, so that she could take their place in the silk-bedecked howdah – the keeper had told her the correct name for the seat – as the docile beast swayed along the terrace. By the time they reached home, she'd convinced herself that it had really happened, giving anyone prepared to listen a vivid account of the accident and her subsequent ride, accusing Lewis of jealousy when he contradicted her.

Kirsty looked solemn. 'Look, Tessa, we both care for Lewis—'

'*Care for?* I don't *care for* my brother. I *love* him.'

'We both *love* Lewis. And I know how close you two are. Unless we find a way of becoming friends, he's going to be permanent piggy in the middle.'

'Go on.'

'And it's got to be a bit more than rubbing along. It's all to do with trust so it's not going to work unless we're completely candid with each other.' Evidently sensing Tessa's reservations, she continued, 'Everything that passes between us would be in the strictest confidence.'

'Like the confessional.' Tessa put her hands together and closed her eyes. 'Bless me sister, for I have sinned.'

Kirsty grimaced, 'If you like, although I've never thought that religion sets much of an example.'

'But what if we go through all this getting to know each other malarkey then come to the conclusion we can't stand each other? '

'God, I don't know.'

'We'll fight a duel. Winner takes Lewis.' Tessa caught her hair in the towel, twisting it into a turban. 'We might as well get on with it straight away. Go ahead. Ask me something. Anything.'

'I didn't mean it quite so literally.'

'C'mon. Ask me a question.'

Kirsty wrinkled her nose. 'Okay. Did you really sprain your hand on the bus?'

Rundle's bedroom; the smell of alcohol and sweat; the sickening pain as he wrenched her hand back. Why couldn't she have asked something straightforward like *Who d'you love most in the world?* Lewis, of course. Or, *Have you ever kissed another woman?* Yes. Diane Stoddy. With tongues. She cried and I felt sick.

'No. To be honest, I'm a bit embarrassed.' She cleared her throat and looked directly into Kirsty's eyes. 'I had too much to drink the other night. I slipped when I was getting out of the bath. I didn't want to tell Lewis. He worries about my drinking.'

'And should he?'

'No subsidiary questions. My turn.'

'Okay.'

'Will you and Lewis have children?' Besides wanting to know the answer, Tessa was interested to see how frank her new friend would be.

'You don't mess about, do you?' Kirsty took a hairdryer from the drawer in the bedside table and untangled the flex. 'Naturally Lewis and I have discussed it. I'm thirty-three so we can't put it off indefinitely but I wouldn't want to have a child until we're married.'

'So you are planning to have children?'

Kirsty hesitated, 'Lewis is keen but I have reservations.'

'What reservations? Age? Career?'

'A subsidiary question, if I'm not mistaken. But I'll answer it. It's partly to do with those things but they're not my main concern. Lewis already has two children and...' she dipped her head.

'He doesn't like them much?' Tessa suggested.

'It's more that he doesn't seem to *feel* anything for them. I've tried to get to the bottom of it but—'

'Surely it's not difficult to work it out. The whole Andrea thing was a mistake from start to finish. He knew that – we all knew that – before he even walked up the aisle. But you know Lewis. He'd promised so he had to go through with it. He must have had some idiotic idea that kids would bring them together

302

– or perhaps *she* thought it would prevent them drifting apart. Not that I think she ever cared much for him. She was on the lookout for a harmless provider – and they don't come any more harmless than Lewis. Lewis Swinburne, pillar of the community. Reliable income. Foreign holidays. Detached house. All that middle class shit. Thank God she pulled out because he would have soldiered on.'

She reached out and touched Kirsty's shoulder. 'It'd be different if you had kids.'

Kirsty smiled indulgently, as though she were listening to a child's simplistic version of a complex event. 'We can't be sure, though, can we?'

There were footsteps on the stair and Lewis popped his head around the door. 'Girl talk? I'll put the coffee on.' He beamed, clearly delighted that they were getting on so well.

Lewis suggested they visit their father. 'I haven't been for a couple of weeks and I know he'd love to see you. He's got some things he wants you to look at. Bits of Mum's jewellery, I think.'

'I've got work to do but why don't you two go?' Kirsty said. 'Then tonight we'll take Tessa to our favourite Italian restaurant.'

Lewis, as usual, drove with the cautious precision of a learner driver but, for once, Tessa was in no hurry. 'Thanks for asking me down. I was feeling a bit low. The hand thing was the final straw.'

'You're missing Dan.' He stated it firmly, an indisputable fact requiring no reply.

Yes, she did miss Dan – his composure, his patience, his wisdom. The sensation was unexpected and heartening.

'You and Kirsty seem to be getting on well.'

'Did you think we wouldn't?' she asked. 'We were fine in Nice, weren't we?'

'Yes, but there was a crowd of us in Nice. And we were on

holiday so it didn't really count.'

'Didn't count? You make it sound like an endurance test. Anyway, don't worry. It'll be fine. We've agreed to share you. We've also pledged that, if that doesn't work, we'll fight to the death. Winner takes you.'

They crossed the Severn Bridge, Lewis enthusiastically explaining the physics involved in the construction of the suspension bridge. Tension. Compression. Bending moments. What a shame to reduce the elegant structure to equations. She stopped listening and peered down at the waters of the Severn Estuary, a gigantic ooze of gravy separating England and Wales.

'Lewis? Can I ask you something? And I shall know if you don't tell me the truth.'

'Why do I suddenly feel nervous?'

'Have you told Kirsty about the doll?'

'No.' He answered without hesitation. 'No. She knows what happened on the day Gordon disappeared. But I've never mentioned … that.'

'And what have you told her about Cranwell Lodge?'

'About Mrs Channing and Mr Zeal. And Blanche. And the stupid business about the police and the cellar.'

Tessa watched the cars overtaking them. 'Did you tell her about Morocco?'

'No. That's ours.'

She smiled. 'I think they must put happy pills in the Bristol water,' she said as they took the slip road off the motorway.

Happy families and fresh alliances. She could go along with that – for a while, anyway.

There was a cloth on the kitchen table, the best china set out in readiness.

'It's only salmon sandwiches, I'm afraid,' Dick Swinburne

apologised but Tessa had spotted the empty tin. *John West Red Salmon* – her father's equivalent of the fatted calf.

Throughout lunch, Lewis entertained them with tales of the classroom. He was teaching in a co-educational school and it seemed that he had already become a heart-throb amongst the female pupils. 'Heaven knows why,' he shrugged, clearly not understanding that, lanky and open-faced, hair flopping across his forehead and gentle eyes, his unthreatening manliness was a soft target for teenage lust.

Uncle Frank used to sit in this kitchen, amusing them with daft anecdotes, transforming jam sandwich ordinariness into something special and their mother into a light-hearted girl. Now she understood that it was more than Frank's unremitting bonhomie that had caused her father discomfort.

She'd visited him twice in the nine months since the funeral. On both occasions they had taken flowers to the cemetery. The first time, a mound of red clay topped with a rudimentary wooden cross had marked her mother's earthly remains, the second time, a drab grey headstone had proclaimed 'At Rest'. Nine months – the gestation period of a human life. Her father hadn't created a new life in that time but he was adapting the old one to meet his circumstances.

The kitchen now boasted two conspicuous additions – a radio-cassette player and a sleek, four-slice toaster. He was quick to point these out to her. 'Great company, the radio.' And, 'No excuse to go hungry if you've got bread and a toaster.'

He'd rearranged the furniture. In the living room, the sideboard was now against the wall facing the door and the television in the opposite corner. Upstairs, the beds had been arbitrarily shifted. Under their father's roof, the old order had been slightly skewed.

'You've shuffled everything round, Dad.'

'Yes. Well, I thought … why not?' A stickler for accuracy,

his woolly reply was conspicuous. 'I've got something to show you.' He led her upstairs, groaning softly with the effort of the ascent.

Her parents had slept in the front of the house, in the largest bedroom, but he took her into the one that overlooked the back garden, the one that had been Lewis's. 'I sleep in here now. It's quieter. Catches the evening sun.'

All her brother's bits and pieces had, long ago, been transferred to Cranwell Lodge. Since then, this had been known as 'the guest room' although Tessa doubted whether a guest had ever slept in it. Lewis's single bed had been replaced by a double bed with upholstered headboard and her mother's pale oak dressing table stood in front of the window.

Her father took a shoe box from the bottom drawer of the dressing table and handed it to her. 'Look through these, if you've got a minute. Take whatever you fancy.' He cleared his throat. 'I'll give your brother a hand with the dishes.'

She sat on the bed. The metallic taste of tinned salmon lingered in her mouth. Cutlery tinkled downstairs. As she tipped the contents of the box on to the candlewick bedspread, the past came tumbling out in a cascade of trinkets.

VI

1980

Chapter 29

LEWIS CHECKED THE CLOCK ABOVE THE DOOR. One-twenty. Over an hour until visiting time although he wasn't expecting anyone to come. The ward was too hot and the air stale, as though it had already circulated through dozens of sickly lungs. It smelled of the lunch they had been served at eleven forty-five – mashed potatoes, mince, tinned carrots – and illness. He ached from lying on his back but he was reluctant to roll on to his side in case he disconnected the drip that was taped to his left hand. When he attempted minor manoeuvres, the bottom sheet slithered on the rubberised mattress and he ended up in the same position but with the additional discomfort of elbows grazed on the starched cotton. His fellow patients were asleep, or pretending to be, and he closed his eyes, longing to join them and escape from the whole sorry business.

It was probably nothing – one of those freak one-offs that might never be explained. He felt fine now but it had been terrifying at the time. It must have been because he hadn't argued when the Head insisted on dialling nine-nine-nine. Then, when the ambulance men turned up, he'd passed out for a second time, not so much with pain as with the relief of seeing them. 'Tests,' the doctor had said, breezily. 'We'll keep you in for a couple of days. Take a good look at you.' That was yesterday morning and, although very much the 'new boy' in Churchill Ward, he was already learning the ropes, guided by its other inmates.

Beyond the tatty swing doors, above the clatter of trolleys and squeak of rubber soles on buffed linoleum, he heard raised voices. Registering that something interesting was on the cards the dozers roused and by the time Tessa flounced through the doors four pairs of eyes were focussed on her. She glanced around the room and Lewis raised his hand, afraid that whatever was wrong with him might have altered him beyond recognition.

She frowned, striding towards him, shaking her head. 'What a load of cretins. They tried to stop me coming in. I explained that I've just flown in from the States and I'm not intending to hang around for hours—'

'You were in America?' Lewis interrupted.

'No, of course I wasn't. But that's not the point.' Tessa bent to kiss him, the whiff of peppermint failing to mask the alcohol on her breath. Perching on the bed, she made a show of inspecting his face. 'You don't look too bad. A tad pale, perhaps. I thought I'd best come and see what all the hoo-ha was about.'

A nurse bustled in, stern-faced and officious. 'I'm sorry, miss, but visiting time doesn't start 'til two-thirty.'

Before Tessa could launch another salvo, Lewis switched on what Kirsty called his 'little-boy-lost smile'. 'Please, *please*, nurse. My sister's only going to be in the country for a day or two. And I haven't seen her for … years.' The nurse's expression softened and he pressed his advantage. 'I promise we'll be as quiet as mice.'

As the young woman retreated, Tessa whistled softly, 'That was impressive.'

'Maybe. But we won't be able to pull that one again.'

'I suppose not. Will we need to? How long are they keeping you in?'

'No idea. "Tests," that's what they said. All they've done so far is siphon off copious quantities of blood and check I've still got a pulse.'

She pointed at the bag of clear liquid dangling from the stand next to the bed and the tube leading from it to his bandaged hand. 'What's that in aid of?'

'Everyone gets one of those. It's the NHS's version of a ball and chain.'

Gingerly, she fingered the sleeve of his hospital gown, 'God, this is pretty basic.' She leaned back and squinted. 'Actually, you look rather sweet. Like a gigantic baby.'

'Maybe that's what the problem is. I'm morphing into a baby,' he grinned.

'I don't know why you're so chirpy. It's very inconsiderate of you to be ill, Lewis. You know hospitals give me the heebie-jeebies. Ughhh,' she shuddered, 'the whole place is full of sick people and germs. Disgusting. And you must have noticed how they warp time.' She pointed at the clock, 'I've only been in here for ten minutes, and I've already aged ten years. You'd better pull yourself together and get out before we both shrivel up and die.'

'Yes, miss.' He saluted. 'How's Dan? Every time I open the Sundays, there he is. "Dan Coates in his stylish East End studio." Quite the man of the moment.'

Lewis was delighted that Dan was successful. He liked the man and was enormously thankful that he had stuck with Tessa. A few years ago, when they'd been in Nice, he and Dan had strolled along the beach. The others had gone off to the Casino but, full moon reflected in the flat calm sea, it had seemed too magical a night to be indoors. They'd had a good meal, drunk several cognacs and the two men had opened up to each other. 'Why d'you put up with my sister?' Lewis had asked. Dan had launched a pebble in to the indigo night, waiting until it plopped in the sea before replying, 'I'm surprised you, of all people, need to ask me that. You know Tessa better than anyone else in the world.' Lewis had nodded, 'Yes, I think I do. That's why I asked. She's selfish, impatient, intolerant and unreliable. Which suggests to me that you're some kind of masochist.' Dan had laughed, 'Maybe. But she's also clever, funny, irreverent, fearless and never, ever dull. It breaks my heart to see her thrashing around, lashing out at anything and everything, hurting herself more than anyone else. Okay, we have some pretty dire moments but all I have to do then is remind myself what she – both of you – went through when you were kids. If that happened now, your whole family would get professional help. God knows how you came out of it so sane, Lewis, because it's damaged Tessa profoundly.' 'That still doesn't explain why you put up with her,' Lewis had persisted. 'To be truthful, I have walked away a couple of times but when she wasn't there I felt sort of … anaesthetised. Unable to function. Does that make sense?' 'You love her,' Lewis had replied, 'and no one has yet come up with a rational explanation for love.'

'Dan's fine,' Tessa said. 'Of course he makes out that he hates all the publicity, but it's certainly good for business. He tells everyone that his success is entirely due to me. Apparently I'm his inspiration and his muse. We get invited to some very swanky parties. I don't think the Great and the Good would be so keen to meet me if I were a stripper rather than an artist's model. In both cases it boils down to taking ones clothes off for the general public to gawp. It's a fine line between fame and infamy.'

Visitors started dribbling in, nodding diffidently around the ward.

'Is anyone else coming to see you this afternoon?' Tessa asked.

'It's Thursday, remember? Everyone's at work. Kirsty'll be in this evening but I'm not expecting anyone else. I certainly don't want Dad driving over here in the dark.'

'Good. I've got you all to myself.' She shrugged up her shoulders and smiled like a child anticipating a treat. 'We can have a proper conversation.'

She took the blanket from the foot of Lewis's bed and, curling up in the bedside chair, she draped it over her legs.

Lewis gave a puzzled frown, 'And what is it we need to have a proper conversation about?'

'C'mon, Lewis, don't play dumb. Tell me again about the mystery woman. You only gave me half the story on the phone.'

Lewis explained that the previous Sunday he'd been summoned by the current tenant of Cranwell Lodge – an American lecturer on a year's sabbatical – to sort out a couple of problems. Before returning to Bristol, he'd called on his father only to find him sitting in the kitchen with a woman Lewis had never seen before.

'Did he seem embarrassed?' Tessa asked.

'Slightly. I usually phone if I'm going to call, so that in itself would have wrong-footed him.'

He replayed the scene, his father sheepishly smiling and talking too much, keen to tell him that 'Barbara was just passing'; the woman knowing exactly where to find the tea bags and the biscuits.

'Actually it felt a bit disturbing, seeing another woman on Mum's territory.'

'Too bloody right. And what was your gut feeling? Did you take to her? If you dare say "I don't know" I'll wrench that needle out of your hand.' She reached out towards the tube and he knew, without a doubt, that she would do it.

'There was nothing about her not to like.'

'Mmmm. Neat avoidance of the question but I'll let you off for now. And how did they behave towards each other?'

He pictured the chubby hand, nails coated with pale pink

varnish, resting briefly on his father's shoulder; the lingering eye contact.

'They seemed pretty easy with each other. Like old friends. Not surprising, seeing as they've been working in the same office for – what did she say? – six years.'

Tessa chewed her lip. 'So this *might* have been going on while Mum was alive.'

Lewis shook his head, 'You know that's not what I meant. Seriously, I think we should be pleased that he has some company. You wouldn't like to think of him spending the rest of his life on his own, would you?'

Tessa ploughed on. 'Describe her. How old is she? What was she wearing? Is she well educated?'

'How old? Fifty-ish I'd say. Short brown hair. Clothes? Smart but certainly not flashy. Educated…? I'm hopeless at this kind of thing, Tess.'

'She sounds like a gold-digger. Why else would a smart fifty-year-old fuck an old cripple?'

Lewis screwed up his face and put a finger to his lips, 'Shhhh. For heaven's sake. Must you make everything so crude? We have absolutely no evidence to suggest that they're … together in that way.'

'"Together in *that* way".' She lowered the pitch of her voice, mimicking his. 'You do realise, don't you, that if he marries her, she'll get the house and the money when he dies?'

'You make it sound as though he's a millionaire.'

It *had* crossed Lewis's mind that his father might re-marry, not with regard to the inheritance he might lose, but as a reminder that anyone's life, can, at any moment, veer off course and hurtle into uncharted territory, dragging a handful of other lives along with it. The notion scared him stiff.

'Let's forget all that for a bit.' Tessa closed her eyes and pulled the blanket up to her chin. 'Talk to me, Lewis. Tell me things I ought to know.'

She yawned and leaned her head back, closing her eyes as if to concentrate on the revelations he was about to utter. He watched her as she teetered on the brink of sleep. Wide mouth, heavy eyebrows, square-ish chin, she was handsome more than beautiful. Bold-faced and fearless. It occurred to him, not for the first time, that she would have been more at ease, more fulfilled, had she been a man.

'Okay. I bet you didn't know that light emitted by—'

She frowned and sighed. 'Not that sort of stuff. Who cares if … I dunno … the average something generates so many somethings?' She heaved herself up in the chair and yawned. 'Tell me things that will help me make sense of my life.'

He smiled, recognising his sister's tactic to extricate them from the dreary confines of the ward and transport them to a place that was theirs alone. But he was tired, his wits refusing to dance to her command. 'That's a tricky one,' he muttered. 'Can I get back to you on that?'

She took his hand. 'No worries. Anyway, it probably boils down to the old maxim.'

'What's that then?' He closed his eyes, rubbing his thumb across the cool skin on the back of her hand.

'You know. "A leopard can't change its socks."'

'Mmmm. I expect you're right.'

He drifted into sleep.

The previous evening Kirsty had phoned Tessa from the hospital. 'He complained of a sharp pain in his back and then fainted. Apparently he was out cold for several minutes. They're talking about a mild stroke or an epileptic fit. Obviously they won't know until they've run tests.'

'But surely he'd be paralysed if it were a stroke. Or bitten his tongue if—'

'I'm only repeating what they told me.'

'But he's okay? He's not … gaga or anything? You'd tell me if he was—'

'Tessa, I'd tell you if he were gaga. But I'm not going to pretend he's fine when we don't yet know what we're dealing with.'

'I'm coming down. I'll get a train first thing in the morning.'

Tessa had expected Kirsty to tell her that there was no need and, when she didn't, her anxiety increased. 'You will let me know—'

'Of course.'

When she saw Lewis, wan-faced and bewildered, emasculated by the hospital gown, she wanted to whisk him away from the prodding and the poking and the paraphernalia of illness. But she had no getaway car, engine running, stationed outside the hospital gates; no miracle man waiting to administer a magic cure. All she could do was hijack his attention. So she cross-questioned him about their father's 'friend', in the hope of geeing him up, but he seemed apathetic and uninterested, satisfied to take the new friendship at face value.

Pulling the blanket up to her chin, she closed her eyes. They were back in Medway Avenue, in the bedroom they'd shared during those months when Gran was living with them. Night after night, they'd lain whispering in the dark, pretending not to hear their mother crying, kidding each other that it would all come right in the end.

'Talk to me, Lewis. Tell me things I ought to know.'

He began, with typical Lewis earnestness, to reel off tedious statistics.

'No, things that will help me make sense of my life.'

She wanted to say that it – the 'it' that was her life – was all such a disappointment and she ached to share her regrets; to have him tell her that it wasn't her fault – at least not all of it – and that there was still plenty of time to have babies and write wonderful books; to fall in love with kind, patient Dan and to kick the drinking. Most of all she wanted him to know how she'd nearly – *so nearly* – freed herself from Rundle.

But Lewis was ill and it would be unforgivable to dump all that on him. Surrounded by tubes and charts and bottles of Lucozade, she felt weary and anxious as she watched her brother fall asleep.

Kirsty unloaded the rucksack on to Lewis's bed, 'Pyjamas. Dressing gown. Slippers.' A discouraging permanence descended with the growing pile of homely items.

'Thanks, love.'

She studied his face. 'You look better than you did yesterday.'

'I feel better.'

He told her everything that had happened in the twenty-four hours since she'd left him there, keeping it light, as if by so doing he could hoodwink his body in to believing that there was nothing wrong with it after all.

'It was nice to see Tessa this afternoon.'

'She said she was going to come, but I wasn't sure…'

'Yes. And she might stay tonight. I told her you'd be home by eight-thirty.'

'She's not coming in this evening, then?'

'No. She thought we'd like some time to ourselves.'

'That was considerate of her.'

In fact Lewis had discouraged Tessa from returning for evening visiting. The truth was that she could, within a second, switch from genial companion to prickly adversary. The last thing he needed was to be caught in the crossfire between her and Kirsty and have his blood pressure soar.

Kirsty sat on the chair next to the bed, leaning forward, her head resting on his hand, her eyes closed. She'd recently had her hair cut in a shaggy bob. He hadn't said anything to her, but he'd preferred it as it used to be, longer and unfussy, more the way a child would wear it. She looked worn out, freckles prominent on her pale cheeks, lips dry and flaky. He knew that she would have gone to work at some ridiculously early hour to compensate for the time she'd lost yesterday whilst the hospital staff ground slowly through the admission procedure.

She raised her head and frowned, as though she'd heard an unexplained noise. 'You didn't tell Tessa about the baby, did you?'

'Of course not. We agreed that we'd wait a bit, didn't we?'

'Yes. But your sister has a spooky knack of reading your mind. And you're useless at lying. It's one of the things I love most about you.' She yawned. 'I'll just have to throw up discreetly in the morning if she's there.'

'You'll have left by the time she surfaces. No doubt, as we speak, she's in a pub somewhere. I wish she'd get help before the boozing gets out of control,' he said.

'It's not your job to worry about that, Lewis. Particularly at the moment.'

He wished he didn't worry but *if wishes were horses then buggers would ride* as Mrs Channing might have put it.

'How did he seem to you?' Kirsty asked.

'Jaded. Battered. But anyone would feel ropey in that dreary hole,' Tessa replied. 'Are you sure it's okay if I stay? I'll pop in and see him tomorrow afternoon, then go straight to the station.'

'No problem. As long as you don't mind being surrounded by toys.'

Toys? *Ah, yes.* It was easy to forget that Lewis had two daughters; that she had two nieces.

'How are the girls? D'you see much of them?'

'They don't come often. They're timid little things. No sooner do they acclimatise to being here, than it's time for them to go home. I don't think they like me much, but that's of no consequence. Did you know that Andrea has re-married? An old flame from her schooldays, apparently.'

'Pity she didn't marry him in the first place. Lewis did mention it but everything to do with Andrea is eminently forgettable.'

Tessa watched her sister-in-law preparing supper, breaking four eggs carefully in to the Pyrex bowl, re-wrapping the butter before returning it to the fridge, filling the pepper grinder.

'How can you stay so calm? Aren't you frantic with worry?'

'Of course I am. But there's nothing to be gained by my getting all steamed up. And we've still got to eat.' Kirsty slid an omelette on to Tessa's plate. 'I'm lucky, I suppose. I'm good at compartmentalising. It comes from the work I do. For example, I have to put Mr Jones's boundary dispute completely out of my mind before I open the file on Mr Smith's probate case. I sometimes have a dozen cases in various stages of completion. I'd go nuts if they were all swilling around my brain at the same time.'

'But this isn't Mr Jones we're talking about, it's Lewis and he's lying half dead in that fucking hospital—'

'Thanks, Tessa.'

Tessa pressed her fingertips against her lips. 'Sorry. Sorry. It's just that it breaks my heart to see him in that bed, all tubes and God knows what. He doesn't deserve it.' She drew in a breath then expelled it slowly. 'Let's talk about something else.'

'Let's.' Kirsty set down her knife and fork. 'How are things with you? It's months since we saw you.'

'Me? I'm fine, thanks. Everything's good.' But no sooner were the words out than anxiety, alcohol and Kirsty's steady gaze made restraint impossible. 'That's bollocks, actually.'

'D'you need to talk about it?'

Was there any point in confiding to someone who could

'compartmentalise' that her whole life had gone down the pan when she was ten years old? To be specific, when her parents had, irresponsibly, produced a third child, then, even more irresponsibly, lost him. If Gordon had never existed, she might have been – *would* have been – a different person. She could have done anything – discovered a galaxy, or a cure for a killer disease, or played Lady Macbeth at Stratford, or won the Nobel Prize for something or another. What's more, her poor mother wouldn't have lost her grip on the world and thus been lost to her children. God, it was all so precarious.

Kirsty wasn't one for histrionics so Tessa kept it factual. 'I was eighteen when I left home. No doubt Lewis has given you his version of what happened that night. I got a job with Jay and Liza Costello, looking after their children if you can call it that. We spent the summer in Cornwall then later we decamped to Ireland with a crowd of their friends. Artists. Writers. That's when I first met Dan, although he didn't make much of an impression on me at the time. It was a magic summer. Everyone was buzzing with ideas; everything was possible.

'I stayed with them for a while but things got a bit … messy. So I went to London to try my luck. For a couple of years I fooled myself that I was having the time of my life. I really thought it was the beginning of something fantastic, what with the success of the book and everything. But it didn't last long. Merely surviving seems to have become an end in itself. Nothing excites me any more.' *Except Rundle.* 'Sometimes it hardly seems worth the effort.' Tired of the sound of her own whining, she threw her head back and shrieked, 'Screw them all, the whole bastard lot of them.'

Kirsty, seemingly unfazed by this outburst, spoke softly. 'Look, Tessa, you're young, beautiful and certainly not stupid. You could do anything you put your mind to. I don't want to hurt your feelings but it seems to me that you're like the little ball in one of those maze puzzles, forever chasing off down blind alleys. You need to focus on a goal – it doesn't have to be anything earth-shattering – and apply all that energy and intelligence to achieving it. God … that sounded like a pep talk to the Lower Fifth.' She paused as if expecting a further outburst, then, when it didn't come, she continued, 'I don't know Dan well but I'm sure he'd support you in whatever you want do.'

'No. A pep talk is what I need. On the hour, every hour. And you're right. Dan would be supportive. Poor Dan,' Tessa smiled ruefully, 'he's kind, patient and sensitive. Quite rich and famous, too. What more could a woman want? Everything would be simple if I could fall in love with him. He says I can take as long as I like which makes me feel even shittier.' She was near to tears.

Kirsty passed her a tissue. 'Spending all that time on your own, in front of the typewriter, can't help. Maybe you should get away for a while; see it all from a distance.'

Tessa blew her nose and smiled forlornly. 'Stop navel gazing and bugger off to Tierra del Fuego, is that what you're saying?'

They watched the ten o'clock news. Iran and Iraq seemed to be involved in a war, although Tessa had only a sketchy idea where those countries were and no idea at all why it was important. She'd never found foreign affairs, or politics in general come to that, of much interest and was surprised to see how seriously Kirsty took it all. Presumably lawyers needed to keep abreast of the world. Tessa had always inhabited the shady regions of 'the system'. She'd never joined a union or put money in to a pension or owned property. Any money she'd earned, she'd spent. She'd never filled in a tax return or paid a National Insurance stamp until Dan insisted that she did, or rather did it for her.

'I'm off to bed,' Kirsty announced. 'Could you take those things in for Lewis tomorrow?' She pointed at a carrier bag on the hallstand. 'He was muttering about sending work in for his

A Level group and he wants his books. It'll help him pass the time.'

Tessa lay in bed. She'd had a stupid row with Dan before she left. Something to do with an unpaid bill. She ought to let him know she was staying the night but he'd be asleep now and, besides, one of the conditions of her moving in with him had been that she needn't explain where she was or with whom.

In the bedroom next door Kirsty coughed. What would it be like to have her sister-in-law's sense of purpose, her certainty and self-assurance? It seemed unfair that as well as those attributes she had Lewis. A plane throbbed low overhead making its descent to the airport. Was Lewis still awake? Was he listening to the plane too? She got out of bed and went to the window, looking out across the twinkling conurbation towards where she guessed the hospital might be.

The following morning, the mystery was solved. The consultant, complete with an entourage of medical students, swept in to the ward and revealed to Lewis that he had kidney stones.

'Is that good or bad?' Tessa asked when, on the dot of two-thirty, she arrived at his bedside with a bulging carrier bag.

'Good, I think. Better than the alternatives anyway. I've got to drink gallons of water and take something to make my urine more alkaline. And I can go home as soon as Kirsty brings my clothes in.'

Tessa frowned. 'But I could have done that.'

Lewis said nothing, giving her time to work out that it was Kirsty's place to take him home.

'What's in the bag?' he asked.

She peered into the plastic bag as though checking that its contents had not been transformed during her bus ride from house to hospital. 'Maths books. Pens. Paper. And...' she grinned, pulling something out with a rabbit-from-a-hat style

Chapter 30

AFTER THE SECOND MISCARRIAGE, Kirsty announced that she wasn't prepared to try again. Lewis had assumed that they would make the decision together but he had no right to persuade her to go through it for a third time. He wasn't sure how he was supposed to *be*. Should he give her 'space'? It was an expression he didn't care for. It conjured up the spectre of a tightrope walker swaying on a high wire, almost sure to fall. Should he arrange lots of events to keep her busy? Encourage her to parade her feelings for all to see? They talked about counting blessings and how lucky they were to have each other but it seemed horribly like dialogue from a second-rate play. For the first time since they met, they were holding back from each other and made him feel wretched.

'Don't worry, Lewis. I'm fine. Honestly,' she said, and he felt undermined by her self-reliance.

Those who knew about the failed pregnancies were sympathetic but embarrassed. They might have been more comfortable had she been suffering from gangrene or diabetes but miscarriage combined an unpalatable mix of sex, death and 'women's problems'. Tessa was the only one to say what she was thinking. 'You must be devastated. When I think of all the irresponsible morons breeding like rabbits … It's so sad and so unfair. You should adopt. Lovely people like you, you'd have no trouble at all. There are so many unwanted children in the world who'd love to have you as parents.'

All the while, a quiet but persistent voice nagged away inside Lewis's head, insinuating, oh so softly, that Kirsty might be a tiny bit relieved at the way it had turned out.

Dick Swinburne reached retirement age. He'd been a Post Office employee since leaving school at fifteen. On the day he finished – his sixty-fifth birthday – the head of his section presented him with a barometer and a cheque for seventy-five pounds. And that was that.

He invited the family to join him for a celebratory Sunday lunch at The Salmon's Leap, a pub a few miles out of the town. 'MY TREAT,' he'd added in red capitals across the corner of the photocopied invitations.

Lewis felt that Kirsty had gone back to work too soon. She looked washed out and had no appetite. She was preoccupied, often pausing mid-sentence to stare out of the window, losing the thread of what she was saying.

'No need for you to come, love. Why don't you have a quiet day at home?' he said. 'Everyone would understand.'

'Don't treat me as an invalid, Lewis. I want to come. It'll do me good to do something normal.'

'Something normal' wasn't how Lewis would describe it. His parents had only given parties when there was no way of wriggling out of them. *Throw a party.* The phrase suggested vigour and lack of inhibition. Arbitrary celebrations were out of the question but birthdays and anniversaries were irritating blips, like molehills on a perfect lawn and Christmas could not be sidestepped. Whenever paper serviettes and crackers had appeared in the Swinburne house so did an invisible hand, hovering above the festivities, ready to clamp down at the first sign of abandon. This made his father's invitation all the more significant.

Tessa and Dan said they were coming and Lewis suggested they club together to buy a gift for their father.

'That's ridiculous,' Tessa scoffed, 'it's only a family get-together. And what would we get him? A pen and pencil set? An engraved tankard?'

Kirsty, practical as ever, suggested that Lewis buy something as back up. 'You can leave it in the car. See how it goes. You can always give it to him for Christmas. Even your family gives Christmas presents.'

Lewis chose a Roberts radio that worked on mains or battery. He signed the gift card 'To Dad, Happy Listening, from Lewis, Tessa, Kirsty and Dan.'

He'd planned to be there in good time, to prime Tessa about the radio and catch up on things but his schedule went adrift when they were held up behind a bicycle race and arrived twenty minutes late.

The Salmon's Leap, with its oak beams and horse brasses, might have been a wonderful refuge on dank winter evenings but it was too gloomy for a June day. Coming in from the sunlight, it was a few seconds before his eyes adjusted and the shadowy figures became distinct. Tessa. Uncle Frank. Dan. Beyond them, his father and Barbara chatting to a man and two women he didn't know.

His father joined them, kissing Kirsty on the cheek and shaking Lewis's hand. He wore the charcoal grey suit which Lewis was sure he'd worn at their mother's funeral and this, teamed with white shirt and striped tie, made him look like an assistant bank manager who had wandered in to the wrong function.

'We were getting concerned, Lewis. Thought there might be a problem. But you're here now so we can get started.'

The dining room smelled of gravy and overcooked cauliflower. 'The Swinburne Party' picked its way to the empty table in the far corner of the room, Lewis manoeuvring so that he was sitting between Kirsty and his sister.

It was the first opportunity he'd had to speak to Tessa and, leaning close, he whispered, 'Who are they?' nodding towards the three strangers.

She directed her reply with the back of her hand, 'Barbara's daughters. And son-in-law.'

Dick Swinburne was on his feet, fiddling with his shirt cuffs, clearing his throat. 'I know it's customary for the speeches to come after the meal but on this rather special occasion I'm going to break with tradition.'

First he spoke about the joy of being part of a wonderful family – a family that Lewis found it hard to recognise. Next he embarked on a series of clichés about 'life's ups and downs'. 'But the important thing is never to give up. Hope springs eternal. Life is what you make it.'

Tessa squeezed Lewis's knee beneath the table and he realised, then, what was coming. Not quite ready to hear the words that would convert speculation into reality, he concentrated on Barbara's face as she sat, straight-backed, an indulgent smile fixed on her lips, like a mother willing her son not to fluff his lines in the school play.

When he'd bought the radio, he'd pictured his father in the shed or the garage, listening to the rugby commentary on the natty little Roberts, and it was odd to think that it would sometimes be tuned to Woman's Hour.

'We'd like you all to come back to the house.' Their father, tipsy with the good wishes of his guests, was clearly reluctant for the party to break up. 'It'll be a chance for you to pick up that box, Tessa.'

Tessa spotted Barbara's daughters exchanging *Oh, no* glances. The last thing she wanted was to spend the afternoon at Salisbury Road, but she was affronted on her father's behalf.

'We'd love to, Dad.'

Dick Swinburne had already given Tessa the bulk of his wife's 'treasures'. He'd presented these to her over a period of years, as if it were too painful to part with them all at once. He'd prefaced each with the story of where it had come from. 'That Toby jug's from Shanklin. We went there for our twenty-fifth,' and 'Your mother fancied the china kitten when we went on that tour around the Royal Worcester factory.' Tessa disliked knick-knacks but it would have been cruel to refuse. She'd wrapped them in newspaper and packed them in her mother's hatbox, promising to take them back to London when she came in the car.

As kids, when the coast was clear, she and Lewis had bounced on their parents' bed, trying to get a better view of the pink and white striped box which had lived on top of the wardrobe. If they bounced high enough, they caught a glimpse of the white satin bow draped across its lid. When the family moved from Medway Avenue, the box had gone with them but, in the new house, the object that had once seemed enchanting became disturbing. Why was it there? What did it contain? Their mother would never have worn a hat grand enough to warrant such a fancy box. The answer came to her one winter's day when she and Lewis were snooping around, trying to discover where their Christmas presents were hidden. It was obvious. The hat box was full of Gordon's clothes, wrapped in folds of white tissue paper.

When, in the course of sorting through her mother's things, she'd finally lifted the box down, she could tell from its weight that it was empty. 'What's the hatbox all about, Dad?' she'd asked. He'd smiled, 'Your mother bought it in a junk shop, not long after we were married. She used to say that when we won the pools she'd buy a posh hat to put inside it.'

'Did she keep anything in it?' Tessa persisted.

'Not as far as I know. I kept doing the Pools and she kept on hoping, I suppose.'

So her mother had been a dreamer as well as an accordion player.

'I've often wondered what happened to Gordon's clothes.' She hardly dared look at him in case she saw pain in his face.

But he answered without hesitation, 'Your Gran packed them all up. Gave them to the Salvation Army.'

'So you never really thought…?'

'The clothes wouldn't have fitted him anyway.'

She laid a hand on his arm to signal her thanks, but he hadn't finished.

'Your mother did keep something. A pair of knitted bootees. She thought I didn't know. But sometimes I'd come into the bedroom and she'd be pushing them away in that little sewing box she had.'

Tessa waited to hear the conclusion of the sad story.

'I put them in with her when…' He took out his hanky and blew his nose.

'She'd have liked that, Dad.'

During the period of their estrangement, she would not have believed reconciliation was feasible. In the beginning it was a little awkward but now they were 'rubbing along' fine. Were she inclined to whimsy, she might be tempted to view it as a parting gift from her mother.

During those first months on his own, Dick Swinburne had learned to cook simple meals and mastered the twin-tub; he emptied the vacuum cleaner bag regularly and made a reasonable job of ironing his shirts. But he was baffled by choice and asked her advice on the most basic things. Which pyjamas to buy – cotton or winceyette? The sort of saucepan to replace the one he'd burnt. Christmas cards – robins or a manger scene? It touched her that this man who had always 'known best' was unable to decide between granulated and caster sugar.

She'd made a point of coming down on his birthday. They went to see *Chariots of Fire* at the Odeon, following it with a fish and chip supper. In the vinegary fug of the chip shop, across the Formica-topped table, Tessa came close to asking him about … *it*. How had it felt coming out of the newsagent's to find the pram empty; to tell his wife that their baby was missing. Had she ever forgiven him? Had he forgiven himself? But his bemused expression as his wrinkled hand thumped the bottom of the ketchup bottle had made it impossible.

Another time, when her father was doing something to the car, Tessa had flipped through the calendar that hung near the telephone. In painstakingly neat writing, her mother had, with unfounded optimism, filled in the birthdays and anniversaries for the year ahead. Tessa, her throat aching from holding back the tears, had studied the entries for 'August' and 'November'. But there was nothing, not even the faintest pencil mark, to verify that, on this day Gordon Swinburne had been born and, on that day, taken from her.

After they had seen the first twelve months through and weathered all the meaningful dates, the force that had drawn them together at the graveside slackened and they began to withdraw a little. Nothing was said; they didn't row or fall out, but their need grew less. When she mentioned it to Lewis he told her not to feel bad. 'The main thing is that you've reached an accommodation. And that's terrific. There was a time when you two couldn't be in the same room without laying into each other. Mum would be pleased.'

Loading the remnants of her mother's life into the boot of the car, it occurred to her that her father's marriage to Barbara wouldn't be such a terrible thing. The woman standing at his side on the pavement, waving them off, seemed very fond of him. Protective, too, as if he needed to be treated with special care, as if he were damaged. Tessa had never considered that.

'I bumped into a bloke called Mark Hollinghurst today,' Dan said. 'He says he met you in Cornwall that summer. Bit of an entrepreneur these days. He's looking for staff for a gallery he's opening. I said I'd ask if you were interested.' It didn't ring true but it was sweet of Dan to find a tactful way of suggesting that she get off her bottom and do something; sweet of him to pull the necessary strings to secure the offer.

She envisaged Lewis, Dan and Kirsty hatching the scheme. *It would do Tessa a world of good to mix with some new people; get out of the flat.* She knew they were trying to help. In fact she'd been thinking that she should find something to occupy her until she got underway with the next book.

'Why not? It might be fun. I don't remember him, though.'

Dan primed her. Hollinghurst had been a second-rate painter who had hovered around the fringes of the art world for years, eventually forsaking fine art for commerce and working on 'visuals' for a successful advertising agency.

'He has fingers in several pies. Jay told me that he's recently inherited serious money from his grandfather, hence the gallery venture. Poacher turned gamekeeper – or *vice versa*.'

She suddenly remembered the journal that she'd kept in St Ives and eventually she unearthed it in a large carrier bag, crammed with letters and postcards. The bag had moved with her several times but, knowing it was dangerously full of the past, she hadn't opened it for years. She flipped through the pages of the journal. There they all were. Liza. Valmai and Connor. Jay, of course, on every page. God, she'd been besotted with him. Occasionally, even now, when he came into a room or when they spoke on the phone, a sweet burst of lust exploded in her gut. 'Suzie', 'Midge', 'Steve', 'Terry', the names stirred memories of flat-chested girls with wild hair; intense young men with nicotine-stained fingers and unattractive feet. But she could find no reference to Mark Hollinghurst. Or Dan Coates either, come to that.

Gallery Seven's glass and steel minimalism was an incongruous addition to a streetscape of shabby houses, family-run businesses and basement sweat shops. The front door was propped open with a couple of bricks, allowing the smell of gloss paint to spill into the street. An electrician on a stepladder was rigging spotlights on a track.

'Is Mark Hollinghurst around?' Tessa asked from the threshold.

He pointed to the corner where a man in a dark grey suit and black brogues was sorting through a pile of papers. His hair was unfashionably neat but, as if to deny that he might be an accountant, his white shirt was buttoned to the top and he wore no tie. Suddenly she felt foolish. She'd come to see if it might be bearable to work here but she'd got it the wrong way round. It was she who was under scrutiny.

Ignoring her extended hand, Mark Hollinghurst kissed her on both cheeks and steered her to his office where they sat in trendy leather chairs surrounded by boxes and wrapped furniture. He assured her that she hadn't changed; she told him that he *had*, which he took as a compliment not a confession that she didn't remember him. He asked about Dan and the Costelloes and, from his accurate recollections, it was clear that he must have spent a good deal of time with them. While he reminisced, she studied him, imagining how he might have looked twenty years earlier, but his was a run-of-the-mill sort of face, without a single remarkable feature. She would have sworn in a court of law that she had never seen him before.

He admitted this wasn't the obvious location for a gallery selling 'cutting edge stuff' but he seemed convinced that the area was on the up.

331

'In five years it'll be buzzing. A couple of good restaurants have opened recently in the area and there's a very trendy furniture shop around the corner. Anyway, I plan to target investors, not passing trade. City boys with red braces. Ad men. Punters with money, prepared to take a gamble; anyone who wants to be in on "the next big thing". I'm out to sign up new talent. Tomorrow's Hockneys and Warhols. Give them their first break.'

'It sounds a bit … cynical,' Tessa ventured.

'No room for sentimentality in Thatcher-land.' He grinned as though ruthlessness was something to applaud.

She asked what the job entailed. He wrapped it up in fancy terms but it boiled down to opening the post, typing letters, keeping lists up to date and responding to enquiries. Glorified clerical work.

'You're not looking for an art expert then,' she said.

He missed the irony. 'I've got one if I need one. You'll be working with Amelie Tanqueray. Degree in History of Art. Nice girl. All you need to do is stick to facts. A bit of background on the artist. The date the work was done. Price, of course, once you're sure they're genuinely interested. But no opinions. Nothing subjective.' He smiled an implicit warning.

The pay was poor and the job unlikely to stretch her but it was a long time since she'd chalked up a success. 'No worries. I can be extremely objective when I have to be.'

'Great. I'll take that as a yes.' He leaned across and kissed her again, this time squeezing her thigh. 'Make sure you drag Dan along to the opening party next week. Jay Costello, too, if you can twist his arm. We need a few big names on board.'

Tessa liked being part of it all; dressing stylishly and joining the troop of workers on its daily march to the Tube; checking her make-up in the staff cloakroom and priming the coffee machine for the first cup of the day; squaring up the pile of catalogues on the low glass table; replenishing the water in the vases containing fresh flowers. Being on the inside for a change.

Amelie Tanqueray was in her early twenties. Blonde and self-assured, a size eight in clothes and four in shoes, Gran would have described her as 'a little china doll'. She was bilingual – her mother, a French socialite, her English father, 'something in the city'. Educated at posh schools and the Courtauld Institute, she skied, rode and sailed. The labels on her clothes read like captions from a fashion magazine. If Mark Hollinghurst employed Tessa for her links to the art world, Amelie was there for her class and family connections.

Tessa couldn't help liking the girl. She was funny and irreverent. She knew how to get things done. She balanced irony and optimism in exactly the right measures. It wasn't her fault that her parents were rich and influential, and naturally they'd wanted the best for their daughter.

Amelie appeared to like her, too. She asked Tessa's advice on dealing with the Ruperts and Ralphs and Hugos who constantly pursued her; confessed that she'd cheated in her 'finals'; confided that she'd taken 'this poxy little job' as a stopgap whilst she caught her breath after a frenzied affair with a married man.

Tessa had never, until now, been called upon to play the wise older sister. Strange, bearing in mind that she had a younger brother.

Chapter 31

THE HOUSE IN SALISBURY ROAD was becoming less and less the place where Lewis had grown up. The front door had always been privet green but now it was canary yellow. A shower had appeared above the bath and a leather three-piece suite filled the living room. The towels smelled different and a musky bouquet of garlic and ground coffee pervaded the kitchen cupboards. In his mother's day, the house had been a Forth Bridge of never-ending domestic duties but, since his father's marriage to Barbara, it had been demoted to a backdrop, setting the scene for more interesting events. The Swinburne Family, as a unit, was retreating from the place.

Barbara continued to be pleasant and welcoming, leaving them to themselves whilst she wrote a letter or went to the library. Not that he visited as often as he used to. There was no longer the same imperative.

Bristol was a lively city where he and Kirsty had a growing circle of friends. Invitations to dinner parties decorated the mantelpiece and their pin-up board was a patchwork of concert and theatre tickets. They spent the half-term holiday in Amsterdam and were planning a few days in Paris at Easter. They were back on their old footing but, once in a while and for no obvious reason, sadness would creep between them, sending one or the other off for a brisk walk or an early night.

Lewis was pleased that Tessa was sticking with the gallery

job. From what he could make out it wasn't anything special but she seemed to get on well with the people there and she'd hinted that she was writing another book. Perhaps, with that on the go, she needed a job that didn't require much brainpower.

Lying in bed next to Kirsty, the back of his hand resting against her thigh, he was a grateful man. Kirsty was well again and his kidney stone crisis was resolved; his father was settling in to his new life and, remarkably, Tessa had a job. Now that his daughters were older, he was finding them easier to get on with. Doug Williams was due to retire soon so there would be a vacancy as head of the Maths Department. Yes. Things were ticking over nicely.

Although the job at Gallery Seven wasn't the most stimulating in the world, Tessa enjoyed it. She should look for something more challenging soon but in the mean time it wouldn't do any harm to use this period to make contacts and get something concrete on her CV. Hollinghurst had signed up a cohort of talented youngsters and she was damned good at selling their stuff. When Lewis phoned or when she was out with friends, she had tales to tell of eccentric artists and celebrities who spent unbelievable amounts of money on unbelievably outrageous items. Most satisfying of all, the embryo of a novel was quickening in the back of her mind.

Tessa was thirty-nine years old, a fact which astounded her. When her mother was this age, she'd written her off as fit only for perms and wrap-around 'pinnies'. Recently she had started colouring her hair and used reading glasses when she needed to look up a number in the phone book. But she didn't, and never would, possess a 'pinny'.

Her doubts about living with Dan were more or less resolved. He was good company and a thoughtful lover. He didn't smother her with attention or demand that she account for her every movement. The flat was spacious enough for her to have her own study where she could write or read or simply be alone. She realised that the 'sell-out' that she'd been fighting against was, in fact, 'balance'. *Balance.* It sounded positive. It implied expertise.

One thing threatened to destabilise everything. Her addiction to Rundle. She'd broken with him on several occasions, the most recent, twelve months ago. 'Okay,' he'd agreed impassively, 'see you around'. She'd held out for four months then, when she'd gone back, he'd neither crowed nor shown any indication that he was pleased. And they'd carried on as before.

It had been up to her to decide when to meet. On the face of it she called the shots but in truth it made her need for him all too evident. She would resist for as long as she could then, when she could bear it no longer, she would phone him. This time it would be different. She would arrive unannounced. Rundle didn't know she had keys to his flat. Once, when he'd been called away to sort out a crisis at the garage, he'd left her a set which she'd 'forgotten' to give back, hanging on to them until her next visit, in the meantime, getting a duplicate set cut.

At Victoria station, she bought the *Observer* and a black coffee. The station concourse was busy with families getting out of London on what promised to be a lovely day. She watched a woman, hand in hand with a skipping toddler, another wrestling with a dog and a cumbersome pushchair. Did she envy or pity them their domesticity?

She chose a window seat in the corner of the carriage where she wouldn't have to talk to anyone. Balancing her coffee on the flap-down table, she laced it with whisky from the flask in her handbag. The train journey held no interest for her. She'd seen every isolated farmhouse, every picturesque village church, and every graffitied railway bridge a dozen times before. She opened the paper. 'Cold War in Space.' 'The Hitler Diaries'.'

336

More trouble in Zimbabwe. Alcohol and the pulse of the train lulled her and she drifted.

It had to stop. She would stop it.

At times she hated Rundle but she knew he wasn't fundamentally bad. He was simply a man who took what was offered. First she'd offered him her virginity then, next day, gone back for more. The *rendezvous* in Trafalgar Square was at her instigation, as was her follow-up visit to Brighton. She'd finished with him several times then been unable to stay away. He'd never attempted to sway her. When she was with him she didn't have to be clever or brave or considerate. All she had to do was let go. No one else had ever had this effect on her and, because of this, he was a threat.

Mrs Channing had shown them a wooden box, every facet of which was inlaid with mother of pearl and ivory. When she shook the box, it rattled tantalisingly but there appeared to be no way to get in. The trick was to find the sliding panel which would allow another panel to slide, and then another, until the box revealed its contents – a miniature wooden lotus flower. Very occasionally, Rundle opened up a little. 'We're two of a kind, Tessa. We're not like the rest of them. We write our own rules. Then break them.' He was a puzzle box which might contain everything or nothing.

From the moment she'd seen him with Mike Stoddy, she'd allowed herself to be controlled by him but she was sure she didn't exist for him unless she was standing in front of him. They might be 'two of a kind' – what a thrillingly conspiratorial phrase – but it didn't follow that he needed her.

The brakes squealed and the train came to a halt. *Come on.* She was impatient to get there but there was a problem on the line and the train limped fitfully through the Sussex countryside. By the time they reached Brighton, she was feeling sick with apprehension and unsteady from the alcohol.

Rundle's car was parked outside his flat and, looking up at the first floor, she saw that his kitchen window was open. She rang the bell, inclining her head towards the entryphone, listening for his voice, ringing again when there was no response. She unlocked the door and went in to the communal hallway then tiptoed up the stairs to the first floor. She tapped firmly on the door to Rundle's flat, giving him another opportunity to answer before letting herself in.

The room smelled of freshly made coffee.

'Rundle?'

In the beginning she'd assumed that he tidied up before she came but she soon realised that the place was always immaculate. He never left dirty crockery in the sink or a tea towel over the back of a chair. Books went back on the shelves, clothing on hangers in the wardrobe. No doubt he was the same at work – tools in the right place, records up to date. She imagined that after she left he'd have changed the sheets and given everything a wipe down with Dettol before she reached the station. Once, irritated by his orderliness, she'd snapped, 'I'm surprised you don't put a plastic sheet down, to save the mess.' 'Sounds kinky,' he'd replied.

She went in to the kitchen. The kettle was still warm. He couldn't be far away. The sensible thing would be to leave a note then catch the next train home. *Dear Rundle, I shan't be coming here again. Thanks for everything. Good luck in the future, Tessa.* Factual. Final. Magnanimous. Why even pretend that she could do it that way?

It wouldn't be a good idea for him to find her in his flat and she decided to come back in an hour or so. Suddenly she felt the urge to take a memento of the man who was fucking up her life, something to punish him and to remind herself never to become this vulnerable again.

There was a small chest next to his bed and she eased out

each drawer, careful not to disturb anything. Hankies. Balled socks and folded tee shirts. Sweaters. In one of the small top drawers, a box containing cufflinks and tiepins. And a man's wristwatch, square-faced, with an expanding metal strap. The shape of it and the elegant Roman numerals slanting in to the corners told her that it was special. She dropped it in her bag.

Then, she found a pub where she spent the next forty minutes bolstering her courage and wondering when Rundle would return home.

The door phone crackled. 'Yes?'

'It's me. Tessa.'

The mechanism buzzed and she pushed the door open. She climbed the stairs, this time knowing he was there, a fusion of excitement and anxiety rising inside her.

He was wearing a white tee shirt and jeans. His hair was damp as though he'd just washed it. His feet were bare and there was a sticking plaster wrapped around the little toe of his left foot. An ironing board stood in the middle of the room, a pile of shirts on the sofa, a couple more on hangers dangling from the picture rail. Dylan was rasping softly from the turntable.

'You didn't phone,' he said. It was a statement of fact.

'"It's lovely to see you, Tessa. I've been counting the days,"' she chanted.

'Is that what you want me to say?'

She must remain detached, say what she had to say then get out, but Rundle, shape-shifted by domesticity, wrong-footed her.

'Take your jacket off and I'll make us a coffee,' he said.

'No.' She held her hand out as if to fend him off. 'No, thanks.'

'Okay.'

He turned back to the ironing board, taking the next shirt off the pile. His lack of interest was more painful than a slap across the face.

'I won't be coming here any more.' It sounded as though it was the *place* that she had taken against and she had another shot at it. 'I don't want to see you again. Ever.'

There was no interruption to the movement of his arm as he pushed the iron back and forth across the shirt front. 'You're the boss.'

Go. Go now. She reached the door then hesitated.

He glanced up. 'Am I supposed to dissuade you? You'll have to tell me if I am.'

'Get stuffed.'

Slamming the door behind her, she ran down the stairs and out into the street, not looking back, running until the stitch in her side doubled her up and brought her to a halt. She found a seat in a little park and waited until the blood had stopped pounding in her ears. She felt fired up yet damaged, like a soldier who had escaped from an ambush but in so doing had lost a limb.

Everything had changed. And *she* had changed it. Suddenly the pillar box on the corner looked redder, the blossom on the street trees, frothier. She put her head back, the sun warming her face. She was free. *Free.* It was a glorious day. Why was she rushing home? Dan was in Italy and she had nothing pressing to do. She would go and find the sea – wasn't that what people came to Brighton for?

The promenade was thronged with people walking mangy dogs or roller skating or gazing at the horizon. On the beach, children screamed as the grey-brown waves churned the pebbles; mums watched to see that their offspring didn't drown and dads read the Sunday paper; teenagers snogged and groped each other under beach towels; Granddads dozed and grannies fiddled with Thermos flasks. Ordinary people doing ordinary things and now she was one of them.

*

Later that evening she wrapped Rundle's watch in newspaper and, placing the parcel on the bread board, she pounded it repeatedly with a hammer. After a while she set the hammer down. 'Abracadabra,' she giggled, lifting her whisky glass and wafting it above the flattened package. But when she unfurled the paper the watch was mangled beyond repair.

VII

1987

Chapter 32

I<small>T HAD TAKEN</small> L<small>EWIS A WHILE</small> to get used to teaching in a co-educational school. Girls were inclined to doubt their own abilities and needed sustained encouragement. Boys, on the other hand, were cocky and boisterous, triumphant when they were right and quick to jeer anyone, male or female, who faltered. Boys shrugged off criticism but girls crumpled.

One girl in his fourth form set, a shrimp of a thing called Michelle Haldane, took the jibes particularly hard. When something she did or said provoked ridicule, she flushed a blotchy scarlet and sniffled into the sleeve of her cardigan. She had no mates, no one to shout up for her and when Lewis spotted her sitting on her own in the school canteen, it struck him that his daughters, pale and timorous, might suffer the same fate.

He picked his way between the tables. 'How did you get on with the homework, Michelle?'

She blushed and stared down at her plate. 'Dunno, sir.'

'Well, don't let on to anyone but I do actually get paid to teach you maths. So if there's anything you don't understand...' He gave what he hoped was an encouraging smile.

Her cheeks reddened further. 'Thanks.'

When he passed her in the corridor, he made sure to nod 'hello'. If they happened to be crossing the schoolyard at the same time, he walked a little way with her, asking about the sort of music she liked or if she'd had a good weekend, demonstrating that there was more to life – hers and his – than quadratic equations. Sometimes, after a lesson, she stayed behind, and, safe from the boys' ridicule, asked him to go over something she 'didn't get'. Standing dumbly at his side whilst he ran through it again, she gave no indication whether she grasped it but, during the course of the term, her maths marks showed a definite, if slight, improvement. She was less timid in class, making eye contact when he addressed her, occasionally flashing a nervy smile. Most satisfying of all, he noticed that she had been adopted by one of the leading fourth form cliques. What Michelle Haldane had to offer them was a mystery, as was most of what went on between girls of that age, but he felt that he was, in some small way, helping.

One Saturday Lewis visited his father and discovered an estate agent's sign planted amongst the rose bushes in the front garden.

His father looked sheepish. 'We thought we'd test the market. See if we get any interest,' he explained.

'And have you?'

'Well…'

'We have, actually,' Barbara chimed in. 'A nice young couple who've got a little one. They want to move into the school catchment area and they're happy to give the asking price.'

Lewis tried to look unfazed. 'So where are you going?'

'Barbara thinks—'

'We *both* think it's the right time to look for something more manageable. A bungalow with a small garden, perhaps. On the flat. Handy for the bus. It'll be a chance to dispose of all the junk we've accumulated.' She smiled cheerily, as though their plan to ditch the family's past was bound to win his support.

'Isn't this a bit … sudden, Dad? You didn't mention anything.'

'No need to get aerated, Lewis. Nothing's settled yet. There's many a slip.' His father evidently thought a dose of pessimism was the best way to demonstrate the uncertainty of the situation.

After a cup of tea, Lewis made his excuses. 'Just a flying visit this time, I'm afraid. I've got to check something up at the house.'

This wasn't true. He didn't need to go to Cranwell Lodge at all. He merely wanted to look at it.

To start with, Lewis had organised the lettings himself. Sorting out inventories, dripping taps and faulty boilers was time-consuming but it kept him closely involved with his house and he liked that. After a while Kirsty had put her foot down – he could see her point – and he'd handed over its management to an agent.

Dave and Sue Brown still lived next door and over the years they had become good friends. Lewis admired Dave's ungrudging commitment to his wife and young family; he liked Sue's honesty and refusal to be 'cool'. He enjoyed visiting them, not only because they were good friends but from their back garden – in colder weather, through their kitchen window – he had an excellent view of the old house, imposing and enduring, little changed by whatever was going on within its solid walls.

'Who's your money on?' Dave pointed at the pile of election literature stacked on the worktop. 'The electorate must be wising up to her by now. The woman's a megalomaniac. I fancy Kinnock.'

'Don't count on it.'

Dave offered Lewis a chocolate biscuit. 'We've just finished Tessa's latest. What's it called? *Obsessed.* That's it.'

'What did you think?'

'Great. A bit saucy in places, mind you.' Dave grinned. 'We couldn't decide if you figured in this one or not.'

Promising to call again soon, Lewis left the homely chaos of the Brown's kitchen. As he drove along Medway Avenue, he glanced at his watch. It was an age since he'd been to his mother's grave. The cemetery gates closed 'at dusk' – an unsettling arrangement during winter months, the prospect of a night amongst the tombstones preoccupying anyone lingering there on a January afternoon. But it was six o'clock on a bright summer's day and, after stopping at a phone box to let Kirsty know what he was doing, he found a corner shop selling flowers then drove the short distance to the cemetery.

Leaving the car just inside the ornate iron gates, he negotiated the maze of solemn paths, preparing himself for what never failed to distress him. As he approached he saw a man kneeling in the grass next to the grave, not in an attitude of prayer but as if he were scrubbing the kitchen floor. He cleared his throat and the man turned around. It was Frank Swinburne.

Lewis hadn't seen his uncle since the Christmas before last when they'd all congregated at his father's house. Frank had been quiet and seemed out of sorts. Later, when he and Kirsty were discussing the get-together, it had occurred to Lewis that Barbara and his uncle might not get on. She might even disapprove of her homosexual brother-in-law. 'Mum thought he was wonderful,' Lewis explained. 'She came alive when he was around. But I'm not sure she knew about his ... inclinations. Probably didn't know that such things went on.'

'Hello, Uncle Frank.'

'Hello, Lewis, old son.' Frank Swinburne struggled to his feet and they hugged. 'Thought I'd come and give your mother a wash and brush up. This sandstone soon discolours. I told Dick at the time he should have gone for granite, but it was three times the cost.'

Lewis felt ashamed. Not only had his uncle spotted that the stone needed attention, he'd toiled here with a jerrycan of water and a wire brush, then spent goodness knows how long scrubbing away the grime. He'd brought flowers too – pink roses, his sister-in-law's favourite – making his own offering of carnations look like the tired afterthought that it was.

'She was a lovely woman.' Frank's tone wasn't in the slightest bit maudlin. 'A shame the way it turned out.'

They stood together, each silently remembering their own Margaret Anne Swinburne.

'Are you still at the same place?' Lewis asked as they walked back to the cars. 'Conway Road, isn't it?'

'We left there six months ago. We're down near the back of the station now.'

Lewis, resolutely ignoring the 'we', continued. 'D'you fancy a drink? I'm not rushing back. We never seem to have time to—'

'No, thanks, Lewis. Next time, maybe. I'm expected home.' He held Lewis's gaze, steady and open.

'No worries. As you say, next time.' Not knowing what else to do, Lewis shook his uncle's hand.

They drove away, Frank Swinburne behind him until, at the traffic lights, he turned left and his uncle carried on towards the train station and whoever was expecting him home.

After an eight year break, during which she'd doubted whether she would ever get another novel published, Tessa had found a dynamic new agent who secured her a reasonable advance on a two book deal. Although she'd given in her notice at Gallery Seven as soon as she'd signed the contract, Mark Hollinghurst had hosted the launch of the new book – set in an artists' commune in Cornwall – and rounded up as many of the 'old crowd' as he could. The event attracted plenty of media attention and the book sold well. Tessa's agent was currently negotiating with a production company who were interested in adapting it for television.

The follow-up, *Obsessed*, was a stark tale of abuse and revenge in which the relationship between her two central characters wasn't quite … healthy. She'd written it in just a few months, the words pouring out in a bitter torrent. 'Terrific stuff,' her agent had enthused. 'Nothing the punter likes more than a *soupçon* of soft porn; a touch of voyeurism.'

The publishers arranged for Tessa to do a series of book signings, one of which was in Hove.

'Why don't I come with you?' Dan said. 'We could stay overnight. Stroll along the prom like a couple of old fogies. Eat fish and chips. Perhaps there's a pier. I love a good pier.'

The holiday season was getting underway. The town seemed charmingly faded and soft-edged after the grind of London. It was a while since they had been away together and Tessa had forgotten how much fun it was to visit a new place with Dan. He had an eye for abstracting things from their context, seeing juxtapositions of colours and shapes where she saw buses and awnings and lampposts. 'That's what artists are for,' he explained, 'to view the world through the eyes of an alien. Oh, and to ravish lady writers.'

They'd intended to stay in a hotel but in the end plumped for a guesthouse on the strength of its ridiculous name – Valhalla. They weren't disappointed. Their landlady had attached explanatory and cautionary messages everywhere, anticipating every possible problem. *Water very hot. Window latch stiff. Extra pillows available on request.* She had an extensive collection of Toby jugs and an alarming enthusiasm for knitting which extended beyond coy toilet roll covers and antimacassars to matching Fair Isle sweaters for herself and her gummy-eyed Labrador.

Tessa's grandmother had knitted a Fair Isle sweater for her when she was thirteen or fourteen – too old, anyway, for home-made clothes – its blue and green intricacies chasing around her chest, swamping her developing breasts and rendering her androgynous. Now, seeing the zigzagging rows, Tessa felt wool rasping on her cheeks, smelled its damp hair scent as, nose flattened and temporarily blinded, she'd pushed her head through the tight neck. She'd detested it but her mother had forced her to wear it. *Forced her?* How had Peggy Swinburne forced anyone to do anything? 'It took Gran months to knit that, Tessa. It would be terribly unkind of you not to wear it. And it's lovely and warm.' That's how.

Dan went in search of the local art gallery while Tessa introduced herself to Howard James, the proprietor of the bookshop. She was looking forward to the afternoon. It amused her to see herself smiling out from posters and fun to sit, surrounded by crisp, un-thumbed copies of her books, being treated as a minor celebrity.

She'd been installed for half an hour and signed perhaps seven or eight books when she became conscious of being watched. It wasn't unusual for an inquisitive customer, unwilling to make eye contact for fear of being shamed into forking out ten quid, to spy on her. Today's observer was standing slightly behind her, to her right, half-hidden by a display of travel books.

'Hello, Tessa.'

She swung round. 'Rundle.'

His un-prefaced surname rang around the small shop as accusatorily as if she'd shouted 'murder'.

The customers froze, staring at her until she forced a smile, releasing them from their paralysis.

She lowered her voice. 'I didn't expect to see you here.'

'Didn't you? You've been all over the local press.' He held up a copy of the book, its dust jacket scuffed. 'I bought it as soon as it came out. Not in this shop but I was hoping you'd sign it for me. Is that allowed?'

Rundle must be over fifty but he had a full head of grey-flecked hair. He was neat and trim, lean without looking scrawny. An observer might put him down as a long distance runner or a swimmer.

The proprietor bustled across, ready to sort out any trouble. 'Anything you need, Tessa?' He kept his gaze fixed on Rundle.

'I'm fine thanks, Howard.' James was a nosy man and she knew she couldn't get away without some kind of explanation. 'Rundle – Tony – is an old friend of mine.'

Yes,' Rundle smiled, transforming himself in to the irresistible young man she had stalked in the church hall, 'but we've lost touch recently, haven't we, Tess?'

James seemed relieved that he wasn't going to be called on to evict a difficult customer. 'Can I bring you both a coffee?'

Rundle looked at Tessa and raised his eyebrows. 'I don't want to put you to any trouble.'

'Not at all, Mr Rundle. Sometimes customers are a bit shy about approaching an author. It helps to have a bit of activity. Milk and sugar?' He disappeared in to his office.

Rundle tapped the pile of books. 'I enjoyed it. Weird, though, knowing how involved I was in your … research. Plot too, come to that.'

A middle-aged woman edged hesitantly towards the table and Rundle stood back while Tessa signed her book and they exchanged a few words.

'You're doing quite well, by the look of it,' Rundle said pointing at the stack of books on the table.

'What d'you want?' she asked quietly. 'Why are you here?'

'I want you to sign—'

'I may be foolish but I'm not a fool,' she whispered. 'Please don't mess me about.'

He cleared his throat. 'I'm not messing you about. On the contrary, I came because I wanted to see you.' He looked her square in the face. 'I've missed you.' There was no trace of mockery in his confession.

'That doesn't sound like the Rundle I used to know.' She

351

waited for him to turn their exchange into a joke or revert to the sneering silence that was his speciality.

'That's because you never got to know me.'

He was out of order, turning up like this, polite and reasonable – and sexy – scattering her good intentions like leaves in a gale.

'Get to know you? How was that ever going to happen? Was I supposed to be a mind-reader or something? Anyway, you couldn't have been that distraught to have left it this long.'

'I was waiting for you to come back.'

She stifled a laugh. 'What, you waited five years for me to come back? I don't believe you.'

Another customer came to the table, interrupting their conversation. The woman confessed to being a fan and set out to prove that she had read every one of Tessa's books by discussing them in detail.

At last she went and Tessa tried again. 'I told you that it was over between us and I meant it. I still mean it. How dare you come here,' she waved her hand towards his navy suit and his red silk tie, using every ounce of willpower to keep from touching him, 'all tarted up like this. What do you want from me?'

Rundle might well be playing a spiteful game but something in his manner denied her suspicion.

'I hoped you'd bring my watch back one day, so I needed to let you know that I'm moving. I was going to write but when I saw the poster I decided to come and tell you in person.'

She'd forgotten about the watch.

'Well you've told me now, haven't you?' She stood up and held out her hand as if ending a business meeting. 'Goodbye, Rundle. And good luck with … whatever it is you're doing.'

He took her hand, gripping it tightly without shaking it and with his other hand slid a folded piece of paper across the table. 'That's where I'll be.'

The bell above the shop door tinkled. She glanced up and saw Dan. He winked at her and held the door open, nodding amiably at the edgy-looking man in the dark suit who pushed past him.

'What on earth did you do to him?' he asked, jerking his head towards Rundle who had raced across the road and was already way down the street.

The wind had coaxed Dan's longish hair into rough curls and pinked his cheeks. He looked handsome in a vigorous, boyish way, and Tessa wished with all her heart that Dan, not Rundle, was the one who made her sick with desire.

Chapter 33

THE RUNDLE WHOM TESSA HAD RESISTED for five years was a cold-hearted loner. But suddenly here he was, vulnerable and confessional. Rundle reconstructed. It was too cruel. She had to talk to someone.

Lewis? Her brother had always treated Dan as if he were her salvation, admiring him with the reverence of first former for Head Boy. There was no doubt what Lewis's advice would be. If it came to the crunch, he would stand by her but disapproving support would do nothing for her self-esteem.

Kirsty? She could be counted on for objectivity but it was impossible to imagine her sister-in-law empathising with her visceral desire for Rundle. Asking Kirsty how to deal with a sexual craving would be like asking a vegetarian how to make black pudding.

Liza? Or even Jay? They were neither prudish nor judgemental but the three of them shared a delicate history. Too many skeletons lurked in their communal cupboard, ready to come clattering out and complicate things further.

She moved on through the list of possibles, eventually arriving at Amelie Tanqueray.

Amelie had moved on from Gallery Seven not long after Tessa left. In her case it was to marry a Tory politician twenty years her senior. Tessa and Dan had attended the wedding, a stultifyingly formal affair somewhere in rural Buckinghamshire. The women often met for lunch when Amelie came to London and Tessa had stayed with them several times. Dan was always included in the invitation but he and Amelie had never hit it off and he found a string of plausible reasons not to go. On these visits, Tessa saw little of Amelie's husband, Sir Marcus Fellowes, who spent most of the time in his study, doing whatever members of parliament did at weekends. This suited everyone.

On her most recent visit, Amelie had admitted that she'd married on a whim. 'Marcus needed a presentable wife – the electorate are dubious about bachelors – and I needed a safe haven. Neither of us pretends that it's a love match but, as long as we're discreet, we've agreed that we can carry on as we wish.' They were sitting on the terrace of the detached Georgian house in its several acres of landscaped garden. 'Doesn't he want an heir for all this?' Tessa threw her arms wide. Amelie had shrugged. 'We're still negotiating on that one. I've got no real objection. For an ex-public schoolboy, he's surprisingly good in bed. Money and status create a potent aphrodisiac, mind you.'

Yes. Amelie was the one to confide in.

They met in a Greek restaurant near the British Museum.

'You were very cagey on the phone,' Amelie said. 'Secrets?'

Tessa had never shared Rundle. He belonged solely to her. She hesitated, unsure, now, if this was a good idea.

'Is everything okay? You look a bit … worn.' Amelie leaned across the table and, placing a finger on Tessa's chin, turned her face towards the light. 'Mmmm.'

'I haven't been sleeping.'

'You're not ill?'

Tessa attempted a smile. 'There's a strong possibility that I'm going mad. Does that count?'

'Spit it out.'

The temptation to offload was irresistible. Starting with her first glimpse of him on the school bus, she revealed her obsession with Tony Rundle. Everything. The 'first time'; the miserable weekend when she'd run away from home and gone to him; their meeting in Trafalgar Square when it had all started up again; the furtive trips to Brighton. She tried to explain the thrill of their sexual encounters and how bad she felt afterwards; how she'd made the break, refusing to give in to her craving. Finally his reappearance – transformed and needy.

'So there you have it, in all its squalid glory. Pathetic, isn't it? Sordid, ridiculous and pathetic.' She paused. 'You're allowed to agree with me.'

Amelie pushed aside her plate and was silent for a moment, staring at the lunchtime crowd hurrying past the window. 'It's sad, actually.'

'*Sad*. How d'you make that out?'

'Well, for all those years, you and this man were having the most incredible sex, the sort of thing all women fantasise about, but you were completely isolated … insulated … from each other. It wasn't even as if it were an amazing secret that you *shared*.' She frowned. 'There was no sharing.'

'No, because neither of us was up for that sort of relationship.'

'Really? In that case, why did he say that you'd never made an effort to get to know him?'

Amelie was starting to annoy her.

'You don't know what he's like,' Tessa muttered.

'Do *you*? Look, the man took advantage of you when you were eighteen. Losing one's virginity is a massive thing, especially if it's *taken* rather than *given*.' She played with her linen napkin, rolling and unrolling it. 'I had a similar experience. But I was only fifteen and he was … well, never mind. I can understand, too, why you got back in touch with him. Laying ghosts. Wiping the slate clean. But you should have had it out with him, there and then. Who knows, you might even have been able to start a viable relationship.'

This superficial claptrap didn't come within a million miles of explaining the hold Rundle had over her.

'With a view to what, exactly? Life with a car mechanic?'

On all sides, flawless women and loud men tucked into fancy food. Rundle's broad accent echoed in her head and she pictured his pen holder knife grip. She couldn't bring him to a place like this. Or take him down to Berkshire for the weekend. Or introduce him to people like Liza and Jay.

Amelie pushed her plate aside. 'Have you thought of telling Dan? At least you'd have cleared away all the crud that's piled up between you.'

'We're not talking blocked drains. Dan's a dear, sweet man. He's never had any misconceptions about me, but to hit him with something so … brutal. I'm not that much of a cow.'

Amelie's raised eyebrows questioned Tessa's assertion. 'So what *do* you want me to say? Yes, it's perfectly fine to go sneaking off to Brighton regularly for some S and M with your dysfunctional bit of rough. No. I'm not prepared to do that.' There was concern in Amelie's voice. 'I don't understand why you're turning this into a problem. You did the hard bit years ago when you gave him up. Just forget the man and invest in a top of the range vibrator.'

There was no point in going on with this. Amelie was probably jealous.

Tessa drained the dregs of her red wine. 'You're right. I'm being stupid. I don't know why you bother with me.'

'*Schadenfreude*. The basis of most friendships.' Amelie stood up. 'Where are the loos? My bladder's about to burst.'

Amelie's Armani jacket was looped over the back of her chair and, while she was away from the table, Tessa unpinned the

357

sparkling brooch from its lapel and slid it into her bag.

Schadenfreude *the bones out of that, Mrs Smart Arse Fellowes.*

Lewis couldn't remember an October as pleasant as this. Blue skies and balmy days had oiled the squeaky wheels of the new school year. The usual range of glitches peppered his working day – timetabling clashes, shortfalls in equipment, staff absences – but, on the whole, teachers and pupils seemed mellow and upbeat.

He was halfway through a double period with Form One, trying to explain why algebra was useful whilst simultaneously watching the caretaker raking leaves off the tennis courts, when the school secretary tapped on the door.

Doreen Lane had worked at the school for ever. She had weathered its transition from grammar to co-educational establishment, and worked for seven different head teachers. She was efficient, enthusiastic and kept her head when things went awry, but this morning she seemed jumpy.

'Sorry to disturb you, Mr Swinburne.'

'Not at all, Mrs Lane. What can I do for you?' The formal charade played out whenever pupils were within earshot never failed to make Lewis feel ridiculous.

'Could I have a word, please?'

Instructing the class to get on with their work, he stepped into the corridor and pulled the door to.

'What's up?'

'The Head wants to see you. Right away. Linda's on her way to cover your lesson.'

'Can't it wait until break? What's the panic?'

'I'm afraid I couldn't say.'

Ken Anson was tidying his already immaculate desk when Lewis entered his office. Despite the heat, the man was wearing the black gown he donned for special occasions and which transformed him from pompous little man into gigantic crow.

Lewis waited in silence.

'Sit down, Lewis.' Anson gestured to a chair. He looked uncomfortable. Shifty.

'I'll stand, if that's okay with you, Headmaster.'

Anson was a small man, no more than five foot six inches, and Lewis sensed that it would be wise to retain his height advantage.

Anson's discomfort turned to caginess. 'I've … we've … received a complaint.'

'About whom?' Lewis already knew but he still had to ask. 'Me?'

'Well. Yes. Actually.' Anson blew his nose and avoided Lewis's gaze. 'Do you have any idea why anyone would lodge a complaint against you?'

My jokes are corny? I wear too much aftershave?
'No.'

Lewis had no clue why anyone would complain. He'd been doing the job long enough to know that he was a good teacher. The kids liked him and they achieved reasonable exam results. He set enough homework to satisfy parents yet not overburden his pupils. He ran the chess club and the jazz society. He was doing okay.

Anson, in nylon shirt, navy blazer and bat-winged gown, was sweating. 'Michelle Haldane. Does the name mean anything to you?'

'Of course. She's in my maths set. Quiet girl. Average ability but, with a bit of encouragement—'

'Her parents contacted me this morning.'

The blood pumped in Lewis's ears. His throat constricted and he couldn't get rid of the spittle that was pooling beneath his tongue. He stared at Anson's glistening face, noticing the

359

flecks of scum at the corners of his mean mouth, the wayward hairs sprouting, like miniature antennae, across the bridge of his nose.

'Michelle says … *alleges* … that you have made improper suggestions. Of a sexual nature.'

What, that I wanted to run my fingers through that limp hair? Kiss those dry lips? Fondle those non-existent breasts?

'Do you have anything to say before we go any further?'

Lewis felt sick with fury. 'Of course I have something to say. But I'd be stupid to say anything until I know exactly what I'm supposed to have "suggested".' It sounded slippery but one word out of place, one flippant comment, and he might be damned.

'I can't go into that at the moment but obviously you are suspended as from now. Temporarily, and on full pay, of course. I've informed Social Services. They're sending someone to talk to Michelle. And … well, I'm sure you're aware of the procedure.'

'What about my classes—'

'Don't worry about that. It's all in hand.' Anson turned away and pretended to study his desk diary.

As Lewis left the room, he glanced at the wall clock in the corridor. The interview with Anson had lasted four minutes. Long enough for a man to run a mile, or the world to end.

'So you did spend time alone with this girl?' Kirsty asked.

'Yes. She was never going to ask for help in front of the class. I was trying to give her a bit of a confidence boost. I felt sorry for her. I kept thinking that Sarah or Jane could be in the same position one day.'

They were in bed, Lewis's restlessness keeping them both awake. Kirsty was lying next to him but their bodies were not touching. Her demeanour was disturbingly neutral, as though she were a disinterested third party.

'Teaching's not just about imparting facts and information.

It's about exposing young minds to life's possibilities.'

She groaned. 'I hope you're not going to come out with that sort of thing to a tribunal. It sounds … suggestive.'

He watched a shaft of light cast by a car's headlights track across the ceiling and down the wall. 'I'm sure that if I could just talk to Michelle—'

'Are you out of your mind?'

Crazy, mad, demented – that was exactly how he felt. 'The kid hasn't got the gumption to dream up a story like this. She's basically a wimp.'

'Look, you can't do anything until you know what action the school is taking.' She yawned, rolling over to kiss his cheek. 'I'll sleep in the spare room. I've got a heavy day tomorrow.'

His wife's matter-of-fact reaction to his predicament wounded him. What he'd hoped for was unconditional support, a champion to take up his cause and transform him from villain to hero.

He must have dozed for a couple of hours but he was awake when the central heating clicked on at six-thirty. He heard Kirsty showering but when she slipped into the bedroom to collect her clothes he feigned sleep, unable to stomach her detachment.

Lewis made an effort to keep busy so that, when Kirsty got in from work, he could report that he had been swimming or gone for a walk on the Downs. He made himself go out but he had little appetite for these solo excursions. He felt conspicuous amongst the young mums and pensioners who were the only people around during the day. He was convinced that everyone whom he encountered must wonder why an able-bodied man of his age wasn't at work. One rainy afternoon, he went to the cinema, sitting in the almost empty auditorium, not knowing what the hell he was doing there. 'Good film?' Kirsty asked but he could remember neither title nor plot.

At the end of his first week at home, Kirsty insisted he contact his union and engage a solicitor. 'Hand it over to the professionals. They're familiar with the procedures. They'll know how to push for information.' These seemed premature steps, the actions of a guilty man, but he wasn't up to arguing with her.

A union representative, harassed and officious, spent a lot of time phoning 'headquarters' and flicking through a fat book of regulations. He left, making Lewis promise to keep him informed of any developments, as though he were the one under the gathering cloud.

The solicitor, an acquaintance of Kirsty's, was overly cocky, constantly reassuring Lewis that he had won lots of cases 'significantly more complex than this'. Considering that no charges had been brought, Lewis wasn't encouraged to hear his circumstances referred to as a 'case'. It placed him a whisker away from being 'the defendant'. He made a statement denying that he had made any advances or improper suggestions to Michelle Haldane. Still without a list of his supposed transgressions, it had to be couched in general terms. His solicitor assured him that, should he be charged with anything, they would be given a detailed catalogue of accusations. *Very comforting.*

Half-term came and went. His full salary was credited to his account, the clocks went back and the shortening days raced on. Then everyone seemed to lose interest in him, as though he had no stake in what was unfolding. He wondered how Michelle was getting on, whether she, too, was feeling high and dry. He didn't know – didn't dare enquire – whether she was still at the school and, if she were, how she was coping. He felt no animosity towards her. It couldn't have been her idea. She had been forced into it somehow, making her as much a victim as he was. They were a wronged minority of two.

Kirsty and Lewis went over the ground so many times that it became treacherous and eventually they steered around it, their conversations dwindling to small talk. 'How was your day?' 'And yours?' 'Anything interesting in the post?' 'Custard or ice cream on your apple pie?' It had been this way when she'd miscarried the second baby.

He held out for a while before telling Tessa or his father. He was certain the business would soon be cleared up and it was pointless worrying them unnecessarily. But, if he were truthful, his reticence was due to embarrassment. The crime he might be charged with was not the sort of thing he wanted to bandy about.

He put it off, and put it off, until, in the end, Kirsty said, 'You've got to tell Tessa sooner or later. Why don't you go up to London?'

Then she added, rather unkindly, he thought, 'You know how Tessa enjoys a drama.'

Chapter 34

'THE LITTLE BITCH. I'm going to come down there and give Michelle Haldane a good slap.'

Tessa's reaction lifted Lewis spirits. 'Brilliant. Why didn't I think of that?'

Tessa hugged him. 'Seriously, Lewis, promise me you're not going to sit back and let this happen. And what's Kirsty playing at? She's the bloody lawyer, after all.'

'She says that it's best to back off. Wait and see if they're going to charge me.'

'Is she a Kafka fan or something?' Tessa demanded. 'We've got to pester them. Make a nuisance of ourselves until they tell us what's going on. And I haven't forgiven you yet for not telling me straight away.'

We. Us. It was wonderful to have a biased ally.

They were in Tessa's kitchen. Dan was in Amsterdam, at the opening of an international sculpture exhibition.

'Why didn't you go with him?' Lewis asked. 'Amsterdam's a great place.'

'A gathering of sculptors isn't as much fun as you might think. Anyway, I've got something on tomorrow night.'

'Boot me out if I'm in the way.'

'You're not. And you're welcome to stay. I'm sure Lotte would be delighted to entertain you if you feel like some company. She always asks after you.'

He raised a hand. 'Thanks, but no thanks. I might see if Jay fancies going to a jazz club. Are the Costelloes around?'

'I think so.' She stood up. 'C'mon. Let's go somewhere. You can treat me to lunch.'

They meandered through the City, a part of London that Lewis had only visited at weekends when it was deserted but for tourists searching for ghosts of Fagin and murdered princes. Today it was open for business. Pavements throbbed with busy, busy, people; traffic choked the narrow streets; loitering tourists, ever present, got in the way. The clang of scaffolding poles and church bells ricocheted between the buildings. There was a building site around every corner, piling an umpteenth layer of history on the capital. Outside banks an armed police presence was a reminder that not everyone wished to be part of the country's history. Lewis and Tessa watched a team of grim-faced policemen checking a white transit van before waving it through the gated entrance to a courtyard.

'Doesn't it scare you?' Lewis asked.

'It's a bloody nuisance. Bag searches, Underground evacuations, road closures. But I'm buggered if I'm going to let the IRA control my life. If it's going to happen, it'll happen.'

Typical Tessa. One minute insisting he be master of his destiny, the next turning all fatalistic about her own.

At lunchtime they were lucky to find a couple of seats in the corner of a crowded pub. Tucking in to bangers and mash, they returned to Lewis's predicament.

'Do I take it you still haven't said anything to Dad? And what about Andrea?'

'I had to tell her. The girls were supposed to come for a visit. I couldn't risk anything unpleasant happening with them around.'

Lewis's conversation with his ex-wife had been prickly. He'd detected exasperation, not sympathy, in her voice, as though he'd engineered the incident to inconvenience her. She'd thought it best if he postponed contacting his daughters until the matter was 'cleared up', as if he was suffering from a contagious disease.

Tessa stabbed at a sausage. 'She can't stop you seeing your own kids.'

'I know. But I'm going to wait until it's all sorted out.'

She shrugged. 'Your call.'

'Actually I wanted to talk to you about Dad. I went to see them last weekend. I thought I'd gauge the lie of the land before I told him.'

'And?'

'Something wasn't quite right. Usually Barbara leaves us to chat but for some reason she stuck around. Like she wanted to keep an eye on him.'

'Funny you should say that. Last time I rang, it sounded as though she was standing next to him, prompting him. As though he'd forgotten his lines.' Tessa groaned. 'She's not going to turn weird on us, is she? It would be nice if *something* went right for this family.'

'Everything's okay with you, isn't it?'

'Don't worry about me.' Tessa leaned across and kissed his cheek. 'Look at those two over there?' She nodded towards a couple at a table near the door and mouthed, 'Spies.'

With Tessa, nothing was ever as it seemed. The man on the opposite side of the street, the one with the velvet-collared overcoat and shiny brogues, had stabbed his wife at the breakfast table and concealed the bloodstained bread knife in his rolled newspaper. The girl with the bright red lips and fingernails, hurrying down the escalator, was on her way to meet her lesbian lovers. The car, engine running, young man at the wheel, was the getaway car for a bullion heist. It was a childish way for two forty-somethings to carry on, but it was fun and he was grateful to Tessa for trying to take his mind off things.

Although his sister often played the crazy woman, she was steadier than she used to be. When she was eighteen, she'd jumped out of their life like a skydiver without a parachute, and for years he'd held his breath, dreading a phone call from the police or a stranger bringing bad news. She would always be a pain in the arse but, thanks mainly to Dan Coates, he no longer feared every late night phone call or knock at the door.

As Tessa travelled south, she thought about Lewis and wanted to punish someone. Lots of people, in fact. She'd line them up. Michelle Haldane, Kirsty, Andrea, Lewis's boss. She'd douse them in boiling oil then string them up by their toenails. Admittedly Lewis had been naïve. He'd made a rudimentary mistake but it was unthinkable that he should lose his job and his reputation merely because he'd tried to improve a girl's life. He didn't deserve any of this. Still, a night out with Jay might do him good.

Rundle's new flat had two bedrooms, a spacious living room and a smart kitchen. It was, as the previous one had been, part of a Georgian house but this time on the northern outskirts of the town where the streetscape was looser and gardens larger. It was some distance from the railway station, but she had her own car and the journey took not much more than two hours, door to door.

Rundle was waiting for her. 'I thought you might not be able to get away.'

'Lewis is out on the razzle tonight.' She took the glass of wine he offered her and drained it. 'That's better.'

'I'm glad you came.' He kissed her, tenderly at first then more roughly.

'Not yet.' She needed to put her London life behind her. It

hadn't been like that in 'the old days' but things had changed. 'Have you got anything to eat? I'm famished.'

He heated a tin of minestrone soup and grated Parmesan cheese on top. While they ate, she told him what had happened to Lewis. She didn't expect him to engage in it – what was Lewis to him? – but eating and talking anchored her in this other existence.

Tony – he'd asked her to call him that – had cried the first time she came here. She'd been embarrassed and irritated by his display of emotion because it made him attainable, which had never been part of the deal. He was still taciturn but she no longer felt intimidated by his silences. These days, when she asked him a question, he answered. Since they'd resumed their relationship, she'd discovered that his mother, who had moved to Brighton in the late sixties with her second husband, had died and left him this flat; that he had an older sister living in Australia; that he played in a band – bluesy stuff these days; that he kept in shape by going to the gym twice a week. She'd even dared to ask whether the teenage rumours that he'd fathered a child had been true. 'Not as far as I know,' was his answer and she'd believed him.

'I met your brother once,' Rundle said. They were lying in bed, in the dark, sipping whisky and smoking.

'When?'

'After you went to Cornwall with the artists.'

'But that was twenty years ago.'

'He came to my flat. Told me to leave you alone.'

'Lewis? Lewis did?'

'Yeah. He was all fired up. Threatened to kill me.'

Tessa laughed. 'You're lying.'

'No. It's true.'

'What did you do?'

'I hit him. Punched him on his shoulder.'

'What?'

'He was a plucky kid. I had to stop him before he did anything daft.'

Tessa pictured Lewis confronting Rundle, terrified yet standing his ground. 'Then what happened?'

'He cried. Then he begged me not to come looking for you. Said it would ruin your life if I did. So I didn't.'

She turned her head and bit hard in to his right bicep. He cried out, pulling away and spilling his drink over her naked thigh. 'Christ, Tessa. What was that for?'

'For hitting Lewis.'

A week before school broke up, Michelle Haldane changed her mind. Mr Swinburne hadn't made any improper suggestions after all. She'd been mistaken.

'Great news, eh, Lewis?' Anson, this time in tweed jacket and grey flannels, slapped him on the back. 'I told you these things tend to blow over. Given time.'

Lewis couldn't remember his saying anything of the sort, nevertheless his initial reaction was relief and gratitude. *Now we can all get back to normal.*

But it wasn't that simple. At the first whiff of scandal, his 'comrades' had abandoned him. During his two months enforced absence he'd received only three phone calls and one note from fellow members of staff, all lukewarm. No one had come to see him or invited him out for a drink. No one had asked him for *his* side of the story, although, come to think of it, he'd never heard the *other* side.

Anson sketched in the details. 'It seems it was that gang of girls, you know the ones – Rachel Philips, Naomi Clark, Chrissie what's-her-name – that put Michelle up to it. They found out that you were giving her a bit of extra tuition and bullied her in to accusing you of…'

The very girls whom he'd thought were throwing Michelle a lifeline were using her to cause mischief. Clever. Cruel.

'How is Michelle?'

'I wouldn't worry about her, Lewis. In fact she's not with us any more.'

Lewis froze. 'She hasn't—'

Anson laughed. 'Good Lord, no. I say "not with us" as in "gone elsewhere". Her parents thought it best to move her to another school.'

Poor little bugger. Mocked, bullied, exposed as a liar then exiled to a school where she knew no one.

'What made her change her story?'

'Mmmm. That was rather odd. Mrs Haldane said Michelle received a letter. She wouldn't tell her mother what was in it but it was postmarked London. Typed envelope. The very next day, she admitted that she'd lied.'

Tessa. How had she got hold of Michelle's address? And what unspeakable threats had she made in her letter?

No longer required to retain his composure, Lewis buckled, like one of those figures made from wooden beads that collapses when its base is pressed. Within twenty-four hours he had succumbed to bronchitis and spent the best part of a week in bed.

Rundle offered to take Tessa to the cinema or for walks along the prom; he worried about her driving back to London on frosty nights; he wanted to know when she might next come.

What had gone on here? A road to Damascus conversion? Therapy? Something to do with his mother's death? She knew from experience that death could precipitate startling readjustments. Or – and this wasn't an easy one to swallow – had he never been the villain she'd made him out to be? Could his surliness have been shyness? His off-handedness, a cushion against her selfishness? She'd cast him as a 'loner' but he must get on with people to have held down the same job for so long; to play in a band. Such a radical reappraisal of the man didn't help because, whatever the reasons for his metamorphosis, the net result was the same. What he now offered Tessa wasn't so very different from what she had with Dan. In fact the last time she'd spent the night in Brighton, he'd brought her breakfast in bed and she'd automatically muttered, 'Thanks, Dan.'

Perhaps she should dump both of them and start again. She might try a toy boy next time. Or a woman.

Who was she fooling? She was almost forty-four. London was awash with gorgeous, confident young women elbowing the likes of her out of the market. She wasn't prepared to join her desperate friends who were clinging to the wreckage. Look at Lotte Jamieson. A few years older than Tessa, Lotte had resorted to surgery and now resembled a younger, startled version of herself. But her thick toenails and crépey cleavage gave the game away. 'I insist the bedroom light goes off these days,' she confessed after a few glasses of wine.

Lewis spotted immediately what was wrong. It was his first visit of the New Year, the first time he'd been to Salisbury Road since October. His father came to the door – Barbara was in the kitchen and hadn't heard the bell – and from the wary look in his eye, Lewis realised that he didn't have a clue who was standing on the doorstep.

'Why didn't you tell us?' Lewis asked when he and Barbara were alone.

'I thought I was mistaken at first. We all forget things from time to time. Then, when it became obvious that it was more than forgetfulness, I thought that if no one else knew, it couldn't be happening.'

Lewis thought back to the day of his mother's death. 'I

understand exactly what you mean. How are you coping?'

She shrugged. 'We're managing. He's fine most of the time. We just have these little … lapses.'

'Is Dad aware…?'

'Yes. That's the cruellest thing.'

Lewis floundered, searching for an on-the-spot solution.

Barbara must have seen his confusion. 'We've talked to the doctor and found out what to expect.' She shook her head. 'Your father's very cross with himself.'

'He must know it's just bad luck.'

'Yes, but that doesn't stop him wanting to take the blame.' She twisted her wedding ring. 'As the present is starting to slip away, he mentions the past more and more often.'

'The past?'

'He talks about your mother.'

'What does he say?'

'How beautiful she was. How it was his fault that she had such a sad life.'

'So he must have told you about Gordon. Talked about … that day.'

'Yes. He remembers it all down to the tiniest detail.'

'Like?'

'The coat he was wearing and the headlines in the newspaper he'd gone to buy; how he felt as he was searching for change to phone your mother.'

'And us? Me and Tessa? Does he talk about us?'

She hesitated. 'Sometimes.'

But Lewis knew she was only being kind.

It was bitterly cold. The daytime temperature didn't rise above forty degrees Fahrenheit for ten consecutive days. It appeared that Dick Swinburne was coming back from taking breadcrumbs to the bird table when he caught the sole of his built-up shoe

372

against the path edging. He fell heavily, breaking his hip and wrist. He was seventy-one years old when he died of pneumonia three weeks later.

It was a blessing, really, in view of what lay ahead for his father. And poor Barbara, of course. That's what Lewis kept telling himself.

'How d'you feel about being an orphan?' Tessa asked. They were at the bungalow sorting through their father's papers and personal effects.

'We are, aren't we? Unless orphan-dom, orphan-hood, whatever it's called, stops when you reach your majority. Technically, that is.'

She wrinkled her nose. 'You mean you could be one day an orphan, the next day, not an orphan. That seems arse about face to me.'

She lit a cigarette. 'So would that make Gordon an orphan too? Lots of technicalities to wrestle with there, Lew. He's way past eighteen – thirty-three, I make it – but he may well have a couple of living parents, if you want to define parents as the people we call Mum and Dad. Does that make him luckier or unluckier than we are?'

Gordon, his mother, Gran and Mrs Channing had all been jostling around in Lewis's head for days but he was in no mood to talk about them. Closing his eyes, he pleaded, 'Could we concentrate on the job in hand?'

'Okay. But even though Gordon *went*, he'll never go away – if you see what I mean.' Tessa held up a paperknife, a small dagger with a vicious blade and *Toledo* inscribed on the enamelled handle. 'Any good to you?'

Later, when Lewis took Tessa to the railway station, she said, 'Everyone's feeling sorry for Barbara but it's worse for Uncle Frank, don't you think? Barbara's got her kids and enough money to live comfortably. She and Dad got on well but they were more companions than soulmates. Losing a sibling – the person who's been in your life longer than anyone else, who's shared the same experiences, the same family crap – must be the most devastating thing that can happen.' She turned towards Lewis and gave a wry smile 'So you and I will just have to go together when we go. Agreed?'

He couldn't let her inaccuracy pass unchallenged. 'You and I have already lost a brother, don't forget.'

She pursed her lips. 'But he wasn't around long enough for us to share anything with him so it hardly counts.'

'We shared parents.'

Suddenly Lewis wanted once and for all to dump the stuff about 'Christopher' and his wonderful life. He wanted to talk about Gordon Swinburne. 'I would have liked a brother.'

'Really? It would have made you the "difficult middle child".'

'But it might have been better for us if there'd been someone else there when we were growing up. Diluting the mix. Shifting the balance.'

'You really think things would be different between us – you and I – if Gordon had been around?'

'Of course.'

'How different?'

'Less intense. Less dependent. Less exclusive. I think that the manner of Gordon's going, our … involvement in it—'

'Involvement? You're not saying we had anything to do with it?'

'Not in *real* terms—'

'In what then?'

'Tessa, we wanted him gone. You can't deny that. We must have felt – and must *still* be feeling – pretty damn guilty or we'd have told someone about the voodoo business. Our wanting Gordon gone, and then the way he went, drove us together. Then effectively losing Mum for the rest of our childhood glued us together. When we should have been out there making friends and acquiring social skills, we were becoming totally dependent on each other. It wasn't our fault but I'm sure it's affected our ability to form stable relationships.'

'What if he'd never been born? Would we be any "less exclusive"?' she asked.

'It's pointless discussing that.'

'No more pointless than discussing the merits of your having a brother to "dilute" me.'

She clearly felt belittled and he regretted having raised the matter. Pointing to the station clock he muttered, 'You'd better get going if you don't want to miss the train.'

She got out of the car and before slamming the door she said, 'Well call me a weirdo but I'm happy with the brother I've got. So screw you, Lewis Swinburne.'

A few flakes of snow tumbled out of the colourless sky as he watched her disappear into the station concourse.

VIII

1988

Chapter 35

'How are things at school?' Tessa asked. 'All back to normal?'

'Yes. Well. Not really. If I could just go in, teach my classes, mark homework, and come home again it would be okay. But the Head's being sickeningly "hail fellow" and roping me in on various committees and steering groups. At the same time he thinks I'm "not quite ready" for the deputy headship that's coming up at the end of the year.'

'What about the rest of the staff?'

'Oh, they're going out of their way to be palsy but it'll take more than a pat on the back and a pint to make me forget how stand-offish they were when I needed support. I used to think of school as a sort of home from home but that's all gone down the drain.'

Tessa's mouth turned down in a grimace. 'Might things improve?'

'Who knows? I get the feeling they think I must have done *something* dodgy. No smoke, etcetera.'

The solicitor's secretary brought them cups of coffee, apologising for keeping them waiting.

Tessa turned back to Lewis. 'And how are things with Kirsty? I got the impression you were going through a sticky patch.'

'Yes. She was getting impatient with me. She said I had to put the school business behind me. When I tried explaining how difficult it was, going on working with people who'd believed me capable of child molestation, she said I only had to *work* with them, I didn't have to *like* them. I told her that might be feasible in her world but it wasn't in mine.'

'Good for you.'

'Anyway, we ended up going to Relate. Our counsellor went on a lot about my "issues"—'

'Sounds disgusting,' Tessa wrinkled her nose.

'Dad's death and the Haldane fiasco.'

'Gordon?'

'No, thank goodness. The sessions would still be going on if she'd got hold of that. She told me it was perfectly natural to be feeling angry, guilty and inadequate.'

'Were you?'

'Only after I realised I *hadn't* been feeling angry, guilty or inadequate.'

'How d'you feel now?'

'Exhausted. In the end it was our mutual lack of confidence in the woman that got us back on an even keel.'

Tessa smiled. 'D'you reckon Relate chalks that up as a success?'

'Undoubtedly.'

Kirsty was offered a partnership in the firm, something she'd been working towards for years. Lewis was delighted for her, even when he heard that the promotion was contingent on her moving to York. Things were no better at school and, for some time, he had been scouring the job ads. There was nothing to keep them in Bristol. Kirsty's parents were living in Edinburgh now; her brothers in Glasgow and America. Now that his father had died, Lewis's only ties with his home town were ghosts and graves.

'Perhaps it's time to make a break; sell Cranwell Lodge. The property market's strong. You'd get a good price for it.' Kirsty ventured.

'It's something to think about,' Lewis agreed.

Anson gave him implausibly glowing references – 'A sure sign he wants rid of me,' he told Kirsty – and he had no trouble finding a job in York. The school gave him a good send-off but, driving out through the gates for the last time, the back seat of the car stacked with the dog-eared contents of his locker and a pile of unimaginative farewell gifts, Doreen Lane seemed the only person sorry to see him go.

Their new home was a detached Edwardian house in a village to the west of York. It stood in a mature garden and the previous owner had converted the substantial outbuildings to a double garage and a spacious garden room. Everyone who visited the house – Kirsty's parents, staff from her office, teachers from Lewis's school – told them how lucky they were. Space. History. Fresh air. Yes, they had it all.

What was the matter with him, then? Why did he feel so 'temporary'?

For a start, the house was too big. After they had distributed their belongings, the rooms still looked bare, as if a second removal van had been delayed by traffic and had yet to turn up. Wherever he sat, in whichever room, he felt lonely. When he was on his own in the house, he increased the volume on his record player to 'max,' inviting Miles or Charlie to help him take possession of this new world.

The school was fine. The Head was enlightened, members of staff friendly, the pupils well behaved and their parents cooperative. But this didn't stop him from feeling as if he were merely standing in until the permanent Head of Maths returned from extended leave. The thing that troubled him most was his reluctance to get close to the children, but he couldn't afford to make the same mistake again.

He kept busy. He joined things. Clubs. Societies. Choirs. He did everything he could think of to weld himself into this new life. Kirsty would never be able to accuse him of not giving it his best shot.

'This house is vast,' Tessa said the first time she visited. 'You can take in lodgers if you're ever short of a penny or two.'

Lewis found the idea appealing. Guests, coming and going; muddy walking boots piled outside the front door; fried breakfasts and a visitors' book on the hall table. But money wasn't a problem. Kirsty's promotion carried with it a considerable salary increase and pupil numbers at his new school pushed him up a grade on the pay scale. On top of that, Dick Swinburne had left an unexpectedly large sum of cash to be split between his two children. And there was the rent from Cranwell Lodge.

While Dan and Kirsty were discussing the best place to site a garden pond, Lewis and Tessa walked to the village shop to get the papers.

'It'll take me a while to get used to your being a Yorkshire lad,' Tessa said.

'Me too.'

'And I can't say I'm crazy about the accent.'

'Me neither.'

Indeed he found the local brogue depressing. He would get used to it in time but it was odd to think that, if he and Kirsty had produced children, they would have spoken with the broad, matter-of-fact intonation he heard every day in the classroom.

His sister looked tired. Her cheeks were colourless and there was an angry sore near the corner of her mouth. Daylight revealed glints of grey at the roots of her dark hair. It was unthinkable that she was nearing middle age. *They* were nearing middle age. As they walked, he draped his arm around her neck and pulled her towards him, her shoulder digging in to his ribcage. 'It's great having you here, Tess. Confirmation that I exist.'

'D'you doubt that?'

'Sometimes. In a what-the-fuck-am-I-doing-in-Yorkshire kind of way.'

'I don't see anyone holding a gun to your head.'

'Probably because it's an invisible gun and I'm the one holding it.'

Tessa stuck her foot out, tripping him, and they laughed as they struggled to stay upright.

'Seriously, Tess, we've got acres of room. Don't wait for an invitation. Come whenever you like. You should get away from London more often. Put some colour in your cheeks. I can picture you now, striding across the moors, plotting the great Twentieth Century Gothic novel. Dan must come too. That goes without saying. The garden room would make a great studio—'

'Stop, Lewis,' Tessa spoke solemnly, 'you're sounding embarrassingly desperate.'

When they reached the shop, they collected the items on Kirsty's list. Milk, double cream, toothpaste and an assortment of Sunday papers. On a whim, Lewis grabbed a bag of humbugs and dropped them in the wire basket.

Tessa pulled the bag open and sniffed its contents. 'It's incredible how smells take you back.' She held it towards him.

He inhaled the minty scent. 'I shall never forget Mrs Channing telling me how she hated Blanche.'

'But she loved life, didn't she? Not that hers was a bed of roses, reading between the lines.'

Lewis raised his eyebrows. 'So you admit you nicked her diaries?'

'What if I did? I was going to return them but she died and there was no point. You got a house, I got a few diaries. Care to swap?'

They started back up the hill. Tessa took a sweet from the bag. 'I've never met anyone like her. She was cantankerous, supercilious, ruthless … and sort of sexy at the same time. Quite something in an old lady. No wonder we couldn't stay away from the place.'

It was a blustery day of bright skies and racing clouds. A rippling shadow chased the sun across the undulating landscape. Something – the wind perhaps – spooked two horses that had been grazing in a field next to the road and they took off, galloping in wild zigzags.

'Remember when Mum and Dad took us to Llangorse Lake and that horse went berserk? It came from nowhere, straight towards me. I would have been trampled to death if you hadn't swung at it with a cricket bat.'

'Did I?' Tessa frowned. 'What was I doing with a cricket bat?'

'We'd been playing French cricket. You almost certainly saved my life.'

It wasn't like Tessa to forget a drama, particularly one in which she'd played the heroine, and Lewis wondered if he might have daydreamed the whole thing one summer afternoon as he'd watched the Spitfire swaying on its thread.

They walked on in silence for a few moments then she stopped, tugging his sleeve. 'If I did save your life, Lew, promise me you won't waste it. Promise you'll put up a fight for what you want. Life's not a dress rehearsal, *blah, blah, blah*. Don't be too eager to please. The meek are never going to inherit the earth, or anything else.'

Lewis raised his hands in the air. 'Here endeth the first lesson.'

Tessa seized his wrist, twisting his arm behind his back in an unconvincing half nelson.

'Ouch. Gerroff. Put me down.'

Two boys, maybe seven or eight years old, watched suspiciously from the safety of their front garden.

'It's rubbish being grown up.' Lewis shouted, loud enough for them to hear.

'How would you know?' Tessa countered, 'You've never left school.'

Tessa presumed that Lewis had only agreed to move because he could find no reason not to. The business with the girl had knocked him for six and it was a good thing that he was out of the place, but it didn't take an expert to see that, whilst Kirsty was flourishing in their new environment, Lewis was struggling. She *would* make an effort to see him more often but, ultimately, he would have to find his own solution.

When their father died, there had been the inevitable sorting out and disposal of his things but, in the move to the bungalow, he had been ruthless and there was surprisingly little to do. His financial matters, too, were in good order. Originally Tessa had assumed Barbara was out for what she could get but time had proved her to be a caring companion to her father. When the will was read, it plainly came as no surprise to Barbara that her husband had left his capital to his children and the bungalow to her. She seemed happy with that which made it easy for everyone. They'd promised to stay in touch but Tessa wasn't sure that this would happen, not because she disliked Barbara but because Barbara had never been part of her world.

When Dick Swinburne died, Tessa had experienced an immediate and deep sense of release. This might have been understandable had she cared for her father through a long illness. But she'd only seen him a couple of times after his dementia became apparent and, on these occasions, he'd seemed neither unhappy nor in pain, merely distant, as though preoccupied with a riddle. Then he'd fallen and it was over almost before it began. Finished. Her parents were gone and it seemed right for Gordon to accompany them, the three of them fading slowly into the past.

Not long after that a story hit the headlines. A woman whose three-year-old daughter had disappeared from a swing park over ten years earlier had, through sheer tenacity and with the help of private detectives, recovered her missing child. The details of the case were all over the newspapers. The child had been abducted by an infertile couple who, in one moment of folly, had given in to their overwhelming need. They had raised the girl with loving care. Despite the furore, no one seemed to have asked the girl how she felt about it all or whom she wanted to be her 'Mum and Dad'.

The story occupied the front pages for days and Tessa couldn't put it out of her mind. She had been too young to know what steps were being taken to find her brother. Her mother was suffering a breakdown; her father was worrying about his wife and trying to look after a young family. Neither of them would have had the energy or confidence to pester the police. Tessa had both and although it might be thirty years late, she made up her mind to find Gordon. If nothing else, Lewis would have the brother he seemed to think was needed to fill the void in his life.

The police had never closed the case but they had effectively given up on it. Ex-detective Hulbert hadn't given up though. Tessa guessed that he'd attended their mother's funeral not so much out of respect as inability to let go of the mystery which had dogged him into retirement.

A rough calculation told her that Hulbert must be in his eighties. A call to Lewis – 'What was the Christian name of that Hulbert man?' 'Brian. Why?' 'Nothing.' – followed by another to Directory Enquiries gave her a telephone number.

Yes, he was still alive, still in the town and pretty on-the-ball by the sound of his voice when he'd answered her call.

'I'll be away for a couple of days,' she told Dan. 'I thought I'd go and see Barbara; take flowers to the cemetery; wander down memory lane.'

'Researching a book?' he asked.

'Sort of.'

Hulbert lived in an unattractive bungalow with pebble-dashed walls and a crazy paving path. It was indistinguishable from dozens that surrounded it and wholly fitting, Tessa decided, for a man who had spent his working life trying to blend in with the scenery. He greeted her with a stiff smile and an outstretched hand but affability didn't suit him. He might be older, smaller and less robust but he was still Hulbert, the copper.

Sipping instant coffee in his neat, soulless living room, she came straight to the point. 'I intend to find Gordon, Mr Hulbert, and I was counting on your help. I've no doubt that my father was the prime suspect so don't feel you have to pussyfoot around that one. But I'm sure you have your own theory about what happened.'

Hulbert said nothing. He's waiting, she thought, until he's sure of my motives.

'You probably think I'm crazy, raking it up again. But now Mum and Dad are both gone, whatever I unearth isn't going to trouble them.'

Still the old man remained silent.

'I've come into a little money, Mr Hulbert. I can afford to employ someone to help me. But you were the obvious place to start.'

He sighed. 'I suppose the story of that girl got your hopes up.'

Tessa was impressed by the old man's deductive powers. 'I suppose it did. It made me think that, with enough media coverage and the Missing Persons organisation, I'd stand—'

He raised a finger. 'Point of order. "Missing Persons" usually know that they're missing, if you see what I mean. As a rule they don't want to be found. Your brother was only three months old when he disappeared. If he's alive, he certainly has no inkling that he *is* "missing". And there's no chance that anyone could identify him from this.' He pulled a creased black and white photograph out of his cardigan pocket.

A baby stared at her, slightly out of focus, propped up against a pillow. Tessa had seen the picture before, of course, and knew that this must be a copy because the original was safe with Lewis in the family album.

'Why did you keep it?' she asked.

'I'll be honest with you. This case became a bit of an obsession with me. My late wife would have vouched for that,' he grimaced. 'I kept thinking that one day I'd crack it. But I never did.'

'Not yet, anyway, Mr Hulbert.' Tessa needed him on her side. 'It would be really useful if I could hear your thoughts on it. You must have a gut feeling. You're the expert, after all.'

'And you always had the gift of the gab, Miss.'

She took a small dictaphone from her bag and held it out towards him. 'Just talk into this. There must be lots I don't know. For example, how long was it before the police decided it was hopeless? Everyone was very protective of Lewis and me. We didn't have much of a clue what was going on.'

Hulbert needed no encouragement. Gordon's disappearance had cast a long shadow and it was obvious that he had been – still was – fixated on the case. Tessa hadn't imagined that she would discover anything new but it was fascinating to view their family's calamity through his plodding objectivity.

He cleared his throat and, staring at some point on the picture rail behind Tessa's head, he began.

'In cases like this we always start close to home. We look at the people who've got the most to gain and the most to lose; the people with inside knowledge of habits and routines. We eliminated your mother, your brother and you—'

'You really thought Lewis and I might have…' She'd intended to remain silent, so as not to break the old man's train of thought, but this wasn't easy.

'I try never to make assumptions, Miss. Many a villain slips through our net because someone makes an assumption.'

It was telling that he'd slipped into the present tense, as if he were still in the throes of the case.

'Your father was the obvious suspect. He took the pram to the shop all right but it could have been empty when he left the house. It was possible that something had already happened to the baby.'

'You mean that Dad had killed Gordon?'

Throughout disaffected teenage years and disgruntled twenties it had suited Tessa to deem her father capable of murder. And it had fitted so neatly with the far-fetched notion that her mother and Frank Swinburne had been lovers, and Gordon their child. But that version of events had always belonged entirely to her. It was a fiction which she'd felt at liberty to use in *Lost,* although no one else seemed to understand that, and it was shocking to hear even an element of it voiced as a possibility.

'Not necessarily. He could have had an accident. Dropped him or the like then panicked. Even the most level-headed people panic, Miss.'

Hulbert shifted his gaze to his hands, clasped across his broad chest. 'Your dad was lucky there. A neighbour was cutting their front hedge and stopped him to admire the baby and chat about the Cup match that was to be played that afternoon. Fred Johnson his name was. Number thirty-two. Johnson's evidence put him more or less in the clear.'

'Did you ever think that Mrs Channing was involved?' Tessa asked.

'Not for a minute. I knew what you were up to though. Trying to protect your dad. Very laudable if a bit misguided. No, someone would have noticed an old lady, done up like a dog's dinner, hanging around a pram. Of course we had to go and see her and the old man. As it transpired they had a watertight alibi.'

When he'd finished, Tessa asked quietly, 'Is Gordon still alive, Mr Hulbert?'

Hulbert took a handkerchief from his trouser pocket and blew his nose, making the most of his big moment. 'I think he was taken from the pram. It might have been a spur of the moment snatch but...'

'But?'

'But, if that were the case, without a plan whoever did it would have slipped up sooner or later, unless they were very lucky.'

'So you think it was premeditated?'

'I do. I do. I think someone set out to steal a baby. Any baby, that is, not specifically your brother. It could have been for themselves or to order. The baby trade is nothing new, you know.

'In those days nobody thought twice about leaving a baby outside a shop. In fact you were considered a nuisance if you took the pram in. They were bloody great cumbersome things. The way I see it, the perpetrator was prowling around with an empty pram, on the lookout for a suitable target. By that I mean a very young baby who couldn't give the game away. Once they were sure there were no witnesses ... wham,' Hulbert's hand shot out and grabbed the cushion from the sofa. 'It'd be over in ten seconds. The abductor would be streets away before the alarm was raised, just another mum or dad pushing their kid out on a Saturday morning.'

Hulbert's theory was persuasive but the old man wasn't finished. 'I'd put money on your brother being alive, barring accidents. But that won't get you very far because he could be anywhere. And you can bet your bottom dollar he won't be called

389

Gordon.' He stood up and pointed to a mock-leather briefcase on the polished sideboard. 'It's all in there. I kept copies of everything. Against the rules, but I did. It's all yours. I'm done with it.' He lifted the shabby, brown case and presented it to her. 'A word of warning, Miss. It can get to you. My wife would have vouched for that.'

They'd lived in Yorkshire for more than a year but Lewis still felt that he was adrift in an ocean, treading water. He might drown or he might be saved.

One day, when he and Kirsty were reorganising the downstairs rooms, she pointed at several boxes of his books, stacked in a corner where they'd remained since the removal men dumped them there.

'It looks like you're in two minds whether to stay.' She hugged him, standing on tiptoe, pressing her cheek against his. 'Is it that bad?'

It *was*, but in such a monstrous, impalpable way that he dared not reply.

He wasn't sure that Tessa's mission to find Gordon was a good idea. What if she were successful? Who would it benefit? Certainly not a thirty-five-year-old bloke who thought he knew who he was. True to form, Tessa had gone off like a rocket, first visiting Hulbert then pestering Uncle Frank and anyone else who was mentioned in Hulbert's papers. When he'd complained that he was the last one to learn what she was up to, she'd talked a lot of nonsense about not wanting to bother him until she had something concrete to report. Of course there *was* nothing. How could there be after all this time?

School finished for the year. Lewis had six weeks off but Kirsty went to work, covering for staff who needed time off for family holidays. 'It's good management practice,' she explained when

Lewis accused her of being over zealous. 'We'll go somewhere special at half-term. Promise.'

So, with the long holiday stretching ahead and nothing much to do, he went to London.

He'd counted on Tessa running out of steam on the Gordon business but she seemed as resolute as ever and was talking about getting the media involved.

'What good will that do?' he asked.

'I don't know. Someone must know something. Or at least have suspicions. You can't produce a three-month-old baby without a relative or a neighbour noticing. You can't just say, "Oh, and by the way I forgot to mention that I gave birth to a son a few months ago."'

'Then why didn't they come forward at the time?'

'Maybe whoever took him is waiting for the right moment. I've been doing some research, talking to people who know about these things. You wouldn't believe how many transgressors want to be found out.'

'What, after thirty-five years?'

'Possibly. There are countless reasons why they might be ready to make a clean breast of matters. Remorse. Fear. Shame. Religion. They might be dying and want to set the record straight.'

'Wouldn't that be a bit ... selfish on their part? It might salve their conscience but it wouldn't do Gordon much good, would it?'

She smiled, knowingly. 'It might if it meant that he would come into money.'

'Money? What money?' Lewis felt as if he had turned over two pages of a detective novel and missed the vital clue.

'I've still got Dad's money sitting in the bank. And, not wanting to blow my own trumpet, I'm quite a successful writer. I've got no children to inherit my estate. A long-lost brother could do quite well out of me.'

'Great expectations, eh?' Lewis grinned but he was troubled by her perverse determination.

'Ward & Cox are going to republish *Lost*. It makes sense for them to cash in on any publicity that's going around. And I'm going to write an end piece, telling the real story of what happened to our family when Gordon disappeared. I'll include an appeal for information.'

Lewis hated the idea of his parents' sad lives being used to drum up interest in a cause that was best left undisturbed.

Dan was worried, too. 'I've never seen her so … focussed. Did you know she's engaged a private detective?'

She hadn't told Lewis but he wasn't surprised. 'She'll soon get fed up. Tessa's never been one to stick at anything for long.'

Dan frowned. 'I hope you're right. I don't know if I can handle being cuckolded by a three-month-old baby.'

Chapter 36

HULBERT'S BRIEFCASE CONTAINED a muddle of carbon copies and handwritten notes, everything tainted with a smell of oil cloth and failure. Tessa sorted the papers, eavesdropping on words that had been whispered in strictest confidence by people who had been the bedrock of her childhood. Her mother and father. Gran. Mrs Channing and Mr Zeal. All of them dead.

There was the routine stuff – statements from her parents, the neighbours and people who had been on the spot when her father came out of the shop. None of them had seen, heard or knew anything. No one had a bad word to say about Peggy and Dick Swinburne who had been, it appeared, model parents. Hulbert had dismissed Mrs Channing and Mr Zeal in a couple of sentences. 'Pair of weird old birds living in a world of their own. No record of hanky-panky with kids.' Below, he'd added the details of their alibi.

The police had taken a great interest in Uncle Frank. Homosexual activity was a criminal offence then and 'queers' – Hulbert had used the term several times in his notes – evidently provoked suspicion amongst policemen. The detective had visited him more than once in the days after the abduction but her uncle had been selling insurance on that particular Saturday morning, an alibi confirmed by several customers.

Then there were the records of local mothers whose babies

had died around that time, their individual tragedies revealed and their guilt dismissed in a few stark sentences.

Hulbert had been incredibly diligent.

Tessa became addicted to the thrill induced by the musty pages, yet it was soon clear there was nothing amongst them to provide a fresh lead.

So she tracked down everyone she knew who had media contacts, anyone who might be persuaded to publicise her mission. She engaged a private investigator then sacked him when he told her that she was wasting her time. She found another – an unlikeable young man who wore nylon shirts and smiled too much but who was ready to assure her, 'One good lead, that's all I need, and we're home and dry.'

She had less time to go to Brighton. This displeased Rundle who was becoming irritatingly possessive. He pried into her life, asking whether Dan was a good lover; what she had been doing since they were last together; when she would next come. Sometimes he would pull away when they were making love and accuse her of 'not being there'. More often than not, he was right – she was light years away, shadowing a stealthy figure pushing a pram down a featureless street; trailing a boy who looked a bit like Lewis as he walked to school, hand in hand with loving parents; spying on a dark-haired young man in a library or on a farm or on the deck of a ship.

Rundle was becoming a drag and she ought to put an end to it. But he was a moody, passionate man and she was fearful of how he would react if she did.

Dan, on the other hand, was drawing away from her. It was evident from his watchful silences that he disapproved of her attempt to find Gordon. It would have been good to have his support but, with or without it, she was going to continue.

'Tessa's on Radio Four,' Kirsty shouted from the kitchen.

Lewis switched on his radio and heard his sister's voice. She was on some book programme, talking about the new edition of *Lost*, contrasting the fiction of the novel with the events that had taken place. She was making a good job of it, too. It was easy to imagine listeners thanking their lucky stars that their own child or grandchild was upstairs safe in bed. It was more difficult, however, to believe that her words would persuade anyone to reveal a secret that they'd kept for nearly forty years.

He'd not told anyone here about Gordon. It wasn't the kind of thing you announced to new acquaintances. But everyone at school and in the village seemed to know. They didn't say anything to him but it was obvious from the way they looked at him and stopped talking, or talked too loudly, when he came into a room. He shouldn't be surprised. Tessa had done a brilliant publicity job, hinting that new evidence had come to light in 'the Swinburne mystery', keeping the story alive.

Swinburne was a distinctive name and local journalists harassed him.

'Don't be so wet,' Tessa snapped when he complained of the intrusion. 'We've got to do whatever it takes.'

'Remind me again,' he said, 'why you are doing this. D'you really want to shatter a young man's life and slam a couple of old people in jail. What would be the point of that?'

'They screwed up our lives, Lewis. Why should they live happily ever after?'

'Look. If it hadn't happened we *might* have been the happiest family on the planet. Mum *might* not have lost it. Dad *might* not have turned into a narrow-minded bigot. On the other hand, Gordon might have turned out to be a psychopath who slaughtered us in our beds.'

'He'd have been a lot more fun than you are.' She tipped her head back and closed her eyes. 'Let's not fall out. I suppose I'm doing it because if *I* don't, who will?'

395

'Are you sure anyone needs to?' Lewis touched her hand.

'You haven't read the Hulbert stuff. It's heartbreaking. Mum's statement. Dad's statement. The phrases they used. The way they put things. I can hear their voices as clearly as if they were speaking.'

He handed her a hanky and she wiped her eyes.

'Why not leave it now, Tess? You're going to make yourself ill. You've done your best. Let them go in peace.' Trite words but it was how he felt.

'It's easy for you. You weren't mean to him. I used to pinch him when Mum wasn't looking. When he was asleep in his cot, I used to shout in his ear and watch him jump.'

He wondered whether Tessa had been drinking. It would explain this sudden sentimentality.

'Brothers and sisters do that sort of thing to each other. It's part of being a family. You were mean but you didn't harm him.'

'Barbarity begins at home.' She blew her nose.

Wanting to rescue her from her misery and demonstrate his steadfastness, he said, 'There's a new test – a bit like a blood test. They take a sample of DNA from one person and can deduce pretty accurately if they're related to another person.'

She stared at him. 'We can use this test to find him?'

'Don't get too excited. Not to *find* him. But if someone came forward we might be able to prove whether he was related to us.'

'Dear Lewis. You never let me down.'

'I do my best.'

Dan was invited to spend a year in America, at the Rhode Island School of Design.

'Won't that interfere with your work?' Tessa asked.

'I think it would be stimulating. It's a highly esteemed establishment and they've got some interesting people working there.'

She shrugged. 'It sounds as if you've already made your mind up.'

He cleared his throat. 'I thought you might like to come. As wife of the Visiting Professor. I could probably swing you a Writer in Residence post. Brits seem to be in favour at the moment.'

'But—'

'Before you say anything, I'd like you to hear me out.' He was staring out of the window, as if the words he was searching for were written on the building across the street. 'I love you. You must know that by now. I've tried bloody hard not to make you feel trapped or limited. It's been tough at times, especially knowing that you were seeing someone else.'

'Dan—'

'But I thought, hang in there, Dan. So I did. And for a while, it was really good.' He gave a dry little laugh. 'I coped with your seeing someone else because you always came back to me. But I'm not sure I can compete with Gordon. He's spirited you away completely.' He turned to look at her. 'I'm going to the States for a year. I would like you to marry me and come with me. You already know everything there is to know about me so I'm not going to try and sell myself. It's up to you.'

He was handsome and dignified, and if this were a Hollywood film she would say yes and fall in to his arms. But it wasn't and she didn't love him, at least not enough to weld herself to him for the rest of her life.

Silent seconds ticked away.

'So that's it then,' he said.

They had been together for fifteen years and it ended there, in ice not fire.

Dan brought his departure forward. He insisted that Tessa stay in the flat, saying that it was ridiculous to pay rent when the place would be standing empty; that she would be doing him a favour by looking after it and ensuring that squatters didn't move in.

The news of their split seeped out. Friends called round on the pretext of checking that she was okay, assuming that Dan had dumped her. Accepting sympathy for a misfortune which she hadn't suffered didn't seem quite right and, over a bottle of white wine, she divulged the circumstances of the break-up to Liza Costello. After that, it wasn't long before Tessa discovered that most of the people whom she considered to be *their* friends were, in fact, *Dan's* friends. Not only did they drop her but some of them accused her of treating him badly then having the gall to hound him out of his own flat.

'Take no notice,' Liza advised. 'What do they know? It's between you and Dan.'

It was a crass thing to say when Dan was thousands of miles away and there was nothing 'between them' any more.

When Tessa told Lewis he took it hard. He'd liked Dan from the start and they'd formed a close, uncomplicated friendship. Although Lewis didn't have a creative bone in his body and Dan had failed O Level maths three times, each appreciated and respected the other's skills.

'Perhaps a spell apart will do you good. Prove that you're right for each other after all,' Lewis said.

'Like your separation from Andrea did?' she asked quietly.

Once in a while, Jay and Liza invited her to share a meal, or go with them to see a film. They were easy company, amusing and original. What could be more agreeable than spending time with old friends?

Then Jay started coming to the flat alone, turning up late at night with a takeaway and a half-bottle of whisky, telling her how much sexier she was these days. 'You mean middle-aged and desperate?' 'I mean luscious and … imaginative.' What could be more harmless than spending an occasional night with an old flame?

But there were days when the phone didn't ring and the only person she spoke to was the girl at the supermarket checkout or the man who sold newspapers on the corner. Voices often echoed up the stairwell and doors banged in the flat below but no one knocked to introduce themselves or invite her down for coffee.

She hadn't realised how few people she could count on. Amelie and Lotte. Jay and Liza. Lewis of course. And, in his own way, Rundle. There had been others. Magda at the temp agency. Linda – or was it Lynne? – in the editorial department at Ward & Cox. But they'd fallen out over something or another – a man or a broken confidence.

So. Three friends, two lovers and a brother. It was a shame about Dan. He'd been a true friend and she'd sent him away.

She took a ten pence piece from her purse. How many times had Lewis's coin come down heads? She flicked hers spinning into the air, catching it on the back of her hand. Heads. Then tails. Then heads again. What did that prove?

Tessa was struggling with her book. It was difficult to keep at it when she knew that it was a poor effort which the publisher would, very possibly, reject.

It turned out to be a gloomy, cold winter which meant hefty gas and electricity bills. Someone snatched her handbag as she was coming out of the flat and she had to pay a fortune to get the locks changed. The car tax and insurance were due. Her boots need replacing. Fares went up. Funds dwindled. Three pounds for this, five pounds for that and – *hey, presto* – her purse was empty. The truth, which she'd chosen to ignore, was that Dan had been supporting her for years.

How did people earn money? Correction. How did forty-seven year-olds without qualifications earn money? Her looks, which would once have counteracted her lack of skills and clinched a cushy job in a posh office, were fading. The brave new world of 'information technology' intimidated her but 'temping' – her old standby – was a non-starter unless she got to grips with it. She asked Lewis's advice, making out that she was thinking of upgrading from an electric typewriter to a computer, not wanting him to twig that she was short of money. He suggested that she sign up for a beginner's course somewhere. It was a good idea but, on making enquiries, she was deterred by the fees and a lack of enthusiasm for the subject.

She nagged her agent to get commissions but the work soon dried up when she failed to meet deadlines.

She looked for ways to economise, determined not to dip into her savings before it was necessary. She'd taken to eating at the local Italian restaurant, enjoying the bustle and banter after her solitary day. But, even if she chose the cheapest dish on the menu, she could no longer afford it.

She dismissed the private investigator. Then, within days, she received a letter from a woman claiming to have information about Gordon and, not able to trust her own objectivity, she re-engaged him. He didn't take long to establish that the woman, a clairvoyant from Leeds, was a charlatan but the short-lived buzz whetted Tessa's appetite and she was drawn back into the hunt.

She scanned faces at bus queues and Tube stations, in restaurants and shops, convinced that sooner or later she would see him. On one occasion she spotted a man who looked as she imagined he would look. She chased him up Tottenham Court Road but when she got closer she saw that he was much too young.

Dan wrote to say that things were going well. He was staying on in the States and was thinking of selling the flat. *I'm in no hurry to put it on the market but I wanted to give you time to find another place. Or perhaps you'd be interested in buying it?* The first time she read the letter, she imagined he was trying to conceal his unhappiness at losing her, the second time she understood that he no longer cared.

Her introduction to the new edition of *Lost* evidently dredged up memories for many readers who insisted on sharing their stories with her, as if she were the patron saint of family tragedies. Amongst these letters was one from Diane Stoddy, saying how much she'd enjoyed the book, wishing her well in her search and inviting her to a school reunion. *I'm sure you would remember lots of the girls and they would love to meet Tessa Swinburne, the famous writer.* Tessa associated Diane Stoddy with failure, a colourless nonentity hovering on the periphery whenever things went wrong. If she'd had more energy and a less dilapidated pair of boots she might have gone to remind herself that, however bad things were, she had at least escaped being one of 'the girls'.

Rundle broke their rule and phoned her at the flat. He didn't know that Dan was no longer in her life and she was determined that he shouldn't.

'When can you come down?' His voice, once electrifying, now got on her nerves.

'Soon. I've been up to my eyes.'

'Tomorrow?'

'Okay. I'll try.'

Why was she going on with this? She and Rundle were like two has-been boxers, slugging it out in the ring, too punch-drunk to throw in the towel. Jay was on hand if she wanted a bedfellow. And, if she fancied something more dangerous, there were always men in bars.

The weather next day was foul and she decided to travel to

Brighton by train. But there had been a bomb scare and the Underground wasn't running. It was the perfect excuse not to go but, having geed herself up for what she'd decided must be their final meeting, she drove.

It was dark by the time she pulled up outside Rundle's flat. Taking the silver hip flask from her bag, she unscrewed the top, comforted by the rasp of metal on metal. She would do the deed then be on her way back to London in no time at all.

She let herself in to the flat.

'Hi.' He stood in the kitchen doorway. 'Steak and salad okay?'

She glanced in to the living room. He had set two places at the table. Napkins. Candles. Bottle of red wine, already open.

'What's the matter?' he asked.

'Nothing. I'm tired.'

'Take your coat off and relax. Here,' he handed her a glass of wine, 'the food's nearly ready.' He returned to the kitchen.

She drank the wine then poured and drank another before joining him. 'I'm not staying.'

He looked up and smiled and she knew he hadn't heard. 'What?'

'I came to give you these.' She held out his keys.

'Look, if it's because I phoned—'

'I can't see you any more, Tony. I'm sorry but I can't. It was a mistake thinking we could get back together.' She paused, wanting him to say *You're right. It was fun while it lasted.* But that was never on the cards. She tried again. 'It's nobody's fault but it's run its course—'

'That's bollocks and you know it. You need me. You need this.' He grabbed her, forcing his mouth against hers, kissing her violently.

She tasted blood where his teeth had cut her lip. 'Fuck you.'

She raised her hand but before she could strike his face he caught her wrist, pushing her back against the table and trapping

402

her other arm against her side.

'This is what you like, isn't it? What you come here for.' He pushed his hips hard against hers, tearing at her shirt and kissing her neck, her breasts. He was strong but she wasn't going to let this happen. Wrenching her arm free, she reached behind, running her hand across the table and snatching up the knife that he had been using to slice tomatoes. She jabbed it hard in to his thigh.

'Christ,' he moaned, letting her go and dropping to the floor. 'Christ, Tessa, I thought it was what you wanted.'

She looked down at him. He was holding his leg, the knife still protruding from it, blood trickling across the back of his hand. The pan was still on the gas ring and the sharp smell of burning steak, the heat and the blood combined to make her feel faint. She had to get away from there, to get into the fresh air.

She drove for a while then, when she could no longer fend off the horror of what she'd done, she drew up at a phone box and dialled nine-nine-nine, requesting an ambulance be sent to Rundle's flat, giving a fictitious name to the matter-of-fact voice on the end of the line.

She drove on. It started to rain again, the *swish-swash* of the wipers and the hum of the engine merging hypnotically. Now and again she rolled down the window, the wet blast first reviving then chilling her. Lights from oncoming cars caught the raindrops on the windscreen, dazzling her. Her eyes ached from peering at the cats' eyes in the road. She felt queasy.

Crawley. She was half way home. *Swish-swash … Frankie and Johnnie were lovers … Swish-swash, swish-swash.* God, she was tired.

Chapter 37

LEWIS WAS HALFWAY THROUGH BREAKFAST when someone from the hospital phoned to tell him that Tessa had been involved in a car accident. They said that she was 'stable' but would give no details of her injuries or the circumstances surrounding the accident. 'Tell her I'll be there as soon as I can,' was all he could think of to say.

He had little recollection of the train ride from York to London, filled as it was with grim speculation. The Tube journey from Kings Cross to the hospital was a straightforward one but, unable to face dizzying escalators and the press of bodies, he splashed out on a taxi. On arrival at the hospital he was directed to the fourth floor, where a nurse led him away from the main ward, down a corridor that smelled of tomato soup.

'She's in here.' The nurse opened a door and he saw Tessa, lying on her back, her eyes closed. 'The medication's making her drowsy,' the nurse explained. 'Don't stay too long. Just five minutes.'

Lewis edged in and lowered himself onto the bedside chair. The room was painted an unsubtle pink, the window obscured by a venetian blind, its slats dusty and misaligned. A plastic jug containing water stood on the bedside locker, a beaker next to it. *Nil by Mouth* was scrawled on the white board above the bedhead and below it, in neater script, *Consultant – Denner-Brown*. She wasn't in the intensive care ward and there were no machines, bleeping and pinging away. That had to be a hopeful sign.

He stood up to get a better look at her. She was wearing a hospital gown, the geometric pattern on the much-washed fabric all but invisible. She had a support collar around her neck and a drip taped to her hand. Her hair was drawn back, her face sallow, her nose prominent. There was a dressing on her temple and another on her cheekbone. The area around both eyes was reddish-purple and badly swollen. Her arms were bruised, too, and the bed covers were mounded up in the region of her right foot.

He concentrated on her face, waiting until she moved her head before reaching down and touching her forearm. 'Hi, Tess.'

She opened her eyes and he leaned over to bring his face into her line of vision. 'It's you.'

'Yes, it's me.'

She stared at him for several seconds then murmured, 'I think I killed someone. I didn't mean to—'

'Ssshhh.' He stroked her arm. 'You mustn't worry. We can sort all that out later. You're okay. That's all that matters.'

'My ankle hurts like hell. They're going to operate. Maybe they have.' The phrases emerged in fits and starts. 'I've got to lie flat. Until they know if my spine's damaged.' She moaned gently. 'God, I ache all over.'

'Don't talk too much or they'll throw me out.'

He wanted to ask whether she'd been driving the car and if she'd been alone but the nurse appeared, saying firmly, 'That's enough for now, Mr Swinburne. Why don't you go and get a coffee? Come back a bit later.'

He kissed Tessa's cheek, 'I'll be back soon.'

He tracked down the doctor on duty and introduced himself. 'What happened exactly?'

Doctor Briscoe, his name on a badge fixed to the lapel of his white coat, cleared his throat. 'Your sister was admitted last

405

night, at about nine o'clock. She's sustained multiple fractures to her right ankle and we're keeping her under observation for other possible injuries. The police will be able to give you full details but, as far as I can gather, the car she was driving collided with a van. Her vehicle mounted the pavement.' The young man studied his shoes. 'Unfortunately, there were several people waiting at a bus stop ...'

Lewis pictured a car, spinning across a wet pavement, mowing down a queue of people. 'Oh, God. She said she'd killed someone but I assumed she was delirious.'

'Several people were admitted to A&E at the same time as Miss Swinburne. Unfortunately one of them...' Briscoe's technique for relaying news seemed to depend on the recipient supplying the endings to his sentences.

'Was my sister alone in the car?'

'As far as I know.'

'Was she ... drunk?'

'I couldn't say. We haven't had the test results back yet. Now, if you'll excuse me...'

Briscoe hurried off towards the lifts.

Lewis pushed a handful of change into the drinks machine in the waiting room. He didn't want the thin, scalding coffee but he had to do something to occupy himself. There was a payphone in the corner and he rang Kirsty, telling her the little that he knew.

'What's the best thing to do?' he asked.

'What d'you mean?'

'The best way to help Tessa.'

There was a pause. 'The best way to help Tessa is to encourage her to tell the truth. There's no wriggling out of this one.'

'But—'

'Lewis,' she spoke quietly and unemotionally, 'if Tessa was drunk and killed someone, the only thing you can do is make sure she has a good lawyer.'

He returned to Tessa's bedside. This time she was awake.

'I've been trying to remember what happened. It was raining. The lights were reflecting off the road and—'

'Don't. Not yet. Concentrate on getting well first.'

She was silent for a while. Her eyes were shut and he thought she'd gone to sleep but suddenly she said, 'I was coming back from Brighton.' She brought her hand up and covered her eyes. 'I didn't plan it. Honestly. He was going to rape me.'

'What are you talking about?'

'Rundle. I killed him,' she whispered.

This made no sense. It simply didn't square with what Briscoe had just told him. She was confused, maybe suffering from concussion. Bizarre, though, that the crash had sparked off memories of that dreadful bloke.

On the train home, he sketched out a plan. He would visit Tessa again at the weekend and, while he was in London, find out from the police details of what had happened. In the meanwhile, he would get in touch with Dan – the Costelloes would have a contact number – and tell him about the accident. He surely still had feelings for Tessa, so it was only right that he should know. Whatever else happened, as soon as she was well enough to leave hospital, he would bring her back to stay with them.

Kirsty took an uncompromising stand. 'She's a middle-aged woman, Lewis, not a juvenile delinquent who's going through a difficult phase. I agree she needs help, but from medics and lawyers not from an indulgent brother. And I don't think she should come here. It won't do her any good. Or us for that matter. It sounds callous but that's how I feel.'

Tessa was his sister not a client, and he'd counted on Kirsty bending a little, for his sake. She'd always been decisive, a quality that he admired, but she was assertive these days too and he wasn't sure how to deal with that. Maybe she would reconsider.

He got hold of Dan Coates who sounded concerned and sympathetic. He asked Lewis to pass his love to Tessa and wanted to be kept abreast of events, saying he would delay the sale of the flat until she was fully recovered and had found somewhere else to live. But he made it clear that he had no plans to return to England – and, by implication, Tessa – in the foreseeable future.

As Tessa's condition improved, her head became less fuzzy and memories of the crash started to firm up. Wipers, flicking across the windscreen; red tail lights of the vehicle ahead, bright and blurred through the slanting rain; dreary rows of suburban houses. The radio droning on – something about negative equity. A jolt and the chilling din of grinding metal; the seatbelt biting in to her neck as the car spun.

The tests showed that she'd had over twice the legal limit of alcohol in her bloodstream when the accident occurred. As soon as the doctors declared her strong enough, two policemen came to interview her. The impassive pair treated her with coolness verging on contempt. Hulbert seemed, at a distance of forty years, benign in comparison. No one would ever know whether she had fallen asleep or merely lost concentration. It didn't matter because, either way, she had killed an old man and injured several other people. One of the injured – a young woman – had needed to have part of a leg amputated. The police told her that she would be charged with a serious offence and advised her to engage a lawyer. Kirsty said the same thing and recommended several firms. Tessa couldn't see the need. She'd done what they said she'd done and she wasn't intending to contest it.

But what about Rundle? Why had no one mentioned him? She'd stabbed the man and left him, his dark blood pooling on the pale kitchen floor, her finger prints on the knife and all over the flat. If he were alive, wouldn't he have put the police on to her? Could his body still be lying there? *Had* she phoned for an ambulance? It was all so hazy. She was sure of one thing though. It would be madness to raise the matter. She was resigned to being punished for killing and maiming innocent pedestrians but it had been her right to defend herself against a psychopath.

Ted Knowles, aged eighty-two, widower and war veteran, was crushed to death by drunken author with tragic family history. Ted was on his way home from visiting his sister in hospital...

The accident was pure gold for the tabloids. It had the lot. Pathos, bad luck, fate and wrongdoing in one tale that was ripe for the telling. Some of what they printed was true and a great deal of it wasn't. On this flawed evidence the world would reach its conclusion and she would be judged. Black and white – no shades of grey.

Single rooms were at a premium and she expected to be moved to the main ward. But they left her where she was. She worked out why when she caught a glimpse of someone peering at her through the pane in the door. She had become notorious and was corralled in this room, isolated from the other patients, to prevent any 'unpleasantness'.

An envelope arrived from America. The sight of the 'Airmail' sticker and the flashy stamps cheered her. But Dan's shop-bought card and the few words that he'd scrawled inside were no more than she would receive from an acquaintance. They had been friends and, although their affair was over, she expected more from the man who had, not so long ago, proposed marriage.

Other letters arrived, anonymous and vitriolic, saying that she should be locked up for life or, better still, hanged. A couple of them contained offers to exorcise the demons in her and save her soul. She kept the letters to show Lewis, thinking they might amuse him, but he insisted on informing the hospital administrators. There was talk of vetting her mail but she couldn't risk that because one day a letter might come from Rundle.

'If something's addressed to me, I have every right to see it,' she said.

Doctor Briscoe, who had become an ally in her occasional run-ins with the staff, supported her. 'You're right. Anyway, people who write this filth are deranged.'

'I'm not so sure they are,' Tessa replied. 'If some drunken woman killed my brother, I wouldn't stop at letter writing.'

He seemed alarmed by what she said, 'Look, if you'd like to talk to someone, I'm sure it can be…'

She smiled and shook her head. 'I don't want to talk to anyone, thanks. I don't want some shrink digging around in my head or some do-gooder nagging me to stop drinking. I'm quite capable of working out why I feel the way I do. Just take away my driving licence and car keys – not that I've got a car any more – and leave me to get on with it.'

At weekends Lewis travelled to London. He stayed at Dan's flat and, although he didn't mention it, Tessa guessed he was dealing with the muddle of bills and final demands that had accumulated. Each time he came, he brought a bag of thoughtful gifts. His choice of books – *Kidnapped*, *Gone with the Wind*, a biography of Mary Stewart – was perfect. He remembered how much she loved anemones and chocolate-covered ginger. He dug out her Walkman and bought new tapes – stuff she'd never heard before but immediately loved. He made her laugh with stories of his week at school and the goings-on in the village. He relayed titbits of news. Uncle Frank hadn't been well; there were new tenants at Cranwell Lodge – a doctor and his family from Iraq; Sarah had been offered a place at Southampton University and Jane was auditioning for the County Youth Orchestra.

They reminisced, swapping memories not only of dens

and make-believe but also the permanent cloud cast by their brother's disappearance. When they were talking like this, she came closest to telling him about Rundle. The whole story. But not sure how the story ended, and terrified of losing whatever respect he still had for her, she couldn't do it.

When her misery spilled out, Lewis was there to soak it up. 'I killed an old man, Lewis. And because of me a woman's going to spend the rest of her life hobbling around on a hideous false leg. Everything I touch turns sour. I must be a bad person.'

Lewis was the only one she wanted to see. She couldn't imagine why the others came. Were roles reversed, she wouldn't visit them. But they did turn up. Lotte, loud and smelling of gin, took the 'what's done can't be undone,' approach; Liza, more other-wordly than ever, prattled about karma and fate; Jay shot her nervous smiles, perhaps wondering why he'd ever got into bed with such a wreck; Cora, her skinny editor, turned up laden with sickly-scented lilies, ate a grape or two then had to dash. Amelie was the only one who talked about the accident. 'It could have been worse, darling. The guy was over eighty. Think how bad you'd feel if you'd killed a child.'

Kirsty visited just once, wanting to know what the police had asked her and how she'd replied. 'Give them honest answers but don't volunteer any additional information. Put the onus on them to find out,' was her advice.

When Kirsty sent Lewis to the cafeteria for some sandwiches, Tessa knew something was coming.

'I won't beat about the bush. You realise, don't you, that you have great power over Lewis? I'm not interested in discussing how or why, it's enough to recognise that you have.' She was sitting straight-backed, holding Tessa's gaze. 'I'm asking you to stop exerting that power. Ever since I've known him, you've been lurking in his life, ready to step in and call him to heel. It has to stop now. Once and for all. You've got yourself into serious trouble this time. Really serious. Drag him in with you and he'll lose everything. Job. Me. Everything.' Her voice was restrained but full of passion.

'I thought that you and I were supposed to be friends,' Tessa said.

'We once agreed that friendship between us was dependent on honesty.' Kirsty shook her head, 'Tessa, you haven't been honest with me from the moment we made that pact. If you recall, we also said that should we ever fall out, we'd fight for Lewis and the winner would take him.'

'You're turning him into a trophy and making me sound like a monster. You know how much I love him.'

'You think I don't? You're in a mess but you got yourself into it so grow up and take responsibility for once. You've wasted your own life and wrecked several others. I'm asking you to set Lewis free – give him a chance of happiness.'

'What'll you do if I don't? Disconnect my life support system?'

Kirsty sighed and shook her head. 'Don't you get it? This isn't about you, Tessa. This is about Lewis. I watch him when you're around. He's … he's diminished. Reduced. Emasculated.'

'I've never thought of my brother as a macho man.'

'You're determined to misunderstand me, aren't you?' Kirsty spoke quietly but her tone was menacing.

'No. You're making yourself very clear.'

Tessa learned to use crutches and to walk without putting weight on her injured ankle. This was exhausting and frustrating, and it made her sweat. But it was a relief to be *doing* something and to be able to venture out of the room which had, for so many weeks, been her entire world.

One evening, when the other patients were eating supper, she hobbled to the payphone in the corridor. Heart pounding from exertion and apprehension, she dropped a ten pence piece in the slot and dialled Rundle's number. She'd rehearsed this moment dozens of times as she'd lain in bed. One of two things would happen – he would pick up the phone, or the answering machine would cut in. Either way she would remain silent. But instead of a ringing tone she heard a series of piercing notes followed by 'I'm sorry but this number is no longer available…'

At first Tessa dismissed Kirsty's accusations and demands. But whatever else she might be her sister-in-law was honest and scrupulously objective. There was no doubt she loved Lewis, in her own competent way. Perhaps she *should* loosen the ties. Hadn't Lewis intimated something along those lines once, suggesting that they'd become unnaturally dependent of each other after Gordon disappeared? The last thing in the world she wanted was to hamper Lewis's chances. She'd always thought that he needed chivvying. Had she been wrong? Would he be happier, stronger, more successful, if she, to all intents and purposes, took the stabilisers off his bicycle, gave him a push and watched him wobble away?

Perhaps it was.

The first thing was to serve her sentence then, when she came out, she would move to a place where no one knew her. A city like Manchester or Birmingham. She'd take a job in a shoe shop or a supermarket, or clean offices at night. She'd rent a flat – a couple of rooms would do. She would check her bank balance regularly and live within her means – not impossible as most of her father's money still lay untouched in her bank account. She might even change her name – people did it all the time. She'd had her fifteen minutes of fame.

It would be unthinkable to cut herself off from Lewis altogether. That would be too cruel to both of them. But she had to put some distance between them. He'd hate it – she'd hate it

– but it would give him a fighting chance.

On the day of her discharge, the faithful Dr Briscoe, who she suspected was a little in love with her, came to say goodbye. 'How d'you feel about…?'

'Going to prison?'

'You can't be sure…'

'I think I can. It's not my first offence.'

'You didn't…?'

'No. I wrote off the car that time. Lost my licence for a year.'

'You don't seem to be too…'

'Worried? I'm not. It's perfectly right that I "pay my dues to society" or whatever the phrase is. Once I've done that I can contemplate making a fresh start.'

IX

1991

Chapter 38

Four years and nine months. Tessa's solicitor had warned her that she would go to prison but even she seemed surprised at the severity of the sentence. 'Of course your previous driving record counted heavily against you. But even so…' She frowned then reassembled her features in a consoling smile. 'You'll be out in three years, unless you do something foolish.'

During the court procedure it was mentioned, more than once, that Tessa was a successful author and the newspapers, eager to wring the final drama from the notorious 'Swinburne Tragedy', reported the case extensively, frequently recapping on the past.

'I expect the judge wanted to make an example of me,' Tessa said. 'Prove that even the rich and infamous are subject to the laws of the land.'

The solicitor shrugged. 'It shouldn't work like that but God alone knows what goes on under those wigs.' She glanced at her watch as though she'd done what she'd been paid to do and now needed to be elsewhere. 'Well, good luck Miss Swinburne.'

They shook hands and she left, the *clip-clop* of high heels fading as she hurried down the corridor.

The 'sweatbox' was parked at the rear of the court building, waiting to transport prisoners who had been sentenced that day. One of the less stony-faced policemen told Tessa that she was lucky to be going to Downham.

'It's okay, is it?' she asked.

He gave her a pitying smile. 'I only meant that it's near London. Easier for your family to visit.' Then he locked her in one of the tiny cubicles within the vehicle.

They'd been travelling for perhaps two hours – Tessa wasn't wearing a watch – when they stopped, edged slowly forward and then stopped again. There was no mistaking the sound of gates slamming and with that, voices from within the van set up a chorus of jeering and shouting. Fists and feet pounded metal. The whole vehicle began to sway. It was terrifying. Isolated in the cubicle, she was without reference points or certainties. Closing her eyes, she clamped her hands over her ears and tried not to cry.

'Swinburne?'

Tessa stepped forward, accepting the drab tracksuit and ugly black trainers thrust at her by the warder. 'One piece of jewellery. What'll it be? Wedding ring?' She sounded bored yet impatient.

Tessa studied her own hands as though, by magic, a gold band might have appeared on her ring finger. Her hands were trembling and in an effort to steady them she clenched her fists, digging her nails hard into her palms. The only jewellery she was wearing was the broad silver bracelet that Dan had given her on the day she moved in with him and wearing it would deny the hurt she'd caused him.

'Nothing, thanks.'

She fixed her eyes on the back of the warder – a squat woman with beefy legs – who lead her across the hall, through the mob of women. Stillness and silence fell over the crowd. Then suddenly the questions came, loud and hostile, bombarding her from all sides. 'Where you from?' 'Got any drugs?' 'Nice arse. Got a girlfriend?'

This moment was critical, yet she had no sense of how to play it. Her ankle still gave her pain but she tried not to favour it in case it marked her out as a pushover. The long-ago screw-the-lot-of-you girl would have found a dozen gritty remarks to yell, or at least have given them the finger. As she climbed the metal steps to the landing above, it was as much as she could do not to soil herself.

Her cellmate, Sandra, was a small, self-contained woman who looked as though she would be scared to go out after dark. She seemed eager to tell Tessa that she had embezzled her employer – a road haulage company based in the Midlands – of two hundred thousand pounds.

'That's a lot of money,' Tessa said. 'What did you spend it on?'

'Roulette mainly. And Blackjack.' She shrugged. 'Easy come… What about you?'

'I killed an old man. And maimed a girl. I was drunk and I drove into a bus queue.'

Sandra's crime seemed heroic and harmless by comparison with hers.

Nothing had prepared her for the indignity of sharing a cell. No bigger than the bathroom in Dan's flat, it contained bunk beds, a small table and two upright chairs, two shelves fixed to the wall, and a radio. In one corner there was a lavatory and a washbasin. The window was a sheet of perspex planted in front of a barred opening. In this cell, she had to pee and snore and cry and fart, never more than a few feet from a stranger.

It took less than a week to learn the routine. Meals in the canteen, 'bang up', roll counts, exercise, 'association time', lights out – all slotted precisely into the day. Letters were pushed under the cell door, as was the polythene bag containing the daily ration of teabags and condiments. Clean clothes were delivered on Mondays; clean bed linen on Fridays. Overall, the food wasn't bad but plastic cutlery and plates did nothing to enhance it. On Saturdays, instead of a cooked supper inmates were served 'finger food' – sausage rolls, sandwiches, pork pie and cake. Tessa never found out why.

'Screws', 'jam roll', 'diesel'. The crude slang was easy to pick up but Tessa avoided using it. To do so might be taken as a sign that she wanted to fit in.

Everywhere stank of cigarette smoke, sweat and the stuff they used to clean the floor. Day and night, it was never quiet. Doors banged; shouts and screams and laughter echoed off bare walls; footsteps rang on the metal staircases. The flickering strip lights gave her headaches.

Lying in her hospital bed, she'd kidded herself that a spell in prison would be fascinating. It wasn't. She was trapped in a mind-numbing environment, surrounded by damaged people, every minute governed by dehumanising regulations. Not so different from hospital but without the option to discharge herself.

The inmates lived for 'association', the hour each evening when they were herded into the hall and expected to play cards or pool or table tennis. Tessa found the whole thing intolerable. She didn't want to 'associate' with any of these women. They had no idea what she was about, nor did she wish to tell them. She was civil – foolish to be otherwise – but she steered clear of them, using 'association time' to shower and wash her hair, occupying herself until she could return to the cell. She wasn't here to win friends or play ping-pong.

Each week, they were allowed to borrow two books from the library and Tessa set out to tackle the authors that she'd spent years pretending that she'd read. Tolstoy. Dickens. Victor Hugo.

George Eliot. But she found herself reading and re-reading the same pages, forgetting who the characters were and why she should care about them.

She had ideas for short stories but when she came to shape them they fell to pieces.

She was permanently tired yet found it hard to get to sleep, rousing whenever Sandra stirred overhead.

Often, and for no reason, she wept.

'The girl before you lost it a few times.' Sandra said. She was bending over a jigsaw puzzle, quietly but doggedly occupying the table. 'She kept saying the walls were coming in on her. In the end she taped the tubes out of two loo rolls together. She spent most of 'bang up' standing at the window, peering through them, like they were binoculars.'

'What was she looking at?' Tessa asked. 'There's nothing to see out there.'

Sandra shrugged. 'I'm just telling you what she did.'

Time and again, Tessa returned to the last conversation she'd had with her sister-in-law. Had anyone else told her to leave Lewis alone, she would assume they were jealous of their closeness. But she'd been warned off by the Ice Maiden, the woman who had left Lewis to sort his own life out and who had stayed away until he did. It galled her to admit it but Kirsty had put Lewis's needs ahead of her own desires. *Screw Kirsty Ross.* She could be equally resolute. She would set Lewis free. If it turned out to be a catastrophe, he would find his way back to her somehow.

She wrote to him.

Dear Lewis,
You are not to come here. There's nothing to be gained and it will only make it harder for me. I know you wouldn't want to do that. I also know you'll fret about me. You mustn't. I'm not going

to phone but I will write once a month so that you know I'm OK.
I don't want to discuss the past or the future.
Love,
Tessa

Of course Lewis did come and although she was within her rights to refuse his visit she didn't have the heart to do so. Beforehand, she was searched, given an orange tabard to wear over her navy blue tracksuit and allocated a numbered table at which she was to receive her visitor. It was her first glimpse of the visiting area – a utilitarian room with two dozen small tables arranged in rows. The tables were fixed to the floor, an orange plastic chair on one side, two blue chairs opposite. Inmates took their seats and waited in silence. At two-thirty the double doors opened and the visitors surged in. Husbands, lovers, children, friends. And her brother.

He came towards her, picking his way between the tables, systematically checking the numbers stencilled on them.

'You've got to sit on a blue chair, Lewis.' She didn't look directly at him, knowing that he was crying. 'Orange is for the baddies.'

He blew his nose and forced a smile. 'Hello, Tessa.' He looked confused and embarrassed, as if he'd walked into a room and found her naked. 'I don't know what to say. What I'm supposed to do.' He dipped his head and she saw a tear drip off the end of his nose. 'I can't bear to see you like this.' He stifled a sob. 'God, I'm useless.'

'See,' she whispered gently, '*you* feel dreadful, *I* feel dreadful. I tried to tell you that there's no point in coming.'

'But I can't *not* come,' he said.

'Why? What difference will it make if you come or not?'

'It'll make a difference to me,' he whispered.

'Trust you to be selfish.'

She looked at his hands, the nails flat and square-ish like her own. This was the hardest thing she'd ever had to do.

'From now on I'm going to refuse visitors.' She held his gaze. 'I mean it. Please go home to Kirsty. Get on with your lives. Do it for me.' She smiled and sat up very straight. 'It's really not so bad in here. I've got a roof over my head and three meals a day. They don't even make us sew mailbags.'

He went to say something but then shook his head, overcome with tears.

Her refusal to see visitors seemed to bother those in charge. Both the chaplain and the social worker sent notes. Did she want to take confession or communion? Would it help to talk to someone? Would it help to pray with someone?

'Holy Joes and do-gooders. They can all fuck off,' she snapped.

'Everyone gets down,' Sandra said. 'Perhaps a chat would do you good.'

'I don't want to be "done good". It's not what I'm here for.'

'Please yourself.'

She wrote to Lewis on the first day of each month. They were notes rather than letters – disjointed lists of trivialities. She was determined not to upset him with the details of her incarceration so even filling a page was difficult.

Dearest Lewis,
Another month has flown by. Did you catch the programme about the Women's Land Army? (Radio 4 – last Tuesday) Wonderful. I'm currently reading my way through the library's collection of Sherlock Holmes stories. Conan Doyle isn't generally thought of as a humorist but they make me smile. Holmes is such a pompous prick and Watson such a dullard.

I'm feeling very well and making sure I get plenty of exercise
while the weather lasts. My ankle is almost back to normal.
I hope everything is well with you.
Love, as ever,
Tessa

When the Tuesday mail appeared under the cell door, there was always an envelope from Lewis. He never missed a week and his letters ran to several pages. He told her the amusing things his pupils got up to; filled her in on the wildlife that visited the garden; grumbled about the difficulty he was having in finding a chimney sweep or a reliable plumber. It was obvious that he, too, was censoring his life, leaving out anything that might draw attention to her circumstances.

She'd been at Downham for a year when Jay Costello wrote – there was no mistaking his bold handwriting – but she tore the envelope into small pieces without opening it. He had no right to impose his words and thoughts on her.

The exercise yard that served the wing was thirty-seven paces long and twenty-one paces wide. She checked it every afternoon. Once when she was out there a helium balloon, shaped like a puckered heart, appeared and drifted idly overhead. Dozens of arms reached up, snatching at the dangling string. A scuffle broke out and while the rest of them pushed and shoved, Tessa stood to one side, watching the balloon rise over the rooftop, willing it away.

Sandra's parole came through. On the morning of her release, Sandra gave Tessa half a bottle of shampoo and a jar of pink nail varnish. They parted with a hug and a mumbled 'you take care'. Tessa was relieved that there was no mention of keeping in touch.

By lights-out, Tessa had a new cellmate.

Jackie had been to prison twice before. This time it was for attacking an ex-boyfriend. She flaunted her crime like a badge of honour, filling the cell with anger and vulgarity, leaving Tessa nowhere to go except inside her own head.

I attacked a lover, too. What d'you think of that? I stabbed him then watched his blood spill onto the floor. They never came looking for me. Why was that?

Isn't it weird? No one ever caught us together. I never met his friends or went to hear his band. I've got nothing – nothing at all – to show for it. It doesn't add up. Unless I was fucking a ghost. Did I murder a ghost?

I stabbed a man then watched his life blood oozing onto the kitchen floor. I did. Didn't I?

Around and around it went. There was nowhere else for it to go.

There was little to see from the cell window, only the four-storey buildings surrounding the exercise yard.

But if she looked up…

On sunny days aeroplanes glinted overhead, stringing white highways across the sky. There were clouds to study. *Nimbus. Cumulonimbus. Cirrus. Stratus.* She'd learned them all in geography. And the weather that went with them. The beautiful names had lodged in her memory, but what difference did it make whether it rained or not? There were birds. Dim-witted pigeons squatted on the prison rooftops but above them gulls and crows free-wheeled. Higher still, tiny *somethings* – could they be swifts? – spiralled up and up.

Sometimes, when she was sure that Jackie was asleep, Tessa stood at the window, letting the moon and stars and chasing clouds remind her that none of this was important.

*

424

Monotony stifled Downham in grey fog, infiltrating her brain, clogging her thoughts, damping her imagination like the soft pedal on a piano. She was de-sensitised, as if she were under an anaesthetic, floating further and further away. Time got out of kilter. Monday jumped to Wednesday; September to November; one year to the next. Time was passing and that was all that mattered.

Dear Lewis
This is the last time I shall be writing to you from Downham.
I'll be in touch as soon as I have an address and know what I'm doing. I have several ideas.
Thank you for every one of your wonderful letters.
Love, as ever,
Tess x
You mustn't worry about me or this whole business will have been pointless.

At eight-fifteen on a bright June morning, Tessa stood on the pavement with four other women. Unlike them, there was no one waiting to meet her, and for that she was grateful. Her shoulder-length hair was heavily streaked with grey. She wore her own clothes but they seemed to be too big and her shoes pinched across the instep. As she walked towards the bus stop, somebody shouted 'Good luck, love,' but she didn't look back.

There was music playing in the café – something South-American-sounding, with a lazy beat.

Tessa walked towards the counter, past the sofa where the young man was reading the paper; past the woman breast-feeding her baby; past the two middle-aged women who were laughing loudly.

The man tending the coffee machine half-turned towards

her. 'If you'd like to take a seat, Madam, someone will take your order.'

Smile. 'Thank you.'

She chose a table towards the back of the room. Dipping into her jacket pocket, she brought out a handful of change, turning it over as if she were a tourist fathoming out the local currency.

A waitress – young, fair-haired, middle-European perhaps – came to the table. 'What can I get you?'

Deep breath and smile. 'A small white coffee, please.'

A lad came in, whistling, carrying a tray of bread rolls; a scarlet-lipped woman in a black suit left an order for sandwiches; the mother sang to her baby. All so sure of themselves and what they were doing.

The waitress brought the coffee. It came in a white china cup, a cellophane-wrapped biscuit resting in the saucer alongside a shining spoon.

Tessa ran her finger around the rim of the cup. 'I haven't drunk out of a china cup in three years.'

The girl smiled and nodded, clearly thinking that she had misunderstood.

Chapter 39

LEWIS DUMPED HIS BRIEFCASE on the bottom stair and scooped the letters off the doormat. Loosening his tie, he went through to the kitchen. While the kettle boiled he flicked through the mail. A postcard from a colleague, a bank statement, the usual junk mail, and a letter from Tessa.

He hadn't heard from his sister for several months and the sight of her untidy scrawl both cheered and alarmed him. Balancing the white envelope on the palm of his hand, he stared at it, as if its weight or the angle of the stamp might give a clue to its contents. If Kirsty were there she'd say, *For heavens sake just open it. Why d'you always try to guess what's in a letter?* The answer was simple. He was bracing himself for the worst as he always did whenever he received Tessa's communications.

He slipped a knife under the flap, slicing cleanly along the fold and pulling out a single sheet of paper. Tessa had moved. She was still in Birmingham but gave no explanation for moving – the third time in two years. Her new address was printed in block capitals at the top of the page. As usual there was no phone number. She'd added a couple of lines. *Not much to report apart from the new address. I'm working at Boots now – better pay and it smells nice. I'll keep in touch. Much love.*

When she was discharged from prison she'd moved to Birmingham. 'Why?' he'd asked when she phoned to let him know. 'Why not?' she'd replied. 'And Lewis, can you do something for me? It's important.' 'Of course.' 'Can you leave me to get on with it?'

He'd done as she'd asked because he hadn't known what else to do.

He'd broken his word only once. His daughters had spent a week in Yorkshire and, having delivered them back to Stafford, he'd continued down the M6 to Birmingham. He'd planned the detour weeks earlier but only told Kirsty the day before, making out that it was a spur of the moment idea. Tessa's address led him to a drab semi, located off a dual carriageway. The row of doorbells indicated that the house was divided into flats. He checked the names and found *Swinburne*, buzzing several times before Tessa, thin and pale faced, opened the door. 'Can I come in?' he asked. 'I'd rather you didn't. Let's go to the pub. Hang on while I get my coat.' He'd kept the conversation light, describing the changes they'd made to the garden and telling her about their forthcoming trip to visit Kirsty's mother in Scotland. She hadn't said much but drank three glasses of white wine to his pint of shandy. After an hour she said that she had to go, adding, 'You're not to worry about me. And if you promise not to come here again, I'll promise to write regularly.' 'You don't expect me to fall for that again?' he asked. 'Don't pressurise me, Lewis. I've said I'll write and I will.'

He'd re-run the moment of their meeting dozens of times since but he still had no idea whether she'd been pleased to see him.

When they did come, her letters told him nothing beyond the essentials. She was okay; had changed her job; had moved again. Once in a while – most recently, his birthday – she phoned. 'Happy birthday, Lewis. Another year gone. Don't panic, you'll always be my baby brother.' Her calls were brief and always from a payphone. He never succeeded in getting much out of her. When he tried ringing back, she didn't pick up.

Lewis wrote to her on the first Sunday of every month, regardless of whether he heard from her or not, printing his name and address on the back of each envelope. At least a neighbour would know who to contact in an emergency.

The forecast was for a blistering weekend.

'Anything you fancy doing?' Lewis asked.

Kirsty grimaced. 'I can't face sitting in a hot car. Let's stay here. We could invite the neighbours round for a barbecue or something.'

'We don't have a barbecue,' he pointed out.

'Phew. The perfect get-out.'

In the end, equipped with sunhats, books and portable radio for the Test score, they set up their deckchairs in a shaded corner of the garden. It was an idyllic day, roses scenting the air, dabs of pure white cloud decorating the sky, Kirsty alongside him deep in her novel.

Lewis closed his eyes.

He'd lost Kirsty once but she'd given him a second chance. They'd come close to fouling up again after the miscarriages. Then they'd drifted further apart when she took over the York office and buried herself in the job as if, having failed to prove her womanhood, she needed to prove herself better than any man.

His childhood had been dominated by women. Tessa. His mother. Gran. Mrs Channing. They weren't all *strong* women but each of them had exerted significant influence over him. What if he'd grown up with a brother as well as a sister? It would have made him the 'middle-of-three' as Tessa had once reminded him. Would it also have made him more self-reliant?

His was labelled 'the lucky generation'. No wars. No rationing. Grammar schools. University grants. Free health care. An era of unlimited opportunity. But mightn't he be a stronger person had it not been handed him on a plate?

When he was a lad, he *must* have peered into the future but he had no recollection of what he'd seen there. It wouldn't have been a life lived in a haze of chalk dust, one failed marriage, two daughters whom he barely knew and a notorious sister.

He'd suffered a dull but ever present ache since Tessa had cut herself off from him but he said nothing to Kirsty. Recently, something had eased between him and his wife and he welcomed the change. These days she rarely stayed late at the office, getting home in good time for them to eat supper together. At weekends, they drove to Whitby and strolled along the beach or played the machines in the penny arcades on Scarborough sea front. They made love, nothing ambitious but something they hadn't done for months. They were drawing closer again and, in order not to jeopardise this, he kept his pain to himself.

'Penny for them.'

He opened his eyes, squinting against the sunlight. Kirsty was coming across the lawn, carrying two glasses of squash.

He pushed himself up in the chair. 'It'll cost you a lot more than a penny.'

Lewis arrived home to a phone message. A Terry Vaughan – he didn't recognise the name – said that he needed to speak to him on a matter of urgency. Lewis's first thought was Tessa but, when he listened to the message again, he realised that the contact number was Frank Swinburne's.

Vaughan told him that his uncle had died the previous day. 'It was quick, thank God. A massive stroke.'

Lewis made an effort to hide his relief. 'Poor Uncle Frank.' He paused. 'I don't think we've met, Mr Vaughan.' The man must be his uncle's partner but it was an awkward thing to ask.

'No. But he often talked about you. You and Tessa. He gave me

431

your phone number, in case anything…' his voice trailed off.

'D'you need me to come down and help with…?' It was Lewis's turn to falter.

'Frank made his wishes quite clear. Wrote it all down and left it with his solicitor. Even chose the music. The funeral's next Wednesday. Twelve noon at the crematorium chapel. I haven't managed to find a number for your sister.'

'I'll make sure Tessa knows, Mr Vaughan. And thanks so much for taking this on. It's very good of you. Let me know if we owe you—'

'We were together for twenty years, Mr Swinburne,' he said. 'I loved him.'

That night, Lewis dreamed about Cranwell Lodge. It was on fire, flames licking up through the roof, sparks twirling into the summer sky. He was standing at the back door, calling through the shattered pane into the smoke-filled scullery. *Tessa. Gordon.* He could neither feel heat nor smell smoke but something had fixed his feet to the ground and he couldn't move, couldn't save them.

Uncle Frank was dead. It was so long since Tessa had seen him that, before contemplating his death, she needed to remind herself that he'd still been alive. He was a couple of years older than her father – which would put him in his mid-eighties. What people referred to as 'a good innings'. But that was if the deceased died in bed not at a bus stop, wiped out by a spinning car.

In his letter, Lewis offered to give her a lift, implying that he expected her to attend. She despised the whole hypocritical ritual. Mourners who, in reality, wanted to jump for joy because they weren't the corpse in that coffin. A vicar, who'd never met the deceased, spouting condescending crap – *We're here to celebrate a life* – although it might be amusing to hear what the Reverend made of Uncle Frank's lifestyle. Then, after Frank Swinburne was incinerated, the gawping and whispering would begin. *That's Tessa Swinburne over there. You know. The one who killed the poor old man.*

She pushed the coins into the slot. 'Thanks for the offer, Lewis, but I shan't be coming. They don't allow us time off for funerals. Not an uncle's funeral, anyway. Too easy to concoct a dozen dead uncles.'

She heard the disappointment in his voice followed by false cheeriness as he invented bits of news to keep her on the line. She watched the seconds counting down. *10 – 9 – 8 –* 'Sorry, I'm out of change. Love you.' *– 3 – 2 – 1 – gone.*

The *trrring ... trrring* of his returned call followed her as she hurried away.

In the beginning it had been an adventure; a series of challenges. Finding a job and somewhere to live. Spinning out her money from week to week. Picking through dented tins and overripe fruit. Trawling through rails in charity shops. She'd fooled herself that, if things became intolerable, she could use her experiences to write a novel, exposing the condition of the working class in the dying days of the Twentieth Century. Gritty. Authentic. Redeeming. That was in the beginning, when it was an adventure and when she assumed that sacrifice would add weight to her side of the scales of justice.

Her first job was at a newsagent's. The shop had an easy-going atmosphere and the proprietor, once he'd shown her the ropes, left her to get on with it. She didn't mind the early start or working on Sunday mornings but her ankle sometimes gave her trouble. It hadn't been right since the accident and, despite her efforts to exercise it every day while she was in prison, after she'd been standing on it for several hours, it started to ache. There were, however, benefits to working in the shop. It was easy to slip a pack of cigarettes or a bar of Fruit and Nut into her pocket as she was putting her coat on to go home. But she hadn't anticipated how chummy the customers would be, and expect her to be in return. They called her 'Tessy' and teased her about her 'posh' voice. Some men made what Gran would have termed 'advances'. One 'regular' ruined everything by inviting her to spend the evening with him at the Con Club – whatever that was – then became abusive when she refused. The proprietor, seemingly more reluctant to lose a customer than an employee, thought she should have accepted. The atmosphere turned sour and she moved on.

There was always work for those who would accept low wages in return for long hours. Newsagent's, dental surgery, coffee bar, bread shop. And now Boots. Tessa had acquired a whole range of useful skills. She'd learned to operate a till; to stack a tray with dirty crockery and balance it as she weaved between crowded tables; to arrange cream cakes efficiently in a box. She'd discovered that postcards in shop windows offered the most affordable accommodation. She became expert in detecting the smell of rising damp and learned the right questions to ask about pre-payment meters and shared hallways. She could make a tea bag stretch to three cups, a tin of baked beans to two meals and discovered that fish paste didn't taste as bad as it smelled.

One morning, kneeling in the aisle, stacking boxes of hair colourant on the shelf, she started crying. She wasn't in pain; no one had shouted at her; nothing had happened to make her feel sad. At first it was a whimper, barely audible and vaguely pleasurable. She blew her nose on a tissue. 'Get a grip, woman.' But she couldn't and the whimpering escalated to sobbing. Her nose streamed with strands of clear snot, salty on her lips. The odd thing was that, although she could taste the salt and feel the racking sobs, she was remote from her body, watching her pathetic self from a few feet away.

The store manager hustled her to the office then sent her home in a taxi, telling her to see her doctor.

Insomnia and mood swings had plagued her for months. One minute she felt fine, the next she couldn't find the energy to raise a cup to her lips or the will to put her shoes on. Now she could add hysteria to her list of symptoms. She thought it might be something to do with the menopause. But the doctor, flicking through the sheaf of notes in the buff slip case, didn't show much interest in what she was telling him.

He gave her a cursory examination – eyes, blood pressure, reflexes. 'I'm going to put you on Prozac,' he said, as if he were offering her a treat.

'Happy pills?'

'If you want to think of them like that. Oh, and no alcohol. That's important.'

It didn't sound like a recipe for happiness.

'The medication is usually pretty effective but it only addresses the symptoms. I'd like you to talk to someone. Sort out why you're feeling ... the way you are. Get to the root of the matter.' From his sing-song delivery, she knew that he'd said it a hundred times and no longer believed it.

'You think I'm depressed?'

'Do *you* think you're depressed?'

She shrugged. There was a time when she would have relished a little cut and thrust with this bumptious prick. But she was too tired.

The doctor signed her off for two weeks, telling her to come back if she needed longer.

She'd not spent this much time on her own since leaving London, neither had she had more than two consecutive days off work. She'd lost the knack of doing nothing. The empty hours were booby-trapped with anxiety and she felt vulnerable as she woke to each unstructured day. She made a timetable, splitting the day into morning, afternoon and evening sessions and deciding what to do with each manageable chunk of time. She went to the library. She walked around the park then treated herself to a coffee from the kiosk. She changed her bedding and took it to the launderette. She listened to the radio. She prepared *proper* meals – as proper as two gas rings and a grill would allow. Her most ambitious project was to visit the City Art Gallery which Dan had once told her housed a fine collection of Pre-Raphaelite paintings. But, as she stood at the bus stop, a vision of large echoey rooms filled with well-dressed, well-informed people flashed through her mind. Her heart galloped and she couldn't catch her breath. She ended up going to the library instead.

After two weeks she returned to work, telling the girls there that she'd had a nasty bout of the 'flu that was currently doing the rounds.

Chapter 40

IF SHE DIDN'T WRITE SOON Lewis would turn up. She couldn't risk that. Not until she was completely well again. She'd already discarded several muddled attempts, knowing that he would detect that she wasn't quite herself. The thing was, when she got home from work, by the time she'd had a bowl of soup or a cheese sandwich, all she was fit for was bed.

In the end she sent a postcard – an aerial view of 'Spaghetti Junction' – saying *Everything OK. Tessa x*.

His reply came back by return.

Dear Tessa

Thanks for the postcard which came today. It was a relief to get word (3 words actually) from you. I must admit I was starting to worry.

Can I try, yet again, to persuade you to come up to Yorkshire? Stay a few days. Longer if you can spare the time. You'd be interested to see what we've done with the house. The garden is looking good and the pond is a triumph. Come in the summer holidays when I'm home and we might have some decent weather. I know that sounds an age away but I imagine you have to sort out your leave well in advance. I won't pester but, in return, promise me you'll think about it.

Lewis xxx

Please come. I miss you.

She missed him, too, with the chronic pain of bereavement. But people coped with separation. Della – one of the women she worked with – was constantly tearful. Her daughter had married an electrician and they'd moved to Sydney five years ago. Della's grandson was three now and she'd only seen him once. 'Just got to grin and bear it,' she said. 'You wouldn't want to spoil their chances, would you?'

Spoil. Chances. Did every person in the world have the potential to ruin the lives of those they most loved?

By the time her hospital appointment came through, she'd given up thinking it would happen. She was tempted to tear up the letter. She'd grown accustomed to keeping herself to herself so did she want a stranger – this 'Dr S Davies' person – ferreting around in her head? Therapy, or whatever they called it in those days, hadn't done her mother much good. But, on the plus side, it would only cost the bus fare to the hospital. Maybe she'd go once – see what it was like. They would give her time off work for a hospital appointment but it was probably best not to mention the nature of her problem.

No more than thirty, intelligent and confident, Doctor Sophie Davies reminded Tessa of herself at that age. Or how she might have been.

She asked a string of questions. 'Can you tell me exactly what happened just before you started crying?' 'How did you feel the day before?' 'What was your first thought on waking up this morning?' 'What makes you smile?'

Tessa had expected something more penetrating but at least the young woman was interested in her and treated her with respect.

Every Tuesday morning she spent forty-five minutes with Sophie Davies. It meant reorganising her shifts but Tuesday was a quiet day in the shop and, as long as she was available for weekend work, there was no problem.

Together she and the doctor excavated the past, two archaeologists scraping away the years, revealing her history – or some of it. Lewis. Her parents. Gordon. Dr Davies was gently tenacious. The car accident. Prison. Sometimes when she felt particularly raw, she'd make a joke or try to divert the conversation but Sophie Davies sieved every throwaway remark as if it might contain a shard of vital information. Uncle Frank. Cranwell Lodge. Jay Costello.

Tessa had never before been invited to develop her thoughts like this, or required to convey her feelings so accurately, and it took a while for her to get the hang of it. After a tentative start, she began to believe that she could reveal anything in that austere consulting room and not be judged. She and Sophie Davies weren't friends but colleagues, working towards the same goal, and Tessa came away from each session worn out but hopeful.

Tuesday mornings became the high spot of her week. She planned in advance what she wanted to talk about. Ted Knowles and the girl at the bus stop. Why she hadn't married Dan. One day, when she was ready, she would ask if she might have inherited this 'illness' from her mother. One day she might *even* tell her about the doll – Lewis would surely understand if it helped to make her well. But she would never, *could* never, tell anyone about Rundle. No one would forgive her for that.

Almost five months into her treatment, she received a letter telling her, without explanation, that Doctor Davies was no longer working at the hospital and that, in future, she would be seen by Doctor Alistair McBride.

Why hadn't Sophie Davies said something when she saw her last week? How dare she plunder all Tessa's secrets then disappear without explanation or apology? What a bitch. Yet another false 'friend'. So, no. She wouldn't be 'seen by Doctor

Alistair McBride' or any other bastard psychiatrist.

The headaches grew worse.

'Perhaps you need new glasses,' Della suggested.

The optician a few doors down, was advertising free eye tests and Tessa made an appointment. Yes. Both her reading and distance spectacles were way off. It was a relief to know that the headaches were nothing sinister but a shock to discover what she would have to pay for the most basic spectacles.

Not long after that, the landlord increased her rent and once more she had to dig into her shrinking savings.

She found somewhere cheaper to live. A bedsit in a terraced house. It was small but it was handy having everything in one room. And the heating bill was bound to be lower. There wasn't much storage space, though. A blessing that she had so few possessions.

Not long after moving, she succumbed to a virus. Everyone referred to it as a 'forty-eight hour bug' but hers continued for days. The little appetite she had, failed to return and she couldn't get warm. When the alarm went off for work, she pulled the covers over her head and sank back into half-sleep.

'Personnel' sent a threatening letter, demanding a doctor's note or her immediate return to work. She forced herself back but it was all a bit of a struggle.

After a month, having been given the statutory warnings – *Unpunctual. Unreliable. Offhand with customers. Unacceptable standards of personal hygiene.* – she lost her job.

There were still a few hundred pounds of her father's money in the bank and she'd just received a modest royalty cheque from Ward & Cox. It didn't amount to much but if she went carefully it would give her several weeks' breathing space. She'd seen an advert in the free newspaper for a cleaning job at the local school. If she could get that, and a couple of others like it, she should just about be all right until something better turned up.

But to be truthful, she wasn't sure she had the energy or the know-how to be a cleaner.

She really should let Lewis have her new address. There must be a stamp somewhere in her purse. God, she was tired. Why couldn't she sleep? So, so tired. What was the best thing to do? Perhaps she should talk to Lewis. She'd done her best not to bother him but…

She went to the phone box on the main road and dialled Lewis's number. Kirsty answered. It was odd hearing her voice after so long. It hadn't changed a bit.

'Kirsty? Can I speak to Lewis?'

'Tessa? Is that Tessa?'

'Is Lewis there?'

'He's not, I'm afraid. He's lending a hand with the Lower Sixth field trip. He's gone to—'

'When will he be back?'

'He's away all week.'

'I need to speak to Lewis.'

'Is there anything I can do?'

'No. It's just that … no, there's nothing you can do.'

There was nothing Kirsty could do. There was nothing that Tessa would *allow* her do.

'But that was three days ago. Why didn't you contact me?' Lewis shouted.

Kirsty spoke quietly. 'Tessa did sound slightly distracted but she didn't say it was urgent. I asked if there was anything I could do but she said there wasn't. Anyway, you were busy in Dorset, doing your job. I'm sure she'll be in touch if it's important.'

He hated her cool logic. 'I don't have time for this now. I'm going to Birmingham.'

'Tonight? Isn't that rather melodramatic? Of course, that's precisely what she wants.' Kirsty reached out and touched his shoulder. 'Be sensible. It's gone eight. You've been on the go all day. Go first thing in the morning.'

'I've made my mind up. I'm going now.'

He stopped at the first service station to fill up with fuel and buy a black coffee then drove on. He was too old for this. His back twinged and a headache lodged at the base of his skull. He'd been up since dawn, dismantling tents, chivvying kids, taking his turn at the wheel of the minibus. Now he was driving half way back to Dorset. The traffic was light but even so he couldn't afford to lose concentration for one second. He lowered the window a few inches, trusting that the cold air would keep him awake.

He took a second break and phoned Kirsty. 'You were right. I should have waited until the morning.'

'You probably wouldn't have slept. I should have come with you and shared the driving.'

He couldn't tell her that he was glad to be on his own.

He made good time down the motorway then lost an hour in the confusion of Birmingham's suburban streets. At last he found it – a four-storey block, its brickwork piebald with graffiti, a scum of litter on the lank grass in front of it. Although it was near midnight, the curry-scented night was restless with traffic noise and the *weee…waaa…weee…waaa* of an alarm. He double-checked that he'd locked the car.

Flat 7, Elgin Court. He'd never imagined it would be such a dump. He rang the bell, hoping against hope that Tessa would come to the door and curse him to hell for being there. He hoped that his journey was a waste of time. He hoped that she'd been phoning to tell him that she'd started writing again or that Dan had come back or that she had decided to do anything but what she had been doing.

442

A young man came to the door. Too young for Tessa.

He glared at Lewis. 'Yeah?'

'I'm looking for my sister. Tessa Swinburne.'

'You'll have to look elsewhere, mate.' That was clearly all he had to say on the matter and he made as if to close the door.

'I know she lives here. Or did live here.' Lewis felt sick.

'Her and this lot.' Using his foot, the man dragged a pile of mail out from behind the door. He scuffed the heap, spreading it out across the doormat.

Lewis spotted his writing on one of the envelopes. He stooped and picked it up, wanting to kick this oaf in the balls and demand to know why he hadn't had the decency to return it. Instead he sorted through the pile and, amongst the fliers and takeaway menus, he found another of his letters and several official-looking envelopes addressed to Tessa.

'How long have you lived here?' Lewis asked.

The man paused, evidently weighing up the implications of such a disclosure. 'Four or five weeks.'

'And you have no idea where my sister went?'

'Sorry, mate.'

Lewis held up Tessa's mail. 'Okay if I take these?'

'Help yourself.'

Driving towards the city centre, he spotted Marriott Hotel emblazoned across a tower block and by one o'clock he had booked a single room and phoned Kirsty to let her know what was going on.

Despite his anxiety, he slept well – not surprising after five nights in a tent and a day shuttling up and down motorways. Before going down for breakfast, he opened his sister's mail. He felt wretched reading his own flippant sentences, knowing that, whilst he'd been wittering on about school trips and his new car, something terrible must have been going on in Tessa's life. The other letters were from the council and the TV Licensing people, reminding her that she owed them money. A bank statement showed that she was four hundred pounds in credit. It painted a depressing picture but there was nothing here to cause someone to run.

He knew she worked at Boots. He would start there. There must be branches all over a city this size but, he wasn't sure why, he'd pictured her in a large store near the centre. Maybe something she'd mentioned? The girls on the hotel reception desk were helpful and he soon had the four city-centre branches pinpointed on a map. He headed for the nearest one.

Once inside the store, it was more difficult than he'd envisaged. He'd assumed he'd be able to find someone in charge who could tell him whether a Tessa Swinburne – he daren't contemplate the possibility that she was using a different name – was employed there. When he eventually got hold of a junior manager, she said she wasn't able to give out that sort of information, spouting a lot of tripe about confidentiality and 'duty of care' to the staff.

He paused for a quick coffee and decided to switch tactics. In the second store he took a more direct approach, avoiding the management, going straight to the women who were working in the shop, enquiring whether they knew a Tessa Swinburne. Drawing a blank on the ground floor he went up the escalator and started again.

Trying his best to look benign, he approached a woman in the standard blue tabard. 'Excuse me. I was wondering whether Tessa Swinburne works in this store.'

'Who wants to know?' She was a woman of about fifty, careworn but well-groomed, and, from the way she said it, Lewis knew that he was in luck.

'I'm Tessa's brother.'

She smiled. 'You must be Lewis, the teacher. I'm Della.' They shook hands. 'Yes, Tessa did work here. But she left about, what, three weeks ago.'

Lewis wanted to kiss her. 'Brilliant. D'you have her address by any chance? I went to Elgin Court—'

'Oh, she moved from there a while ago. Went to Windsor Street. I'm positive of that because my sister used to live in Windsor Street. Don't know where she's working now.' She frowned. 'She's okay, is she? She hasn't been well recently.'

'I'm not sure but I think she may be in trouble.' He felt disloyal revealing this to a stranger but he needed Della as an ally.

They were interrupted by a hard-faced woman in a navy suit. 'Any problems, sir?'

Della looked flustered and, not wanting to get her into trouble, he replied 'None at all. This lady has been most helpful.'

He walked towards the stairs, returning when the woman had gone. 'If you give me your number, I'll ring you later. Let you know how I get on.'

The taxi dropped him at the corner of Windsor Street. The terraced houses, their front doors set no more than a metre back from the pavement, were neat enough and, tiny though they were, many of the properties were subdivided into flats. He was pleased that Tessa had moved here; it seemed more civilised than the shabby block he'd visited the night before. Suddenly the confidence with which he'd approached the task of finding her in the vast city dissolved. He'd cracked the difficult bit and all he had to do was knock on thirty or forty doors but, having got this far, he was terrified of what he might unearth.

It was midday on a Saturday. People who weren't at work were likely to be out shopping or making the most of the good weather. Steeled for disappointment, he worked his way along the street, up the odd numbers and back down the evens. As he knocked on each door, rang each bell, he could see how dodgy he must look – a middle-aged stranger wearing yesterday's grubby shirt, enquiring about some fictitious woman. But on the whole, the people to whom he spoke were cooperative and he wasn't too concerned that he had no luck on what he estimated to be a thirty per cent response. He decided to go back to the hotel, take a nap and freshen up. Maybe he'd buy a new shirt.

At seven twenty-five that evening he found Tessa at number four Windsor Street. And that was only because the neighbour at number six was pathologically nosy. 'There's a new person next door,' she'd confided. 'A woman. About sixty, I'd say. Short hair. Thin. Doesn't go out much. Listens to the radio a lot.'

Standing in front of the drab brown door, he knew that Tessa was close by. He just knew. There were two unmarked doorbells and he rang both. To be sure, he pounded on the tarnished door knocker, not caring who came as long as someone did.

Tessa opened the door a few inches and stared at him. She made no move to let him in, gazing at him as if he might disappear if she looked away.

'I knew you'd come.'

Tears filled his eyes, dissolving his sister into an indistinct figure. He brushed them away with the back of his hand. 'I'm sorry I took so long.'

Her short hair was entirely grey. She was wearing a brown sweater, several sizes too large, the wool pilled and snagged, and shapeless navy trousers. The corduroy slippers on her bare feet were grubby. She led him along a narrow passageway, shuffling ahead of him, her head, bowed slightly, revealing the tendons running up the back of her thin neck. Extending her arm behind her, she twiddled her fingers in silent instruction that he should take her hand.

She opened a door. The room they entered was no larger than his study yet this was where she lived. It was chaotically untidy and smelled of cigarette smoke and decaying rubbish. Her 'kitchen' – a small sink, a miniature fridge, something that

446

looked like a camping stove – occupied an alcove in one corner. Alongside it was a door, which he hoped led to a bathroom. Everything else – bed, table, chair, plywood wardrobe – was in that room.

He ought to shake her and ask her if she realised how impossible it was to find a person in a city the size of Birmingham; to point out that if she'd worked in a different branch of Boots or if Della had been taking a lunch break, he wouldn't have found her. She would have the last word, of course – *But I did work there and Della wasn't at lunch.*

She was clinging to him, not speaking, her body trembling and he couldn't bear to spoil that moment with recriminations.

'I'm sorry, Lewis. I shouldn't have phoned. I promised her I wouldn't interfere—'

'What? When?'

'A long, long time ago. Before…' She stopped as though she were peering into the past, unable to make out whatever she was seeing there.

The confusion on her face distressed him. 'Let's not worry about that now. Put a few things together. I'm taking you back to my hotel.'

She smiled. 'What do I need?'

When they got to the Marriott, he booked a second room and while Tessa was soaking in the bath, he phoned Kirsty, ignoring the coolness in her voice when he told her, 'She's in a bit of a state so I'm bringing her back with me.'

Then he called Della to thank her for everything. 'I'd never have found her without you. I'll let you know how things work out.'

He was alarmed to see how his sister had let herself go. She looked and smelled better once she'd bathed but scented water failed to wash away the melancholy that clung to her. She gave him a disjointed account of the last few months. She'd obviously suffered a breakdown of some kind but, recognising how fragile she was and fearful of exacerbating things, he didn't press her for details. There would be plenty of time for that.

Tessa slept most of the way back. Lewis drove steadily, rarely exceeding sixty-five miles an hour, as though he were transporting a frail cargo which would disintegrate if jolted. He felt irrationally happy and more than a little pleased with himself. He had succeeded in his undertaking and he wished that he could remain forever in this moment.

Not far from home, she woke up. 'Do you believe in God, Lewis? I don't think I've ever asked you before.'

'It all depends…'

'Yes or no?'

'I don't think I do. What about you?'

'Of course I don't. It would make life unbearable. The idea that we might be called to account – as if we haven't already gone through the mill down here. It would be like being charged twice with the same offence. And what could be worse than ending up in heaven with all those people we never gave a stuff about? Then having to pretend we liked them all along and were sorry for … whatever terrible things we did.' She paused. 'D'you suppose we'll recognise Gordon? Will he be called "Gordon" or will he use the name he was given by the people who stole him?'

There was an encouraging hint of the old Tessa in the inconsistency, an echo of the games they used to play, although he was in two minds whether to distract her from Gordon and the pitfalls surrounding him.

She persisted. 'What d'you think?'

'Christopher. That's what he'd be called. But we've just agreed, haven't we? There *is* no heaven. Or hell, come to that.'

'"Hell is other people." Who said that?'

'Oscar Wilde? It usually is.'

So what does that make heaven? Ourselves?' She frowned. 'That can't be right.'

Chapter 41

HAD LEWIS PASSED HIS SISTER IN THE STREET, he would not have recognised her. The skin on her face resembled a sheet of crumpled tissue paper, and one deep vertical crease bisected each cheek. Veins, visible beneath the translucent skin, snaked across the backs of her hands. Her hair had thinned. She was scrawny. In fact her whole frame had shrunk.

Lewis could accept the physical changes but it was her state of mind that concerned him. One moment she was commenting on their new kitchen and asking after his daughters, the next sunk in silence, picking at the cuff of her sweater, humming to herself.

Their GP agreed to see her first thing next morning as an emergency patient. Lewis notified the school that he wasn't feeling too good – perfectly true – and took her to the surgery.

'I can give you something to help you get through the next few days, Miss Swinburne, but you need to see your own doctor as soon as possible.' He glanced towards Lewis then back to Tessa who sat silent and disengaged.

'Thanks,' Lewis said. He hadn't thought beyond today let alone when Tessa might return to Birmingham.

Kirsty was courteous towards Tessa but kept her distance. Lewis knew that his wife was reserving judgement, waiting to see how things would develop. He hadn't tackled her about some promise that she'd apparently extracted from Tessa.

He didn't like the sound of it but now wasn't the moment for confrontation. He was standing at the fulcrum of a see-saw, maintaining equilibrium, making sure that neither Tessa nor Kirsty was catapulted to disaster, and this required every ounce of his energy.

'You can't watch her all the time. You'll have to go to work tomorrow,' Kirsty said as they were getting ready for bed. 'She's doped out on tranquilisers. She'll sleep all day.'

Next morning, as he was leaving, Lewis took Tessa a cup of coffee. 'I'm off now. Don't forget to take your pills. I've left the school number next to the phone if you need me. I won't be late back.'

'Thanks.' She pushed herself up in the bed. 'Thanks for everything. I'll be fine. I'll have a slow start; a soak in the bath; read the paper. A few days of country air and I'll be good as new. Off you go.'

It was years since Tessa had been there but she had no difficulty in finding her way to the village. The shop was remarkably well-stocked considering the size of the place and, seeing the range of goods, it was obvious that it catered for an affluent clientele.

She wandered between the shelves. A horsey woman in waxed jacket and fancy wellington boots was dropping items into a wire basket, things Tessa hadn't tasted for years. A tin of anchovies; a jar of duck pâté; a bottle of olive oil that cost half of Tessa's food budget for the week.

Checking how much money she had in her pocket – money she'd scooped off the kitchen windowsill – she calculated that she had enough to buy a Chelsea bun and a bag of treacle toffees.

By the time she got back to the house, she was looking forward to the coffee she would have with her bun. As she was hanging up the jacket she'd borrowed from the hallstand, she felt something hard in one of the pockets. It was a minute tin of caviar. While the kettle boiled, she went upstairs to her bedroom and pushed the tin to the back of the drawer beneath her bed.

'I went out for some fresh air this morning,' she told Lewis later when he asked how she had spent her day. Tossing the toffees towards him, she smiled. 'All the way from … the village shop.'

The house was empty when she woke next morning. Kirsty had stuck a Post-it on the fridge door, inviting her to help herself to anything she fancied. The fridge was full, the bread bin contained two loaves and a packet of croissants, the fruit bowl was piled high with grapes, plums, kiwi fruit, even a mango. Confronted with so much food, so much choice, she felt bewildered.

She wandered through the empty house, sipping black coffee. There were mirrors everywhere. In the hall; the bathrooms; above the fireplace; on each wardrobe door. Too many mirrors. And as she moved from room to room, a woman, gaunt and sexless, stared back at her from every one of them.

What a shame that she'd not been there to keep an eye on what was going on. Kirsty had gained such a hold over Lewis. There always had been something creepy about her. For one thing, how come she never looked any older? Tessa pictured her sister-in-law – white teeth, smooth skin, lustrous hair. And then there were those penetrating eyes. Ruthless. Icy. From the very start Kirsty Ross had set out to freeze Lewis's heart.

By the end of the week, a jar of peaches in brandy, a packet of dried porcini mushrooms and a bottle of truffle oil had joined the caviar under Tessa's bed. It was as well to have a few bits and pieces in, just in case.

'I might have a look around York tomorrow,' Tessa said as they were watching the Sunday evening news.

Lewis frowned. 'I'm not sure that's such a good—'

'The bus goes from the village,' Kirsty chipped in. 'The timetable's on the pin board.'

Lewis reiterated his reservations. 'You shouldn't overdo it. Why not wait until I can take you? We could all go together next weekend.'

Kirsty looked up. 'Tessa might not be here next weekend. And it's very straightforward on the bus.'

Tessa nodded. 'I'll enjoy a bus ride.'

What did she need? A jacket. And some cash – enough for the bus ticket and a coffee. There was a cache of change in a brass ashtray on the chest of drawers in Kirsty and Lewis's bedroom; another on the mantelpiece in the sitting room. Her best find was a five pound note in the pocket of Lewis's gardening trousers. Nine pounds forty. That should be enough.

As the bus carried her away from the village, she found it progressively more difficult to regulate her breathing. Her heart pounded and there was a tingling in her lips as though she'd had a tooth filled and the anaesthetic was still wearing off. She tried counting cows in the fields next to the road but the bus was speeding along and she kept losing track.

She took the bottle of pills from her handbag. Had she forgotten to take one this morning? Was that why she was feeling so jittery? She unscrewed the top and shook two pills on to her hand, studying them – pink, round, conspiratorial – lying there between her life and love lines.

The bus terminated near the city centre. She felt better once she was in the fresh air. More relaxed, less edgy. The early morning rain had blown over, bringing everyone out. The pavements were thronged. She walked briskly along, acclimatising to the city ambience, getting used to being surrounded by strangers. The smell of coffee reached her nostrils, dark and inviting, reminding her that she'd had no breakfast. There were numerous cafés stitched in between the high street stores and she slowed down as she passed each one, peering in, trying to make out what was going on in the shadows. How to choose? How could she know which ones were safe? She solved her dilemma by buying a coffee from a kiosk in the street. As she walked along, sipping from the polystyrene beaker, she felt pleased with herself for keeping a cool head

It came to her out of the blue. She should buy a gift for Lewis. A 'thank you' for driving all the way to Birmingham to fetch her. What would he like? She studied the window displays in the gift shops. Cufflinks. Watches. Wallets. Fountain pens. All of these, nice though they were, weren't quite Lewis. She was looking for something more personal, something to show that she hadn't forgotten.

On she went, glancing in the shop windows as she passed. Top Shop, Smith's, Littlewoods. She was beginning to despair when she spotted the HMV sign. She smiled. Music. That was it. Why hadn't she thought of it straight away? Lewis adored jazz.

The jazz department was on the first floor. It was peaceful in here, breathy saxophone notes barely disturbing the air. There were only half a dozen customers and she made for the far corner, where neither they nor the boy standing behind the counter could watch her.

She flipped through the CDs, the cellophane-wrapped packets toppling forward, clattering gently. *Dankworth. Davis. Dean. Dorsey.* She moved to her right. *McGreggor, Marsalis, Mingus, Mulligan.* She edged along, taking one from here, one from there, until she was holding seven square packets. Seven was an interesting number and square was a pleasing shape. But their square-ness was spoiled by a lump of grey plastic on the opening edge of each case. She frowned, not sure what to do about these imperfections.

She glanced up. The boy was coming towards her. Heat spread

from the small of her back, enveloping her whole body.

'Can I help you, Madam? Were you looking for anything in particular?'

'No. I made a mistake. Lewis hates jazz.' She thrust the CDs towards him. 'I'll get him a wallet.' She hurried away, scanning the store signs, looking for the exit.

From the descending escalator, she had an aerial view of the ground floor. Dozens of people were milling around. Loud music and the clamour of voices rose to meet her. Suddenly the man studying the display of video tapes at the foot of the escalator caught her attention. Although he had his back to her there was something familiar in his stance and the clothes he wore. Jeans. Leather jacket. Short, reddish hair.

It was Rundle.

She stepped off the escalator and, turning her face away from him, she made a dash for the main door. Once clear of the shop, she pulled the hood of the jacket over her head, holding it close around her face, scurrying along as fast as her aching ankle would allow.

There were stupid people everywhere, watching her, getting in the way, trying to trip her up.

Shit. Rundle was on the other side of the street now, with a child in a pushchair.

She took the next turn on the left, her throat scorching as she gasped for air, a stitch nagging her side. She kept going, looking to left and right. Oh, fuck, *there,* there he was again, by that white van, lying in wait for her. *Oh, please God, no.*

She was sweating, the hood funnelling the sound of her fear back into her ears.

Ahead was a sign – Ladies Toilets – and, with one final effort, she pushed through the shabby door. Making for the furthest cubicle, she locked herself in.

*

When Lewis returned from school and found the house deserted, he contacted the police. It didn't take long for them to make the connection between his call and the woman found in the public lavatories.

When he got to the hospital, the sight of Tessa curled up, rocking silently, terrified him.

'Tess?' he called softly.

She looked up but no flicker of recognition crossed her face.

He drove home, hating himself for abandoning her there, yet – he was ashamed to admit – relieved that the matter had been taken out of his hands.

Chapter 42

AT FIRST KIRSTY WAS SYMPATHETIC, saying the things that he wanted to hear.

'You couldn't have done more, Lewis. I've made a few enquiries. The hospital's got an excellent reputation. They'll take good care of her.'

As the days went on, her tone modified.

'Are you sure that your spending so much time at the hospital with her isn't dredging up bad memories?'

This thought had occurred to him but Matthew Collins, Tessa's counsellor, explained, 'Seeing you regularly, someone she's had beside her as long as she can remember, keeps her connected to the world. It provides stability and reassurance. Both are vital if she's to get well. Don't worry too much if she doesn't want to talk. Never press her. Take your cue from her.' He hesitated. 'One thing concerns me slightly. This is a heavy burden for you to shoulder alone, Mr Swinburne. To be frank the worst thing would be for you to burn yourself out and not be able—'

'I won't let her down,' Lewis said.

'Is there no one who could share the visiting?' Collins persisted, 'A friend? A relative?'

'No, there isn't,' was Lewis's despondent admission.

Tessa didn't know where she was or how she came to be there.

She'd wondered if she was back in prison but the people who brought her food and helped her dress were gentle and patient. And Lewis was here, in the room with her.

'What is this place?' she asked.

'You're in hospital,' he explained.

'Am I ill?' she asked. 'What's the matter with me?'

'You've been … overdoing it,' he said.

'Can I trust these people?'

'Yes.'

The doctors looking after Tessa were always ready to talk to Lewis. They made no promises, offered no fatuous reassurances, emphasising that, unlike a broken limb or slipped disc, the mind's recovery process was unpredictable and couldn't be rushed. The surroundings were austere and the staff could be a little brusque at times but he had faith in them. Despite this, the spectre of his mother and her lifelong struggle lurked obstinately in the back of his mind.

He visited every weekend and tried to get to the hospital at least once during the week. Kirsty never commented on his absences but her silence was more telling than any criticism. To compensate, he booked tickets for the theatre and concerts, they went to the cinema and he took her out for meals. It was very civilised but about as effective as applying a sticking plaster to a ruptured artery.

'I'm thinking of going to Greece in August,' Kirsty announced one evening. 'Will you come with me?'

He took her hand, hoping that his touch would temper what he had to say. 'You know I can't go anywhere at the moment.'

'Why not? It would only be for a couple of weeks. Tessa would want you to have a holiday, wouldn't she? Can't you explain to her? Can't she grasp that?' Kirsty raised her eyebrows. 'Or perhaps you don't want to come.'

'She has no one else in the world.'

'And why is that, I wonder? You've got to ease off, Lewis. Take a step back. Anyway, from what you tell me, she's out of it half the time. She's probably got no idea what day it is so how would she know if you missed a few visits? I'm worried for you. You're starting to look … haunted.'

'Thanks.'

She folded her arms across her chest. 'If you don't watch it you'll end up being as crazy as she is.'

'She's not crazy,' he said quietly. 'And it's not as if she's *chosen* to be … ill.'

'I'll go ahead and book my holiday, then.' She stood up, signally the end of their conversation.

He was saddened that Kirsty – a strong, well person – couldn't find it in herself to be more compassionate.

Tessa liked Matthew. He was very young – no more than forty – but there was something solid about him. He didn't look a bit like Dan but he reminded her of him. He had Dan's way of not crowding her. She assumed he was a psychiatrist but he didn't prod or poke her mind like that Sophie woman had done. Where was that? Somewhere else. Not here, anyway.

When term fished Lewis had more time on his hands but, as Matthew Collins had recommended, he stuck to the same visiting regime.

Kirsty had been right. He *was* tired. Exhausted, in fact. But it wasn't the sort of fatigue that a few weeks on a Greek island could dispel. He'd been carrying a weight, on and off, for the whole of his life. At the moment it was as heavy as it had ever been. But he had no intention of giving up. And it was altogether easier for him once Kirsty went away, taking with her the need for him to pretend that Tessa, and his concerns for her, didn't exist. He pottered about, listening to his records or tinkering with the old pushbike he'd picked up in a junk shop. He creosoted the fence at the side of the house. Occasionally he went for a walk on the moor. Whatever he did, Tessa was always with him.

Sometimes when he visited her she was withdrawn. He couldn't be sure if this was because of the medication she was taking or if it was just an 'off' day. She would sit, staring out of the window or bolt upright with her eyes closed, whilst he pretended to read the paper. When he left, she would smile her goodbye and then retreat to wherever she had been. Even though she barely said a word, he knew that she was glad to have him there.

Sometimes she was restless, pacing the room, edgy and unable to settle. 'There you are at last, Lewis. Let's get out of here before we suffocate.' And she'd lead him round and around the garden as though something horrid would catch up with them if they stopped. Another time, after she'd read an article on Feng Shui , she decided that she'd sleep better if her bed faced the other way and she wouldn't let him go until he'd moved it. 'That's much better. Can't you feel the increased energy?'

Sometimes she was brimming with inconsequential gossip. 'Have you seen the new woman across the landing? She's lauding it about, telling everyone that she's Michael Heseltine's mistress. I said I'd keep quiet about that if I were her.'

The doctors assured him that they were making headway, but each time the porter released the latch to let him in, he felt anxious for fear that, since his last visit, she'd veered off course.

'D'you feel like company?' Matthew asked.

Tessa was sitting on her favourite bench, watching butterflies working on the lavender bushes. She moved her cardigan to make space for him.

'D'you think they know we're watching them?'

He laughed. 'Interesting question. I shouldn't think they do.'

'I know you're watching me,' she said.

'Does that bother you?'

'It would if you denied it.'

It was some while since she'd been able to find the words or the wit for banter and she felt euphoric, as though a plug of gunk had come away from inside her head.

Kirsty returned with a deep tan and photographs of hillside churches and azure seas. She brought Lewis a soapstone chess set and a pair of slippers with absurd pom-poms on the front. Peace offerings.

They inspected the garden to see what had come into flower while she'd been away. Lewis showed her the freshly painted fence and made a few circuits of the yard on his renovated bicycle.

It was almost an hour before she asked, 'How's Tessa?'

'She seems a lot better.'

'I'm glad. Now perhaps we can start getting back to normal. D'you have any idea when they'll discharge her?'

Did she really think it was as simple as that, no worse than a nasty dose of glandular fever – all over and done with in a few months?

Tessa could see that Lewis was avoiding talking about her breakdown. She understood why and it was fine. She and Matthew were working on it and she felt more at ease discussing the complex issues involved with an outsider. In a way she was sorry that Lewis had been caught up in it at all. Poor Lewis. He must be going through a helluva time at home. But she'd done nothing to force him to come, and to keep on coming. It was his choice and Kirsty had always been keen on the individual's freedom to choose.

She half-expected her sister-in-law to turn up and give her another talking-to, but time went on and Kirsty didn't come.

Increasingly often, the *real* Tessa was waiting for Lewis. After months of passivity it was wonderful to hear her sniping and moaning again. 'Haven't you brought me anything to eat? I've got a craving for smoked salmon. Oh, and artichokes. We may be a bunch of loonies but that doesn't entitle them to feed us slop.'

She was regaining herself. She looked healthier – fuller in the face, less hunched. He noticed that she was wearing make-up and that her hair was always clean and brushed. She was encouragingly caustic and self-deprecating; attentive and able to maintain concentration. There was usually a newspaper on her bedside table and they often discussed the news – the latest theories surrounding Diana's death or how the BSE crisis was affecting the sales of beef.

'I've started keeping a journal,' she said one day. 'Jotting down a few thoughts. I've got an idea for a short story. Maybe a linked sequence.'

It sounded as though she was opening up to Collins too. He knew it for a fact when she asked, 'Matthew and I have been talking a lot about Gordon. How would you feel if I told him about the doll?'

After it being entirely theirs for so many years, it hurt him to think of her sharing the secret but he knew that this was absolutely the right time.

'Tessa, you have my permission to talk about anything and everything if it's going to help you get well.'

Then she began to speak about 'when I get out of here' and, as he drove home, he found himself whistling and giving thanks to the God that neither he nor Tessa believed in.

Tessa frowned. 'I don't think we were wicked children.'

They sat in Matthew's office-cum-consulting-room, drinking tea, talking again about how close she and Lewis had been as children and how Gordon's birth had made them so angry.

'Can children be wicked?' he asked.

'You tell me. You're the expert.'

'I can certainly tell you that no child welcomes a new sibling with open arms. Attention-seeking, puking, mewling interlopers. Why would anyone want one of those? It's years before the newcomer becomes useful as playmate or accomplice.'

'I never hated Lewis,' she said.

'Believe me you did, in a very basic way. But you don't remember it because you were only twelve months or so apart. Eventually the "hate", or whatever it is, mutates and we all end up with a cocktail of feelings towards our sibling. You were unlucky. Your "hate" never had time to mutate.'

'But the thing with the doll…'

'Leaving a lump of plasticine in a phone box is a very mild manifestation of hatred if you ask me. The world would be a happier place if we all left our hatred in a phone box.'

As if on cue, the telephone on Matthew's desk rang and Tessa left him to take his call.

The weather mellowed. Tessa and Matthew took advantage of the Indian Summer and went into the garden for many of their sessions.

'Let's talk a bit more about your parents,' he prompted.

'I despised them. Isn't that an appalling thing to admit? I knew why they were like they were, but that didn't excuse them.'

'For what?'

'Letting me down.'

'And what were they like? In your eyes?'

Tessa waited a while before saying anything. 'My mother … this sounds ridiculous but it's as if she was a sort of film extra who was given a few lines to say once in a while. But nothing that moved the plot forward. I try so hard to remember what she was like before Gordon was born. I've got this picture of an attractive, energetic woman who laughed all the time and was such fun. Have I invented that?'

'And your father?'

'Dad was a bully. No, not a bully. A bigot and a pedant.'

'Did he ever hit you? Abuse you?'

'No. But I'm sure he came pretty near it now and again. He was like most fathers of his generation, I expect. And of course he had to contend with a damaged leg.' She sighed. 'I *did* push him to the limits. It's just that I wanted him to be…'

Matthew nodded, 'You wanted him to be…?'

'Oh, you know, the man who walked on water, I suppose. At least we patched it up before he died. I'm glad that we did.'

Matthew offered her a mint. 'Had enough for today or d'you want to go on?'

'You mean take the money or open the box?' She chewed her lip. 'I might as well open the box.'

She told him about Rundle, the whole thing from breathless start to bloody finish. For the first time since she began exposing her life to him, she wept. 'The way I carried on was … despicable. Disgusting. Indefensible.'

He pushed a box of tissues towards her. 'You weren't married, you had no children. You had an affair. It's not that unusual.'

'But it was so sordid. It made me feel constantly dirty.'

'You're referring to the sex?'

'Of course. That's what the whole thing hinged on.'

'From what you've told me, nothing you two did was outside what might be considered normal behaviour.'

'But it polluted my life. It impinged on everything.'

'For example?'

'My relationship with Dan. My choice not to have children; not to get married; not to get a decent education.'

'Really? Have you considered that Rundle might be an excuse, not a reason?'

She felt let down by his calm appraisal of her obsession. 'So you're not going to allow Rundle to be the villain who screwed up my life?'

'No. It seems to me that Rundle provided excitement. A secret to be kept from everyone. When, for whatever reason, you no longer had the need for that excitement, you finished it.'

'Finished him, you mean.' She was cross with Matthew for making it out to be no more than an ordinary little affair. 'Stabbing ones lover with a vegetable knife can't be considered "normal behaviour".'

'No. I'll grant you that. But you were provoked and clearly you didn't kill him. The police would have tracked you down in a couple of days if you had. And Rundle didn't report the attack or they would have found you within hours. You said you phoned him?'

'Yes, once. From the hospital. But the phone had been disconnected.'

Matthew stood up and stretched. 'Rundle isn't a common name. It shouldn't be difficult to find him if you feel the need to. I'd be prepared to help, if that's what you want.'

'Is that what you lot call "closure"?' she asked.

'Blimey. Don't tell me you've been reading *Teach yourself Psychiatry*, Miss Swinburne.'

As Lewis was leaving after his weekend visit, Tessa asked, 'Could you dig out the family photos? I've spent months talking to Matthew about the past. I reckon I'm ready to take a look at it.'

Next time he came, they spent a couple of hours going through the photographs in the old shoebox, studying and reliving each moment captured within the borders of the dog-eared snaps. Everyone was there. Their parents. Gran. Assorted aunts and uncles, cars and family pets.

And there were numerous photos of Tessa and him, side by side on beaches and promenades, in parks and gardens. Dark-eyed and open-faced, what a striking pair they made. One image touched him more than the rest. They must have been four or five years old and someone had taken them – Gran, maybe – to see Father Christmas in one of the posh stores. There they stood, in matching coats, staring directly into the lens, Tessa clutching a small parcel in her gloved hands. Two bright, brave creatures, full of hope.

XI

1998

Chapter 43

TESSA STIRRED HER COFFEE and watched a pat of butter melt into the toasted teacake on the plate in front of her. Opening the newspaper, she turned to the crossword.

The café was no more than fifteen minutes walk from the house – a pleasant stroll through a leafy park – and, over the months, she had become quite a 'regular' here. Whenever possible she sat at the table in the corner, an excellent vantage point from which to observe the general comings and goings, and to enjoy being part of something satisfyingly ordinary. The proprietor didn't seem to mind how long she stayed but, in return for his forbearance, she made sure to vacate the table before the lunchtime rush.

On her way home Tessa called at the corner shop for a few bits and pieces. Lewis was coming for supper and she needed to buy mushrooms for a pasta sauce.

She saw her brother less often these days. He had his own life to lead and, although he never let on, she knew that he had a great deal of patching up to do with Kirsty.

Matthew had devoted many of their sessions to Lewis. He'd fished around, clearly trying to establish whether there was anything 'unnatural' in their relationship. Initially she'd found it offensive but, as time went on and her trust in him grew, she accepted that it was necessary to rule this out. 'It's unusual for sister and brother to remain as close as you two have. They tend to drift apart once they reach puberty.' 'We drank a lot of potions; mingled a lot of blood,' she'd confided. 'Potions, incantations, voodoo dolls. Never fails.'

She was sharing a house with four other women. They were all at varying stages in their rehabilitation. Living there gave them a breathing space before they had to – what was that phrase? – 'get back on the horse'. Marilyn had been working at the council offices for some time and was about ready to move into a place of her own. Dee had arrived only two weeks ago and was still finding her feet. Tessa had been the same when she was 'the new girl'. In the communal kitchen or on the way to the bathroom, she'd been forced to exchange a few words with the others. But having lost the knack of exchanging small talk with strangers, she'd found it easier to keep to herself, listening to disembodied voices on the far side of her locked door. Her socialisation took a leap forward when, one evening, the lights in the house fused. They'd pooled torches and know-how and, once the power was restored, they'd sent Alice to the 'chippie' for celebratory fish and chips. That evening, the house began to feel like home and the women with whom she shared it became if not friends then certainly allies.

'Something smells good.' Lewis held out a carton of ice cream. 'My contribution.' He kissed her. 'You look well.'

'I can't say the same for you,' Tessa countered.

They carried their meal up to her room.

Sometimes when Lewis came, they ate in the kitchen with whoever happened to be around. Lewis was a ladies' man, although he didn't know it. It was obvious that Marilyn, Dee, Alice and Leanne found him utterly charming and it was amusing to watch them adapt their behaviour when he was there, toning down bad language and even flirting a little. Polite and gentle, amusing and considerate, he was, from what Tessa gleaned, a different species from the men they usually met. She was absurdly proud that he was her brother.

'Everything okay?' This was Lewis's shorthand for *Are you taking your medication?*

'Yes, fine thanks. How about you?' *Are you as unhappy as I suspect you are?*

'Oh … you know.'

She kept a kettle in her room and, when they'd finished eating, she made coffee in the cafetière which Lewis had given her for her last birthday. 'I've been thinking about what I should do next. A "halfway house" is, by definition, not the final destination. I need to make plans.'

Lewis looked anxious. 'Have they said anything?'

'No. And I don't think they will. It's up to me. I'll have to decide when I'm ready to move on.'

'And are you?'

'I think I am.' It was the first time she'd dared voice this thought. 'I've done my sums and as long as I'm sensible I should be fine. The State is surprisingly charitable to the elderly ex-nutter.'

Lewis frowned. 'It's not economics that concern me.'

She smiled. 'I know it's not. You're wondering why it should be any better next time.'

He tugged his ear but said nothing.

'I was ill, Lewis. The accident really shook me up. And then prison…' She laid a hand on his forearm. 'A lot of complicated stuff went on – stuff that you don't need to know about. It was all festering away for a long time. And before you start beating yourself up, there was nothing you could have done to prevent what happened. Nothing.' She patted his hand. 'That's all done with now.'

Lewis nodded and they sat for a few minutes in thoughtful silence.

'Dan was a nice guy.' There was regret in her brother's declaration.

'He was. I made a lot of duff decisions but *not* marrying Dan Coates was one of the few correct ones. We *did* have lots of good times together but I was using him as a sort of human lifebelt, to stop me drowning in one load of shit after another – some of it real, some of it imagined, but all of it my own making. Dan didn't deserve that.'

'I read in one of the supplements that he's married an American woman. An artist, I think.'

'Yes. I heard from him a couple of weeks ago, actually.'

'You keep in touch?' He sounded surprised.

'Not really. He sent the letter to my publisher and they forwarded it. But I will write back. Nothing heavy. Just to wish them a happy life.'

'"A happy life." It sounds so bloody simple. I'll take a couple of those, please.'

She reached across the table and pulled his cup towards her, spat in the coffee and stirred it. Closing her eyes, she lifted the cup and drank from it. 'Now you.'

He laughed and shook his head. 'You're round the bend.'

There had been months and months when Lewis wouldn't have dared accuse her of that and she loved the sound of it.

'Do as I say. Drink it and then make a wish.'

He hesitated then raised the cup to his lips.

When it was time for him to leave, she went down to see him off. A fine drizzle moistened the air and they both got in the car to keep dry.

'Had any thoughts on where you might like to live?' he asked.

'Matthew was asking me that last week. It's not straightforward. I've been trying to work out where I belong. Where my heart lies, if you like.'

471

'And?'

'Not Birmingham, that's for sure. And although I spent years in London and I know – or used to know – a few people there, the prospect of living in a city is too daunting.'

'So that leaves here? Yorkshire?'

'Here. And home.' She shrugged. 'Weird, isn't it? I left the place when I was eighteen but I still call it "home". It's been bugging me why that is and I've come to the conclusion that it might have been different if I'd ever made a *proper* home anywhere. A one-husband-two-point-four-kids-and-a-dog sort of home. But I've spent years avoiding that sort of commitment; never putting down roots, never unpacking my baggage – the mental variety, I mean; always eyeing the greener grass.' She smiled. 'Sorry to sound so corny.'

'Actually its rather quaint coming from you.' He reached across, opening the glove compartment and pulling out a bag of sweets. 'If Matthew Collins were to ask me the same question, I could pinpoint the spot where I belong.'

She unfurled a sweet wrapper and popped the stripy mint into her mouth. 'Cranwell Lodge.'

He nodded. 'I belonged at Cranwell Lodge from the instant we went through the door. How old were we?'

She didn't hesitate. 'Nineteen fifty-three. I was nine, you were eight. You had blood trickling down your arm. I can still smell Germolene and dusty cushions; still hear the bird twittering away in the corner.'

'Mrs Channing?'

'Blanche, you idiot.' She punched him gently on the thigh.

'I didn't really understand that I belonged there until I moved to Bristol.'

'Who's in the house at the moment?'

'No one. The decorators are in. Kirsty thinks I should put it on the market now that house prices are rising again. I'll have to come up with a pretty good reason not to.'

The rain was getting more persistent and the light fading. 'Best be on your way. Thanks for coming.' Tessa leaned across and kissed Lewis's cheek. 'Drive safely.'

She stood on the pavement, barely noticing the rain, waiting until the tail lights of his car disappeared around the corner.

Kirsty was stacking the dishwasher, Lewis bundling newspapers for recycling. They hadn't spoken since supper when Lewis had mentioned that, when he'd seen Tessa the previous evening, she'd talked about leaving the house.

Kirsty pressed the button and the machine began its cycle. 'I'll say this now, so that you know exactly where I stand. I will not have her here.'

Lewis took a deep breath, 'But she has no one else in the world. Not one single soul.'

'As you've mentioned a hundred times before.' Kirsty closed her eyes. 'Look. What if you – *we* – lived in Australia? She'd have to cope on her own, wouldn't she?'

'Yes but we don't live in Australia so I can't see how that helps.' He cut a length of string and tied the last bundle of papers. 'If we converted the garage, she could be virtually self-contained.'

'She *could* but she wouldn't. This is Tessa we're talking about here. I've watched you two for years and I've seen how it works.'

'That's not entirely fair. When she was with Dan, I only saw her once in a blue moon. And I had scarcely had anything to do with her when she lived in Birmingham.'

Kirsty shook her head. 'That's bollocks and you know it. What did Diana say? "There were three of us in the marriage." She may have been barking mad but I can sympathise with her on that score.'

'I can't help what I feel, can I?'

473

'No, I don't suppose you can. But d'you know what? I've given up caring what you *feel*. It's what you *do* that matters. You've allowed your sister to dictate every decision you've ever made and to wreck every relationship you've ever had. I could understand – *understand* mind, not condone – if there were something physical between you. But there isn't. It's worse than that. Tessa fucks your mind. She always has.' It sounded doubly obscene coming from his rational wife.

He looked out of the window. The cherry tree was in full blossom, the tips of its branches weighed down with a froth of pink florets. They'd planted the tree when they moved in, almost ten years ago. As he watched, a breeze swooped through the garden, sending a cascade of petals swirling across the lawn.

'I might as well finish.' Kirsty sat at the table, leaning on her elbows, her forehead cupped in her hands. 'Gordon's disappearance was a terrible, terrible thing. But terrible things happen to people all the time. And they survive. Life goes on. Not your family, though. They wallowed in it. Your father became bitter and dictatorial. If your poor mother showed the slightest sign of fighting back, he slapped her down. It was criminal the way he convinced her, and everyone else, that she was an invalid. And you, Lewis, you revelled in the role of little boy, eager to please, scared stiff of making waves. While all this was going on, Tessa just ran wild. She treated you all appallingly. She worried your parents to death, running away like that. Then writing those trashy novels, cashing in on the family tragedy. And she hasn't changed. You'd think that causing an old man's death and going to jail would have brought her to her senses. But no, she had to play the martyr and get you running around the country after her. Can't you see how calculated her every action is?'

'You're being very harsh. Her breakdown was real enough.'

'Was it?'

Pink petals danced across the grass. There had been a flowering cherry at Medway Avenue, at the far end of the garden just this side of the vegetable plot. Up in its branches, he'd been safe from everything. He shut his eyes, feeling the smooth bole beneath his hands, watching his feet in scuffed sandals, as they sought out a decent toehold.

'Why have you stuck with me?' he asked.

'Pride. Obstinacy. Delusion. The usual suspects.' She picked at the skin next to her thumbnail. 'I did love you, Lewis. That's the shame of it.' She laughed but there was no mirth in it. 'I sound like Celia Johnson. All stiff upper lip and common sense. I don't feel like that, though. I ought to be coming at you with a meat cleaver.'

Did. I *did* love you. So there it was – the past tense that would shape their future.

XII

2005

Chapter 44

LEWIS HAULED HIS BRIEFCASE off the back seat and locked the car. Its bodywork, covered with dust after the dry week, was disfigured with initials and witticisms – *also comes in silver, wish Shazzer was this filthy*. Nothing innovative but the spelling was better than usual.

He walked up the path and let himself in through the front door. 'It's me,' he shouted into the silence. 'Anyone at home?'

A voice came from upstairs. 'No.' Followed almost immediately by, 'Put the kettle on. I'll be down in a minute. I'm printing something out.'

He draped his jacket over the newel post and went to do as he'd been instructed. The kitchen smelled of burnt toast and overripe fruit. He studied the table. A dictionary. A spiral-bound notebook. Several pens – minus their caps. A pair of secateurs. Three dirty mugs. Half a packet of digestive biscuits. A banana skin – completely brown.

He opened the windows, rolled up his sleeves and was clearing the table when Tessa appeared.

'Stop. Leave that.' She pushed him aside. 'You must be home early. I was just about to tidy up.'

She was wearing a velour dressing gown over a thick shirt and jeans, the bottoms of which were tucked into woollen walking socks.

Lewis frowned. 'Why on earth have you got all those clothes

478

on? It's way up in the seventies.'

'I'm freezing. Feel.' She grabbed his hands and he was shocked to feel how cold hers were.

'You've been sitting in front of that screen too long. You should take regular breaks. Go for a walk. Get the blood circulating.'

'Yes, Mum.' A smile took ten years off her tired face. 'Actually, I did. I went to the park – threw stones at the ducks.' She raised a finger to her lips. 'Sorry. I mean *bread*. I threw *bread* at the ducks.'

'Did you hit any?' he laughed, glad to be home.

They sat at the kitchen table drinking tea. Whilst he flicked through the evening paper, Tessa studied her notebook, every now and again striking something out or scribbling in the margin.

Their first contact of the day was generally around this time. Tessa referred to it as their 'Typhoo Tea ceremony'. She was asleep when he left in the morning, then once she started working she preferred not to be distracted. If they needed to 'talk' during the day they texted or emailed. She'd only once come to the school. The secretary had interrupted his lesson. 'Your sister's here, Mr Swinburne. She says it's very important.' Full of foreboding, he'd followed her back to the office. It was raining but Tessa wasn't wearing a waterproof and her wet hair was dripping on to her blouse. 'Are you okay?' 'Of course I am. I had to tell you straight away. My collection won the Darrio Prize.' She'd hugged him, pressing a letter into his hand but he was too busy calming his heart to make sense of the words.

'Any post?' he asked, tossing the paper aside.

Tessa picked up the clutch of envelopes that were propped against the microwave and shuffled through them. 'A gas bill. Something – nasty I'm sure – from the Inland Revenue. A card from the optician's saying your specs are ready. And,' she held up a cream envelope, waving it like a miniature flag, 'a letter

479

from Kirsty.'

He took the envelopes, pushing the one from Kirsty into his trouser pocket. 'I'm going up to change.'

'Spoilsport,' she said.

He swapped his shirt and grey flannels for polo shirt and chinos. He went through his emails but there was nothing of any consequence. Next he checked the weather. It seemed to be set fair until Monday. So, jobs for the weekend: wash the car, have a go at the back hedge before it got completely out of hand, mark the rest of the Lower Sixth's exam papers. Maybe he and Tessa would go to the cemetery. It was nearing Gordon's birthday – he would have been fifty-one – and they always marked it by putting flowers on his parents' grave.

When he could put if off no longer, he opened Kirsty's letter.

Dear Lewis,

As it's neither Christmas nor your birthday, I expect you were anxious when you received this. Please don't worry – it's nothing important but I do need a decision from you.

Over the past few months I've been reorganising the loft – getting rid of as much as I can before the ceiling comes down! We were rather premature (smug?) in thinking that you'd taken all your belongings. The bad (or good, perhaps) news is that I've unearthed four more boxes of your stuff. They were in the far reaches of the loft, beyond the water tank. It would seem from the labels that they contain books and models. What would you like me to do? Should I arrange for them to be delivered to Cranwell Lodge?

The garden is looking lovely this year although the cherry tree has had to come out. It was completely rotten in the crown. At least I shall have plenty of logs for the winter.

That's it for now. I hope the rest of the term goes smoothly and that you have a good summer break. Any plans to retire? I've

*contemplated dropping down to part-time but I'm not sure I'd
know what to do with myself.*
Best wishes,
Kirsty

Efficient. Factual. Correct. Yet she must have known that the
fate of the tree would touch him.

From start to finish, their separation had been 'civilised';
the divorce achieved without histrionics. Kirsty had reduced
their marriage to lists and schedules and clauses. Of course
she would. It was what she spent her professional life doing.
After they signed the final papers, she'd shaken his hand. 'Good
luck, Lewis.' The death of love – of anything – deserved to be
mourned but their marriage had died because of what he'd
done, or failed to do, and it seemed inappropriate for him to cry
or make a fuss.

'So?' Tessa prompted when he returned to the kitchen.

He filled her in on the contents of the letter.

'It's six years. What's the matter with the woman? I'd have
bunged the whole lot in a skip.'

'Yes, well, we're not all the same.'

'Thank God.' She swiped at a fly with the tea towel.

'What d'you fancy tonight ?' he asked. They'd fallen into the
habit of getting a takeaway on Friday evenings.

'Chinese? No. Fish and chips. We haven't had fish and chips for
ages. But could we leave it a bit? I'm full of digestive biscuits.'

'Fine. I think I'll sit in the garden for half an hour,' he said.
'Blow away the chalk dust.'

They didn't use chalk these days but no one had come up with
an evocative phrase about whiteboard markers.

Tessa watched as Lewis dragged the deckchairs into the far
corner of the lawn, beyond the shadows cast by the straggly

apple trees. She'd noticed that as he grew older he was starting to stoop, as though his head had become too heavy for his gangly frame. But he still had a fine head of hair. He must have inherited the hair gene from Uncle Frank although, thank heavens, not their uncle's penchant for dying it.

She hadn't told him but she, too, had received a letter in the morning post. There was no need to worry him. Not yet. The whole point of a biopsy was to find out what was going on. Once she had some hard facts she would make up her mind what to do.

Taking her notebook, she went out into the garden where Lewis was already sprawled in a deckchair. His eyes were shut but he was rolling a ball of silver foil between his forefinger and thumb.

'Asleep?' she whispered.

'Not any more,' he groaned.

She lowered herself into the chair next to him. 'How was your day?'

He opened his eyes, squinting and raising his hand to shield them against the low sun. 'Frustrating. Ends of term get too free-form for my liking. If the kids turn up at all, they don't expect to do any work.' He flicked the silver paper across the lawn towards the bird bath. 'Catherine Thomas came to see me today. Have I told you about her? She's my star pupil. But Miss Thomas has decided that she won't be applying to Cambridge after all. She's going to do Environmental Sciences at Newcastle. She intends to save the bloody planet.' He shook his head. 'Such a waste.'

'Saving the human race sounds quite a laudable ambition to me. We didn't even consider trying.'

He sighed. 'You're right. It's just a bit … demoralising.'

'*You* were once someone's star pupil,' she reminded him gently.

'And *you* could have been too, if you'd wanted to be.'

'Could I?'

'Of course you could. You were brighter than all the other kids. You can't deny that.'

'But bright isn't the same as clever, Lewis. I was bright and you were clever. What was the phrase Mum used to use? When the day started sunny and by lunchtime it was bucketing with rain?'

'"Too bright too soon"?' he offered.

'Exactly. I was too bright too soon.'

The sun was starting to warm her and she pulled her socks off, burying her bare feet in the grass. 'Right. I'm going to ask you a question and I want your gut response.'

'Oh, God, I already don't like what's coming.'

'Don't be so stuffy,' she chided. 'I know you like teaching but what would you *really* like to be?'

His answer came flashing back. 'A Spitfire pilot.'

She pushed herself up in the deckchair and peered at him. 'What? Killing people? Destroying cities?'

'No. *Defending* people. Soaring above the earth in the most beautiful machine that man has ever made. And, for your information, Spitfires aren't bombers.'

'For your information, we don't have Spitfires any more.'

'Nit picker.' He poked his tongue out and prodded her shoulder. 'Your turn. Quick.'

On her first day at school, Miss Drake had asked, 'Children, what would you like to be when you grow up?' The boys wanted to be engine drivers or policeman; the girls, ballet dancers or nurses. 'Tessa?' she'd prompted. 'What do you like doing? Cooking? Helping Mummy.' 'Telling my brother stories,' Tessa had replied. 'A writer. Tessa is going to be a writer, everyone. Isn't that grand?'

She leaned back and folded her arms. As she did so her right hand brushed her left breast. *Fuck, fuck, fuck.* So dreary and so

483

predictable.

She drew in a deep breath. 'Okay. I'd like to be … a magician.'

Lewis threw his head back and laughed. 'I can picture it now. Top hat. Sparkly cloak. Magic wand. Sawing ladies in half—'

'No. Not an illusionist. I'd like to be a *real* magician who does *real* magic.'

'Cheat. That's unfair.'

'What's unfair about it? Your answer wasn't exactly rational.'

'At least Spitfire pilots existed. There aren't, and never were, "real magicians". It's tantamount to saying you'd like to be God.'

'No thanks. Too much responsibility. Not enough fun.'

Laughing, he held his hands up in surrender.

She delved in her pocket and brought out a packet of cigarettes. 'Don't you dare say anything.' She lit one, inhaled then blew the smoke out provocatively. 'You have to allow me one vice. Besides it deters the midges.'

Lewis nodded to the notebook on her lap. 'You're writing a new story?'

'No. An old one, as a matter of fact. I suppose you'd call it a memoir.'

'For publication?'

She shook her head. 'No need to panic. Not this time.'

'Who for, then?'

'*For whom.* We don't want to raise any pedantic ghosts. Actually I'm writing it for us. For you and me. I thought it would be a good idea to get it down on paper. The definitive version.'

'Why now? Any particular reason?'

'The time seems right. Far enough away to get everything in perspective yet near enough to recall the detail.'

He nodded. 'I always think "memoir" sounds a bit … untrustworthy.'

'What are you insinuating?' She raised her eyebrows in mock horror. 'If you're concerned about the truth, perhaps you should write your version of events too. Who knows, you might find the exercise cathartic. We could stitch the two together.'

'Mmmm. I'd have to think about that. It sounds rather frightening if you ask me. So what are you planning to call this memoir?'

'Give me a chance. I'm just jotting down a few notes at the moment. Working out the best way of telling the story.'

Blanche appeared from under a laurel bush, prowled elegantly across the lawn and flopped between the two deckchairs, purring noisily. Tessa reached down and fondled her ear. 'It must be a bugger being a white cat. I'm going to make her a jacket out of old combat trousers. At least she'll stand a fighting chance of bagging a bird.'

The sun disappeared behind the roof and the shadow of the old house enveloped the garden. Tessa glanced at her watch. 'It's getting on for seven. Who's going for the fish and chips?'

Lewis sat up abruptly, as though he'd been stung by something. 'I've got it. The title for our story. We should call it … "Sweets from Morocco". What d'you think?'

'Mmmm. Not bad for a beginner.'

She closed her eyes, the bittersweetness of sherbet lemons erupting on her tongue. '"Sweets from Morocco". Yes. That'll do fine.'

Jo Verity

Having worked as a graphic designer and medical graphic artist, Jo started writing 'to see if she could'. Her previous very successful novels were *Everything in the Garden* and *Bells*, which was awarded a commissioning grant by the Welsh Books Council. She's also had short stories, poems and articles published or broadcast on Radio 4. She won the Richard & Judy Short Story prize in 2003 against 17,000 other entries, won the *Western Mail* short story competition, was shortlisted for the Asham Award and was a runner-up in the 2008 *Myslexia* International Poetry Competition. Jo lives in Rhiwbina, Cardiff.

Q&A

What started you writing?
Jo: I'd arranged to meet an American friend (Ruth, an eccentric sculptress) whom I'd first met in Prague when I was inter-railing around Europe in the early nineties. We'd kept in touch and I'd visited her in Rhode Island and she'd been to Cardiff. We'd met a couple of times in London to go to art galleries. Ruth and I were planning to rendezvous in Budapest and spend a week together. At the last minute she pulled out and I was left with a week's leave and nothing special to do with it. Jim suggested that, as we had a new PC, I take the week to get to grips with it. So, as a way of doing that (and just to see if I could) I wrote a short story, basing the central character on my American friend.

After a week I was hooked on writing, although I had no ambition to be published. I just loved the whole process. From that moment on I've written almost every day.

I attended a 5-day Arvon course at Lumb Bank which was hugely important in convincing me that, if I applied myself, I could be a writer. Then I had the lucky break that all writers need - I won the Richard & Judy Short Story Award, which led to Janet Thomas (Honno) contacting me to see if I'd 'written anything longer'.

What themes inspire you?
Jo: I always write about people and relationships – nothing is more fascinating and worthwhile. Put a few human beings together and something will surely happen – a story will unfold. Husbands and wives in *Bells*; friends and families in *Everything in the Garden*; sisters and brothers in *Sweets from Morocco*.

It's my job to help the reader appreciate how extraordinary 'ordinary' people can be; how well or badly or crazily they behave when a spanner is cast in the works. I want my characters to be recognisable to the reader – to be people they know, or maybe even themselves. I hope the reader will connect with the characters and the situations that they have faced so that when they put the book down they think, 'Yes. I know people like that. I've had those feelings. That had a lot of truth in it.'

Other titles by Jo Verity

Jo Verity was the winner of the 2003 Richard and Judy 'Write Here Right Now' short story competition.
'Jo leapt out as the clear winner of our competition and we are over the moon that her writing talents have now been recognised.'
Richard and Judy

Everything in the Garden
When Anna and Tom Wren join together with three other couples to buy a rambling farmhouse in Wales, the intention is to grow old with the support of tried and trusted friends. But life turns out not to be the bed of roses Anna had imagined. As

she teeters on the brink of an affair, the relationships that have shaped her life begin to crumble and she is forced to confront the changing nature of her own desires and the consequences of giving in.

978 1870206 709 £6.99

Bells

Jack has fun playing away – not with loose women, but as part of a Morris dancing team. But when a gig is cancelled and he falls for the young woman behind the desk at The Welcome Stranger, he is launched into a world of love-struck subterfuge. Meanwhile, his wife, Fay, rashly offers a home to one of her son's ex-bandmates just days before she's forced to house her frail but argumentative mother-in-law. To top it all, she's in the throes of an illicit passion for her best friend's handsome son.

Will Jack and Fay's marriage survive the promise of new and exotic liaisons? Will the chime of Morris bells turn a woman's head in the days of iPods?

'Excellent' *The Bookseller*

978 1870206 877 £6.99

About Honno

Honno Welsh Women's Press was set up in 1986 by a group of women who felt strongly that women in Wales needed wider opportunities to see their writing in print and to become involved in the publishing process. Our aim is to develop the writing talents of women in Wales, give them new and exciting opportunities to see their work published and often to give them their first 'break' as a writer.

Honno is registered as a community co-operative. Any profit that Honno makes is invested in the publishing programme. Women from Wales and around the world have expressed their support for Honno by buying shares in the co-operative. Shareholders' liability is limited to the amount invested and each shareholder has a vote at the Annual General Meeting.

To buy shares or to receive further information about forthcoming publications, please write to Honno at the address below, or visit our website:www.honno.co.uk

Honno
'Ailsa Craig'
Heol y Cawl
Dinas Powys
Bro Morgannwyg
CF6 4AH

All Honno titles can be ordered online at
www.honno.co.uk
or by sending a cheque to Honno.
Free p&p to all UK addresses